"Do you believe in Mojo? Me, I believe in Nalo, and I've yet to be let down. MOJO shows that Nalo Hopkinson is every bit as talented an editor as she is a writer—and that's a lot of talent."
—Mike Resnick, author of *The Outpost*

## MOJO: CONJURE STORIES
### Edited by Nalo Hopkinson

Fall under the spell of nineteen tales of passion and darkness, including:

**Daddy Mention and the Monday Skull** by Andy Duncan:
"Much that is said about Daddy Mention is not true, and much of the rest is lies. Many of these lies were told by Daddy Mention himself to begin with, and he is always pleased, at a general store or a hog-killing or a shrimp boil, when one he invented is told back to him . . ."

**The Horsemen and the Morning Star** by Barbara Hambly:
"Their anger, their desperation, their fear, melded and changed with the drumbeat and the cicada voices into something else, something clear and burning and perfect, bright as the core of the sun. And then he was there. An old man in rags, molded out of the night . . ."

**She'd Make a Dead Man Crawl** by Gerard Houarner:
"It wasn't the black man, or the white one. It wasn't me before I came to be what I am. But she doesn't care. There's nothing worse than a dead man with a broken heart . . ."

**Fate** by Jenise Aminoff:
"She wept a little then, knowing her son was truly dead. Then she thought, *To hell with that* . . ."

**Lark till Dawn, Princess** by Barth Anderson:
"A month after the death of my tea-mother, I graced the Laughing Jag in disguise, wearing men's blucher-cut wing tips, trousers, and a silk tie. I say if a girl is going to cross-dress, she better do it with *style* . . ."

**The Skinned** by Jarla Tangh:
"I have come to wicked America. Where, if I breathe in too deeply, my nose burns and my skin itches. No wonder bad things happen here. The air is thick with spirits . . ."

## Books by Nalo Hopkinson

*Brown Girl in the Ring*
*Midnight Robber*
*Skin Folk*

## Anthologies available from Warner Aspect

*Dark Matter: A Century of Speculative Fiction
from the African Diaspora*
edited by Sheree R. Thomas

*A Woman's Liberation: A Choice of Futures By and About Women*
edited by Connie Willis and Sheila Williams

# mojo

## conjure stories

edited by

# NALO HOPKINSON

ASPECT®

WARNER BOOKS

An AOL Time Warner Company

Compilation copyright © 2003 by Nalo Hopkinson

Contributions copyright: "Fate" © 2003 Jenise Aminoff; "Lark till Dawn, Princess" © 2003 Barth Anderson; "Heartspace" © 2003 Steven Barnes; "Death's Dreadlocks" © 2003 Tobias S. Buckell; "Cooking Creole" © 2003 A. M. Dellamonica; "Notes from a Writer's Book of Cures and Spells" © 2003 Marcia Douglas; "Trial Day" © 2003 Tananarive Due; "Daddy Mention and the Monday Skull" © 2003 Andy Duncan; "White Man's Trick" © 2003 Eliot Fintushel; "The Prowl" © 2003 Gregory Frost; "Bitter Grounds" © 2003 Neil Gaiman; "The Horsemen and the Morning Star" © 1994 Barbara Hambly. First appeared in *South From Midnight*. Richard Gilliam, Martin H. Greenberg, and Thomas R. Hanlon, eds. Southern Fried Press, USA. 1994. Limited edition printed specially for the 1995 World Fantasy Convention; "She'd Make a Dead Man Crawl" © 2003 Gerard Houarner; "Shining through 24/7" © 2003 devorah major; "Asuquo, or The Winds of Harmattan" © 2003 Nnedima Okorafor; "Rosamojo" © 2003 Kiini Ibura Salaam; "The Tawny Bitch" © 2003 Nisi Shawl; "The Skinned" © 2003 Carla Johnson; "How Sukie Cross de Big Wata" © 2003 Sheree Renee Thomas

Original lyrics on page 41 are from "Fever" by John Davenport and Eddie Colley © 1956.

All rights reserved.

Aspect® name and logo are registered trademarks of Warner Books, Inc.

Warner Books, Inc., 1271 Avenue of the Americas, New York, NY 10020

Visit our Web site at www.twbookmark.com.

An AOL Time Warner Company

Printed in the United States of America

First Printing: April 2003

10 9 8 7 6 5 4 3 2 1

Library of Congress Cataloging-in-Publication Data

Mojo: conjure stories / edited by Nalo Hopkinson
    p.cm.
    ISBN 0-446-67929-1
    1. Short stories, American—African American authors. 2. African American magic—Fiction. 3. Short stories—Black authors. 4. African Americans—Fiction. 5. Fantasy fiction, American. 6. Hoodoo (Cult)—Fiction. 7. Blacks—Fiction. 8. Africa—Fiction. I. Hopkinson, Nalo.

PS647.A35 M65 2003
813'.0108896073—dc21

2002034922

Cover design by Julie Metz

Cover photo by Elizabeth DeRamus

# Contents

# Editor's Note

Religion and magic are two different things. Religion is an institutionalized system of spiritual beliefs and rituals through which one worships one's gods. Magic, on the other hand, is the practice of altering the fated progression of events to suit one's desires. In some ways, magic is an ultimate act of presumption. It is tricky, powerful, and often dangerous.

There are lots of theories about the etymology of the word "mojo," but one thing seems true: It originated with people press-ganged out of West Africa and brought to America to work as slaves. It refers to a small cloth bag with magical contents that is kept on the person as protection; but more generally, "mojo" can simply mean magic—a magic imbued with African flavor and with the need of indentured peoples to take some control over their lives. And yes, it's tricky, powerful, and dangerous if not used wisely.

The spirit of mojo—of personal magic—shows up right through the diaspora: in root-working, conjuring, and ouanga; in obeah and the ability of "four-eye" people to see into the otherworld; in the West African magics that the Portuguese dubbed "juju." I hope that these nineteen stories conjure up some of that spirit of mojo.

—*Nalo Hopkinson*

# Introduction

Reader, Be Aware!

There's a conjuring going on.

You are being lured, with the turning of each page, into the myth and mystery of our DeepBlack magical heritage.

Put on your beads, pocket your jujubag, and cross yourself several times. Do what you do. Do what you must. But do turn the page and remember what Grandma told you! The old sayings are here. The beliefs are manifested. The formulas cook on the stove.

Eshu, the Trickster will meet you at the Threshold. He stands there in the crossroads between power and fear.

A door will open into the darkness of these pages. You will see in the dark that all are accounted for. The deities are here; the ancestors have arrived. This is the council chamber of those who hold sinister wisdom and serve up justice.

The demons and shape-shifters pace around the corners of this book. They pant and salivate, they snarl and sniff, awaiting your arrival, human. Gather up your courage, child. Do not be frightened by howling laughter and deep guttural moans.

Go ahead; turn the page. Come in and meet your past, your present, and your future.

These stories take us across the varied landscape of our DeepBlack magical heritage. They recall our experiences in the African bush and on the plantations of the Old South. They entice us to feel again the murky waters of the swamp and the hard hot concrete of the northern ghettos.

These stories speak to the conditions of slavery and the secrets of the struggle for freedom. They wrestle with the demons: addiction, incest, and insanity. The healing sacrifice is made with our blood!

Turn another page and you are led to the inner room of your own mind, where madness and genius, wild imagination and common reality, perform a "danse macabre."

And if you make it, dear reader, through these pages, the Trickster will meet you once more at the Threshold where, having survived the darkness, you are in grave danger of being blinded by the light.

Come now. Turn the page. I dare you!

*—Luisah Teish*

# mojo

# DADDY MENTION AND
# THE MONDAY SKULL

*Andy Duncan*

**W**hen old Wilmer guarded Block Twelve, there was no radio, because old Wilmer mistrusted people sitting around a box harking at nothing. But one summer the warden made old Wilmer use a month of his hoarded vacation time, for fear he'd cash it all in at retirement and turn out the lights of Tallahassee as he went. The first thing the guards did once old Wilmer was dragged onto the Trailways bus to his mama's in Pensacola was plunk a long-hidden radio onto old Wilmer's desk and get that thing cranking.

Daddy Mention, in Cell A for obvious reasons, was so near the guardroom that he got to listen to the radio, too, whether he wanted to or not. With one part of his mind, though both wood and blade were denied him, he whittled, without medium or tool or external motion, and with the other he listened, at first with resignation and then with sluggish interest, beginning to study how he might put this racket to use.

"And for all you folks who requested it, here's that hot new song from the Prison Airs, 'Just Walkin' in the Rain.'"

Prison Airs?

"Hey, Narvel," called the desk guard to the corridor guard. "It's those jailbirds from Tennessee."

Daddy Mention jerked a little, and in his mind his whittling knife jumped the grain and sliced his thumb. In his cell Daddy Mention sucked his bloodless thumb and listened to the Prison Airs, which sounded to him like a half dozen colored men trying to sing white.

"They good, ain't they?" Narvel said. "When the governor brought

1

'em to the mansion, to sing for Truman, Truman said, 'Governor, you ought to pardon every damn one of 'em.' "

Now Daddy Mention was two big ears and nothing more.

"Did he pardon 'em?" the desk guard asked.

"Hell, no," Narvel said. "You don't earn no votes in Tennessee by pardoning niggers—just by dressing 'em up and waxing their hair and putting them on the radio."

Amid their laughter, another song started, something about a tiger man who was king of the jungle. Daddy Mention planned never to see a jungle outside a Tarzan movie, but he thought he'd be loose in good honest swampland again before long. If these Prison Airs could go through the wall by singing to white people, Daddy Mention figured he could do that, too. He stopped listening to the radio or to anything except the reasoning inside his head, and an hour past lights-out, he achieved the perfect ironclad silver-dollar plan. For the next hour he turned the plan every which way and saw it shone from all sides, was in fact a plan without flaw, excusing only the technicality, the barely visible chink in the gleaming surface, that Daddy Mention could not sing one blessed lick, sang so bad from the cradle in fact that the mothers of the church had come to the house when Daddy Mention was seven and told his aunt she'd be doing a boon to the Lord if she yanked Daddy Mention out of the children's choir and gave the children a chance. "Well, Daddy Mention," Aunt Ruth had said after the mothers left, though she had called him not Daddy Mention but his true name. "Well, Daddy Mention, I reckon you and the Lord got to drum you up some other skills." The Lord had been so generous on that score that Daddy Mention, by using only a few of his God-given talents, had earned permanent room and board from the taxpayers of Florida. He knew he had improved his whittling by just thinking about it all this time in Cell A, because whittling was that kind of skill, like robbery and book learning and laying down a woman, but he knew singing was different, like carpentry and conjuring and marriage, a thing you needed a talent for.

Still, as Aunt Ruth said, there's no problem invented that a root somewhere won't cure, or help with, or at least distract from a little.

The next afternoon in the prison yard, Daddy Mention checked with the four-on-four players that it wasn't Monday and then paced the west chain fence and stared at the swamp. He stared through the links until they blurred and thinned and flew apart, and the sound of the game behind got farther away until it was just the basketball bouncing *thump*, *thump*, *thump*, into a wad of cotton, and then just Daddy Mention's heartbeat in rhythm with the bullfrogs. On the five hundredth beat, a rippling V appeared out in the green water. It was like a current around a stick where there was neither, just the V point heading for Daddy Mention. When the point reached the edge of the reeds on the other side of the fence a moss-covered snout lifted streaming, and way down at the far end of it a slitted yellow eye gazed at Daddy Mention. The other socket was a scarred knot like a cypress knee. The gator's head was so wide that Daddy Mention had to move his head, like watching horseshoes, to look from eyeball to eye socket, which was left to right today. It was to this scaly hole that Daddy Mention spoke, knowing the good eye was only for appearances.

"Hello, Uncle Monday," said Daddy Mention, though no man chained to his ankle could have heard him.

"Hello, Daddy Mention," said a voice like the final suck of quicksand as the head disappears. That chained man would have heard and seen nothing but a swollen green bubble peck the surface. "I'm sorry," the voice went on, "that I can't rise from this water and shake your hand like a man, Daddy Mention, 'cause you done called me on the wrong day of o'clock. You know you ought to call on a Monday, if you want me at my best."

With the sliver of his mind not holding on and holding off, Daddy Mention vowed he'd sit in Cell A till Judgment before he'd call up Uncle

Monday on the second day of a week. But Daddy Mention knew better any day than to flap gums with Uncle Monday, because that just gave him more time to work at you like the Suwannee working its bank. With most of his mind Daddy Mention stuck with the program, and said:

"Sunday's dying
"And Saturday's dead
"Friday's crawling
"Into Thursday's bed
"Wednesday's drunk
"And Tuesday's fled
"And Monday's bound
"With a piece of—"

The vast scaly thing in the water thrashed in place as if speared, roaring and slamming up sheets of water with its railroad-tie tail (and even the guard in the corner tower thought maybe he heard a beaver slide into the shallows, then forgot it before he could turn his head); but it was too late for Uncle Monday, for Daddy Mention already had flung down a three-inch piece of thread, which stretched taut as barbed wire when it hit the ground. Uncle Monday writhed and puked and snarled horrible things, but he finally settled down, his white belly heaving in the murked-up water. He blew a long blubbery breath and said, "Name it, then."

"Make me sing," said Daddy Mention.

"You'll sing," said Uncle Monday, grinding his many teeth, "when I gnaw off your generations."

"Make me sing," said Daddy Mention, sticking to the program. "Make me sing like a mockingbird's mama, like a saint, like a baby, like the springs on a twenty-dollar bed."

"Huh," said Uncle Monday, and the hard-packed dirt at Daddy Mention's feet boiled like an ant bed. By the time he jumped back, the dirt had stopped moving around a moss-covered, snaggletoothed, hang-jawed human skull.

"What devilment is that?" blurted Daddy Mention, and Uncle Monday nearly got his mind. Wrestling it back was a near thing, and Daddy Mention had to bite his own tongue bloody to do it.

"Old bullets well up in my hide," said Uncle Monday, pleasant and dreamy as if cross-legged on a veranda, as Daddy Mention gagged and choked and reeled, "and work their way out as the months pass, and leave a scar. This skull is one of the Earth's old bullets. Rub it, Daddy Mention, and it will smile at you, and while it smiles at you with favor, you will sing."

Daddy Mention spat in the dirt, wiped his mouth with his sleeve, gulped air, and—focused on Uncle Monday all the while—leaned down and rubbed the skull. It was hot and wet and grainy and barked his fingers like an emery board. He stepped back. The skull sat in the dirt, a vacant, crusty hunk of bone with a kick-sized crack in the temple. Daddy Mention stared and stared, and then, before his disbelieving eyes, the skull . . . just kept lying there, deader than dead. It kept on doing that for a long while. And then, just as Daddy Mention was about to lose patience and give that old skull a matching dent with his foot, just as he realized Uncle Monday had made a fool out of him again from age-old habit and cruelty and contempt for all who go two-legged daily, just as he could taste the bitter burn of years climbing his throat to be swallowed again, why, at that precise moment, the old skull that had shown no previous sign of life . . . did not do one goddamn thing. Daddy Mention kicked it across the yard. It rolled nearly to the feet of two blurred prisoners pitching horseshoes in real time, one gray U drifting through the air like a milkweed.

"Damn your evil soul," Daddy Mention said. "You told me this skull would smile on me with favor, and make me sing."

"And so it will," said Uncle Monday, subsiding like an eroded sandbar or a rotten log. "And so it will . . . on Mondays." A smoke curl rose from the string, which burned out like a fuse, and then Uncle Monday was gone.

When they blew the coming-in, Daddy Mention, in real time again, walked back inside with all the others. No one noticed that beneath his shirt, under his arm, Daddy Mention cradled something.

No one noticed, either, because Daddy Mention already looked twice as old as Methuselah, that in the exercise yard that afternoon, from going-out to coming-in, he had aged exactly three years, one per minute of Monday's time, one per inch of thread.

The next Monday, an hour before lights-out, Daddy Mention wrinkled his nose, rubbed the nasty skull, hid it beneath the cot behind the bucket, and began to sing.

He had given no thought to material. He'd just sing any of the many songs he picked up in turpentine camps and sawmills and boatyards and boxcars and prison after prison after prison. He decided to start with "Gotta Make a Hundred." He cleared his throat and hummed, *Hmmm*, as preachers sometimes did to launch a song, as if tuning themselves. Then he took a deep breath and began:

*Lord, I'm running, trying to make a hundred*
*Ninety-nine and a half won't do . . .*

Except it didn't come out. He thought the words, but his mouth and tongue and lungs and gut didn't cooperate. What came out instead was one of those happy, bouncy, dumbass songs on Narvel's radio all week, a song Daddy Mention didn't know he knew. What came out of his mouth was "If I Knew You Were Coming I'd Have Baked a Cake."

Uncle Monday was having some fun.

Daddy Mention sat dumbfounded. It was his voice, all right, and not the gal's on the radio, but it sounded too damn good to be him. Held a tune and everything. His mouth and equipment were a bellows being worked by other hands, something Daddy Mention sat above and apart from, the balcony looking down on the band. He was about two words ahead of his mouth in knowing the song, as if someone were dictating into his ear.

"What the hell?"

"Pipe down!"

"It's him. It's Daddy Mention."

"Get out."

"Yeah! Look!"

When that song finished, the next one started, then the next. Not work-camp songs. Popular songs. Hit-record songs. White songs. They poured from his gullet like he had taken syrup of ipecac and couldn't empty himself fast enough. They left a taste like ipecac, too. The second song was "Rag Mop," then "The Cry of the Wild Goose," then "Bonaparte's Retreat," and Daddy Mention knew them all just in time to sing them, and knew their titles, too. In front of his cell stood the guards of the block, gray-faced, jawstrings popped. The prisoners in their cells whooped and hollered. Daddy Mention sang "April in Portugal" and "A Guy Is a Guy" and "The Little White Cloud That Cried." He had no control over what came up. He was like a nickel jukebox. The whole corridor was full of guards, coming from the four corners to stare like Daddy Mention was an after-hours sideshow. Daddy Mention's face hurt from being worked in strange ways, but still the songs and the guards kept coming. He sang "Glow Worm" and "Tennessee Waltz" and "How Much Is That Doggie in the Window?" Some of the guards barked along; "Woof! Woof!" He sang "On Top of Old Smokey" and "Sweet Violets" and "How High the Moon" and "Harbor Lights." The guards laughed, whistled, snapped their fingers, danced, cut shines. The guards got louder, the prisoners quieter. Too many guards meant trouble, and so did an obvious hoodoo job. Now the warden was on tiptoe behind the guards like Zacchaeus, come down in his flannels to see for himself that the whole goddamn Hit Parade was indeed venting from the coils and recesses of Daddy Mention—who was now taking requests, things that weren't even English: "Vaya con Dios" and "Eh Cumpari" and "C'est Si Bon" and "Auf Wiedersehen Sweetheart" and "Abba Dabba Honeymoon." He had no

7

more control over the singing than a cow the milking, but he had possession of the rest of his body, and so he started to work the crowd a little, add dance steps, hand gestures, a wiggle of the hips, some flash. He high-kicked his way through "Music Music Music," and that was the showstopper. As the warden led the cheers of "Encore!" Daddy Mention tensed, mouth open, for a next outburst that didn't come. He swallowed; his throat was dry and sore. He waited.

Nothing.

"Show's over," Daddy Mention said, all energy gone.

And he now realized, as the guards and the warden hollered for more, that for quite some time, while playing Mister Bones for the white folks and getting beyond himself, he had not been alone in his mind. That second barely-there presence now ebbed, but not before Daddy Mention clearly heard, more as an inner-ear tingle than a sound, someone—some*thing*—chuckle.

The trusties had moved three rows of cafeteria benches into the exercise yard, with folding chairs up front for the warden and the governor and the yes-men. All the prisoners were locked up tight for Daddy Mention's semipublic debut, but the benches were full of invitees—school board members, Rotarians, preachers, city councilmen, Junior Leaguers, Daughters of the Confederacy, Sons of Confederate Veterans, White Citizens' Council officers, turpentine magnates, all the quality for miles, eating Woolworth's popcorn and drinking pink punch and murmuring in expectation of helping (as the warden had put it) a wayward Negro boy rehabilitate himself through song. Several had shiny pennies to give the performer after the show, if the warden would allow it. Stapled to the benches, leftover Christmas bunting flapped red and green in the rising breeze. The atmosphere was as festive as it gets with a prison in front and a swamp behind.

Up front, the warden, his bald head beginning to sunburn, chatted with the governor, who sat cross-legged and fidgety, wiggling his right foot, exposing a length of shiny new sock with clocks on it. He was technically only the acting governor, because the real governor lay on his deathbed in Tallahassee, watched always by rotating shifts of the acting governor's yes-men. He had lain there for ten months. The governor had hundreds of infant constituents named for him who had not even been conceived when he began to die. Month after month the minions of the acting governor sat at the governor's bedside, keen for cessation of breathing. More than one lifted a pillow and punched it and hefted it and checked the door and was tempted, but set it down again because he was a Democrat and had standards.

"Tell me again, Warden," the acting governor said, "why your caged mockingbird sings only on Monday?"

The acting governor encouraged everyone to call him simply "Governor," as a time-saver. "Well, Governor," the warden began, then faltered. His head began to hurt whenever he was asked this question. Daddy Mention had explained this peculiarity at great length—it was something about a family gopher—no, wait, that would be silly—a family *goopher*, a hex on all his kinfolk that enabled singing only one month per decade, and that on Mondays—but the warden couldn't remember the half of it. And whenever he tried to reconstruct the conversation, which had seemed convincing at the time, he had an unsettling trace memory of Daddy Mention leaning across his desk blotter and blowing dust into his face, but that couldn't have happened. Could it? He tried to tell some of this to the acting governor, who waved him off.

"No, no, never mind, I'm sorry I asked. Do *I* care what day I'm summoned to take part in a penitentiary minstrel show? It's not as if I have any other claims on my time. I only have a state to run, that's all. Why, I am at the disposal, the utter beck and call of your grandpa Mumbly, or whatever his name is. Why, he can't even vote. Even if he wasn't in jail."

The circumstances of the acting governor's quasi administration had left him with an unbecoming streak of self-pity.

"Warden, do you know how many miles of coastline alone I am responsible for, de facto if not de jure? Do you? Oh, come on, guess. You know you want to guess. Total miles."

The warden squirmed. "A thousand?"

"A thousand, hmm? A thousand. Nice, round figure. Wholly inadequate, but even. Try four, try six, try eight thousand four hundred and twenty-six, hah? Hah, Rand McNally?"

"Here he is!" cried the warden, vastly relieved.

They had come for him at two, Narvel trundling back the cell door.

"Let's go, Daddy Mention," Narvel said.

"Go where?" He glanced at his cot, where the skull lay amid a jumble of sheets, covered by his pillow. "Thought the governor was coming."

"You don't think the governor's coming all the way in here, do you?" Narvel said. "He's waiting in the yard. Come on."

In the yard meant in reach of the swamp, and today was Monday. Daddy Mention grabbed the bars. "Hold on, now. I got to think about this."

Narvel laughed. "What fool talk is that? Daddy Mention wants to stay *inside* the prison." The others laughed as they took hold of his elbows. "Come on, I said."

Daddy Mention hung on to the bars still, with surprising strength for an old man. He looked at his bedclothes again, for longer this time. "No, Mr. Narvel, please," Daddy Mention said, his voice quavering. Those in neighboring cells caught this new note in his voice, and those who could, exchanged glances across the corridor. "Bring the governor in here," Daddy Mention went on. "I'll sing for him just as pretty. Oh, please, Mr. Narvel, please don't make me go outside."

"Come forth, Daddy Mention," Narvel said, jaw set. The strong hands on Daddy Mention's arms redoubled their efforts, and a fourth guard grabbed around his waist, pulled backward till he was off his feet, still hanging on. Narvel worked to pry loose Daddy Mention's fingers. "Come forth, Daddy Mention, come forth," Narvel repeated, in a voice not his own, a voice like a cottonmouth gliding into a pool.

"Come forth, Daddy Mention, come forth," said the other guards, sounding not like three men but one using three mouths. Narvel, eyes shining faintly yellow, whipped out his pigsticker and went for Daddy Mention's fingers with the blade. Daddy Mention let go of the bars, and the guard at his waist stumbled backward. The skin of the guard's hands looked pebbled up and scaly. "Come forth, Daddy Mention, come forth."

Daddy Mention looked long and hard over his shoulder at the cot as they hauled him out. What did he have to do, hit these crackers on the head?

"Hey, Narvel!" cried Creflo the bootlegger in Cell B. Narvel jerked, startled, and blinked the yellow out of his eyes. He shook his head as if to clear it. "What is it, Creflo?"

"I think Daddy Mention's got something hid in there," Creflo said, "s" sounds whistling through the gap in his top teeth.

"Is that right?" Narvel was himself again. "Check it out, Dell."

Daddy Mention scowled at Creflo and thought, *Thank you, brother.* Creflo, who lacked the gift for sending, just nodded and grinned. *You're welcome,* that meant, clear to anybody, gift or no gift.

Dell jumped back with a cry, bedclothes in hand. "Damn, Narvel, look at this! Daddy Mention's a body snatcher!"

There sat the skull, the sheet around it stained brown like tobacco juice.

Narvel snatched Daddy Mention close by the collar. "What the hell you up to, boy? Trying to lure the governor down here, work some hoodoo on him?"

"No, sir," Daddy Mention said. He cringed and teared up and trembled, proud and disgusted at pulling the mushmouth so well when he had to. "I don't know where that skeery thing come from. It's hainted, I swears it is. Oh, please sir, leave it be. I don't want nothing to do with it."

"Oh, no? Dell, bring Daddy Mention's play-pretty with us. We'll have a talk with the warden later about your witchy ways."

Daddy Mention rolled his eyes and sobbed and pleaded and exulted.

Dell made no move. "Huh-uh. I ain't touching that thing."

Narvel flipped out his pigsticker again and twirled it in his fingers like a little baton. Narvel could be scary even when he wasn't possessed. Dell sidled forward and yanked free the corners of the sheet. He gathered them up and held the sheet, skull and all, away from his body like it was outhouse dirt.

Daddy Mention stumbling in front, Dell creeping behind, the little procession walked down the corridor. The other prisoners listened as one door, a farther door, an even farther door was unlocked and relocked behind. The clanks got fainter, the echoes more ghostly. When they were half memory, Creflo spoke.

"I got a quarter says he won't be back."

There were no takers.

The sight of Daddy Mention disappointed a number of spectators, mostly female, as they had hoped for a younger, more robust specimen of repentant male Negritude.

The warden joined the little party at the single microphone, which he covered with one hand to ask, "What's in the bag?"

"Hoodoo contraband," Narvel said.

"Scary shit," Dell cried, at the same time.

"Tell me later," the warden said. "Just keep it out of sight till they go." He removed his hand and spoke. "Good afternoon, ladies and gentlemen . . . ."

As the warden droned, Daddy Mention smelled the air: a whiff of rot, growing stronger. He tasted the breeze: out of the swamp, picking up. He listened past the warden, past the rippling crepe, past the weary sighs of the acting governor, past the cranes hollering in the trees, and heard wet footsteps coming closer, *squelch*, *squelch*. Then applause drowned them out, and Daddy Mention stood alone.

He figured he was ready. Daddy Mention had nearly worn out the skull rubbing it before Narvel came for him. The wind from the swamp was really whipping now. A popcorn box tumbled to rest, spraying white puffs, at Daddy Mention's feet. He knew Uncle Monday was coming, but he had to speed him up some, for the gift he had fashioned in his mind wouldn't last, and Uncle Monday had to be a whole lot closer when he got it, if this was going to work at all. And so Daddy Mention found himself doing that thing he once vowed never to do: calling Uncle Monday on his very day.

Not that the crowd could hear him, of course. As far as they could tell, he was just standing there, leaning into the breeze, his eyelids half-closed and fluttering.

Someone coughed.

"Well, this is fun," the acting governor told the warden. "Is there no end to the man's talents? He doesn't sing, and he has seizures, too."

"God damn, I'll make him sing," muttered Narvel. He stood and strode forward, fists clenched, only to stop dead with a grunt about three feet from Daddy Mention, as if he had bellied into an electric fence. As the crowd murmured, Narvel slowly turned.

"What's wrong with his eyes?" a woman asked.

Narvel's jaw slowly sagged, dragging his mouth open. Deep inside, something gurgled. Then a voice not Narvel's own emerged, as his jaw worked up and down, not in sync with the words:

*"Raw head and bloody bones, rise up and shake yourself. He's halfway here."*

Dell jumped to his feet shrieking, because from within the sheeted bundle beneath his bench had come a sound like a cricket chirping: *Rick-de-rick, rick-de-rick, rick-de-rick!*

*"Raw head and bloody bones, rise up and shake yourself. He's mostways here."*

Dell's bundle slid forward several feet, caught no doubt in a sudden gust from the swamp, though it might have kept moving after the gust died. *Rick-de-rick, rick-de-rick, rick-de-rick!*

Not even the acting governor was joking now. Everyone but Narvel and Daddy Mention sat, frozen. Something yanked up Narvel's right arm, so that it might have been pointing, had the hand not flopped at the wrist like a scarecrow's.

*"Raw head and bloody bones, rise up and shake yourself, for Monday's here!"*

The wind ripped open the sheet, and the skull tumbled out, rolled to a stop at Daddy Mention's feet. *Rick-de-rick, rick-de-rick, rick-de-rick!*

Daddy Mention opened his eyes and smiled. As he squinted into the wind he could make out, in the distance, a tiny dark two-legged figure in a hat, striding ever nearer across the swamp, across the surface of the deep water.

Daddy Mention sometimes wondered why he always took free and bedeviled over locked up and safe, but he couldn't change how he was, any more than Uncle Monday could choose his walking days. There are higher powers in this old world, his aunt Ruth used to say, and that old woman didn't know the half of it. One day Daddy Mention was going to find those higher powers and open up a can of whupass. But right now Uncle Monday was laying hold of him. Narvel dropped like an empty sack as Uncle Monday, still a hundred yards distant, pried open Daddy Mention's mouth and began, through him, to sing. It was a song that got amongst the audience like a moccasin in a swimming hole. It carried without need of amplification, without need of eardrums. It was Uncle Monday's song.

*"Uncle Monday's on his way, better strike a deal*
*"You know he ain't never one to miss a meal*
*"Uncle Monday*
*"Uncle Monday*
*"Uncle Monday Uncle Monday Uncle Monday*

*"Uncle Monday's been dead for many a year*
*"But he keeps hanging round 'cause he likes it here*
*"Uncle Monday . . .*

*"Uncle Monday likes to crawl up onto the land*
*"Go two-legged dancing like a natural man*
*"Uncle Monday . . .*

*"Uncle Monday goes a-strolling on the second day*
*"He'll let you keep your money, steal your soul away*
*"Uncle Monday . . .*

*"Uncle Monday has so many teeth sharp as a file*
*"Can take you seven days just to watch him smile*
*"Uncle Monday . . .*

*"Uncle Monday walks Okeechobee like it was dry*
*"While bobbin' up behind him are the fish that have died*
*"Uncle Monday . . .*

*"His breath blows hot but his blood runs cool*
*"And his nuts swing low like a Georgia bull*
*"Uncle Monday . . .*

*"When Uncle Monday wants a woman he just gives her a shout*
*"She goes skipping into the swamp and never comes out*
*"Uncle Monday . . .*

*"Uncle Monday knows the swamp ain't all that it seems*
*"And you know that wasn't just a panther's scream*
*"Uncle Monday . . .*

*"Uncle Monday made a raw head and bloody bones*
*"Rise up and be a-walkin' just to hear it moan*
*"Uncle Monday . . .*

*"Uncle Monday, there's a poor man got no legs*
*"Yes, I swum up beneath him, cut him down a peg*
*"Uncle Monday . . .*

*"Uncle Monday took a trip down to hell and back*
*"Toting seven governors in a croker sack*
*"Uncle Monday . . .*

*"Uncle Monday says have you a drink and a smoke*
*"You'll soon enough be swinging from a cypress oak*
*"Uncle Monday*
*"Uncle Monday*
*"Uncle Monday Uncle Monday Uncle Monday"*

His walking form was now a dozen yards away and closing, and Daddy Mention could feel him pouring in, opening the skull-door wider, ever wider, in his eagerness to get in. *Rick-de-rick, rick-de-rick, rick-de-rick!* But here's a true thing: a Monday skull is a two-way skull. And while Uncle Monday was sending Daddy Mention his song, Daddy Mention was sending him something in return, something powerful, something he had spent several days whittling with his mind: a little squatty man carved from black oak, with Uncle Monday's true name cut into its stomach; this wrapped with black cloth and tied with black thread around a bundle of blackberry vines.

While Uncle Monday dealt with that, he lost his grip on Daddy Mention, the way a man who steps into a hive has concerns more immediate than honey. In the moment Uncle Monday was distracted, a moment in which Daddy Mention aged more than any human life span, Daddy Mention snatched up the microphone stand, swung its weighted base over his head like a hammer, and bashed the Monday skull into graveyard dust.

Then lots of things happened at once.

Daddy Mention, as near as Uncle Monday could tell, ceased to exist—for a few minutes, anyway.

The bad energies Uncle Monday had funneled through the skull sped out in all directions from the impact, like pond water fleeing a chunked-in brick. Snowballs pelted roofs in Key West. A sudden, pervasive hog-pen smell emptied the white high school in Tampa. In Orlando, the screens of televisions showing a roller derby telecast flickered and, for just a few seconds, held the grainy silent image of a black man howling. In Tallahassee, the governor in his deathbed sat bolt upright with black orbs for eyes and rasped to the yes-man, "I have come back from where you are going," and fell back dead.

The full brunt of the flood, however, was borne by all those people in the prison yard, who briefly and horribly became aware of Uncle Monday's true nature.

Each reacted after his own fashion. There was wailing and sobbing and puking and tongue-speaking and Saint Vitus dancing. Some just sat and moaned, and some ran, knocking their heads into the stone wall or tangling themselves in the fence where they might have been shot had the guards not been jibbering mad at the moment, too.

None of those doused by Uncle Monday that afternoon could remember it afterward, and you could say they all recovered within the hour, none the worse for wear. But the seeds had been planted. And so they found themselves, in the next month or so, for perfectly good everyday reasons (they thought), switching churches or getting saved or writing letters to the editor denouncing Jim Crow or preaching atheism in the town square or taking grocery-store bagboys as lovers or beginning to drink heavily or taking the pledge or buying two-tone Buicks or joining the Klan or the Masons or the Anti-Defamation League or giving all their possessions to colored orphanages or declaring for the fifth congressional seat or burning their hats or crying for two days, all because it's always Monday somewhere.

In the immediate aftermath, as everyone rubbed their heads and picked themselves up off the ground and tried to remember what had happened, it was Dell who first asked, "Where's Daddy Mention?"

That seemed another uncanny mystery beyond human ken, until they found a cafeteria bench standing on end against the west wall and discovered the acting governor's limousine was acting gone.

Daddy Mention's latest escape made neither the papers nor the radio, but every inmate in eight states knew about it by Tuesday at three, when it was the talk of the yard at Tennessee State.

"Picked up Uncle Monday by his tail and slung him right over the wall!" said Marcell, the bass.

"God damn! I'd like to have seen that," said John D., the second tenor.

"Then he dusted the governor with some essence of bend-over and made him hand over the keys to his limousine," said William, the baritone.

"Lord amighty!" said Ed, the third tenor. "Tell it, now."

During all this, Johnny Bragg, lead tenor of the Prisonaires, whom armed guards had escorted to the Sun studio in Memphis to record "Just Walking in the Rain" and then escorted back again, stood in the corner of the yard, facing the wall, practicing a song titled "That Chick's Too Young to Fry." It was a song with meaning for Johnny Bragg, who at sixteen had caught his girlfriend half full of another man, her eyes focusing on Johnny Bragg only long enough to wink. The police got there in time to arrest Johnny Bragg, somehow, on a rape charge, and as they had a file drawer of unsolved cases at the station house, Johnny Bragg was now serving six ninety-nine-year sentences, which was entirely two many threes for comfort. But Johnny Bragg knew he had not been delivered from blindness at age seven just to stare at the walls of a six-by-eight cell, so he practiced, food bucket over his head for reverb, while his sorry excuse for a vocal group woofed the hour away.

Johnny Bragg wondered whether Bill Kenny ever had this trouble with the Ink Spots. He doubted it. He yanked off the bucket, found the outside air just as hot and close as in, and said, "Daddy Mention this, Daddy Mention that, Daddy Mention shit. How many times Daddy Mention ever got your asses over the wall? Huh? Marcell? Even you can count up to nothing. Are we going to practice today or not?"

The others made no move. "We was just talking," Ed mumbled.

"*Some* of us," said William, his shoulders back, thumbs seeking purchase on absent suspenders, "think a whole lot of Daddy Mention."

"I done time with him," Marcell said. "South Carolina, summer of '52. He whistled down an eagle and flew off over the Congaree. He did! I knew a man who talked to a guard who was in the yard with his back turned and heard it happen."

"Wait, now," William said. "It was Parchman he busted out of that summer. Raised so many sparks gnawing his bars he started a fire that he walked right through and out the door, Shadrach, Meshach, Abednego."

Now all the others chimed in with their own competing accounts, and Johnny Bragg shook his head.

"My people, my people," he said. "My race, but not my taste. What does it matter how many prisons Daddy Mention got out of at once? Here we sit when Daddy Mention goes in, and here we sit when Daddy Mention goes out. You are four sad gum-beaters."

Johnny Bragg cast down his bucket and tried to walk away, but the effect was spoiled by a guard who made him pick it up. Those damn things cost money, and he didn't want to eat out of his *other* bucket, did he?

That night he woke to find Daddy Mention standing beside his bed, looking down and smiling. He was a lot older than Johnny Bragg had expected. Johnny Bragg asked, You come to spring me? and Daddy Mention said, Hell, no. Johnny Bragg asked, Why you here, then? and Daddy Mention asked, Why are you? And then Johnny Bragg—who would never escape, who would serve another three years and be let out and be sent back to serve six more and then be released into a world where even the Ink Spots were forgotten—woke up a second time and woke up mad, that he had fretted his sleep on such useless dreams as that.

Late in the day of Daddy Mention's concert for the governor, old Wilmer, sunburnt and swollen like a boudin sausage, stumped down from the Trailways at the turpentine thicket on the highway, not real close to the prison but as close as the Trailways ran.

Old Wilmer mopped his neck with a scrap of tablecloth as he trudged the shady back road toward the coroner's entrance. Bluebottle flies zummed past. A faraway woodpecker fired off messages: send help send help send help. Old Wilmer set down his case, unhooked his suspenders, and made water in the road, just to watch his stream cut channels in the clay. Old Wilmer was in no hurry, because he knew that in his absence, the prison surely had gone teetotally to hell, and his mind projected Technicolor slides of chaos and ruin.

He stopped on the plank bridge for a cigarette. As he slung his match into the scum, he thought someone was watching beneath the surface of the water, and the sweat beaded cold on the back of his buzz-cut neck. But then it was just a big old gator, still as a cypress log and playing dead. Full of deer, probably, or coon dog. Every time the hounds were let loose in the swamp, one or two didn't come back, and the warden would cry like a woman. They lost a lot more dogs than men. At that moment, old Wilmer heard the hounds baying, as if he had summoned them.

Old Wilmer smoked and stared at the gator, and the gator's one eye stared back. When he was done, old Wilmer felt strangely respectful, did not throw the butt into the water but wedged it into the crack of his shoe between leather and sole, to save for the trusty who collected tobacco and was two-thirds of his way to a Winston by now.

Wilmer found turning his back on the gator surprisingly difficult. He looked back once. Standing stiff-legged on the bridge, arms hanging at his sides, was an old Negro in high-water britches, face shaded by a preacher's hat in the gathering dusk. Wilmer nodded once, the wary acknowledgment one Southern man gives another, and after a pause the figure nodded back—less a nod, really, than a jerk, involuntary, like a flinch from an unseen blow. With the nod was a brief pyrite sparkle in the shadow where the right eye might have been.

Old Wilmer turned and walked on, his fatalism stoked at every step by the baying of hounds and, now, the splashing and cursing of men. The first to stagger into view was that idiot Narvel, now rightly subordinate to the ass end of a hound, Narvel so muck-crusted and bedraggled and snarling that he clearly was on his third or even fourth fruitless sweep through the swamp—and then old Wilmer knew who, of all of them, had got out.

He set down his suitcase till he was done laughing. Then he picked it up and swung it as he walked, and whistled a nasty song his mama's nurse had taught him over a Mason jar of coondick. Maybe he could get Cell A for a proper office, once it was cleansed. Surely no prisoner would be moved in there. Who knew what Daddy Mention had left behind?

Guards ran in and out the back gate like roaches from a matchbox. Old Wilmer handed his suitcase to one, really just held it out so that the rushing other's pistol arm thrust through the handle and snatched it away as a train snatches mail. Old Wilmer wouldn't need it again for a long, long time. All he needed was here, inside a pair of boots in his locker. Narvel and the other guards might put their faith in locks and walls, muscles and guns, and the color of their skin, but old Wilmer kept his eyes open, and believed in whatever worked. If he laid down an X of Draw Back Powder, corner to corner of the cell, and burned a black-over-red candle at the crossroads, that would be a start. Uncle Wilmer reached into his pants pocket, touched the little nine-knotted bundle of devil's shoestrings, and strode whistling into the prison.

Much that is said about Daddy Mention is not true, and much of the rest is lies. Many of these lies were told by Daddy Mention himself to begin with, and he is always pleased, at a general store or a hog-killing or a shrimp boil, when one he invented is told back to him. They were whoppers to begin with, but my how they grew!

One night beside a campfire beneath a trestle, Daddy Mention held forth to a group of travelers about his many exploits: how he hacked through a prison wall with a single sharp toenail that wasn't even his; how, one August, he swam out of a jailhouse in a river of his own sweat; how he had so many garters from grateful wardens' wives and sheriffs' daughters that he was paying a granny woman to stitch them into a quilt; how he used a singing skull to reel in Uncle Monday himself like a bream on a line and then threw him on the governor; how he escaped a chain gang by holding his breath till they declared him dead and buried him; and all such tales as that.

Finally a man just beyond the firelight said, "I God, mister. You sound like Daddy Mention himself."

"That's what they call me," Daddy Mention said.

The man stepped forward, flashed a badge, and said, "Well, do you know who I am? I'm the sheriff, I'm the father of two daughters, and you are under arrest."

Daddy Mention replied, "How do, Sheriff. Allow me to introduce myself. I am the lyingest nigger on the face of this Earth."

# ROSAMOJO

*Kiini Ibura Salaam*

**E**yes half closed. I see the dark denim of Daddy's legs. My bedroom door swings open. Light rips into my room, then disappears. I am alone now. Daddy's footsteps get softer and softer. I relax when I can't hear them no more. I turn my head to the wall real slow. My neck is sore, but that's better than it being broke. My breath goes from fast to slow. Then I start to notice other things. Like the moon glowing outside my window. My leg shaking so hard I can't stop it. My fists clenched tight. I open one hand. It's empty. I hold my fingers up to my face. It's dark in my room, but I can see the two white marks my fingernails made when they were digging into my skin. I squeeze the other hand tighter. The soft springy clump of Daddy's hair shifts in my palm. It would tickle if I would let it. But I don't. I can't laugh while I still hear Daddy's voice whispering that I'm his favorite.

Sunlight is creeping under my eyelids, climbing into my eyes. I curl over on my side and draw my knees up to my chest. I don't want to move, not ever. I hear Mama screaming at Lola to hurry up in the bathroom, and my heart catches in my throat. Benny is crying at the top of his lungs. I know I better get up. Unless I want Mama to know, I gotta start moving. I jump up and pull my nightgown over my head. At first I go to throw it in the dirty clothes hamper; then I stop. I shove it under my mattress instead. My head feels dizzy, but when I hear Mama's voice in the hall, I know I gotta make everything look right.

I stumble over to my dresser and pick out a clean nightgown. The new nightgown is soft on my skin. It smells like soap powder. I wanna go lie down again. I wanna close my eyes and sleep with the fresh smell, but I don't. I yank the edges of my sheets and tuck the corners under the mattress. I climb on top of the bed and throw the top sheet high up so it can fall down flat. Before the sheet reaches the bed, I see them: two dark streaks—one short, one long. I go to pull them dirty sheets from the bed, but then I start thinking about how far away the clean sheets are. It be smarter to hide the stains from Mama than try to get some fresh ones from the hall closet. I grip the edges of the top sheet and pull it smooth. If Mama comes to check on me now, she'll be real happy with how tight I made the bed. She'll be so proud, she'll never even see the stains.

When I peek out into the hall, nobody's looking. I run straight to the bathroom and shut the door behind me. Before washing up, I wipe the warm washcloth between my legs. When I look at it, I see the same dark red streaks that were on the sheets. I rinse the washcloth and wipe till it shows no more red. Then I wash my face and brush my teeth.

Mama is already at the stove cooking when I sit at the table.

"No kiss for me this morning?" she says.

But I don't move. I just sit at the table still as a stone.

"Rosamojo, you wake up on the wrong side of the bed?" Mama laughs. Then she comes and kisses my cheeks.

Daddy kisses me on top of my head like normal. I sit on my hands because if I didn't, I'd scratch his face and Mama would know something is wrong. Mama drops my plate down in front of me. The two huge yolks of my eggs is still jiggling from their journey from the stove. I don't say nothing. Not even when Benny starts to tease me about how long it take me to get out of bed. Not even when Lola steals two pieces of bacon from my plate while looking me dead in the face. Not even when Mama says, "Rosamojo's having a bad day," and puts cheese on only my grits. Lola looks at me and squints her eyes. When Mama goes back to the stove and Daddy goes to the coffeepot, she balls up her fist and says, "You better not be doing no magic no more." I shake my head.

"I didn't do no magic, I swear," I say in a flat voice.

"What you said, sweetheart?" Daddy asks.

"Nothing, Daddy," I say, and stir my cheese into my grits.

Benny and Lola are loud in the backyard. Daddy and Mama been left, but I'm still sitting at the table, dirty dishes spread all over the tabletop. Lola runs into the kitchen while I'm trying not to think about last night. Benny comes in right behind her carrying two sticks. Lola hits her stick on the floor.

"Wanna go scare some neutra rats?" she asks.

I just shake my head no.

"We got you a stick," Benny says.

I shrug my shoulders.

"We goin' then," she says. "And I don't wanna hear nothing 'bout them dishes."

I shrug my shoulders again.

Lola looks close at me. "What's wrong with you?" she asks.

I don't say nothing. Lola bangs her stick on the floor. She sucks her teeth and turns away.

"Come on, Benny. Let's go to the canal. Rosa's acting funny today."

I feel like the air around me is thick and I gotta move real slow. My favorite overalls be the only thing I can think of to make me feel better. I put them on before I jerk the sheets from my bed. In the tub, I wash out the dark spots. I bring the sheets down the hall, down the stairs through the living room, through the kitchen to the back door. Just when I am about to step outside, I see old nosy Mrs. Roberts looking into our backyard. I back up, arms still full of sheets. If Mrs. Roberts see me hanging up a sheet with a few wet spots, she gonna ask Mama if I got my cycle. And Mama gonna come asking me questions like she did Lola. So I go back upstairs to my room. I let the sheets fall out of my arms onto my bare mattress. Then I sit on my bed a while, thinking and staring out the window. I jump up onto the mattress with my slippers on. I strain to lift the windows and struggle to get the screens out. I hang the flat sheet out one window and the fitted sheet out the other. Them wet spots should dry real quick. But if I can't get them screens back in before Mama gets home, I'm gonna have to do some explaining.

In Mama and Daddy's room everything is cool and quiet. It's like they room ain't part of the rest of the house. It's so dark in there I can't see my reflection in neither of Mama and Daddy's two mirrors. I get real close on them, but I can barely make out my face. Then I start snooping around. I don't even know what I'm looking for until I see it: Daddy's favorite harmonica sitting on top of the dresser with Mama's combs and jewelry. I slip the harmonica into my side pocket. On the floor next to Daddy's side of the bed is the sports section. I crouch down and look at it. His hands left black ink fingerprints all over the paper, so I roll it up and stick it in my back pocket. I go down the hall to the bathroom and stand on the step stool. In the medicine cabinet, I see lots of little bottles with words I can't read. Then I see Daddy's toothpicks. I put a handful in my front pocket and I go to the kitchen.

Beneath the sink is a big burlap bag full of Daddy's favorite coffee. I grab the bag by the edges and drag it through the kitchen, through the living room to the front porch. Back in the kitchen, I find the metal bowl Mama uses to soak burnt pots and pans; I bring that to the porch too. I stick the toothpicks into the harmonica holes. Then I wrap the harmonica in the newspaper. My hand twitches. I look at it and suddenly remember— Daddy's hair! I run upstairs and scoop up the hair from my dresser drawer. On the porch, I unwrap the newspaper and stick Daddy's hair into the harmonica holes too. Then I rewrap the package. I put it in Mama's metal bowl and set the whole thing on fire. I squat, watching it burn. My lips begin to move. Words come spilling out of my mouth quickly. It's a protection prayer that I didn't even know I had in my head. When the fire burns itself out, the whole porch is cloudy with smoke. I use a dishrag to pick up Daddy's burnt things, and I shove it deep into the coffee beans. It seem like it take forever for me to drag that bag of coffee upstairs, but I do it. By the time I stuff the bag under my bed, my arms are wet with sweat.

When Lola and Benny come home, all the smoke from the fire is gone. I'm back sitting at the kitchen table, looking like I didn't move. My pockets are stuffed with cotton balls I took from under the bathroom sink.

When Lola sees the dirty dishes still spread over the table, she punches me hard.

"Why didn't you clean the dishes, stupid?"

I give her the same evil look she gave me this morning, and she backs off. She hates my magic. She liked it better when she could beat me up for anything. Now she be a bit more careful.

"Come on, Benny. Let's do the dishes," Lola says.

"Yeah," Benny says, like doing the dishes is a treat.

After Mama tucks me in and turns out my light, I grab the cotton balls and put them under my pillow. Then I sit on top, and those protection prayers start coming out of me again. This time, they come so fast it's scary. I sit there for hours, mumbling to myself, waiting for Daddy to come home. When I hear Daddy's car creep into the driveway, I jump out of bed and drop down to my hands and knees. The front door is opening as I grab hold of the burlap bag and pull it toward me. Daddy's footsteps are on the stairs. I'm tugging on the bag, but it won't move. It's stuck on the wood frame that holds my mattress and boxspring in place.

Daddy's closer now. I strain against the bag, but it won't come loose. When I hear Daddy's footsteps at the top of the stairs, I run to my desk and snatch my scissors from the desk drawer. I stab the scissors into the bag and yank downwards. The bag splits and coffee beans spill out. I thrust my hand into the coffee and feel around frantically for Daddy's stuff. He's so close now, I can almost feel him breathing down my neck. Instead of my door, I hear Mama and Daddy's door squeak open. I don't relax, though. I keep searching until my fingers touch something hard. I grab the burnt bundle of Daddy's stuff.

• • •

Mama and Daddy's door squeaks closed. I listen for a second, thinking maybe Daddy just got in bed, but no. I can hear his footsteps coming closer and closer. I stick my hand under my mattress and feel around for my magic pouch. Squeezing it, I can feel that it's full already. Daddy's footsteps stop in front of my door. I turn the pouch upside down and shake it wildly. Marbles, gum, and a picture of Ronald, the boy I have a crush on, spill onto the floor.

Daddy's turning the doorknob now. My fingers are shaking as I reach for the cotton. I stuff a little cotton into the bottom of the pouch and drop the bundle of Daddy's things on top. I turn to face Daddy as I fill the pouch up with cotton and a handful of coffee beans. Daddy's face is confused. He stands in the doorway as I tie the pouch closed and hang it around my neck. When I am finally still, he starts to walk toward me.

"Don't be scared, baby," Daddy says.

I put my hand out in front of me, and Daddy stops short. I turn my palm up to the ceiling and imagine Daddy's heart resting in my grasp. The second I feel his heart's weight in my hand, I snap my fingers shut. Daddy gasps and bends over. I squeeze until the thing stops beating. Daddy stumbles away.

The next morning, Mama's not in the kitchen. Me, Lola, and Benny go to Mama and Daddy's room. Lola pushes the door open, and me and Benny creep in behind her. Mama is sitting on the bed crying. She doesn't ask about the missing bag of coffee or her burnt metal bowl. She never even notices how I bent the screens. The only thing she notices is Daddy. He's lying next to her breathing heavy. His hands are shaking. His skin looks gray.

"Lola, honey, go call a ambulance. Your daddy is sick. Benny, come with me downstairs. You'll help me make Daddy some tea. Rosamojo, stay here with your daddy. Call me if he starts to look worse."

I nod my head, but I can't speak. When everyone leaves I'm too frightened to move. I stay with my back against the wall, close to the door.

"Rosamojo," I hear Daddy whisper. "Rosamojo."

I don't say anything.

"Rosamojo, make me well. I won't do it again; make me good again."

"I didn't mean to, Daddy," I whisper.

"Rosamojo, can't you see how upset you're making your mama?"

I put my hands over my ears.

"Daddy, I didn't mean to," I say a little louder.

"Take the hex off me, Rosa, please," Daddy says.

But I can't. My mind is blank. Nothing comes. Not like the protection prayer that just spilled out my lips. Not like I knew what to do to make Daddy never touch me again. I can't think of anything at all. When Mama gets back, I'm crying.

Mama kisses me. "Don't cry, sweet baby. Daddy will be fine."

But I just cry harder because I know he won't.

Mama hugs me. "Go downstairs with your sister and brother, sweetie. Let me talk to Daddy."

But I don't move. I'm terrified Daddy will tell. Mama pushes me toward the door, but my body is stiff and won't budge.

"Go 'head, honey," she says. "Go on downstairs."

"Can I tell Daddy something first, Mama?"

"Go ahead, Rosa."

I'm terrified, but I force myself to walk close to the bed.

"Don't tell, Daddy. Don't tell Mama, and I promise I'll fix it."

Daddy grunts. He can't see my fingers crossed behind my back. It's not that I don't want to fix it; it's that I can't. If Daddy dies, I don't know what's going to happen. But I know I don't want Mama to find out. Ever.

I sit between Benny and Lola on the couch. Benny is crying; Lola is picking a scab on her knee.

"You think Daddy's gonna die?" Lola asks.

When I don't answer, she shoves me, but I still don't say nothing. When the ambulance sirens get close, Benny stops crying. Before they even pull up in the yard, I feel a fire burn inside me. Mama screams loud. I don't say nothing to Lola, but that's how I know Daddy died. When Mama comes downstairs to let the ambulance people in, she don't say nothing. She points them upstairs and sits on the couch with us. She spreads her arms wide and squeezes us tight.

After the funeral, all I can think about is Grandma's pineapple pound cake. Lola and Benny are eating big plates with fried chicken and red beans and rice, but I don't want no food. All I want is Grandma's cake. Seem like I gotta wait forever for them to unwrap the cake. Finally, I get a piece and I go find a private place to eat it in. I don't want nobody else to ask me how I'm feeling or if I'm going to miss Daddy. Before I even take my first bite, I feel somebody hit me on the shoulder. I look up, but I'm scared to look back. If I'm leaning on the wall, can't nobody hit me from behind, can they? I feel it again. This time I turn and look back. Ain't nobody there. I take a bite of Grandma's pound cake and start chewing. I take another bite, and I hear Daddy's voice inside my head.

"Is it good, Rosa?" he say.

I coulda screamed out loud. I wanted to, but I ain't no fool. So I get up and take my cake to the backyard.

"Daddy, that you?" I whisper.

"Rosa, you have to forgive me," he whisper back.

"Me? Forgive you?" I ask.

"Yeah, I wanna go where my soul supposed to go, but . . ."

"But what, Daddy?"

"But you holdin' me back."

"How, Daddy?"

"By not forgiving me."

I stay quiet for a little while, because I don't know what to say. I take another bite of my pound cake. Then he start whispering for me to forgive him. This time I smile.

"Daddy, can I be glad you dead and still forgive you?"

Daddy take a long time before he answer. I know he don't want to hear me say I'm glad he dead, but it's true.

Finally he say, "Did Daddy hurt you that bad, Rosa?"

I say, "Yeah. And you was gonna do it again."

Then Daddy quiet again. He quiet so long, I got time to eat my whole slice of pound cake.

Finally he say, "Rosa, you the only one who can hear me. And I know you don't want to help me 'cause I done you wrong, but I want you to think about forgiving me and letting me go where I need to go."

"Okay, Daddy, I'll think about it," I promise.

And I do think about it. Every day.

# LARK TILL DAWN, PRINCESS

*Barth Anderson*

A month after the death of my tea-mother, Magnifica the Crimson, I graced the Laughing Jag in disguise, wearing men's blucher-cut wing tips, trousers, and a silk tie in a perfect Windsor knot. I say if a girl is going to cross-dress, she better do it with *style*.

I swear I wasn't being melodramatic, but Magnifica passed away, and with her passed her nightclub, Cabaret Sauvignon, my sole singing venue. I thought I would never sing again, but the Laughing Jag, I decided, might serve as a good place to get back on the boards. The only charm it offered was that it smelled like boys, a rather thrilling smell, heady as a gym class full of ruffians who might be persuaded to have their way with a girl.

Consciously keeping my hips from swaying, I made my way to the bar, where an ugly, natty-bearded thing was pouring beer. "Excuse me?" I said. He looked hypnotized by the suds.

When I spoke, a customer wearing a John Deere baseball cap low over his eyes turned from the bar. Though his face was half covered with that cap, I could see he was a handsome little biscuit. "What in the name of—?" He looked shocked, almost offended.

The Laughing Jag was sort of an older, sadder sister to Cabaret Sauvignon—it had fallen out of the artistic club circle years ago, opting for an open microphone instead of full-fledged cabarets. "I'm here for the open mike."

"Sign-up is in the back of the bar," mumbled John Deere, lowering his cap, hiding his face with his brim.

Was he a spurned flame of mine, or an old Stage Door Johnny at Cab Sav? "Oh . . . back there?" I turned away, ready to give him the old *I Declare* (turn, fingertips on collarbone, lashes fluttering for eye contact), but I caught myself. Something wasn't right about John Deere. Rather than find out what, I walked off through a room full of pool tables and dartboards to find the sign-up sheet. The men playing there glanced at me, sizing me up, perhaps, in my tie and French cuffs, their eyes flat and mouths set in the poker face of masculinity.

Two sets of double doors at the back of the bar led into a little theater where the open mike was held. I imagined that bands probably played here too, though only fifty or sixty people could really fit around the stage. A man stood at the door, reading a clipboard in his hand.

I recognized him. He'd come to check out the show at Cabaret Sauvignon several times. "Doors will open in a few minutes," he said without looking at me. Men were so abrupt and rude with each other. I was used to a little more eye contact from them.

"Actually I was hoping to get on the list."

He pinched a pen from his breast pocket. "And you are?"

I gave the name I hadn't used in twenty-one years. "Hector Dominguez."

He smiled as he fumbled with the spelling. "All right. What do you do, Mr. Dominguez?"

"I'd like to sing a couple songs. Is there good piano accompaniment?"

He laughed at me. "We got a karaoke machine."

*Oh my God*, I thought, *what have I done?* Sing-along machines?

Picture this: me, one month ago, honoring my mother Magnifica's last request by singing for her as I promised I would. I was standing center stage, starting song number two of my three-song finale for Cabaret Sauvignon's drag show, hair in perfect beehive, the blue sequins of my tightest gown popping like firecrackers in the spotlight, singing "Witchcraft" in full throat. From a table right in front of me, I heard someone mutter, "Did you hear? Cabaret Sauvignon is going to close shop after the show."

That's how I found out, while I stood singing my signature number on Cab Sav's stage, and I felt that my childhood was finally over, with Magnifica gone and her club going.

"So you just"—I swallowed and looked at the emcee—"plug in the music?" I really tried to take the karaoke machine in stride, but I had been spoiled to death by the professional accompaniment of Stan the (Ten Inch) Pianist at Cabaret Sauvignon.

"Yeah. But listen," said clipboard man, "I should tell you. We only have one slot left." He nodded matter-of-factly, as if he had to break some bad news. "It's after the Elvis impersonator."

I did a quick inventory of the night as it looked so far: suffocating in men's clothing, singing to karaoke, following an Elvis impersonator. I was getting too old for this nonsense. *You've come to sing for Magnifica*, I told myself like a mantra. *You promised her. You promised.*

I must have looked queasy, because clipboard guy said, "How about this? I'm the emcee. After Elvis finishes, I'll keep a fifteen-minute slot open for you and you can come up if you're ready."

A true gentleman knows how to treat a lady even if he doesn't *know* he's dealing with a lady. I reached out to loop my hand through his arm, but he thought I was offering to shake hands. So we wound up shaking instead. I said, "Thanks, man."

He said, "Just flag me down when you're ready."

In a gown, my reply would have been *I was born ready, sweetheart.* But I wasn't so sure that was true anymore.

Picture a svelte boy in 1984 with ink-black hair, coffee-and-cream skin, and knock-out thighs. Picture me in a high-waisted dress made for birdseed boobs. I'm fifteen, gracing through Sally's off of Times Square at my first drag ball, high as a soap bubble and ready to sell my tail to any man with the drugs or cash to buy me. After the girls all walked, a suburban troll slumming for something young pinned me against the bar. He scared me. Whispered frightening requests in my ear. Not that I minded.

"Par doe nay mwa," said a drag queen, grabbing my arm and yanking me away from the bar. "Girl, come here!"

Picture a bantamweight with eyes like a fawn and narrow hips in a tight hobble skirt. That's Magnifica the Crimson, nee Anita Fix, nee Pussy Darling, nee Filipo Peres. She was seventeen years old going on forever because she'd drank it all, shot it all, smoked it all, fucked it all, and she was about to become my true mother. "You don't even know what kind of cruel bastard he is, do you?"

I looked back at the horny troll, who was staring after me with demand in his eyes. "No. What did he want?"

"Bad rumors about that one. He likes it way too rough, I hear. Shit, don't tempt fate with someone like him," she hissed, making an odd gesture in the air in front of us. "You don't even know how gorgeous you are, do you, Honey?"

I went by Honey Deux, even in those days, and I couldn't believe that Magnifica the Crimson knew my name. At Sally's, Magnifica set the standard for young drag queens less concerned with Las Vegas wardrobes and more concerned with passing. They called her "the Crimson" because it was said she was so "authentic" that she menstruated. As a result, Magnifica unilaterally "poured the tea" (tea for "T," meaning "truth"), deciding whether queens truly passed or not. And Magnifica looked at me like I was a twenty-four-karat woman. "Really? You think I'm gorgeous?"

She stopped and looked deep into my eyes like they were crystal balls filled with tragedy. "Way too naïve and trusting. Jesus. How *have* you made it this far? You'll wind up dead if someone doesn't do right by you." She looped her arm in mine and led me out of Sally's. "Far as I'm concerned, you my daughter. That's the way it is now, okay? And you just let me be your mother, girlie girl."

She pulled me close, and I tell you I melted like a boy. Not a girl. I was never really a girl in my life, only a woman. But in that moment, I was a little boy in his mother's arms.

After getting my name on the Laughing Jag's open mike clipboard, I went back to the bar and ordered myself a Beck's Dark and a peppermint schnapps. I had never sung in public dressed as a man, so my stomach was jittery with preperformance anxiety. My friend in the John Deere baseball cap saw me and said, "You get your name on the list there?"

My body responded as if a cute boy were flirting with me: I turned toward him and smiled, probably too long. I caught myself, scrunched my nose as if signing up were all handled, yessirreebob, and finished my schnapps. I could impersonate women, but I could only parody men.

Suddenly we were alone at the bar. John Deere leaned close to me and whispered, "Why are you in drag?"

Fear jetted like a fire inside me. I knew I'd get bashed someday, but I didn't think it would be while I was wearing a tie. "I'm not in drag," I told him.

John Deere smirked. He looked so familiar.

I lowered my voice and said, "I can prove what I am in a *flash*, fella."

He gave me a smug smile, as if he were charmed by my anger. Or maybe it meant he planned to kick the shit out of me. The fact that I couldn't tell told me that our little conversation was over. Behind me the theater doors opened, so I turned and hurried into the theater in important, manly strides. I took a place in the back at the bar and sat with my head bowed, avoiding the mirror behind the bottles of liquor, my hands shaking.

The morning after the Burial of Magnifica the Crimson, which was covered in three alternative papers and lavished by well over four hundred drag queens from all over the five boroughs, I sat in front of a mirror in my bathroom, trying to convince myself I could still pass without makeup, wig, or the other props that made me "Honey Deux" in my thirties. The light was harsh white, and I had just showered. Cute creases at my eyes were becoming crow's-feet. The hair at my temples had retreated farther than I had been willing to admit. Even my mouth seemed old. I looked like the ancient photos of *mi abuelo* Miguelito—handsome, perhaps, but a very old man. I felt sure that I was at the end of my run as a woman.

"Honey, you got the prettiest skin, the prettiest hair, the prettiest eyes," Magnifica had said to me in her efficiency, I mean, the House of Magnificence. "So I'm going to tell you something that I've never told anyone."

This was right after we had met, so I'm sure I glowed like a coal. "Oh, Mama, you want to pour me your tea just because I'm pretty?"

"I'm pouring you tea because you aren't gonna stay cute and cuddly forever, girlie girl. Get the hormones and the plastic surgery after the age of twenty, and you're just gonna be a man with tits. Time's precious; that's why I'm pouring."

She was two years older than I was, but it seemed like two generations to me.

"Now listen. My auntie taught me what to do. I know how to work it right because she learned from her auntie, who was from the Delta where all the strong mojo comes from. Everything I say is true." Her down-home accent was getting stronger, so I knew she was getting serious. "I can fix it so you pass like Audrey Hepburn in Tiffany's for the rest of your life. Or you can start getting hormone shots to protect that baby's-butt skin of yours. Your choice."

At Sally's, I'd seen Doc Cocktail, the moonlighting physician who sold hormones to drag queens for $75 per injection. Pretty steep for 1984. That, and when they hit their late thirties, those poor queens looked like something out of a medieval medical manual—warped bosoms, rippling skin, crow's-feet like knife scars.

I wanted to avoid that fate if I could. "How? How can you fix it, Mama?"

Now. Picture me at the corner of Jamaica and Vine. I'm wearing an ankle-length cashmere coat. In my handbag is a satchel of cat bones that Magnifica gave me, and my lipstick, Mercury Red by Geoffery Armataud. On two corners of this intersection are wide, abandoned lots. No traffic light, just stop signs, so I'm literally in the dark. At Magnifica's request, it's my ninth Sunday of visiting this godforsaken piece of the city. It's almost dawn.

I was sitting on a curb when someone appeared, walking up Jamaica. By the way she moved in her heels and trench coat, I could tell it was a woman. When she reached the intersection she said in a smoky voice, "Put down the bag. What do you have to offer me?"

"I'm here to meet someone." Magnifica had told me to wait for a big, black man—an African. Was this an elaborate practical joke? Who was this woman? "I was told to wait for a big—for a man."

"Funny," she said. "I was told to meet a *woman* at the crossroads." She gave a low laugh. "What do you have for me?"

When I heard her say *crossroads*, big black man or no, I figured this was my cue. I reached into my pocket for the "offering" that Magnifica had told me to bring: a tube of my favorite lipstick, Mercury Red by Geoffery Armataud, which they don't make anymore. A shame, too. That lipstick was everything I wanted to be—classy, sexy, raunchy in a certain light—and when I wore it, I was. I held it out to the woman.

She took it, passed one hand over it, and applied the lipstick carefully in the dark. I couldn't see her face, only the halo of her short, curly hair. When she was done, she closed the lipstick with a snappy twist of her wrist and then slipped it into her trench coat pocket. "Walk like I walk."

I wasn't a true queen, back then, just a boy who could cross-dress, so I followed her, imitating her as best I could. There was something in the toes that I hadn't noticed before. She pivoted in a way that made my heels turn a bit, made my ass sway. Something in her arms, too. Wrists turned slightly forward. We walked in line like this until she turned and told me to walk as she followed.

We walked back and forth across that black intersection until somewhere a few blocks away, a rooster gave a very human scream. As the sky over Jersey turned a luscious indigo, the light came up in the weedy, trash-strewn lots, and I could see that this woman was a man. "Amazing," I breathed.

"Enjoy your talents. But I warn you. Beware of my twin brother," she said, and suddenly she was standing some fifty feet away, down Jamaica, her voice in my ear like an ocean breeze. "He's the exact opposite of me, and he'll come to steal your gift from you someday. Lay you low if you get too talented."

Then Jamaica was empty.

Later that morning, I told Magnifica what happened, and she listened, rapt. "Legba came to you! It really fucking Holy Sacred Heart of Jesus worked!" She nervously rolled a joint, one of her "midnight specials" laced with coke and hash oil, which she dealt to keep herself in lush fabrics. Outside, church bells were ringing. "That twin brother she mentioned? That's Aflekete. His name means 'I have tricked you.' She's right. He'll try and steal what you got, Honey, but don't worry, I'll figure out a way to keep him at bay, okay, girlie? Mama will figure it out."

I always assumed that Mama handled it with her herbs and Tarot cards and so on, because what followed was nothing short of miraculous. Miss Loweastsider. Miss Fire Island. Miss P-town. Miss Boston Uncommon. I was a total natural (or "supernatural," as Magnifica put it).

But damn, the ride of youth is over so quickly, even when precautions have been taken, and the world you thought you were seducing at nineteen won't even look you in the eye at the age of thirty-seven. Two decades, hundreds of shows, and forty-three first-place drag ball trophies after my night at the crossroads, there I was in necktie and wing tips, alone at the bar. Not even Magnifica the Crimson's spells are meant to last forever, I realized then, finally looking at my old man's face in the mirror behind the bar.

The theater doors closed, trapping me inside, and the open mike began. I felt better in the dark, I must say, and the open mike wasn't half bad, karaoke machine or no. Several of the singers were old Cabaret Sauvignon regulars, performing, like me, in straight drag. Even the offbeat acts, inevitable in an open mike, were fun. An Iranian comedy team did the whole "Who's On First" bit in Farsi, which worked thanks to crisp, Vaudeville timing.

But halfway through the fourth singer, I realized this wasn't going to be anything like Cab Sav. Drag show audiences whoop and holler, and men tip you while you're singing. But this group was as stoic and hetero as Mount Rushmore, and with everything that had happened to me in the last month, I didn't think I could sing without a kinder, gentler audience. Just as I was about to bag it and leave, the emcee announced that "Elvis" was up next. It seemed bad karma to leave before a fellow impersonator took the stage, so I ordered one last drink and stayed to watch the King sing "Fever."

The crowd reacted the way all crowds react when an Elvis impersonator takes the stage, crossing their arms and shifting uncomfortably in their seats. I'd been expecting the Elvis cliché: sunglasses and absurd amounts of padding in a Vegas jumpsuit.

But when my intrusive pal from the bar in the John Deere cap took the stage, I realized something strange was happening. He'd taken off his cap and threadbare windbreaker and wore a nice, black shirt and Levi's (tight, I couldn't help noticing). But here's the thing: this young man really looked like Elvis. I hadn't noticed it before, but now, under those lights, his unruly black forelock and even unrulier hips were all Elvis. How had I missed it? The crowd went silent as they uncrossed their arms and sat forward.

John Deere didn't have a guitar. He didn't even use the karaoke. He just started snapping his fingers, and then he slinked up to the microphone stand without touching it, like a bad but cautious boy seducing a timid lover, crooning in a low sweet voice that was all Elvis. The impersonation was absolutely, unequivocally flawless. Every hip thrust, every swallowed note and cigarette-stubbing gyration of his right foot was perfect.

I slid back into my barstool and put down my beer.

*"When you put your arms around me,"* he sang, brow wrinkled. Sneer. Pursed lips.

Snap. Snap. Snap.

Sure, the song was the fabulous Peggy Lee's first, but Elvis made it his when he covered it — and John Deere make it even more Elvis's song with the impersonation. Because I'm telling you this guy *was* Elvis — pretty, juvenile-delinquent Elvis with the killer charisma.

Imagine it. Imagine being one of those people hearing Elvis for the first time back in the fifties. When John Deere unleashed the word "fever" in the refrain, his straight, white teeth gleamed in the spotlight, and my heart melted until I felt like I was one of those teeny-bopper girls who lost it in the presence of the King. His shirt was soaked with sweat, and every woman in the theater (including me) wanted to jump his bones when he sang, *"I get a fever that's so hard to bear . . ."*

As soon as Elvis finished singing, the audience, as a horny man/woman, made a dash for him. A bouncer saw the crowd press forward, and he yanked Elvis from the stage. Then he and a waiter smuggled him out of the back of the theater with a tablecloth over his head. A moment later, the emcee took the stage, looking shocked and shaken. "Everyone! Please! Elvis has left the building!" Then he shaded his eyes from the spotlight with both hands and made eye contact with me.

I shook my head an emphatic no and immediately felt a stab of guilt in my heart for breaking my promise to Magnifica.

Picture me dressed to the nines (in my sea-foam green open-backed evening gown, her fave; canary yellow sling-backs; elbow-length gloves; turban) attending the deathbed of Magnifica the Crimson, cancer ward, Brooklyn Medical. "Mama!" I wailed, clutching her in my arms. "You won't go, right? Your auntie taught you a way to stop this, right?"

"Ears, Honey. Ears, see voo play."

"What will I do, Mama? Who will I—where will I—?" I held her hand to my face, her fingers thin as bird bones. "I'm nothing without you, Magnifica!"

"Ears, Honey." *Listen. This is important.* Magnifica the Crimson gave me her very last words, which only I could have understood. "Grace the House of Magnificence." *Go to my apartment.* "Lamp the Atelier of the Crimson Goddess." *Look in my sewing room*, which was a warehouse of cloth bolts, muslin mock-ups, and unfinished dresses. "Crack the bottom cask in the Tower of Memory." She had all these massive trunks ("casks") used to store her most precious dresses. "Beneath my children"—*my most precious dresses*—"there's a . . . a present . . . and it's . . . yours, daughter."

She was losing her breath, and the light in her skin started fading. "A present? What are you talking about?"

"Promise me you'll lark till dawn, Princess." *Promise me you'll never stop singing, Honey Deux.*

"I promise!" I pressed the button calling for the emergency medical team. "I promise! Nurse!" Magnifica's very last words were tossed on waves of hospital turmoil. I stood in the back of her room, realizing that I did not have a key to Magnifica's apartment and that my no-smear mascara wouldn't work in this situation, because every boy is a queen when he's with his mama, but he's a shattered diva when she dies.

The emcee next called to the stage a kid with an accordion, saying this guy did the best hip-hop covers at the Laughing Jag.

"Wise choice," said a man sitting at the bar next to me. "Never follow the King."

Taking a barstool and stretching his legs, effectively blocking my path out of the theater, was John Deere. He had his windbreaker on again, but there was absolutely no way he could come around from the back, change, and reenter the theater that quickly. I frowned at him and said, "What's going on here?"

"I'm practicing," said John Deere. "I just can't seem to get my late Elvis right."

Suddenly I had a very good idea what was going on, who this might be. *The bad twin.*

If I was scared of John Deere before, I was petrified now. "You're—you're—"

"See, that song 'Fever' was from 1963," he said, ignoring my stammers, "a particularly hard Elvis for me to imitate. Eight years earlier, he's Jailhouse Rock Elvis. Eight years *later*, he's a parody of himself," said John Deere, gesturing to the stage as if he were watching himself perform and not the kid with the accordion, who was doing "Push it," by Salt-N-Pepa. "I didn't mean to, but I was singing 1955 Elvis. I still haven't perfected post-'58 Elvis without lapsing into his earlier, raunchier self."

My throat hurt, it was so dry. Magnifica had never prepared me for this. Whenever I had asked her about the bad twin, she always said that she had handled it. "How very interesting," I said, wondering if I could talk my way out of a second, scarier trip to the crossroads with the twin. "Listen, I'm late. Would you excuse me? I—"

"See, 1958 is when Elvis—" He turned and looked at me hard before saying, "That's the year his mother died."

*He'll lay you low.* I shut my mouth, tried to swallow. Couldn't. Too dry.

"Her death destroyed Elvis, and he was never the same afterwards." John Deere shook his head. "He spent the rest of his life trying to recapture that younger passion, but he never got it back."

I edged forward on my barstool, ready to jump over his legs and dart out the door when a stage light pulsed or maybe the spotlight brightened against the accordionist's white shirt, but suddenly the light shifted, and I could see John Deere perfectly now. "You're—you're a woman," I whispered.

The drag king flashed his smile at me. "Doesn't mean I can't do Elvis."

"You're not the bad twin. You're Legba."

"*Papa* Legba." He smiled ironically. "And you aren't supposed to be here like this." He pinched the fabric of my trousers and whispered, "You haven't gone to Magnifica's apartment yet. You haven't seen your gift."

"I couldn't bring myself to—I was just too broken up."

"Well, it's time." He took my hand and pulled me from my seat.

Three girls got up on their chairs, rolling their fists over their heads in time to the accordion. "Baby, baby! Ooo, baby, baby!"

He led me down the aisle toward the stage. "Where are we going?"

No one seemed to notice as we walked to the front of the theater, stepped onto the stage, scooted behind the accordionist with the spotlight blaring at us, and passed through the part in the red curtain.

It was disorienting, like walking across a frozen lake that you'd swum in just the summer before. On the other side of the curtain? Magnifica's apartment. Yes. The hallway outside her sewing room, which I knew as well as the hallway of the House of Glory—I mean, my own apartment. John Deere and I stood there for a moment, as if getting our bearings. A faucet dripped. Outside, a car alarm went through its clichéd sequences. I could hear Magnifica's deadbeat roommate/lover watching the Mets in the living room, smell the musky midnight specials he was smoking.

John Deere flipped on the hall light and opened the sewing room door.

I followed and grabbed the Carmen Miranda dress that always hung by the door for guests and started to strip.

"You know that's not your present, right?" said John Deere.

"Of course." I kicked off my wing tips. "But only those in drag may enter the Atelier of the Crimson Goddess." I eyed John Deere's windbreaker and jeans. "Since you're already the 'Drag Kang,' you're set." I shimmied into the orange-and-red dress, asked him to zip me up, then stepped into a pair of high heels with plastic grapes and strawberries on the straps. "Okay. Let's find my present."

It took some effort, but we unstacked the Tower of Memory. The "casks" were light but anywhere from six to ten feet long, filled with over twenty years' worth of hoop skirts, petticoats, and headdresses. The deadbeat roommate never seemed to hear us crashing around in the Atelier. When we got to the bottom cask, John Deere stepped back and let me open it. I lifted the heavy lid, and there, beneath Magnifica's most precious children, was my gift.

A body.

Or at least, it was shaped like a body, wrapped in layer after layer of chemically treated cloth, covered in what looked like coarse salt. Pinned to the wrappings across the "torso" was a note.

John Deere said, "Read it."

Leaning over the cask, I brushed some salt aside and read the note without unpinning it from the mummy.

*To Whom it May Concern:*

*This evil thing came to rob the glorious Honey Deux of her magic. So I shot him in the heart three times with the gun I charmed, and now I've admitted to what I did, all as Auntie Reina's spell prescribed. I've wrapped him up in bandages and packed him in salt to protect Honey from him.*

*Yours fabulously,*

*Magnifica the Crimson,*

*July 1991*

At the bottom of the note was her lip imprint.

I looked at John Deere. "Do you know what this means?"

John Deere nodded. "It means Magnifica the Crimson was the greatest hoodoo priestess of her generation." He took off his cap and worked the brim in his fingers, eyes filled with Magnifica's mummy. "And that's my twin brother. Aflekete. Paralyzed in salt."

In those weeks after my tea-mother died, the only thing I could think about was the dull world that Magnifica had left me in. I hadn't thought much about Jamaica and Vine, or cat bones, or my nine Sunday mornings in many, many years.

"Aflekete?"

A name from my childhood, that, from a time when I was the chosen princess for the House of Magnificence. Though it was a name of warning and danger, it reminded me of my deep bond with Magnifica. The mummified body smelled vaguely of pickles and soap. Formaldehyde, I guessed.

"This mummy is the twin brother that the spirit—" I said, glancing at John Deere, "—that you warned me about?"

"He was coming for the talent I gave you." He put his green cap back on.

"He was?" I said, feeling suddenly vulnerable. "Why?"

"Because he balances me. He did it to traveling musicians who came to the crossroads back in the old country, stealing the talents that I gave away." John Deere smiled sadly at me. "Do you realize, Honey, you were slated to be killed the night Magnifica met you? Strangled. Left in an alley like you didn't matter. Every day you lived after that night was a gift, and Magnifica knew it. She even gave you her one trip to the crossroads."

Magnifica had said she always wanted my life to be a lark. That's why she'd made me make that promise on her deathbed. The room got all misty and the floor, unsteady. That was me crying and almost passing out, not anything wondrous from the crossroad spirit.

Wondering if some vengeance would be demanded for this loss of her brother, I felt afraid and apologetic, standing here next to Legba. "Did you love your brother?" I asked.

"Hmm?"

"Are you mad? At Magnifica, I mean, for you know, killing him?"

"Oh, no, no, no. We're not really into the whole death thing, my family." John Deere shook his head. "My brother is so much more than just this mummy. Besides," he said, removing a handful of salt from the cask, "now that Magnifica is dead and you've seen the feat she accomplished, I plan to wake him up."

I straightened on wobbly knees and backed away. "What?"

"Don't worry. You'll be dead and buried before he's ready to start balancing my generosity at the crossroads again." He gave me a devilish grin. "But if the thought of him waking up scares you, you might want to get out of here now."

I looked at my pile of shoes, trousers, and panties on the sewing room floor, then down at Magnifica's Carmen Miranda gown on my body. "Where am I supposed to go? *How* am I supposed to go?"

"Don't worry about how. You have a promise to keep," said John Deere, taking off his windbreaker. "To your mama."

Even knowing that Magnifica had saved me from the crossroads twin couldn't fill me with a passion for singing again. I was still stranded in a world without her. My "larking" had been for her. I went to the crossroads for her. I performed in drag shows and won trophies, all for Magnifica. I headlined at Cabaret Sauvignon because she was always in the audience, the first on her feet when I finished my signature song. With Magnifica, I felt like a glorious songbird singing in her garden. But without her, I was a ridiculous old man wearing high heels with fruit on them. "I can't do it anymore. I wish I could." I looked down at my unpainted fingernails. "I'm just too old."

"I'm not supposed to do this," said John Deere, looking down at the mummy and reaching into his jeans pocket. "With no Aflekete in this world, however, all the rules have changed. And a promise to a woman like Magnifica must be kept." He put something cold and metallic in my palm and closed my fist around it.

I knew what it was before I opened my hand, because this tube of makeup had once been as much a part of my body as my own face. I clenched my fist around it. "It isn't. It isn't really."

John Deere smiled at me.

"They don't make it anymore," I breathed.

I opened my hand. There it was. The shade of my youth. Mercury Red by Geoffery Armataud.

Suddenly, John Deere put his hand over his face. "Look, this is hard to explain, but I shouldn't have done that," he said, leaning against the disassembled Tower of Memory, looking unsteady. "I'm performing as Elvis in seventy-three different clubs across several different Americas right now, and I really shouldn't have just done that for you."

I held out the lipstick. "Do you need it back?"

He smiled as if I had just offered him gold. "Oh, please no. It's yours. Yours alone," he said. "But brace yourself."

"Thank you." I lunged for John Deere and hugged him. "I think you do Elvis better than Elvis *ever* did Elvis!"

A parted curtain of shadow.

Exhilarating coolness.

A taxicab passing through the midtown tunnel, a funnel of roaring and light.

When we got to the Laughing Jag, the cab driver got out and opened the door for me. I shifted across the backseat as if moving along the bottom of a swimming pool. Where was I? Would I have enough money to pay the driver? I found a twenty in my handbag (when did I pick up a handbag?), and he offered me his hand. As I stepped onto the curb, the slit in good ol' Carmen Miranda parted, and I flashed leg, ankle, and the fruity sling-backs.

Down the street, someone wolf whistled, God bless him.

I uncapped the Mercury Red, turned, and looked at myself in the taxi's window, applying my beloved lipstick. God. With my dark eyebrows and black hair, Mercury Red made me look twenty. Or at least, it made me *feel* twenty.

I graced through the Laughing Jag, back to the theater. I cracked the door, and the emcee let me in. He whispered, "We're almost through for the night, ma'am, do you—" His eyes adjusted in the dark. "Oh my God, you're Honey Deux," he hissed in excitement.

"In the flesh. Can you make room for me on the list?" I was beside myself that he knew me. "I heard there was a slot left open."

A fat Elvis in white vinyl was onstage singing "Hunka Burning Love," dancing with a Kentucky Fried Chicken bucket while the audience laughed politely.

"I don't know." He winced, looking back into the theater. Then he beamed at me with such affection. "Wait. You're here to sing for Magnifica the Crimson, aren't you?"

I had to look away, or he'd get my tears going. "Yes," I said, "and for whatever happens in the world without her." I kissed his cheek, leaving a Mercury Red print in gratitude. "My signature song, 'You Make Me Feel Like a Natural Woman,' see voo play."

He smiled like a conspirator. "Are you ready *now?*"

"Sweetheart," I said, adjusting my tits with both hands, "I was born ready."

# HEARTSPACE

*Steven Barnes*

**M**y father is dead to me, I thought as the 6:14 from Portland rolled to a halt at LAX. *What am I doing here?*

The 6:14 ayem is the worst kind of red-eyed monster. No sane person enjoys getting up at three to make it to the airport for the two-hour security window demanded since 9/11. Just one more reason to hate terrorists, I guess.

A mirrored snack machine reflected an image of the man I had become since last breathing Los Angeles smog. Thirty pounds heavier and thirteen years more fatigued, a big, round-shouldered brown man dressed for a cooler climate. A man who seemed prosperous but not affluent, soft-gutted and soft-eyed behind wire-rimmed glasses.

*My father is dead to me.* The thought banged around in my mind as I waited on the passenger pick-up island, watching cars crawl past. Don't get me wrong: not all my memories of Dad were depressing. Once upon a time we'd chased rainbows together. At some point Corbin Wiley started chasing money. Might have been his third wife, the second one after Mother died. He had wandered into a labyrinth of endless work and had never emerged. Now, after all these years, he wanted to see me again. Despite the pain, a glimmer of hope still burned in the darkness. Work had taken the heart right out of Corbin Wiley, my father. But sometimes, love could give it back.

The sky was bright, pale, cloudless—the opposite of the billowing gray canopy the 747 had pierced rising from Portland tarmac. A battered black station wagon pulled up. A plump, latte-colored woman waved at me from behind the wheel. Bebe. My half sister.

"Well, get in, Cal." Both face and voice were impatient. "They give me a ticket if I blink too slowly."

As if in emphasis, the driver of the eggshell blue Subaru behind her leaned on his horn. Bebe's doughy face sharpened. She leaned out of her window and screamed, "Hold your fucking horses!"

Bebe popped the trunk for me, and I shoved my carry-on inside. As I did, she and the Subaru driver exchanged obscenities. Bebe is my half sister, by Father's second wife. Whatever poison burned in our family's veins had worked overtime on poor Bebe. She'd had four husbands, at last count. I hadn't heard from her in eight years; she might have added and subtracted a few since then.

She'd pulled us onto Century Boulevard and the freeway before I ventured further conversation. "How are you, Bebe?"

Her eyes were fixed on the traffic, hands hard and nervous on the wheel, as if expecting cars to deliberately attempt to ram her. "I've got bills," she said, as if that explained everything. "Jody's going to be graduating high school. How's she going to college?"

"Good," I said. "Good. And I'm fine." So we hadn't connected. We rarely did, anymore. Once upon a time Bebe had cuddled on my lap, a laughing angel the color of old pennies, her hair as fine and dark as spun shadows. We'd play hugging games and watch Bugs one-up Daffy, and the Road Runner evade becoming Coyote brunch.

We cruised.

"I need the money, Cal," she said. "But not enough to watch that island bitch poison my father. She's kept doctors away from him for almost a year now."

"He's gotten worse?"

"Yes!" Then: "No." She hunched over the wheel, her plump hands clutching and releasing in a confused rhythm. "I don't know. I'm a schoolteacher, not a doctor."

"What makes you think he'll listen to me?"

"Dad will do what she tells him. You're a lawyer—she'll be scared of you. She probably tried to talk him out of seeing you."

I pushed back into the seat, but found no comfort there. Billboards lining the 405 hawked cell phones and designer water, models with perfect skin and dazzling teeth promising intimacy and health for pennies a day. "Not everything's about time. Some pretty hard things got said."

She paused. "How's Dick?"

"Rick."

"Whatever. Are you still together?"

"Fourteen years."

She snorted laughter. "Who'da thought, huh? That's eight years better than I ever did. I thought you guys just played musical beds."

I looked out the window, feeling a bone-deep weariness that had little to do with the flight. Bebe glanced at my waistline. "Thickened up a little."

"Thanks for noticing."

She brayed again. Then suddenly she brightened. "Hey! Wanna look at the old neighborhood? He's not expecting us until two."

"Sure," I said. "Is that a bother?"

"This whole damned thing is a bother. What the hell?"

*The apricot tree was tall and strong, its branches laden with golden fruit. A tall, handsome man held a boy with my eyes and heart by the wrists, spinning him in gloriously dizzying circles. A smiling woman a little darker and prettier than Lena Horne stepped off the back porch, carrying a platter of lemonade and Oreo cookies, the perfect addendum to a perfect day. . . .*

*"Calvin?" Mom said. "It's time to come in."*

*Father and I planted our feet. It just wasn't fair. "Aw, Mom. Can't we stay out a little while? Just a little while?"*

*"Calvin, it's time to go," Mother said. "Time to—"*

Svelte Mother thickened into Bebe as I clawed my way back to consciousness. I was sand-jointed and lead-limbed, the early-morning rising catching up with me in a tidal wave of fatigue. Bebe was shaking me back to a world where broken couch springs dug into middle-aged backs, and everything smelled faintly of mildew. Bebe held a steaming cup of tea out to me, balanced on a porcelain plate older than either of us.

I sighed, and sipped peppermint. I felt the tightly wound spring in my gut loosen a bit.

Bebe and I were two adults halfway through middling lives. The house I had grown up in was a roach trap, its floorboards warped, its tile discolored. The apricot tree that had once given fruit and shade, in which my friends and I had built the only treehouse of my life, was long gone, victim of time and termites. In some odd way Bebe had skidded blindly through her prime of life, her only tracks a series of failed dreams that had wrenched the living heart out of her. Inevitably, perhaps, she had returned to our childhood nest like a crippled pigeon limping home to die.

"I was dreaming," I said.

"About the house?"

I nodded, tasted the tea. It was good. "Yeah."

"I used to have dreams when I first moved back," Bebe said.

"Now?"

"Sometimes. But it's all so vague."

"For years I had dreams. Walking down the hill, waving to neighbors who weren't there. All the houses were empty."

The silence stretched uncomfortably. Then she said, "Well. Let's go. Time for hearts and flowers later, maybe."

I put my hand over hers. Despite the years and the wear, they were still warm. "It's good to see you, Bebe."

She sniffed, and her huge brown eyes filmed with tears. "Can you help me?"

"I don't know," I said. "I'm a lawyer, not a miracle worker."

Bebe took the 405 up through the Sepulveda Pass to reach the San Fernando Valley. It hadn't changed much in thirteen years—a few more office buildings, a little more haze, the same bad traffic. Father lived at the top of the valley, in a gated community called Chatsworth. "You've never been here?" Bebe asked as we wove through a series of narrow, tree-shaded streets.

"No."

"You were at the old house?"

I nodded.

"That's where it happened?"

"More like: that's where it un-happened. When he said those things . . . called me and Rick those names . . . it just felt like something came undone."

"But he asked you to come to see him."

"Five years ago. Yes. When he thought he was going to die."

"Why are you here now?"

"Because you asked."

Her heavy lips curled into a tight smile as we pulled up in front of the gate. A guard leaned out of a white hut just large enough for the ex–police officer currently in occupation. "Yes?" the uniformed retiree asked.

Bebe rolled down her window. "We have an appointment with Mr. Wiley."

The guard checked his clipboard. "Your name?"

I leaned across Bebe. "Calvin Wiley."

"Yes, sir." He went back inside the gatehouse, and the gate swung open.

"Wow," I said. We drove through a maze of two- and three-story houses—a dozen different styles, from French colonial to California hacienda, so that it looked more like a movie back-lot than a residential neighborhood. A quarter of the lots were still under construction, and half the expansive lawns weren't in yet. The entire development reeked of new money. "The dry cleaners must be doing well."

"Two hundred of them, last count. One of the largest chains in the country."

"I've seen them in Portland."

"There you go. You'd think he could afford to take care of his kids."

"We're grown, Bebe, We're not supposed to need Daddy anymore."

Bebe tightened up. "Well, maybe if he'd been there for me, I wouldn't. But then, you knew him longer, Cal. You got more of him. I'm not much. Maybe I never was. But he should have loved me. I was his. He was all I had." Tears started from her eyes again, and she dabbed at them with the back of her hand.

"You had me," I said.

She bit her lip and tried to smile. Then, perhaps before she could say too much, she parked in front of a white mock Tudor that looked rambling enough for a state orphanage. She got out of the car and headed up the curving, tiled drive. I followed her.

We waited a full minute after she rang the front bell. The music of saws and hammers drifted from a distant lot, and I shifted my weight to the beat. "Are you sure we're expected?"

Even as I spoke, the door opened. A short, plump, stately black woman in a floral-print wrap opened the door. Her face had once been pretty, but now it was grave and almost expressionless, with a slight Asian cast to her eyes. She might have been in her forties or sixties. Gray streaked her severely bunned hair. She regarded Bebe and nodded in recognition. Something passed between them, and it couldn't have been mistaken for affection. When she looked at me, she tried to smile. "You must be Calvin. The lawyer." Her voice had an odd lilt to it, suggesting umbrella drinks and lush tropical beaches.

"Corporate law, not personal. This is just a family visit."

"I see." She paused. "I am Monique."

"May we come in?"

"Yes, of course." She opened the door. Bebe and I entered.

The mansion was beautifully appointed. Exotic, largely earth tones, with much Caribbean and African influence. Tapestries and pottery and paintings of earth and sun and lines of women working in cultivated fields. The human images made me more aware of the mansion's vast empty spaces. They yearned for parties, children, dinner companions, pets—shapes and joyful sounds to relieve the monotonous void.

Monique had tried: there was much art and pottery. Especially eye-catching were several hand-crafted earthen vessels, their shapes vaguely feminine. Hadn't I seen something like them before? Their glazed, dusky surfaces drew my eye and hand. I brushed my fingers briefly over them.

"What are these?" I asked.

"Udu pots," she said.

I *had* heard that term before, but still wasn't certain where. "What does *Udu* mean?"

She paused, giving me a brief, wary consideration. "There are at least two meanings. A vessel to carry water . . . and peace."

Together, we climbed the stairs.

Despite her years, Monique's hips moved with a liquid grace. "Where are you from?" I asked.

"I am sure that your sister has already told you."

"I didn't mean anything by it."

"Saint Simons," she said.

"One of the islands off the Georgia coast?"

She looked back over her shoulder with pleased surprise. "Have you visited?"

I shook my head regretfully. "I saw a special, once." Was that where I'd heard of Udu pots?

"Rapturous," she said. "Sunsets no painter could imagine. Scuppernong grapes and melons so sweet and rich you can make a meal of just one. The best crabmeat in the world."

My mouth watered, and I suddenly remembered I hadn't eaten in eighteen hours. "We have great history," she said. We had finally crested the stairs, and were now walking down a silver-white carpeted hall.

"The people who live in that island chain are descended from West African tribesmen. We have more of the old culture than most Americans."

"I can still hear it in your voice," I said sincerely.

"Things were different on the islands. They could not break us as easily. We tell a story of my own people, the Ibo. Once, when a group of warriors were mistreated, they simply walked out into the ocean to drown. The masters could not break us; so they let us be. We worked during the day," she said. "But the nights were ours."

She stopped, turned to look at me. "I love your father. Yes, he came to our clinic. I know your sister thinks us frauds. But your white doctors had already given up on him."

"People get better sometimes," Bebe said. "Other people take advantage."

"I take advantage of no one."

"He's an old, rich, lonely man. You've kept him away from his family, his friends. He changed his will."

"I am his wife." Her shoulders squared as she said it, and despite Bebe's misgivings I found myself liking Monique.

Feeling a bit like Mills Lane I stepped between the two heavyweights. "Listen. I'm tired. I'm here to see Dad. Fight later?"

"I am sorry," Monique said. "I'm sorry. Yes. You're right. This way."

We came to the top of the stairs and turned down a long hall decorated in shades of blue and deep gold.

57

"You've not seen your father in . . . ?"

"Fourteen years," I said.

"As you can imagine, he has changed." Her voice took an officious tone. "He will see you, but please do not approach him closer than five feet unless he invites you. Please do not touch him unless he invites you."

My ears perked up. "Why is this?"

"He is concerned with . . . infection."

We paused before the third door on the right. "Can you follow this rule?"

Bebe and I exchanged a brief glance. "Sure," I said.

Monique nodded and opened the door. We hesitated at the threshold. Bebe pulled at my arm, tugging backward like a little girl afraid to enter a doctor's office. "It smells bad," she whispered. It was a sickroom smell, a whisper of alcohol and dry, spoiled lunch meat, but not as bad as I'd feared.

"You can wait out here, if you want to."

"No," she said after a moment's hesitation. "No. I'll come in."

The room was filled with flowers that I didn't recognize. Another of those glazed Udu pots was snugged into an enclave in the wall. This one was sealed, and around the rim was etched writing, or symbols I could not read.

Father's bed sat in the center of the room, a vast canopied resting place with mountainous black pillows and white sheets under a gold-and-silver blanket. The bed was draped with clear plastic panels. Yellow plastic hoses ran from a standing bank of pressurized bottles into the tent.

He was propped up on those onyx pillows, wearing a pair of black silk pajamas.

His body remained motionless, but his head turned as I entered the room. Once he had been the biggest, strongest man in the world. Now, he was something less than a child, and the contrast was shocking. His dark skin was more like paper than leather, ashen and sickroom gray. His eyes were deeply sunken, but bright, and he actually smiled when he saw me.

"Father?"

"Calvin? Please," he wheezed. "Come in."

Very carefully, I moved forward. "It's been a long time."

"Yes." His voice sharpened. "Please—no further."

I stopped, confused but obedient. "Why not?"

"Monique thinks—and I agree . . ." He fought for breath. "The outside world and I . . . aren't very compatible anymore." That was a touch of the old humor, something I was surprised to realize I had missed. "Monique keeps me well, but she can't protect me against everything at once."

"I'm sorry." For a long moment we listened to the sounds of hissing gas aerating creaky lungs.

"Have you been well?" he asked.

"As can be expected."

"I hear your law practice is thriving."

In this, at least, I could have pride. "Yes. It's fine."

His face was largely immobile, but his eyes rolled to scan me up and down. "You've put on a little weight."

My hands knotted into fists at this. The first in a series of insults? Or just an honest observation?

"Good, healthy flesh we used to call it," he said, as if reading my mind. "Sign of success." He closed his eyes. "All this obsession with showing your bones. It's not healthy."

I managed to relax a bit and found that my legs felt unsteady. Monique supplied me with a folding chair before I had a chance to ask. Behind me, leaning against a flowered wall, Bebe watched in silence.

As withered as he was, it seemed that every breath Father took should have been his last. Somehow, he continued. "Some terrible things were said the last time, Calvin. I . . ." He sighed heavily, and it was impossible to ignore the regret and the . . . well, the *sweetness* in his voice. This wasn't the man who had cursed my lifestyle or threatened to disown his own daughter. Not the man who had abandoned wives and built a marginal enterprise into a thriving West Coast chain at the cost of love and health. This was, instead, the man who had once held his son by the wrists and whirled him until both were too dizzy to laugh. Who had taught his daughter to read *And to Think That I Saw It on Mulberry Street*, sharing happy hysteria at the impossible, Seussian bestiary. "A father wants his name to go on," he said in that dry-leaf whisper. "To see his grandson. That makes it hard sometimes."

I allowed my heart to harden a bit. "That's no excuse for what you said to us. Love is love, Dad."

"You're right," he said. "It is. I was wrong. A business is unforgiving. A balance sheet has no heartspace. I was a terrible father." A pause. "I'm sorry."

If I hadn't already been sitting down, I would have needed to. "*Sorry?* I'm not sure I've ever heard you say that."

Despite his infirmity, my father managed to smile. "Would you like to hear it again?"

"No, that's all right."

"Tell me. How is . . ." He struggled to find the name.

"Rick."

"Yes. Rick."

"He's fine." *And won't he be shocked to hear about this conversation?*

We talked for the better part of an hour. Nothing earthshaking; nothing horribly impersonal, either. Just two people making a genuine effort to come to some kind of understanding, to touch instead of fence. Bebe hung back, watching without joining in, standing near that sealed Udu pot without touching it. I spoke of the Northwest, of corporate subterfuge and making partner by thirty-five.

He made a few tax suggestions that were actually quite sly and workable. We laughed together.

The sun was a bit lower in the sky when I looked up. Bebe had brought me here to find something wrong, and I had slipped into a comfortable daze, a cocooning illusion: *Just me and Dad, talking about life. Here's a macho topic, should keep the ball rolling.* "Did you watch the Super Bowl last Sunday? I know you love football."

Now, suddenly, and for the first time, Father seemed to struggle. He looked to Monique, momentarily as helpless as a child. "Monique?"

"Yes, you watched the Super Bowl." Her mouth was stretched into a taut line.

"I did?" His eyes were almost comically wide. "Who won?"

"I don't remember."

He sagged back, his face riven by regret as well as time and disease. "I'm sorry. Age can be a terrible thing. I can remember so many things from the past, but recent things . . ."

"How recent?"

"The past five years is a blur. It's as if memories don't stick anymore."

I struggled with that. You hear about memory loss, Alzheimer's . . . how it feels to watch a loved one's mind dissolve. Somehow, loss of mind is more terrible, more final and horrifying than loss of bodily function. "Do you think you'll remember me?" Despite my best efforts, my voice cracked a bit. "Remember this visit?"

"I hope so. Cal . . . I never wanted things to be like this. You have to believe me." He sank back into his pillows, utterly exhausted.

Silence stretched between us until Monique stepped into the breach. "I have to ask you to leave now," she said. Her island lilt added warmth that the naked words lacked. "Perhaps you can return soon?"

"I'd like that." I took a halting step toward him. "May I . . . ?"

She shook her head. "Germs."

I kissed my fingertips and placed them against the walls of the plastic tent. Summoning strength that had been denied him until that moment, Father reached out a thin dark arm and touched his to the other side of the plastic.

Now, finally, Bebe stepped forward. "May I take a picture? I'd like something to remember."

Perhaps she expected Monique to protest, but instead the little woman seemed happy to cooperate. "Why don't I take it?" she asked. "That way you can both be in it." A peace offering?

We both stood, framing Father. Monique fumbled a bit with my Minolta. Father struggled to sit upright. When I glanced at him, his eyes were vast and dark, as though they had already glimpsed the far side of the veil. Monique snapped the picture before I could turn around, and the flash erupted.

Father didn't blink. "Another one," I said. "I wasn't ready." We *cheesed*, she flashed. I took the camera from Monique. "Thank you," I said. "Dad . . . I could come back down for a conference in six weeks. Would you like to see me?"

"Yes," he whispered. "I'd like that."

"Please," Monique said, indicating the door.

On my way out, unable to resist, I let my fingertips brush the soil-rich glaze of the ceramic Udu pot. It seemed warm to me, warmer than that surrounding air. An odd illusion. Also, it seemed to *hum* as the pads of my fingers brushed across. Yes, I was right: I had heard of these on a television show. The Learning Channel, I thought, a show about household artifacts with spiritual or artistic significance. What was the sound quality called? *Aqua* something. I knew my mind. It would produce the required datum if I didn't poke at it too much.

Downstairs we donned our coats and prepared to leave. "Strange," I said. "He seems . . . I don't know, *sweeter* than I remember him for a long time. Some kind of magic potion?" I attempted to bite that gaffe back, but was too slow. "Listen: I'm not against alternative medicines. I've had acupuncture twice."

Monique didn't bat an eye. "I met him when he was sick, when he came to our clinic to try a naturopathic herb cocktail. He was desperate, and desperation pulls down ego walls. He was frightened, and small. . . . I didn't see the money. I saw a man who needed hope. He needed *me.*"

Her eyes were very direct, her face placid. Smooth skin, old eyes, orbs with unexpected depths. I felt myself reel at their brink, suddenly believing that Father might have fallen in love with this woman, even if he had not been in mortal anguish. "Well . . . take care of him."

Bebe snatched my camera from my hand. "May I take a picture of you and Cal?"

Monique looked at her suspiciously. "I don't know. . . ."

"Why? Your people believe cameras steal the soul?"

Only a shadow of irritation crossed her face at Bebe's blatant rudeness. My respect for Monique elevated another notch. "Of course not."

"Of course. Or why would you let us take a picture of Father?"

"It's just that I would prefer—"

In Monique's midsentence, Bebe snapped the shutter. An expression of naughty little-girl triumph twisted her lips. Monique stared at her, suppressing anger. I wanted to crawl away somewhere and hide. "There. That wasn't so painful." Bebe's smile was as fake and adolescent as a whoopee cushion.

Monique turned to me. "*You* are welcome to return."

I recognized the emphasis without acknowledging it. "Thank you." There seemed sufficient rapport between us for me to finally ask the question that had been on my mind since Bebe's initial phone call. "Bebe is concerned about our father. We'd like to have our own doctors examine him."

"Why? They gave him three months to live, five years ago. What can they offer now?"

"Still . . ."

"Does he seem happy to you?"

"Honestly, he seems happier than I've seen him in over a decade."

I watched carefully, perhaps expecting an expression of victory. Conspiratorial success. *I put it over on them. . . .*

Instead, there was a quiet sadness, dark and warm as a moonlit summer ocean off the Georgia coast. "Please," she said. "Leave us now."

We left.

Bebe pulled away from the house slowly, cruising the private streets like a shark.

"That was rude."

She made a hissing sound. "She's killing him by inches. Poisoning him for his money. She's a vampire, Cal. She didn't want us to take the picture because she won't show up."

"It's daytime," I said wearily. "And it's a *mirror* she won't show up in." Trivia triumphant.

"Doesn't matter. Can't you get an injunction? If you do it, maybe he won't cut me out of the will."

"Oh, I could do that," I said. "But he's lucid enough. And he'll know you put me up to it. If he threatened to cut you out, he will. Leave well enough alone, Bebe."

Her face wrinkled with anger, and then finally acceptance. She didn't like my answer, but had to live with it. "Can we take the pictures to a one-hour photo?"

I sighed. Enough was enough. "No. I'll send prints from Portland."

She wouldn't look at me, her eyes glued to the street before her, piloting the car with almost imperceptible nudges of the wheel, her hands trembling with rage, a big, fleshy woman trapped by her past and uncertain of her future. She'd called big brother, hoping for a miracle. Sorry, Bebe. None here.

Except that just maybe, there was love in that gigantic, sterile house. And that, at this phase of Father's life, was miracle enough for me.

We pulled up at LAX at 6:50, two hours before my homeward flight. "Seems ridiculous, this kind of in and out," I said. "I feel like a thief in the night."

"It's daytime," she said, a pout in her voice. Finally, Bebe turned to me. "You don't see anything wrong? You *really* don't see anything wrong? She's killing him. Can't you see?"

I shrugged. "He seems happy. He was supposed to be dead years ago. So he went to a wack clinic of some kind, believes he was cured, and came home with an island nurse. She seems to care about him."

"But—"

I shifted on the seat to face her. "Bebe. Listen to me. I'm tired. You said it was an emergency. There are ways he seems better than he has in twenty years. If they're happy, let them be."

I expected a scream, a tantrum, an accusation. Instead, her eyes overflowed, and tears began to stream down her face. "He's all I've got, Cal. And she's a dragon."

I put my hand over hers. "He's not all you have, Bebe. You have me, too."

Slowly, seeming almost to wince at the contact, she leaned her forehead against my shoulder. "You were always my big brother. I'm not much, am I?"

"You're a mother and a daughter. And you're my sister, and I love you." Her hand clutched for mine. "You'll make it, Bebe. We'll both be okay."

She wiped a tear away from her cheek and managed to shape her lips into a shy smile. "You take it easy, Big Brother."

"You too, Little Sister."

"Call me?"

"You know it." I heaved my bag out of the back of the car and headed into the terminal.

The security line was moving like a glacier. I spent the time focusing and unfocusing the last few hours' kaleidoscopic words, actions, and emotions. I made it through the metal detector without incident, collected my bag off the conveyor belt, and headed to the gate.

I was early. I sat, gazing out watching the planes landing and taxiing. Something was wrong.

When I closed my weary eyes, images roiled the darkness. I saw us arriving at the mansion, the greeting at the door, and my first view of its cavernous interior. Again, I saw myself brush fingers along the jar, feeling the cool surface. Then, a moment later, saw myself touch the jar upstairs.

That one had been strangely warm. A nameless irritation had been chewing at me since leaving the house, a sense that there was something wrong that I could not label, and therefore usefully conceptualize. Damn it—even that was a useless intellectualization, and this sense was more of an emotional thing.

Something was incomplete. Undone. Or . . . there was a puzzle with too few pieces in place . . . or . . .

I couldn't get a handle on it, and that lack of understanding was killing me.

A Beaver Cleaver family was saying its pastel good-byes at the gate. "All right, all right—now you remember to call," the father was saying.

"Every day," his big-haired teenaged daughter replied. "For the first week."

"Ah hah hah," Mrs. Cleaver said. "Very funny. All right—get together; let's take a picture."

"Oh, Mom, my hair's a mess."

"And when isn't it?"

Father and daughter squeezed together into a more easily photographable configuration. Ward Cleaver glanced around, saw me. "Excuse me. Could you . . . ?"

I pushed myself up off my seat.

"Just push the button."

I aimed the camera and pushed. The flash erupted. The daughter flinched and rubbed at her eyes. "Ow."

"Big baby," Ward Cleaver said. "Thanks."

"Don't mention it."

They hugged, mother melting into daughter, father hugging briskly and then kissing a rose-petal cheek.

An emotional sledgehammer slammed against the back of my knees, and I sagged back into my chair. I heard the announcer's voice direct first-class passengers to the front of the line, but didn't move. I kept seeing the daughter hugging her father, envied her that contact so much, so ravenously, it was a hunger more brutally blunt and consuming than any I could remember.

Anger. *How dare Monique tell me I can't touch my own father?*

Fear. *He could die before I come again.*

Hurt. *How long? How long has it been since your only father hugged you, told you in that simple, direct way that it's all right?*

And confusion. Something was wrong. Something about the house. The tent? The photograph? The . . . the *what?* Monique *was* pulling something over, had seemed so plausible and polite that I hadn't pressed for the only thing my sister had asked of me in almost twenty years. Rage born of confusion and half-formed fears boiled up so strong it felt like I'd eaten something rotten. I had. I'd swallowed Monique's act without chewing. The other passengers filed onto the plane, but I couldn't move, just couldn't. Couldn't leave until . . .

Until what?

Heart pounding, vision blurring, I picked up my bag . . . and left.

Luckily, the same elderly guard was on duty when my taxi pulled up to the gate. "Oh, it's you, sir. Mr . . . Wiley? Forget something?"

"Yes. I'm expected."

He pushed a button, and the gate opened. I managed to remember my way through the maze. The cabbie, a night-school student with an engineering textbook spread upside down on the seat beside him, leaned around. "Want me to wait? No bother."

God, twenty-three looked young these days. "No. I don't think so." I shoved some bills in his hand without looking carefully, my heart pounding.

"Say, thanks, buddy."

"Study your ass off," I said. He drove off laughing as I knocked on the door. After a long pause, Monique answered.

"Calvin?" she said, surprised. She seemed nervous, and I was betting I knew why.

I let my rage, boiling for the last seventy minutes of foul traffic, burst free as I pushed past her. "I want to see my father."

"Calvin? No!"

"No?" I dropped my carry-on and stalked straight up the stairs, past the tapestries and pottery and the artifacts of a grasping woman's life.

"No!"

"No?" I pivoted, enraged. "Just try to stop me, and I swear I'll have a sheriff here in two hours. He's my father. He wanted to touch my hand. Can't you understand?"

Her face was slowly distorting with . . . what? Fear? Anger? Guilt? Something. Suddenly a piece of the puzzle spun into place. He hadn't flinched away from the flash, as the big-haired Cleaver teenager had. And his pupils hadn't contracted afterward. My actions and reactions weren't such a mystery to me anymore. "You *do* have him drugged, don't you? How much is left in the accounts? I don't know what you're using, but I'll bet that a toxicology test will detect shit that no pharmacist ever put in a bottle. Hell, you're not a doctor anyway—"

"Not the kind *you* know." She said it with fingers spread and hooked into claws, eyes bright, and before I could more than blink she leaped at me, all teeth and nails and frantic, feral hunger. Surprised at my own strength I grabbed her wrists and damn near threw her back down the stairs. Instead I swung her into the wall harder than I intended. The entire wall vibrated, and a painting slid off its hook and struck the ground, glass shattering.

Monique sagged, sobbing, the fight temporarily hammered out of her. Momentarily the fog lifted, and I was aware that I could be liable for assault, that on one level this made no sense at all, unless I could prove that she . . .

What?

I stormed into my father's room.

Anger had distorted my vision as it had my judgment. The bedroom seemed off-kilter somehow, the angles somehow discordant, as if I were running a low-grade fever. I trailed my fingers along the Udu vase, calmed momentarily by its low, mournful tone—then pulled them back. I didn't *want* to be soothed. This was going to get ugly. Monique stopped at the threshold, as if one of Bebe's vampires, supernaturally afraid to cross running water.

"Calvin?" said the withered figure behind the plastic. "Is that you?"

"Yes, Father."

"Weren't you . . . I thought you were just here. My memory isn't what it was. I'm sorry. . . ."

"It's all right, Dad."

"Don't!" Monique screamed.

I looked at the woman, eyes blurred with fury. I brushed aside the plastic curtain and sat at his bedside. The air was cool and tangy, rich enough to dizzy me. I looked into his eyes, which were vast and unfocused.

"What in the hell is he on? He's doped to the gills."

I looked more deeply. "He didn't even react when the bulb . . ." I touched his cheek.

"There was no pupillary response. . . ."

Suddenly, I was afraid. "His skin is cold."

"Don't," she whispered. "Please."

Hands shaking now, I felt for his pulse. Would it be adrenaline fast? Or morphine slow. . . .

There was no pulse at all. None. Checked both wrists, and then the sunken veins at the sides of his throat. Nothing.

"Calvin? What is it?" He seemed genuinely confused and vulnerable. The air was too rich, so rich it was suddenly too thick to inhale.

"Nothing, Dad," I lied. One thick-fingered motion at a time I unbuttoned his pajama top to expose his chest. I leaned in—and froze.

Puckered flesh around heavy black thread, dreadfully neat stitches and pale scars like furrowed earth in the Mississippi Delta crisscrossed his prominent ribs. All centered on the left side of his chest. A voice in my head whispered that the scars would *never* heal. I stumbled back away from the bed. I looked at the Udu vase. Without any memory of crossing the room, I was suddenly touching it. It was warm, and the slightest stroke across the glazed surface freed a featherlight tone to drift through the air. *Aqua resonance.* That was the term my subconscious had worried at. There was liquid in that jar. Almost imperceptibly, it beat with a subtle, unliving rhythm.

I capped my hand over my mouth in time to stop an acrid gout and rushed out of the room.

Behind me, Monique was trying to comfort my father. "What is it? Is there something wrong?"

"Rest, Corbin. Rest. No, no."

"My boy. Is he all right?"

"Fine. I'll see to him."

I managed to find a bathroom and vomited a sour, thin stream into the sink, glad that the airlines rarely serve food anymore, that I hadn't taken time to eat since landing. Monique appeared in the door behind me. I stared up at her and could not speak.

"Three years ago," she said. "His heart finally stopped. I resuscitated him, but it was clear he was going. I took his last breath, and his heart, and placed them in that jar."

"Why?" I sat on the floor, suddenly catapulted into an infant's role, begging for understanding before the weight of the mystery broke my rational mind.

"Because I love him. I know what you remember of him, but when Corbin came to Saint Simons he was beaten, and afraid. His heart was open to me. As he drank his herbs he spoke to me of his regrets."

I stared at her.

"It was a little clinic on a cove. They used herbs to treat cancer. Corbin had heard of it on the Internet, and came. I knew the doctor was a good but deluded man. I worked there to help people with their passage, and Corbin was, in his dying, so beautiful." Her hands fluttered like little dark birds. "He asked me to come back with him, to administer the herbs." She laughed, a touch of bitterness seeping into her voice. "I knew he would die. I knew. Perhaps at first all I wanted was a bit of time with him. Perhaps the money as well. I will not lie. But in time . . ."

"What did you do?"

"It was not the way of the herb doctors. I did a thing my great-grandmother taught me, and made me swear never to speak of. What I did was wrong."

I managed to ask the words. "Why then? Why did you do it?"

Heavily, as if her confession had drained her strength, Monique sat at the tub's edge. "I love him."

I ran the water in the sink for a long time, and then shut it off without using it. A little spot behind my left eye hammered with pain no aspirin could vanquish. "How long will it last?"

"As long as he does not know."

I mopped my face. Stared at my reflection in the mirror until I didn't recognize myself. Minutes passed. Then slowly speech returned. "You love him?"

"I am bad, perhaps. I do things I swore never to do." A pause. "Am I very bad?"

"I don't know," I said. The dizziness was passing, but what it left behind was a strange sense of seeing the world through eyes so new that color was intoxicating, daylight blinding. "I don't know anything. My father said he was sorry. He never said that before." I cradled my head in my hands. "Oh, Jesus."

"What will you do?" she asked, anxiety flattening the music from her voice.

"I don't know," I said, and had never meant those words more in my entire life.

I walked out, and she followed me downstairs. I looked at the vases. Udu pots. Vessels to carry water . . . and peace.

Yes. That was what I had seen in the thing upstairs, the thing that looked like my father. *Was* my father. Peace.

She had disappeared from my sight, and now reappeared. "Your taxi will be here in a few minutes."

I nodded, grateful that she had done that. I wanted, needed, to be gone. "Would you do me a favor?"

"Whatever I can."

"My sister. Half sister, Bebe. Give her her inheritance now. Just . . . give it to her. I promise she won't trouble you any more if you do that."

She watched me narrowly. "And you?"

"I . . . don't want anything. Need anything. Except . . ." I shook my head, momentarily clearing the cobwebs my mental spiders were spinning for dear life. "I don't know if I'll be back, but I'd like you to take care of . . . him. I want . . ." I suddenly stopped, realizing that words were entirely insufficient to express what I wanted, or felt. "I'm going home," I said finally. "To Rick. Take care, Monique." I paused before I picked up my carry-on and walked out the door. "God save you both."

The taxi arrived, its driver old enough to be the college student's grandfather. As it pulled away I looked back at the figure of the small, plump, pensive woman standing there.

*Am I very bad?*

I leaned back into the seat. Closed my eyes.

Love is strange, and precious. *Each in our own way, Dad,* I thought.

And then, one last thought, causing a spate of almost hysterical laughter before I fell into a brief, troubled slumber:

*My father is dead to me.*

# THE PROWL

*Gregory Frost*

**Plateye:** *A ghost or spirit that can assume many shapes, from animal to human to monster. Believed by some Gullah people to be the incarnation of spirits of dead pirates, killed to protect the location of buried treasure, the plateye is retributive and mischievous. It is particularly fond of whiskey.*

Sure, I know what you want to hear about. You want to hear about the Civil War. I've already been interviewed, and that's all anybody wants recollected. Yes, I know, I *do* look too young to have seen it. I suppose now that there's been this so-called "Great War," people think they need to hear about others, to acquire some perspective. Me, I've seen enough to tell you there's no such thing as a *great* war. They're all ugly, stupid things, and I could relate far more interesting stories on other topics if you cared to listen.

You want to know what? How I learned to speak so eloquently? Hunh. You expected something a little less educated from an ex-slave, is that it? Well, as it happens, my speech is one of those more interesting stories—part of the best story of all, if I may?

Young man, do you know what a *haant* is? Well, it's a Gullah word. They're my people, the Gullah—live on the coast down south below Charleston. No, I don't mean I was born in South Carolina. I wasn't. I was born in Africa. And I was a free man until . . . Tell me, what are you? Maybe twenty-two, twenty-three? Unh-huh. Try to imagine that, at twenty-three, you'd been robbed of your future.

I was sixteen when they captured me. No, not whites. Not my own people, either, but other black men, who swept down upon us. They took me and some of my friends. They set fire to my village, and I don't know who lived or died that day. Those of us they kept were put in chains and marched to the coast and sold to the white men with ships. I didn't know the name of my country then—it was just home. I know now that the world calls it Angola.

The blacks who sold us got a pittance for us compared to what we were worth at this end of the journey. They sold us for silver, for guns, for rum, for beads, and even for pots and pans. While they negotiated with the ships, they locked us up in big cages on the shore called barracoons. People were jammed up together, pushed against each other's stink, but it was heaven compared with what awaited us. There were people from all over, and half of 'em spoke languages I didn't know. Almost everybody was naked. The slavers preferred us that way. We were nothing but beasts to them, and you don't put clothes on a mule, do you? We were there not even a full day before we were purchased and dragged up on a ship.

The captain, he barked at us like a hyena. None among us knew his language, but we understood him well enough, since failing to do so meant you got beat with a rope end till you figured it out. People wonder why we didn't do anything, why we didn't fight. After all, there were hundreds of us and hardly anything at all of them. But they had us terrified. We didn't know where we were. We were hungry and exhausted. I think we all believed that if we were just good and quiet, we wouldn't be harmed. If we'd known the truth . . . There *were* some ships where the slaves mutinied, but not many.

Crewmen came along and pulled some of us out of the crowd and stood us in a line. There was a redheaded fellow who, if anybody was too slow to move, lashed them across the face, and he was smirking all the time and shouting at us. He liked for us to be too slow.

The tall ones like me, we were all lined up together. Then the middle heights and the shortest. Men and women were separated, too.

Then they drove us down into the belly of that ship. They'd fixed it up special for their cargo. Made three tiers of what could be called pigeonholes, but what were more like coffins stacked on top of each other. You climbed in at the foot and dragged yourself up inside it, trying not to lie on the chains that shackled you there, 'cause you were going to lie on them for a long time if you did. The bottom tier was the biggest, which is to say, the longest, for the tallest of us. The first man in line, he didn't want to go in, and that redheaded bastard beat him unconscious with the rope. The man had to be picked up and shoved into his hole. He became the first to die on the voyage, but not the last. The rest of us saw how it was, and most crawled into their coffins willingly. We had no more than fifteen inches across in those holes. There was hardly room above to lie on your side. If you could turn over. Take you half an hour to turn over in that space, and you had to hunch your shoulders and wriggle like a tadpole. You'd end up with splinters in the meat of your arm, and if you weren't careful you could strangle in your chains.

It stank like no pigsty you've ever known, too. But we were property, and worth a good deal, and they didn't want us getting sick. They could lose thousands of dollars if some fever swept through their cargo, so they hosed us down regularly.

I had big wrists then, too big for the shackles they supplied, so that the skin was rubbed raw on me in no time. To either side there were uprights, supporting the second and third tiers, which was all that kept us from being squished. During the day enough light got in that we could see the fear in one another's eyes. They wanted us to see that. They wanted us to pass our fear around. I guess you boys who fought in the "Great War," you had it bad in the trenches, with mud and mustard gas and all. But you haven't been anywhere as near hell as I have. You never lived three weeks in a coffin narrower than your shoulders. If the person on the upper tier above you got scared and pissed himself, it dripped down on you and there was nothing you could do about it till they next hosed you off with seawater, and then a soup of human waste from above came raining down between the boards.

They stuffed in a man beside me who had been beaten all over. His eye was swelled up, and his head was bloody, crusted. The flies were at him, but he was smiling, like he felt nothing at all, and even over the stench of that place I smelled him, smelled the booze on him, for he was drunker than a man can get. I think they could have beaten him to death and he wouldn't have noticed for a week.

They locked us all in, then hoisted their sails. People soon started to moaning; some grew seasick and threw up—yet another stench in which to lie. A couple of people went crazy the first days in those tiny stinking holes. I expect I should have. I'd never been confined in my life till then.

That evening they fed us. We could smell the cooking, and most of us hadn't eaten in days. It was gruel, thick and nasty, but it was enough to keep a body alive. Of course, when you eat, you shit, and there were some couldn't help themselves, couldn't wait till the next time they were danced up on deck.

That's what they called it when they let us walk around—*dancing* us. One group at a time, they led us up on the deck, letting us wander about, tasting fresh air and exercise, every day, for maybe an hour before they put us back down in those coffin holes. Dancing, I guess, 'cause some began to sing and some swayed to the singing, their bodies taking them home. It was the only means they had to escape. Then and after.

The second night aboard, the thing happened that changed my life. That beat-up drunk beside me, he made this quiet sound, like a gas jet. It wouldn't have wakened me, but I was lying on my back and barely asleep. I was looking at the boards above my nose, so close that my breath came back on me. I turned my head to see, but it was black as a coal mine.

I heard a slithery sound, like a big snake twisting, and more hissing. The chain rattled just the tiniest bit. My hair started creeping up on my head. Bristling like a dog. After a time there was only the absence of sound. I knew that hole beside me was empty and that man had gotten free somehow.

I couldn't see as far as my feet even. Couldn't turn my head to know where he'd gone or what he purposed to do. There was no escape from that place for anyone.

An hour maybe went by like that before he came back. There wasn't a sound until he was slithering into that hole again. I stared so hard into that dark that it burned, but all I could make out was a general shape, twisted up like something made of molasses. Then of a sudden two eyes glistened there, looking right back at me, and a voice said, "Best git ta sleep now, friend." Then he gave this big sigh, and his eyes closed into the darkness. He fell asleep, which was more than I did the rest of the night.

Next day they hauled us out for our dance on the deck, and I had a good look at him in the light. All his contusions were gone like they never had been, and he looked like he'd eaten about forty bowls of gruel, instead of the one. The crew hardly paid us any mind. Something had happened, but I couldn't tell what because I couldn't understand what they said. That strange fella was kind of tilting his head as if listening, and damn me if he wasn't smiling to himself like he knew a big secret. He noticed me looking and gave me a wink and talked to me, as a Gullah would say, all *sweetmout*. "They lost that redhead lasher," he said. "He just up and disappeared last night, and nobody kin find him."

I asked myself how he knew their language. Right then I almost guessed the truth about him. But I kept my own counsel on it, as he'd only have to slide over a foot or two in the night to silence me for good.

What was the truth about him? Just wait a bit and you'll see.

After that, he would talk to me while we lay side by side. Most everyone else was wailing or moaning, but he hardly seemed bothered by the inconvenience of being chained up. He told me things—I couldn't figure how he knew 'em. Said some of the women were being led off by crewmen, to be used, and then locked back up at night. Some of the small boys, too. "We lucky we's so tall," he said. "They's afraid of us, don't think they're not. They keep you skayred so's you won't git a notion of fighting back. Don't give you 'nuf food to do much more than lie here in your own stink."

I asked how he knew so much, and he replied, "I listen to 'em talk." So I asked how he'd come to know their speech. He chuckled and answered that he knew *everybody's* speech. He asked if I wanted to know their speech, too. I said I did, and he just nodded, then seemed to doze off.

I guess it must have been a week later that fella got into trouble. The ship was riding calm. He'd slipped out again without waking me, and for all I know he did that every night. Anyway, I woke to shouting and feet thundering across the decks. I heard him beside me, scrambling into place. His chains rattled, and he grunted and cursed under his breath— nothing quiet and careful this time.

They came down with torches, shouting at all of us, screaming. And I still didn't know a word of it, but I knew what it meant same as I knew what it meant when they raised a whip.

Next thing we were dragged out of our holes, kicked and flogged with ropes, and pushed up the steps to the deck. It was a perfect night, and I stared at the clear sky, the stars strung up there, the moon off the horizon, the breeze so cool and salty-sweet. They lined us up as on that first day, and I glanced at that fella—his mouth was all sticky dark. He wiped his hands over his face, and his eyes stared at me above them. He said, "You want to know? This is as good a time as any." And he reached over with one of his bloody hands and grabbed my shoulder.

It was as if lightning struck me from all directions. The deck lit up bright white for an instant. I could still see everybody, but they were hollow, just outlines against the whiteness. He let go, saying, "There," and went back to wiping his hands down his thighs.

They got us all out finally. Then I saw the body. It lay in the middle of the deck, and it was something to see. The head had been almost chewed right off at the throat, and hung sideways. It was a white man, too, one of *them*.

The captain marched back and forth in front of us with a long leather cat that he thrashed in the air. He bellowed, "You foul black beasts, I'm gonna whip each 'n' ever' one of you till I find out who did this! Who got free! Mr. Johnson?" he screamed to one of the others.

"All present, sir. No one's missing."

"Damn me, sir. That means one of these vermin is gettin' loose and then back again."

"Sir."

"Well, dammit, man, get a torch and inspect them. Whoever did *that*, he gonna have blood all over hisself."

That Mr. Johnson picked up a torch and come over and began to inspect us, holding the torch close in one hand, keeping a wood truncheon in the other. I hardly noticed, for all at once I realized that I'd understood every word they spoke, and I stared at the fella next to me, and he just made a face that told me to keep quiet.

When Mr. Johnson come to him, he says, "Captain, this one's got blood on him." He grabbed the fella's arm and held it up, seeing the blood on the hand.

"Let me see that," the captain answered and started over.

I did something then I can't account for. I stepped in between the two men. I shook my head. I tried to say to Johnson that this man hadn't done anything. But even though I could *understand* his speech, I couldn't talk it. So I held up my own hands, and pointed at my wrists where I'd worked the skin raw on their too-small shackles. There were plenty of us had done that.

Johnson looked at me, then with a snarl raised up that truncheon, and I slunk back out of the way before he could hit me. Of course, the fella had no torn wrists, and in a moment they would have known that. But providence saved him—probably saved us both.

One of the shortest men, on the far side of the deck, suddenly cried out, "No more, I can't go down there no more! You can't put me back. Let me go!" He knocked down two of the crew and ran right up and sprang over the rail, and dropped into the night sea.

It wasn't long before we heard his screams. They only lasted a moment.

You see, sharks followed the slave ships. When one of us died, they just pitched the body overboard, and the sharks found out about this and took to trailing slave ships all the way across the Atlantic.

None of the crew understood what the man had shouted. The captain said, "Well, sir, I guess we found our villain. Mr. Johnson, get 'em all stowed again."

"Yessir!" Johnson snapped. He gave me a funny, suspicious look and muttered, "Stupid nigra." Of course, he didn't know I understood him. I was just a dumb beast that had risked my life over nothing.

They herded us back into the belly of that ship. Had to hose us down again, so many had thought they were going to die.

In the darkness, the fella said, "Pleased to make your acquaintance." Then he said my name, which I was sure I hadn't told him.

That's how I met the *palatyi*.

I'd heard of him—the old people around my home used to tell us stories about him, stories to scare us children. He was a shape-changer, could turn into about anything he liked, provided it was as big as him, which seems a mighty powerful skill to have. His only problem was he liked his drink too much, and when he was drunk, he lost his skill. And, son, the *palatyi* liked to drink more than you like to breathe.

The ship arrived in Charles Town—it's called Charleston nowadays. Back then it was a center for slaving. Ships that didn't go to the Caribbean sailed into the bay there direct. Charles Town had a big market square for slave auctions, and people gathered from all over. We were sold off almost the moment we arrived.

They drug us up on a platform a dozen at a time, almost all of us stark naked. The men who bid would climb up and pull back our lips, look at our teeth like we were horses, squeeze our muscles.

Most of us were bought for field work. Me and the *palatyi* got bought by a plantation owner named McTeer. He grew rice down on Saint Helena Island. The cypress swamps and the marshlands there were fertile ground for rice, but you had to dig canals and grub out the stumps and build little dikes to control the water so's you could flood things when you wanted. They grew cotton elsewhere, too, but we worked the rice.

Bunch of slaves he had already came from Madagascar, and they knew how to cultivate rice. Since I could understand what they said, I picked up their skills fast, same as the *palatyi*.

We were branded with an "M," and they gave us all new names. I got called John Brown, just like the abolitionist. They named the *palatyi* George Wellington.

McTeer called his place Hampton House. The whites around there, you see, had decided they were some kind of aristocracy. Like McTeer, they'd arrived from England with indentured servants already—mostly poor Irish who'd gotten arrested for stealing bread or something else innocuous, and who'd chosen to be slaves rather than get hanged back home. These Irish were mostly house servants; a few were slave drivers. Their masters—our masters—believed themselves to be the swells of the world; here, whatever they'd been back home didn't matter. They put on grand airs. George Wellington relished every opportunity to play on their snobbery.

At first, I couldn't figure him out. He could have escaped anytime, I thought, but he stayed and worked. One reason, I found out, was that he was sneaking out of the shack at night and into McTeer's storehouse, where there were kegs of liquor. He got into the whiskey pretty good; after a month or so they discovered that their supply was disappearing and put a guard named Landis on it. That didn't suit George Wellington at all. One night, I woke up to a gunshot and a lot of yelling, and everybody came stumbling out from Hampton House. We all ran outside, too. I knew it was the *palatyi*, 'cause he was missing in the crowd.

Landis came running past us, two or three other men on his heels, the bunch of them with rifles. He was shouting, "It had to come this way, boys! Wait till you see it!"

When I turned around, George Wellington was standing right behind me, just grinning.

"I s'posed they'd shot you sure," I told him. Back then, I spoke like everybody else round that place, and so did he.

"Those fellers is dainjus," he answered, chuckling. "But mos'ly to demself." Then he rubbed his belly and said, "I jis' had me some buckruhbittle, an' it was mighty good. I b'leew I'm developin' a taste for it."

"Buckruhbittle" was the word Gullah slaves used to distinguish white man's food from what they fed us. When they'd locked him out of the whiskey supply, George had switched to the kitchen in the Big House. Tonight Landis had caught him leaving, and George, quick as a wink, had transformed. Landis had seen a monstrous bay lynx, a wildcat. He'd shot at it, but missed. I'm not sure it was possible to hit it.

The next day Landis showed everyone the cat's prints in the dirt. Otherwise, I think they would have adjudged he'd been into the whiskey himself. The cat, though, didn't explain the disappearing food. McTeer blamed the Irish house slaves, but just to be thorough they chained us up at night, too. It didn't bother George, of course, as it didn't bother him what happened to us. He just liked his mischief.

He might have kept stealing their food, but he was bored with that jape already. After a while, things went back to normal. George snuck off at night, and I didn't know where he went now. But I found out. One night he woke me and said, "John, you come wid me. We going to have some fun."

I wasn't sure I wanted to, but he insisted it would be good for my education: "Gib' you a chance to sample the pledjuhs of life."

Now, they didn't guard us much, 'cause there was nowhere to run to. It was an island, so they didn't need to keep an eye on us. George and me walked right to the road and inland. I'm not really certain how we got to Beaufort, but we did. Seems like one minute we were on the road with the lights of Jack Mullaters bobbing in the swamps, and the next we were coming up on the lights of a town. In my astonishment, I looked to George, and my heart nearly jumped out of my breast. I was walking along beside a white gentleman wearing a fine coat. He had a grand ginger mustache. He gave me a slantendicular glance, then smiled that wide grin, and I knew it was still George. I started to babble, but he shushed me and took my hand and held it up for me to see. My hand was white, too, and there was brocade at my wrist. I could even *feel* it. He'd changed us both. I still don't know how. He told me, "Now, you let me do the talking, 'cause no matter how you look, you gwine talk the same's you always do. You hab no skill yet."

And I thought, well, neither did he, seeing as how he talked like any Gullah, but I was happy to keep quiet—I was too scared to do anything else.

He led us right down the main street of that town. People nodded to us, said, "Evenin', gen'mun," and didn't give us a second glance. My terror turned to sly relish.

So we arrived in front of this house with balconies and open windows and lights burning bright. He knocked on the door, and this big woman opened it. She smiled, then went all quizzical. "Why, sir," she said, "do I know you?" George, he took her hand and kissed it.

"Not yet," he told her, and she giggled like a child half her age and moved aside to let us in.

Then I swear he talked to her just like any white man would, without a trace of the Gullah he talked to me and others. He sounded every note. Reached into his coat and took out a handful of gold coins and closed her hand around them. She giggled some more and led us into a parlor. George whispered to me, "Remember, you say as little as you can. Don't speak to your girl, and keep the lights off once you're in her room. Let her think it's some kind of ritual."

That was what I did. A black-haired girl took me by the hand and led me into a private room. She'd disrobed down to her corset before I blew out the candles. "Shy, are you?" she said, her voice full of laughter.

"Yes'm," I answered, softly. Carefully. She didn't seem to mind.

I guess I tumbled her a couple of times before George knocked at the door and stuck his head in to say, "John, it's time to go."

I dressed hastily, pulling on my work clothes in the dark. He gave me some coins, and I set them beside the bed. The girl said, "You pass this way again, John, you look me up."

I answered, "Ma'am, I surely will."

We returned to the shack before daylight. I can't even tell you what moment I changed back again to myself. George, he just thought it was the funniest thing in the world, but I was too exhausted to laugh.

I guess I went with him two or three more times. The money, he was stealing from the Big House—but he couldn't do that too often.

I stopped accompanying him, though, after a while, 'cause I fell in love with a girl named Alike. That means "the girl who drives away beautiful women." They didn't call her that, though, here. They called her Annie. She was an Ibo woman, tall and sharp-boned and beautiful, and we kind of took up together. You have to understand, in that shack, you had no privacy. You had sex with everybody watching, everybody knowing.

The *palatyi* took me aside and told me not to fall in love with her. He said, "No good gwine come of it. In this here land there's no room for love. Them Hampton House people will see it and use that love as a weapon 'gense you." I didn't listen to that talk. Alike gave me a son, and she named him Orji, a name from her people that meant "great tree." He was a big child. For two years we were as happy as you could be, living like that.

Then one night the *palatyi* came lurching into the shack, falling down, laughing and snorting. Everyone woke up. Outside there were dogs barking and lots of yelling. He crawled into his bed and flopped down drunk. I didn't have to smell him to know it. What had happened was that he'd gotten liquored up in town and forgotten his shape. He said later that he'd been with two whores and all of a sudden they'd begun screaming, because the man entertaining them had turned into something else.

He'd escaped, but with a makeshift posse on his tail that followed him back to the plantation. The damned fool led them right to our shack. Men with torches burst in. Everybody was screeching, wailing. Alike cringed on our bed with Orji, and I shielded her from whatever was coming. The men knocked people aside. They had no idea who they were looking for, however. George was too drunk to stand. They might have figured him out, I suppose, but they were hungry to punish someone quick.

They grabbed hold of one of the men nearest and hauled him outside, tied him up and whipped him near to death. We stood and watched, not daring to intercede for fear of being whipped to death ourselves. McTeer, when he got there, was none too happy, and he made them stop. They were killing his property, and they didn't have a story that made a lick of sense to anybody.

Landis came forward with his gun and drove them off. But the next night, we were all shackled again.

When George sobered up, I cussed him a blue streak. He'd inflicted harm on someone else for his amusement. It wasn't funny anymore, his mischief.

He got all peculiar then and withdrew from everybody. They knew he was strange, but they didn't know what he was. That poor other fella suffered awfully. They'd about stripped the skin from his back. He couldn't work, and he rocked on his belly, delirious.

The second morning he was dead. It looked as if the blood had leaked right out of him. The women wailed like Sirens. Landis and the drivers came, carried him off, and buried him.

We went back to work, went out to thresh the rice. George walked beside me, and after a time he said, "I couldn't help him. He was sufferin', gwine to die. Alls I could do was make it quick for him."

Afterward, he seemed to be more cautious about what he did. He didn't talk to any of us much, even me, and I wondered again why he stayed on.

Maybe two weeks after that incident, with the rice harvested, another group of whites showed up at Hampton House. They were traders. McTeer had us all line up outside the shack. We could see that he was edgy and unhappy about something, but we couldn't imagine what he was about to do. He'd decided he had too many slaves, and was determined to sell some of us off.

The traders wandered back and forth, looking us over. They preferred to acquire slaves who'd been born into slavery, as such slaves wouldn't know anything else and would be easy to handle. They liked in particular to buy children. I didn't appreciate what that meant until one of them grabbed Alike and Orji and pulled them out of line. I jumped after them, got one hand on the man's shoulder, and then something smashed into the side of my head. I stumbled, fell. I could hear Alike crying my name, but when I tried to get up, something hit me again. I didn't pass out exactly, but the whole world spun round my head, and somewhere my baby was crying, far away.

When I came to my senses it was night, and George Wellington was sitting beside me. He looked into my eyes and said, "I tol' you not to fall in love. It only sump'n' they kin tek away from you." I understood then that I would never see my wife and son again. I started to cry. George leaned down and shushed me. "Listen up. I'm gwine go now. You wun't see me again. I got no ansuhs for you, but I do owe you sump'n'." He touched me, and the world lit up all white as it had on board ship. When it turned dark again, he was gone.

Before the sun came up the next morning, there was a great alarm from the Big House. We got up, huddling, clutching at each other. We'd already seen loved ones dragged off, and we were sure now it was our turn coming. People began to pray to Jesus, some who'd never been Christians till then.

But it wasn't anything to do with us. Someone had broken into the Big House and killed McTeer's wife and children. Torn them to shreds. Landis had heard a terrible wail and come out in time to see a white man run off into the woods. He'd recognized the man, too, as one of the slave traders from the day before. The man had stolen McTeer's money, Landis said. Mrs. McTeer must have caught him in the act.

They left us—the entire pack of white drivers and servants. They set off after that group of slavers. We could have fled, but we didn't. Some of us did enter the house, though. We found the family. It was horrible to see, but I'd seen that kind of slashing before, and I knew who'd killed them. I knew he'd done it for me, out of revenge. McTeer had robbed me of my family. And so the *palatyi* had robbed him of his. We didn't expect McTeer to be alive, but he was. The *palatyi* had slashed his hamstrings so that he couldn't walk, but had left him alive, if demented beyond words. I was cold then. I didn't mind what had been done to him.

They caught up with the slavers in Beaufort, Landis and his men. They hung the lot of them for the crime they hadn't committed, but that was good enough justice and all we could hope for, who'd watched our loved ones legally taken away.

The plantation went up for sale, but it was a tainted place. I think people believed it was haunted, which might have been George's doing. None of us saw him, though. We were all auctioned off, separated.

I ended up on a big spread outside Charles Town, met a woman there named Kaya, and married her. Her name meant "stay here and don't die." But after our third child, she did die, of a fever. Me, I never got sick at all. Other women round the place took care of my babies and helped raise them up. By the time they were young men, I was past fifty, but I didn't look a day older than them. I knew the *palatyi* had done something new to me. Folks pretended I was just aging gracefully.

I developed my gift for language, and learned to speak as well as my masters, better in fact, although I was careful not to let on how well. I taught my sons how to speak proper English, too. I gained a position in the house, put in charge of other house slaves, and I did what I could for them. Our owners were decent-enough people, I suppose, if you didn't mind that you belonged to them. I kept expecting George to turn up again, but he didn't. Eventually, I'd worked and saved enough to buy my freedom and that of my boys, and I took 'em north to Boston. I enrolled in a university there, and put the boys in, too. We caused something of a stir, the four of us like four brothers. Nobody believed I was their father. The boys almost didn't believe it, either!

I took a law degree and set up practice there. I met your Mr. Lincoln once, some years before the war.

Eventually, though, I had to go back to South Carolina. A newspaper article was what finally drew me. From the city of Charleston. People told of being haunted and stalked by a spirit—a *haant*, you see, which they called the Plateye, or sometimes the Plateye Prowl, 'cause of the way the thing seemed to select people to terrify. It would come to the back door of white people's houses and scratch like some pet to be let in. If they were fool enough to let it in, they didn't live to tell about it. It seemed to appear in various shapes, and I suspected it had to be George. I didn't go right away. None of my sons was still in Boston. One moved to Chicago. Another had gone off to France, and the third had made his way to San Francisco. They were in their thirties, one of them turned forty, and it had become increasingly difficult for me to pretend to be their elder. In fact, I'm sure they put distance between us because of it.

I saw to my affairs, settled some things. I didn't know exactly what I was going to do afterward, you see—just that I was going to vanish.

After the war, I took a train south. I made sure I had papers defining who I was. Reconstruction was under way, for the few years that it was allowed to work.

I kicked around that town a bit, asking people about the Plateye. Everybody had a story about it, and a couple people claimed they'd heard it scratching at their door but they'd had the sense not to let it in.

Finally, I found one old Gullah fellow who talked just like George, and who put me onto him, although he did ask, "Whyfor you wanna go and meet the Plateye? He fist tear you open if he don' tek a likin' to you. You go, jist be sutt'n you armed with whiskey." He told me there was a peach grove the Plateye supposedly frequented, on the edge of the town. I purchased a bottle of bourbon and carried it with me. I set it under one of the bigger trees; then I sat down a ways off and waited.

Sometime around midnight, a big bay lynx came slinking across the road and into the grove. Even though I knew what it was, I found the hair standing up on the back of my neck just like when I was in that coffin hole the first time I'd met him. The cat looked around suspiciously, sniffing the bottle. Then he took it and clambered up the tree. No cat ever moved like that. But that was the restraint on the *palatyi*'s magic. He could *look* like an animal, but he didn't gain its powers. He couldn't fly off as a bird, couldn't swim far as a fish. He was still *him*—whatever that was. Humanlike, but decidedly not human.

The cat sat on a low limb, dangling his legs like a kid fishin' off a dock. I got up and walked out into view. He kept right on drinking while I approached.

"Evening," I said.

The cat licked his lips a while. Then he answered me. "You lookin' purdy good, John."

"You never came back."

"Didn't I? Well, shuh! It's early still. There plenny more time."

"Not for me. I'm more than eighty years old now, George."

The cat shrugged. "You don' look a day over twenty." He took another pull from the bottle.

"And how is that?"

He didn't answer directly, but when he did, he'd dropped the Gullah façade in his speech. " 'George,' " he mused. "Nobody's called me that in a very long time. Guess it *has* been a while, hasn't it?" He set down the bottle. "You stuck up for me once. You shielded me when there was nowhere for me to go but into the belly of a shark. And all my shape-changing wouldn't have meant a thing to a shark—dinner is dinner for all God's creatures. You risked your life. You forced me to recognize something decent in a human being. Something worth saving, and something I don't have in me at all." He tilted his head a bit. "About the only real power I have is to protect myself so's no one'll know me as different. I blend. *You* know. But I got a little bit to spare, and so I gave that to you. Might be a blessing; might be a curse. I can't say. Ain't gonna make you last forever. But you'll sure last a sight more than eighty."

I said, "What about you? You could find a ship, go home now, back to where we came from."

He chuckled. "I got dropped here against my will, and I have to say, I'm not much persuaded to board another ship with these people. Besides, there's just a whole lotta folk in Charles Town I ain't scared yet." That cat face split as wide as a barn with the biggest grin you ever saw. Then he disappeared out of that tree just like that. The bottle came rolling down the trunk, empty. He'd drunk a fifth of bourbon in as many minutes.

I never saw George Wellington again. I suppose he's still there, having his mischief. I came up here to Canada and started over. But someone spoke erroneously of the Civil War, and I corrected him and had to admit to having lived through it. And the next thing I know, you journalists show up to write your articles. It's hard to stay anonymous.

Anyway, that's the story of how the Plateye Prowl of Carolina came to be, and how I learned to speak—as you say—so eloquently.

You're confused as to the time frame of these events? I'm not surprised. Near as I can figure, it was 1783 the year I was captured and brought to this continent.

That's right, that *does* make me more'n a hundred and fifty years old. But between you and me, I don't feel a day over sixty.

# FATE

*Jenise Aminoff*

The day they both fell, Cass knew the moment she'd always expected had come. She'd known the moment after she'd pushed her son into the world, the very moment she first held him, that he was too good to last. His creamy tan skin had glowed against her chocolate breast, and he'd wailed and screamed at the injustice of his minuscule life, and she'd laughed and wept and stroked his forehead and put one fingertip into his tiny grasp.

She'd known, then, that he was holding her only so that he could later let her go. She knew these things, like when it would next snow, and who was calling even before the phone rang. She knew her son's life and her life would be full of tricks and changes, joys and reversals, and so she named him Eshu, after one of the trickster gods in the stories her grandmother had told her, when she was Eshu's age. She held him tight, knowing she would have to let him go.

Hank laughed at her and told her she was going to give their son a complex, holding him that tight, that close, never leaving him even for a moment, even leading Hank in swift and silent sex while Eshu slept in the crib by their bed. Over time, she began to think that maybe Hank was right; nothing had happened yet—it was postpartum depression talking, or superstition, not premonition.

On the day they both fell, Eshu was just past three, walking with proud, uncertain legs and talking incessantly. In the nursery/playroom on the third floor of their condo, Cass was paying him little mind as she carefully moved a batch of baby geckos into a new, larger tank. They were coming along nicely, their adhesive feet clinging fast to the glass walls of their home.

"Mama, look!" Eshu cried.

"Mmm," Cass said, busy disentangling a tiny gecko from her sleeve.

"I'm high! Look, Mama. High, I'm up, up."

She turned to glance at him, and froze. He had climbed up the low futon onto the wall that bordered the staircase and was standing, precarious, above a ten-foot drop, grinning for her and all the world.

*This is the day*, she thought. And then she thought, *To hell with that*. And instead of shouting or jumping up or doing anything to startle his toddler body out of balance, she smiled at him.

"Look at you," she said, standing fluidly. She started slowly across the room. "Look how high up you are! Shall we see how high you can go?" She held out her arms, and Eshu reached for her, and she held one smug moment of triumph for not having panicked, for having cheated Eshu's fate.

So she stepped on the fire truck on the floor and something in her ankle went *snap!* She wailed and very nearly fell on her face. Eshu jerked back, and she saw him start to fall.

Somehow, she made that ankle work. She made a dash across the room and lunged, her ankle going *crack!* And she nabbed him by the collar just before it passed from view, and then her arm came down on the edge of the wall with a *crunch!* And still, she bit back the pain, dragged him up over the wall, and set him down on the floor beside where she collapsed.

His face had gone white, but because she did not cry, he didn't either. Instead, he just said, "Mama, Mama? Was that up?" while she held her right arm in her left and hissed with the pain. In her right hand, she still clutched a few hairs from her son's head, and she could not bring herself to let them go.

"No, Eshu, that was down," she muttered.

"Oh," he said, frightened now.

"Tricky boy," she said to cheer him up. "Help your mama out. Go get me the phone. See it over there?" She started to point, winced, and stopped. "Over there, on top of the table, see it? Go get it and bring it here, tricky boy."

Eshu levered himself up and bobbled across the room, giggling. He brought her back the phone. "Down! I go down! You go down!"

"That's right, my tricky boy. We all fall down."

"Not him," Eshu said, pointing. The gecko, all but forgotten to Cass, must have gone flying when she caught Eshu. It clung to the wall high above the staircase.

"Right. He can go up. But let's you and me stay down here for now."

Cass called 911, gave them her address, and told them to get the key from her neighbors, May and Elliot. Then she called Hank.

"Hi, honey," he said. "How's your day been?"

Cass looked over at Eshu, playing now with the damned fire truck, bellowing "London Bridge."

"All things considered, I guess it's been pretty good," she told him, and she started laughing and couldn't stop until the paramedics came to get her.

After that, with her ankle in a cast and her arm set with steel pins, she told herself, *I did it. It was worth it. I changed my son's fate. I saved him.* But a smaller voice inside her kept saying, *Better hope so, girl, 'cuz if anything happens now, there sure isn't a thing you can do about it, not from this wheelchair.*

Hank took a week off from work, but he began to fret and chafe at home, so Cass arranged for her friend and fellow lizard breeder, Stevie, to come and stay with them both during the day until she had to pick her daughter up from school at 3:00. They found a good rhythm, putting Eshu down for an afternoon nap so that he would sleep until Hank got home.

Of course, this didn't always work. Sometimes he would wake up early; sometimes he wouldn't nap on schedule. For times like these, Cass invented a game: Mama's Helper. "Eshu, go get me that book and I'll read it to you."

"This one?"

"No, the one with the duck. That's right." And he'd brought it, climbed carefully into her lap, and listened to her soft voice until he fell asleep there in her arms.

The next day, she said, "Eshu, go get me a glass of water, and I'll tell you a story." And she sipped and told him one of her grandmother's stories about Anansi and how he won storytelling from the sky god, and Eshu drifted off.

The next day, he began begging. "What can I do, Mama? What can I bring you?" She started having to make things up: a pen, a pillow, a toothbrush.

One day, listening to the radio, Eshu did a wild, ecstatic dance in the living room, and Cass and Stevie laughed and clapped and sang along until the song ended. "Come here, tricky boy," Cass told him, "and I'll tell you your story."

Surprised, he said, "I didn't bring you anything."

"No, but you just gave me something wonderful," she replied, and he beamed and charged up to her, banging her leg cast and climbing up it, exultant and expectant.

After that, he began to do and find small things to delight her: toys, books, songs, food. On the day Eshu left her, on a warm hazy spring afternoon with Stevie already gone, Cass heard the back-door screen slam.

"Eshu?" she called.

"I'm here, Mama," he yelled back. "I'm gonna get *floors*," by which he meant, but could not quite pronounce, "flowers." Cass chuckled to herself, knowing he would pull up some marigolds and bring them in with a scattershot of garden mud. A minute later, she heard his astonished laugh, just once. Then silence.

"Eshu?" she called again, then again. "Eshu? Tricky boy, come on inside now."

The answer came from that small voice, saying, *You knew better all along, didn't you? Now it's come, and he's let go. He was too good to keep.*

It was hard to use the chair's control joystick with her left hand, but she maneuvered over to the back door and looked out through the screen and across the yard, where there was no sign of Eshu. She kept on calling him for nearly an hour; then she fetched her own phone this time and called the police.

At nightfall, with Hank, his strong, ruddy fingers wrapped tight around her one good hand and the police lieutenant coordinating the search from their living room, Cass suddenly knew that he was gone. She felt his life part from hers as keenly as the snap of her ankle, and she let the tears run down her face for a while, quietly, to keep from alarming Hank.

Hours turned to days, and her ankle cast came off. With effort, she could get up the stairs to visit the lizards. To her astonishment, the baby gecko was still loose on the ceiling and had grown. "I just can't reach him," Stevie told her apologetically. And still, Eshu stayed gone.

Weeks grew into months, and her arm finally knit and came out of the cast so thin and pale, she ached. It was the color of Eshu's skin. That day she went up to the nursery and said to the gecko, "You be my judging gecko now. Tell me which direction he lies. I'll come back tonight for your answer."

Hank had taken to searching the streets himself each night; it made him feel useful, somehow less helpless, and he came back exhausted and slept deeply. So it was easy for her to be alone at night in the nursery.

From under her pillow, she took out the small sachet with the hairs she had torn from Eshu's head. She took it upstairs and found the gecko clinging to the wall at eye level, pointing south.

She wept a little then, knowing her son was truly dead. Then she thought, *To hell with that.*

She lit incense in a cradle and added Eshu's hair to it. Then, as the smell of burning hair filled the room, she took out a small knife and sliced her palm, letting it drip, drip, drip into the incense.

Cass sat on the floor and rocked and sang to him, calling him,

*"Tricky boy, tricky boy,*
*Mama has found you,*
*Come to me, tricky boy,*
*Come back, my Eshu."*

He came to her in the small hours of morning.

He was worse than she'd imagined, face pulped and nearly unrecognizable. His ankles and neck were raw and swollen, his shirt rent and caked with mud and blood, and dirt fell from his mouth when he spoke.

"I went down, Mama."

"Tricky boy," she whispered. "Yes, you did, tricky boy, my baby, my Eshu. Who was it that put you down there in the dirt?"

"Elliot," he told her.

Cass felt numb. "Elliot? From next door, Elliot?"

"He said he had a surprise for me, and he lifted me over the fence. Then he took me to his basement, and he called me a lot of names, you and Dad, too. He called me bastard half-breed and abomination, and he hung me from the steps like a punching bag and hit me and kicked me and choked me so I couldn't breathe. And when he was done hurting me, he left me down there in a hole under the stairs."

Cass stayed silent for a long time, weeping, until finally he asked, "Am I home, Mama?"

"You know you can't come home, my Eshu." *You were never mine.*

*I should never have tried to keep you so close.* "But I will tell you one more story before you go. It's a secret. Don't tell anyone else."

Eshu smiled. Some of his teeth were missing. He came and climbed into her lap, his flesh cold and gritty to the touch. And he waited for his story.

Cass wrapped her arms around him and whispered in his ear, "Did I ever tell you about duppies, tricky boy?"

"No," he said.

"Duppies are the spirits of people who have died, but their spirits stay around. Sometimes they stay to help and protect people, and sometimes they stay because they are angry at how they lived."

"Or how they died?" he asked.

"Yes, that's right."

Eshu wriggled out of her arms, slithered down out of her lap, and grinned up at her. "I'm a duppy, aren't I, Mama? That's what you made me."

"Yes, I did, tricky boy. Do you know what you need to do?"

Eshu nodded, and soil fell from his hair. "Yup. I have to earn my story." And he left.

After that, Cass saw him from time to time, in the shadow of Elliot's meticulously clipped hedge, or under their car, or slipping into the backyard. Once, he waved at her, and she shivered.

Elliot began to look tired, then haggard. Two weeks after Cass conjured up her son, police cars and ambulances pulled up next door. Cass watched them push a gurney into the house, then pull it out again with a large body in a bag. Too large for Eshu.

The doorbell rang. Cass heard Hank answer the door. "Suicide note," the policeman murmured, and "basement, buried, coroner, regrets." They had found him at last. A second gurney, a smaller bag. And dirt, again, on the clean white gurney sheets.

Eshu came to his funeral. He stood beside Cass as she cried, and sometimes he cried, too, and sometimes he held her hand, though no one else noticed. Even Hank did not notice his dead son tugging at his pant leg, wanting to be held. It broke Cass's heart. She threw a handful of earth into Eshu's grave, thinking, *Now he can be at peace.*

But he followed them home, riding in the backseat. He played noisily in the living room while Cass held Hank, letting him weep here, in private, because he could not cry in public. Eshu hid under the bed as they made mournful love that night. And he was at breakfast the next morning. And the next, and the next, until she wanted to scream. But she held her tongue for Hank's sake.

At last, when Hank returned to work and they were alone, Cass told Eshu, "It's time for you to be moving on, tricky boy. Your work is done."

He shook his head. The skin had begun to peel away from his scalp; his eyes had sunk back into his skull. "No, Mama. You said I can't go home."

Then Cass knew she was doomed to lose Eshu a third time, because she would die and move on while he would be stuck here, a duppy wandering the site of his murder forever. And she thought, *To hell with that.* She took Eshu by his soft, skinless hand and led him up to the nursery.

The walls were covered with geckos, everywhere. They pointed every which way, and they set Cass's head to spinning. She fell to the floor, confused, unseeing, lost.

A gecko dropped from the ceiling and sauntered up to her. It had too many legs, exactly twice as many as it needed, and Cass suddenly realized that it was no gecko at all but a spider. "Anansi," she whispered.

The spider laughed at her, and it grew and grew until it seemed to fill the room. "Hello, Cass. Hello, tricky boy, Eshu, sweet baby o' mine. What a mother you got." Anansi's wrinkled face stretched into a leer. "Tricky boys come from tricky girls. You reckless, Cass, invoking trickster gods and then cheating them of they right. You tricked your boy's fate twice already, sweetness; and look how far it get you. Each trick you play, things get worse and worse. Now you think maybe a little more incense, a little more bloodletting going to set things right?"

"He's my son," Cass told him. "I have to set him free."

"He a duppy, girl. Is you turned him, you bind him to the earth. No changing that back, not with your weak *simidimi* magic."

Cass wailed and beat the floor with her fists. "Then what? What can I do? Tell me; I will do anything."

"Anything?"

Cass gulped. She knew Anansi the Trickster meant trouble, no matter what. Slowly, she said, "Anything that is mine to give. Not Hank, nothing that will harm anyone else. Just me. Whatever is mine to give, if you take Eshu to heaven."

Anansi laughed. "Now you being careful. Well, late is better than never. I like tricky girls, and their tricky boys, so I going to help you. I going to release this boy to his rest, but you got to give me something in return."

"What?"

"Something precious. Something you can't buy in store nor replace like blood. Something special." And he leaned down and whispered in her ear.

It's not true that black women can't turn pale. Cass felt the blood drain from her face, and she thought, *How will I know? How will I know anything?* But she looked at Eshu, and she looked at Anansi, and she knew there was no going back. So she nodded. "Yes, take it. Take it."

Anansi laughed and danced about the room on all eight feet. Then he lowered himself gently until his face was level with hers. With spidery fingers, he caressed her neck, drawing her close, kissing her deep. And with that kiss, he sucked away his price.

The trickster god let her go, stood up, and smacked his lips. "Is a fine price, Cass; a fine, tasty gift for Anansi. Come on, Eshu. Let we go home." He picked Eshu up and swung the laughing boy onto his back. As he turned, Cass saw Eshu wave to her, whole again, before they both disappeared into the long shadows of twilight.

"Good-bye," she told him, her voice hoarse from effort and loss.

Nine months later, Cass gave birth to her second son. She knew from the moment she pushed him from her womb, the very moment she first held him in her arms, that absolutely nothing about his life was certain, that she had no idea what course his future would take, and anything could happen. And she loved him and named him Hank Jr.

# TRIAL DAY

*Tananarive Due*

etitia was a few months shy of ten the summer Brother was scheduled to stand trial.

Brother was only her half brother, and his name was Wallace Lee, but Letitia had always called him Brother because, to her, the warmth and strength of that word suited him best. In turn, he'd always called her Lettie, the sassier nickname she preferred, instead of the more prissy and cumbersome "Letitia" that Daddy and her stepmother insisted on calling her by. Her stepmother thought nicknames were low-class, and Daddy usually went by whatever her stepmother said, so Brother called her Lettie in secret.

Brother lived with his mama in Oak City, which was a day's drive south in Daddy's shiny new 1927 Rickenbacker, farther than most people she knew had traveled in their lives, so she didn't see him as often as she wanted to. During the summers, and sometimes for Thanksgiving, Brother took a train to stay with them. He would visit for as long as two weeks, arranging his long limbs into knots so he could sleep on the living room couch. Brother was only fifteen now, but he'd always been tall. Letitia had never met Brother's mother, but Daddy was tall enough for two. Letitia and Brother had different mamas in different towns— although Daddy had never been married to either woman—and her stepmother told Letitia the whole thing was a disgrace and ought to be a source of personal shame to her, as if Letitia could be responsible for any of the doings in the world before she was born. By studying Brother,

Letitia decided that his mama must be dark-skinned like her own, and probably pretty too, judging by Brother's long, thick eyelashes. When he had visited them last summer, Brother had been nearly as tall as Daddy, and his voice had dropped to a lower register. Letitia had listened to the two of them laughing on the front porch late at night, having a conversation she wasn't allowed to listen to, and they had sounded to Letitia like two grown men having a gay old time, not a father and son. She still remembered the way they'd laughed, barking out into the night wind. Listening to that sound, which seemed to surround the house, Letitia had fallen asleep with a smile, rocking in their happy noise.

Even her stepmother, Bernadette, stayed out of the way when Brother was here. Bernadette didn't talk to Brother with her voice shrilled high the way she talked to Daddy, and sometimes Brother could make her laugh, too. When he did, she'd hide her mouth behind a napkin or her hand as if she didn't want anyone to witness a smile on her face. Most times, no one did. Bernadette's smiles were hard to come by, and always accidental. Letitia had long ago given up trying to think up ways to bring out Bernadette's smiles. But Brother could. Laughter and smiles of any kind were hard to come by during Brother's impossibly long absences, when Letitia began to wonder if she would see him again or if she'd just dreamed him. Of all the reasons Letitia had to love him—and his kindness toward her was unlike anyone else's except her father's and poor Mama's—perhaps she loved Brother most for bringing the laughter and smiles.

So it came as a shock to Letitia when she learned that Brother was in jail. Bernadette told her about it as if she were discussing a stranger she'd read about in the newspaper. "Got himself thrown in jail for armed robbery! That's what these young boys get for being so wild. They'll probably give that foolish boy the Chair, robbing a white man like that," she said. "Your daddy took up with every tramp and hoodoo woman who looked his way, so what else can he expect?"

Letitia was too scared for Brother to be angry about Bernadette's insults. She knew what the Chair was. The Chair was the electric chair at Raiford State Prison, where colored men were sent to grow old—or to die, if they were destined to take their seat on the Chair. As much as Letitia had heard about the state prison and the Chair in her tender nine years of life, she had never imagined she could *know* someone who got sent there. Those were the hard-luck stories from people with hard-luck lives.

Daddy was Richard Reaves. He had his own grocery store and a cotton farm. He had a house with two stories and three bedrooms on a thirty-acre parcel of land that had once been owned by slaveholders. Daddy and Cecil Johnson, who owned the colored mortuary, were the two most envied men in the county—and Daddy was most envied of the two because Bernadette was so much more light-skinned than Mr. Johnson's wife. (Daddy and Bernadette looked like twins, with their straight hair and honey skin.) When Daddy installed the new upstairs bathroom, neighbors flocked to the house because they were still using outhouses and they wanted to see with their own eyes how a colored man right there on Powell Street had a working toilet and bathtub *upstairs* in his house, in addition to the one downstairs.

Letitia's daddy did not have hard luck, so Brother could not have been sent to Raiford.

"That's just a misunderstanding, and it's being worked out. I'm sure Wallace Lee's home by now," Daddy said when she asked him, mussing her hair. But he never looked her in the eye when he said it, and Letitia felt a growing, heavy pool of disdain in her belly when it occurred to her that Daddy was lying to her. She had never thought of her father as the kind of man who would lie to a stranger, much less to his daughter. To *her.*

That summer, suddenly, everything in Letitia's world began to feel all wrong. Hearing about Brother's arrest was the first thing. Hearing the lie in Daddy's voice had been the next. But the hardest, the worst, was yet to come. Letitia just knew it.

Letitia knew many things, mostly things she wished she didn't. Her teacher called her *unusually perceptive*, which sounded like a grand thing, but Bernadette instead accused Letitia of mischief and lies, helpless to find anything but wickedness in her. Despite Letitia's efforts to behave as well as she could at all times to make her presence less burdensome, she knew that Bernadette considered her the very living image of everything that was wrong with her life. Letitia had learned how Bernadette felt about her when she was as young as five, the first time Daddy had brought Letitia to live with him because Mama was too poor. Bernadette had hated her right away, at first glance. Letitia had not known exactly *why*, but the hatred had been as plain as the moon in the sky. In later years, Letitia had come to realize that Bernadette hated her because she was proof that Daddy had known other women before her, and because she hated mothering a strange woman's daughter when she could not have children herself.

But knowing *why* Bernadette hated her hadn't made Letitia feel any more welcome in her father's house. She only felt welcome when Daddy came home at night, when Bernadette locked most of her hatred for Letitia away and concentrated on finding things to dislike about Daddy. Letitia was afraid to enjoy anything about her father's beautiful house, because none of it was really hers. She could be sent away at any time, and she would hardly ever see Daddy if that happened, like it was before. When Letitia brought powders from Mama to slip into Bernadette's bathwater, she only wanted her stepmother to stop hating so much.

Bernadette never said these things aloud like an evil stepmother in a fairy tale, but she didn't have to. Letitia knew words were only part of who people were, and usually the least important part. Sometimes, she felt she could just see *through* people, as if they were standing before her naked. She could see into people's hearts.

At church, people who were stealing from their bosses, cruel to their children, or wooing someone other than the person they were married to avoided locking eyes with Letitia, for fear she might tell on them. When she was younger, she'd blurted things out that made adults gasp, and once a minister had plain slapped her face from the shock of hearing his business told. Now, she'd learned to keep quiet. Letitia's aunties and neighbors near Mama's house had theories about why Letitia had her gift: It was said that she had been born with a caul covering her face, which gave her the seeing eye, the third eye. Others thought it was because Mama was a roots-woman, and she had tied a piece of High John the Conqueror root around Letitia's neck the moment she was born. Letitia knew things, and usually knowing brought her only disappointment and trouble, so speculating over the reasons why brought her no joy.

And there would be no joy for some time. That much she knew, too.

This problem with Brother was going to change everything. The problem with Brother was going to make every other problem seem small from now on. The problem with Brother would be up to her to fix, in the end.

One afternoon when Daddy was at his store and Bernadette was taking a nap because she'd overheated herself working in her garden, Letitia went to the corner of the parlor Daddy used as his office, with his oak rolltop desk and electric lamp and stacks of papers in different piles. Letitia climbed up into Daddy's leather chair and surveyed the desk. Before she could decide exactly what she was looking for, or where to begin, the return address typed on a piece of mail caught her eye: LIVE OAK, it said.

The letter had been opened with a letter opener's neat incision across the top. Letitia brought it out to read by the sunlight stealing in beneath the drawn shade. The whole letter was typed, which told Letitia it must be important.

*Dear Mr. Reaves,*

*Regarding the matter of Wallace Lee Hutchins, I cannot impress upon you enough how urgent it is that you appear at the County Courthouse at 1 P.M. Friday, July 20. Many cases like this one are disposed of in the blink of an eye, to the defendant's disadvantage. As an attorney for the National Association for the Advancement of Colored People (NAACP), I am investigating the rising number of very troubling capital cases in this county. Your son's case is one of an alarming pattern.*

*Please allow me to be frank: two eyewitnesses, including the shopkeeper, have told police they saw the two boys with a .22-caliber pistol at the time of the robbery. The witnesses and the defendants have quarreled in the past, so one party's word goes against the other's—but since the witnesses are white, I don't have to tell you which version will have more credibility. Mrs. Kelly is fighting the charges against her son with all her soul—she was the one who contacted the NAACP—but I'm afraid she is in a similar position to your own son's mother. Both ladies are ill-respected in this community.*

*Again, Mr. Reaves, it is vital that you contact me as soon as possible to help me prepare your son's defense. My resources in this matter are limited, but I believe if the jury heard the testimony of a respected colored business owner in his son's defense, we may get a lesser sentence. You are his best chance. My great fear, sir, is that the prosecutor will seek execution. Two young men were executed earlier this year after being tried in very similar circumstance, where a robbery was committed, but there were no injuries or fatalities. Armed robbery, it seems, is a capital offense for colored boys.*

*Plainly put, I am asking you to help me save your son's life. I think we can both agree that if these two young men committed an armed robbery—and although they both maintain their innocence, it's very possible that they did—they deserve a severe punishment in the eyes of the law. They will go to jail for a long time, as is only proper.*

*But these are sixteen-year-old boys, and neither deserves to die for the ignorant work of one night, especially not under a legal system that is a sham, in a county where hunting colored men is virtually legal. (There was a lynching not a mile from where I'm lodging the night I arrived—my first exposure to the heinous phenomenon. But it is your son's case that has been sent to the top of the docket.)*

*Please help me in this matter. I am trying to prevent another lynching, this one in a courtroom.*

The letter was the most important thing Letitia had ever found. It seemed to howl in her hands. She held it so tightly she was afraid she might rip the neat paper clean in two, reading it and rereading it until she'd memorized the words that mattered. She knew she would want to draw upon the memory of this letter for a long time to come, because there was so much to think about. So much to ponder. She wanted to steal the letter and lie about its disappearance, but she couldn't steal from Daddy.

Letitia understood it all, now: Brother and a friend had been charged with robbing a store with a gun. The shopkeeper and another witness who didn't like Brother claimed Brother and his friend had a gun, and it was Brother's word against theirs. The court was rushing to take the case to trial, and they would probably ask for the Chair. A lot of colored people had been getting the Chair lately, and the problem was so bad that a national association for colored people had come to see about it. And if Daddy didn't go, Brother might die. It was all so plain to Letitia, it was as if she'd known the whole story the first time Bernadette mentioned that Brother was in jail.

The letter said the trial was going to start on July 20. Letitia hadn't thought about what day of the month it was because there was no reason to track time in the summers, but she checked the kitchen wall calendar and learned it was Tuesday, July 17.

Brother's trial was in less than three days.

"You're going, aren't you, Daddy?" Letitia said at dinner, when she finally dared.

Bernadette looked angry before she knew if she should be. "Going where?" she said in a suspicious tone. She expected to find wrong everywhere. "What are you talking about?"

Daddy's face became stone. He looked at Letitia quickly, then his eyes passed over to Bernadette's. "She ain't talking about nothing," Daddy said.

"Aren't you going to Brother's trial?" Letitia said.

When she said the word "trial," Daddy's shoulders hunched as if a huge weight had suddenly been hoisted upon them.

"Richard . . . Washington . . . Reaves," her stepmother said. Her voice whispered, but her face was shouting, changing colors in the queer way it often did.

"Now, come on, Bernadette . . . ," Daddy said, pushing himself away from the table. He stared at the floor. "Don't start up again. We're sitting to a pleasant meal."

"We settled that, Richard. You promised." Her voice was creeping toward a shout now.

"Yes, we settled it," Daddy said. "Of course we did. Pay Letitia no mind."

"But you *are* going, aren't you, Daddy? If you don't, Brother could die."

Daddy started cursing under his breath then, something he rarely did. He stood up from the table quickly, throwing his napkin onto his plate. Then he took Letitia's arm in a way that felt nearly rough, bringing her to her feet. "That's *enough*, Letitia," he said, thundering. Letitia's heart seemed to rock backward and then fall still. "You come on with me right now."

Letitia was nearly in tears by the time Daddy took her to her room and closed the door behind them. Daddy had only beaten her with his belt once before, when she'd sassed at Bernadette, and she'd cried for two days straight. Letitia couldn't imagine she'd earned another whipping just for asking about Brother. Midnight, Letitia's stocky black cat, mewed softly from the bed, and the sight of his curious green eyes comforted her. On days like this one, Midnight was her only friend. He rarely left her room the whole day long.

"Have you been into my mail?"

"Yessir," Letitia said. "But I only wanted to know about Brother."

"Well, I'm very sorry you did that, Letitia, because that letter was not for your eyes. That letter was from a lawyer from New York who's just trying to scare us so we'll do what he says. He hasn't lived down here, and he doesn't understand my position. He's asking me to do something I can't do, and I want you to put it out of your head. Your brother got himself in some trouble, so he'll probably go to jail. But I sent some money, and he'll be just fine."

Letitia did not remember any part of the letter that said Daddy should send money.

"Daddy, he says you have to *go*, or Brother will get the Chair."

Letitia's father was perspiring now, and Letitia didn't think it was just because the upper floor was stifling after so many daylight hours of rising heat beneath the angry summer sun. Daddy looked nervous. No, not nervous—he looked *scared*, the way he looked when he brought his hunting rifle out of the closet because a strange car was driving slowly past their house at night. Some people were jealous of him, he said— some *white* people—and jealousy was apparently something to fear.

111

There was a bead of sweat on the bulb at the end of his nose, and he could barely make himself keep his brown eyes fixed on hers.

"You're too young to take all this in, Letitia," Daddy said, his voice sad and gentle. "You can't believe everything somebody says just because it's typed on a piece of paper. That lawyer's job is to help your brother. But I'm not a lawyer, and I'm no help to him. And besides that, there's no chance they'll give Wallace Lee the chair. He didn't kill nobody."

"The letter said—"

He shook her, just enough to make his words sink in. "What did I just tell you about believing everything that's typed on a piece of paper? That's a spook story he wrote in that letter. That's so I'll do what he says."

"But why *won't* you, Daddy? You have a car. You could drive there."

Daddy sighed, and his breath smelled like pipe tobacco. "Nothing's that simple, little princess. Wallace Lee's mother and me knew each other a long time ago. She's shamed herself in that town in ways that have nothing to do with me, and if I get all tangled in this mess, running off to a courtroom where there's newspaper reporters and such, then I'll be shamed too. A businessman can't afford to be shamed. All a colored man has in this world is his name, Letitia. And besides that, there's no use me going trying to stir up trouble. The Klan runs that county, and there's Klan in this county, too. People in a place to make life very hard for all of us. Now, my heart aches for Wallace Lee—but I've seen how such things come out in the end, and it wouldn't do any good for any of us. I would just make this situation worse. Far worse."

For the first time, Letitia realized that Daddy had a whole list of reasons why he was not going to Live Oak to save Brother, one having little to do with another. As she stared up at him in that instant, he shrank in her eyes, although he was still three feet taller, with thick arms and thighs as solid as the trunk of an oak. He began to look very small, the way he looked to her when Bernadette chased him from one corner of the house to the other with her sharp tongue, his shoulders wincing with every blow.

"It's 'cause of Bernadette, isn't it?" Letitia said. "*She* don't want you to go."

Daddy was not the slapping sort, but Letitia realized from the stewing cloud that crossed her father's eyes that he had probably come as close as he ever had to slapping her in the mouth. She had learned long ago that the truth made people angry, and to speak of it was considered evil. If she hadn't been so upset about Brother, she would have known better.

Letitia's room was directly across the hall from Daddy's, and even when their door was closed, she knew what went on in there even when she wasn't trying. She knew how Bernadette expected Daddy to account for his whereabouts every minute of every day. She knew how Bernadette told him no when he said he was thinking about buying more land or expanding his store, because she preferred him to buy pretty things for the house. And worst of all, Letitia knew how Daddy had to beg—how he had to make his voice sound silly and ask a dozen times or more, each time sounding sillier than before—just to convince Bernadette to lie in his bed with him like a man lies with his wife. Most times, begging or no begging, her answer was no. Letitia did not know much about the private things men and women did together, but she knew that the sound of her father's begging made her feel sick to her stomach.

If Daddy understood how much she really knew, he would have slapped her for sure.

"Letitia," Daddy said, a low thunder still roiling in his voice. "Don't you dare put that magic eye on me, gal. You best learn to stay out of grown people's business. I've made my decision, and that's the last I have to say about it."

*You're so weak, Daddy,* Letitia thought. *You look big and strong, but you're weak through and through.* And she began to cry. Daddy left her to sort out her tears for herself instead of kissing them from her cheeks the way he usually did. Letitia cried late into the night, stroking her cat, wondering how the whole world could have gone so wrong in so little time.

The next day, as she always did when she had nowhere else to turn, Letitia walked the half mile's distance on an unpaved road to see Mama. Whenever Letitia went to Mama and cried about how mean Bernadette was to her, she knew how to fix it. She knew which powders, which doll, and which combinations of roots, bone, and blood would make Bernadette more humble, more tolerable, more kind. Bernadette never got completely quiet—something Letitia had wished for often—but after a good ritual or two, Letitia noticed she had two or three weeks in a row when Bernadette did not say a single unkind thing to her. That was all the proof she needed that Mama's magic worked.

After she heard the story, Mama clucked her tongue in the space where she'd lost three of her front teeth in a riding accident when she was a very young woman. The work of a curse, people said. Everyone considered the lost teeth a great tragedy, since Mama would be very pretty otherwise, but Letitia knew that Daddy must not have minded. Maybe he hadn't loved Mama because she had no teeth, but he had thought she was pretty enough to court.

"That man, that man." Mama sighed. "Well, don't nothin' change. Always too skeered of what people think." It was rare that Mama said anything bad about Daddy in her presence.

"I think it's 'cause of Bernadette."

"Well, shoot, we know that," Mama said. "What ain't the fault of that devil-woman?"

"Do a spell, Mama. Make it so Bernadette will say Daddy can go save Brother. Make her go out her head, or get her real sick." Or kill her. That was what Letitia really wanted to say. Once, when Mama had made a little rag doll of Bernadette when she was being more unpleasant than ever, Letitia's fingers had itched to tear the doll's tiny head clean off. Instead, Mama had given the doll's leg a good twist, and Bernadette had been laid up in bed for two weeks because she hurt her knee after falling in a ditch near Daddy's tomato patch.

But this time, instead of consulting her doll or her large leather pouch where she kept vials of powders, or gathering herbs from the woods alongside the roadway, Mama sighed and shook her head. "Cain't, Letitia. We hexed that woman five, six times. I told you that kinda magic comes back on you. She got protection, and she's comin' back strong now. Naw, chile, we mess with any bad juju now, and yo' brother's gon' die."

*Brother's gon' die.* Meeting Letitia's ears, those three words turned her blood cold. Tears appeared in her eyes, but froze there. Her entire world felt frozen.

"The spirits is playin' tricks," Mama said, running her hand across her tightly braided hair. Her bracelets of shells and cheap metals tinkled together. "Somebody got a curse on that house, and we got to do a higher ceremony. I think it's got to be you, 'cause you're blood kin to your brother. You need a sacrifice ritual, Lettie. You seen me bleed chickens, and that's what you got to do. But if you want the message to get across, don't use a chicken. That might not get what you want quick enough. Use your black cat."

Letitia had been filled with horror since her mama said the word "sacrifice," because no matter how important the cause, she hated to see animals killed. For that reason and that reason alone, Letitia considered it a lucky thing she'd moved away from Mama's house, because people came for favors, and Mama routinely slaughtered chickens, goats, and pigs for rituals or for meals, or usually for both. Letitia had been mortified enough at the idea of killing her first chicken, but nothing compared to her horror of hearing her mama mention her cat.

Although Letitia didn't speak, Mama saw it in her eyes.

"Lettie, I know you love that cat. But you'll make the spirits *listen* if you bleed something you love. You see how I keep my bleeding chickens apart from my stewing chickens? I treat 'em special. And I had to do this, too, when I was your age."

"I won't," Letitia said.

"Then you don't wanna save your brother, do you?"

Letitia's stomach hurt as she thought of Brother's row of smiling teeth. Brother was in a cage somewhere, and soon he would go to the Chair.

"Daddy will go see about him," Letitia said.

"Chile, yo' daddy ain't goin' nowhere. I know yo' daddy. I *know* him. If he was gonna go, he'd'a gone from the start. He would'a been there an' back. Nothin' can't keep that man from somethin' he wanna do, and nothin' can't change his mind, neither. Bernadette's got him stuck bein' wrongheaded, to let his own boy die. There's ways for women to get ahold of men until they can't fight, an' that's how Bernadette's got him. An' she was too strong for me, chile. Else, you an' me *both* would be livin' in yo' daddy's fine house, wouldn't we?"

That was true, too. Letitia had always known it, but it hurt to hear Mama say it. The idea that Bernadette was more powerful than Mama suddenly terrified her. But of course she was! By now, Letitia's tears had freed themselves, glistening across her face. She hitched back a sob.

"This is one o' them times you got a choice, Letitia. You can do what you want and hope things don't turn out wrong, or you can do what you *know* will make things right."

Letitia's next sob escaped from her throat fully formed. She suddenly wished that her parents had never met for the secret Sunday-afternoon meetings Mama had told her about, because then she would never have been born.

"If you gon' do it, do it clean and quick, like you seen me. When the blood's spilt, say this prayer: *Spirit, release my daddy an' give him strength to fight the curse.* An' do it at midnight. See how you named that cat? Like you known it from the start. Mama'll come bring you a new cat someday."

That was a lie, too, in its own way. Mama could not afford to bring her hardly anything.

"By myself?" Letitia heard herself ask.

"Just take the cat out back, to yo' daddy's barn. Do it quick." With that, she handed Letitia a slender, shiny knife from the pocket of her stained old apron. Just the size for Midnight.

Letitia did not remember her walk home, nor did she remember most of the day. She told Bernadette she didn't feel well—which wasn't the least bit untrue—and she sat on her bed stroking Midnight's velvet-soft fur, rubbing her chin against the top of his head while his purr's roar seemed to fill her ears. As much as she hated to believe Mama's words, she knew their truth. Daddy had made up his mind, and he would not go see about Brother on his own. And Brother, most certainly, would die without Daddy's help. If there was a curse on her house, like Mama had said, then the curse on the town where Brother was in jail was a hundred times bigger. A hundred times stronger. It was a curse that had touched many families already.

And the trial day would ruin everything, Letitia knew. If Brother went to the Chair, Daddy would be a changed man. The bourbon bottle he kept hidden in the pantry for special occasions would become his constant companion. Bernadette, full of her own guilt, would be more hateful than ever. And Letitia would grow to despise them both. For all her life, she would judge men as weak and act accordingly, learning from the lesson of Daddy and Bernadette. She might hate them, but she would imitate them all the same. She knew these things as sure as she knew her name. Letitia felt her future unfolding like a clear-minded dream. It was so imminent, poised with terrible ease, that she marveled that Daddy and Bernadette couldn't see it, too.

But they couldn't. If they could, Daddy would have left for the trial by now.

Midnight's green eyes shone up at her like two perfect marbles; then he mewed at her. In Sunday school, Letitia had studied Judas Iscariot, the Betrayer, and the thought made her cry harder. Midnight wasn't the same as Jesus, of course, but he trusted her. For the past year, since Daddy had said she could keep the cat who had planted himself on their doorstep, she had taken care of Midnight, and he had taken care of her. How could she kill a creature that loved her?

But then Letitia remembered Abraham and Isaac from the Old Testament. God told Abraham to sacrifice his son—which she had thought was very mean of God when she'd heard the story, to tell the truth—but in the end it was only a test. Just like Abraham, she only had to show her *willingness* to do what Mama said, and God would provide another way to save Brother. Or maybe this was the only way, and she and Midnight were making a sacrifice like Jesus had, to save another's soul.

By sunset, Letitia made up her mind with a deep, ragged breath. She would do it. Just before midnight, she would take the cat to the barn. She would bring Daddy's catalog-ordered gold pocket watch, which he kept on his desk at night, and as soon as the tall hand and short hand pointed to midnight, just like Mama said, she would . . .

She would . . .

"I have to do it, Midnight," Letitia whispered to her cat, who was curled in her lap with none of Jesus's inkling at the Last Supper that his sacrifice was waiting. "Maybe God will save you. But even if He doesn't, you can save Brother. I know you can."

And it seemed to Letitia, miraculously, that the cat mewed a tiny yes, the way a cat would say yes if it could speak, as if Midnight understood it all and it was perfectly fine with him.

Midnight was happy to be in the barn, because Letitia had brought out a dish of milk first. He found the dish and crouched comfortably beside it, lapping it up. She watched him drink, enjoying the slurping sound he made and the sloppy droplets of milk dotting his whiskers. Midnight was two parts cat and one part hog, Daddy always said. That thought made her smile through her tears.

Then, she felt her resolve melting. Watching Midnight, she felt frozen with disbelief at the very thought of what she planned to do, and she wanted nothing more than to scoop Midnight into her arms and run back to bed before she got caught outside the house. Then, she remembered that wonderful sound of Daddy and Brother laughing on the porch, how that sound had lulled her to sleep. How he called her Lettie. How he hugged her and said he loved her every time he came to stay, never tugging on her hair or teasing the way her friends' older brothers did.

Only two minutes until midnight. How had the time gone so fast?

Quickly, watching Midnight drink his milk, Letitia said a series of prayers. *God, please let Midnight forgive me for what I'm about to do. . . . And please let this just be a test, so you will stop my hand at the last moment. . . . And please don't let Midnight die. . . . But if Midnight has to die, please let his sacrifice stop the curse so Daddy will go look after Brother and keep him safe.*

Her prayer gobbled a full minute. With as heavy a heart as she had ever known, nearly choking off her breath so that her head felt light, Letitia realized it was time. Time to take out the shiny knife Mama had given her. Time to hold Midnight tight and feed his blood to the spirits.

Midnight had once gotten himself covered in mud, and Bernadette had demanded that she fill up a tin tub and bathe him or else he could not come into the house—so Letitia knew from experience that it was hard to hold Midnight still for something he didn't want to do. She knew to watch out for his claws, especially those powerful back claws, and she would have to hook her arm tightly around him. And she knew she would have to keep no space between her knees, because he would back up against her as far as he could.

Now, just like then, she told herself she would think of the *task*, not of Midnight himself, or else with all his thrashing and complaining, she might feel sorry and forget what was at stake. Daddy was weak, so she had to be strong, and that was that.

Sure enough, Midnight put up a fight. Even if he didn't know what she was planning, he was angry to be pulled away from his milk, and he was wriggling from the start. Letitia was startled when she felt razor-thin stripes of pain across her forearm from Midnight's claws, and then she felt angry. The anger helped. She clamped her knees around him and hooked one arm around his middle, tightly. Despite the perspiration dampening her palm, she kept a firm grip on the knife and raised it to Midnight's throat. Mama always used the throat.

Letitia wanted to close her eyes, but she couldn't. She poked and then slashed with the knife, quickly, and even though the cut wasn't nearly deep enough, she was amazed to see a ribbon of blood seep through Midnight's fur, right above his tiny collarbone. While Midnight screeched and renewed his escape attempt, Letitia watched, fascinated, as two fat, crimson drops of blood fell to the dusty barn floor at her feet.

She kept her grip around the cat. Until the very last second, she almost forgot the prayer, but then she began, reciting it as well as she could remember: "Spirit, please help lift the curse and make my daddy strong so he will go see about Br—"

"What in great red hell are you doing?"

It sounded like it might be God's voice at first, albeit not as kindly as she'd thought God might sound, but when she gathered her senses above her racing heart, Letitia realized it was only Daddy's voice. She looked up, and she saw him standing in the doorway of the barn, wearing only his trousers. She saw his chest heaving up and down with his breathing. His expression was a combination of rage and shock she had never seen on her father's face, and it seared her. The sight of him made her drop the knife, and Midnight scrambled from her arms, scratching her chest through her nightgown as he launched himself from her with his powerful hind legs. Letitia did not know if the blood on her gown was hers or Midnight's.

"Letitia, what are you *doing?*" Daddy said.

"Mama said . . . she said . . ." But Letitia couldn't finish, because she felt too overcome.

Abraham and Isaac, she remembered. God had stepped in and sent Daddy.

Daddy fumbled for his belt before he realized he wasn't wearing it. His sleep-wrinkled face was growing more alert, more angry. He wanted to beat her, she saw. He wanted to beat her in a way he had never beaten her before.

"Mama said if I sacrificed Midnight, I'd break the curse and you would go see about Brother," Letitia said, finally finding the words. She pointed to the droplets of blood that spattered the floor. "See, Daddy? I had to bleed Midnight, but I did it for Brother, Daddy. I did it so you'd go to the trial."

Daddy stared at her pointing finger, then back at her face, then back at her finger, and his own face seemed to transform. The only light was the dim lantern she'd brought with the bowl of milk, but Daddy's face wasn't the same anymore. The only word for it, really, was *haunted.* He cradled his abdomen, as if a grown man had kicked him in the stomach hard.

"We have to save Brother, Daddy," Letitia said, a whisper.

Daddy rocked in place, like he did when he'd had too much to drink. Then, he took a lurching step until he was no longer facing her. One step at a time, he walked away. He did not look at her or speak to her. She saw him climb the steps of the back porch, and he was back inside the house. He left the back door wide open. Bernadette wouldn't like that, Letitia thought. All the mosquitoes could come in.

For a long time, Letitia called for Midnight outside. She finally heard him growling somewhere out in the bushes near the cotton patch, but he would not come to her. Maybe he would never come back, she realized.

But this time, she did not cry.

Letitia quietly washed her bloody scratches clean in the kitchen sink; then she blew out the lamp and climbed the stairs to go into her room. Daddy's door was closed, but she could hear Bernadette's voice through the door, wide awake. "Richard, what's into you? I said to talk to me, goddammit. You put that suitcase down, you hear me? Do you know what time it is?"

Quickly, Letitia stole into her own room and shut the door. She suddenly needed to tear off every piece of clothing she was wearing, even though her body was shaking. She climbed into her bed, under her covers, seeking sanctuary while her breathing came hard and deep from her lungs. She had a headache. The memory of Midnight's blood on the knife made her stomach twist, and she was afraid she would be sick.

She had left Daddy's pocket watch lying on the barn floor, she remembered. And Bernadette's bowl from the kitchen. They would be mad about that, she thought. She thought she'd best get out of bed and go fetch them, but she couldn't move from where she lay.

Letitia heard the door to Daddy's room open across the hall, followed by his heavy footsteps. She couldn't see him, of course, but somehow she knew he was wearing his best brown suit and white shirt, with his brown Sunday derby. He was wearing the clothes that told everyone that he was Richard Reaves, a business owner, and he was not a hard-luck sort of man.

Bernadette had given up shouting, but now she was outright begging instead, the way she liked to hear Daddy beg. "Richard . . . you aren't thinking clearly. Do you know what they'll *do* to an uppity yellow nigger who thinks he can just walk in there and have a say? Think of it,

Richard! Don't be a fool. Don't get your name mixed up in this mess. That boy's gonna be all right. You aren't *thinking*. What about your family? What about me and Letitia? I swear to Jesus, if you don't stop this foolishness, I won't be here when you come back."

Bernadette's voice trailed the heavy footsteps down the stairs. Through her open window, Letitia heard the front door open, and the sound of Bernadette's voice in the night, suddenly shrieking like a woman in pain. "Richard, *don't do this*—I love you!"

But Bernadette's professed love, to Letitia, just sounded like the same old hatefulness. No matter, though. She had bled Midnight, and the curse was broken. Daddy's ears belonged to himself again, and he had his strength back.

Letitia heard the engine to Dad's Rickenbacker choke and sputter, then roar to life. Letitia closed her eyes, smiling. The sound of that purring engine as it drove away was as sweet as the memory of Daddy's laughter with Brother on the porch that night. As sweet as Christmas morning and as gentle as the stinging of Mama's loving hands when she pulled her hair into tight plaits between her knees, the way only Mama really knew how.

For once, Letitia's third eye—what Daddy called her magic eye—wasn't working. Brother's future was very blurry and far away, not for her to know. All she knew for sure was that Richard Reaves was on his way to the trial in his good suit to try to save Brother. And that knowledge would last her as long as she would live.

# THE SKINNED

*Jarla Tangh*

## TEEN TORN APART BY DOGS

***July 18th***—*City Animal Control workers are yet again on the lookout for a pack of feral dogs blamed for the mauling death of sixteen-year-old Tawan Charles of Graves St., Roxbury. The incident occurred at 11:30 P.M. on the quiet, dead-end street. There were no witnesses to the attack. Residents say they heard nothing unusual last night. A thirty-eight revolver recovered from the body and spent bullet casings found in the area raise questions for investigators that the attack might be gang related. Charles died of massive blood loss and asphyxiation. His partially clothed body was found only doors from his home. His is the third such death to occur this year in the vicinity.*

The *nganga* who taught me everything I know said, *Beware guilt*. It is a poison stronger than the strongest juju. He would laugh at me now. *Guilt takes you by the heel*, he said, *and you are the one lost*. Now I am.

This is not the first time I, Sinza Barantsar, have heard a neighbor scream. Back home, it was nearly always a Tutsi—child, woman, or man—whose cries filled the darkness. I want to forget about the trouble there. I meant to forget, but the boy Tawan's scream brings it back: neighbors bashing in the skulls of neighbors with machetes or using nail-studded clubs—*masu*. When evil hunts us, sometimes it wears the faces of people.

So many lights. Americans think they can burn away the darkness. Branchless, concrete trees cast the same dim yellow from their single blossoms. Those sterile sticks spaced evenly apart offer no handhold, no security. They give only light. Why so many of them taking up space that the real trees should have? We should have more real trees on Graves Street. Even with all this bright, the wooden and brick houses do not look any clearer to me at night. I do not have to see every shingle or doorstep to know they are there. My neighbors leave their doors unlocked most of the time, but not tonight.

One apartment building, three single-family homes and four two-family homes huddle together on both sides. The paint-peeling houses are of little use except for managing to keep the Skinned out. So far. I am told I live in a peaceful part of town. Our street is not like Intervale, Homestead, or Columbia Road. We have no gang bangers congregating. No muggers. Carjackings. Rapes. The Skinned have done their work well. Graves Street seems forgotten by the world until another one of these deaths hits the papers. Then what happens here become everybody's business.

Secrets are odd things. Sometimes they float away into forgetfulness unspoken. Others roost in our minds. The new moon leaves the sky clotted with stars. The moon has its own secrets. I have mine.

I smell the coming of death before it happens. I gasp for breath. A stink stronger than musk or human waste attacks my nose. The Skinned are here. My eyes water. I rub at them, but stick my head out the window. Night brings out the jackals and hyenas in my homeland, but here it is the Skinned who rule. I look down the empty street. The lights dim. The heat settles onto me.

The stick-tree streetlamps fail.

A bullet whizzes past my cheek. I hear a raw young voice.

*"Getthefuckawayfromme!"*

I see sleek, bare-muscled animal bodies leap into the air and land on a human one. I hear the screams. The retort of a pistol. For once, I am disturbed by my own helplessness. I am too old and too slow to consider jumping from the window to the ground one story below. I have a game leg from a Tutsi fighting for his life who used my own *masu* on me. A brick building is all that separates me from the Skinned. It is wise to stay where I am. The Skinned. A boy lies crumpled. Dying. Throat torn open. Ripped Nike tank top and shorts expose his entrails and genitals. Blood dries on the sidewalk, leaking in strange patterns. The Skinned finish the kill and run. Tongues loll. Bloodied jaws gleam. Cataract-covered eyes glisten.

"My baby!" his mother squeals in the apartment next door to mine. I can hear her through the thin walls. "Tawan!"

I hear another voice deeper than her own. "Shush up. Can't do nothing for him now. You know the rules."

The mother keeps safe inside her home. She will not come out until after the Skinned have gorged and left. No one who is familiar with their lore will do any differently. The doors stay closed. My terrified neighbors wait behind them. Wait for this night, out of the several nights a year, when the Skinned collect their due. The Skinned are no different from the *nganga* who blesses the body of a soldier so bullets do not find him. The Skinned extend a protection. They are free to set their price. And so it is when one deals with the invisible powers. I, of all people, should be able to understand this. Just because I live now in the new world does not mean this is not a place where the invisible powers cannot reach. *Nganga* understand the paradox. Give the Skinned human faces and human names and their function would be the same.

I hear the pack leader calling to the rest. A long, throaty howl. The Skinned lope into the dark. Into the edge of vision. I watch them go. They make very little sound, actually. Once they close in on a victim, it is the first time one hears them. I knew this boy Tawan. I know he did not believe his mother's tales. I know he thought that if he was to be a man he should be out at night with other men drinking beer, talking big talk and carrying a gun. We all heard the gun. It went off many times. Still the Skinned came.

And the boy is dead.

His ghost will stagger home and wonder why his kinfolk do not see it. I close my eyes.

Now one of us must call the police. It will be done because it must. Because there is no hiding something this terrible except by putting it out in the open. Soon, we will hear the sirens, but the Skinned will have gone and the body will have stiffened. The ghost will come. I hear Tawan's mother weeping. I hear the deep low voice say, "Get yourself together. Don't let nothing slip."

"I can't," says Tawan's mother.

"You gotta talk to the five-oh."

"I can't."

"You will," says the voice. "You want them to take you away?"

"Let them."

"Like the Skinned won't sniff your sorry ass out?"

The woman sucks in her breath. I can almost see her straightening her shoulders, wiping her eyes, finding the words that will be what the men and women in blue want to hear. She will say nothing of the truth. She will say what she has to say, and her neighbors will back her up. There is nothing wrong here. There are no problems. Tawan's death—well, it was an accident. Someone let loose their dogs. Gunshots? Well, we thought it was kids with firecrackers. I say *we* because my silence means I am practically helping them to murder. But that is the guilt talking.

I don't need to hear any more. I retreat deeper into my apartment. Shadows blight the furniture into one coherent darkness. My window is still open. The air is so still, the curtains don't move. The stink of blood and death follows me. I take in a burning breath. I turn on the radio. The international station soothes me with the sound of drums and bells. Loud. The Latinos learned these rhythms from their black slaves. It is almost like home. My daughter, Kize, will be upset she left me alone when another death happened. She cannot help it. She has the graveyard shift. Come morning, she will walk into our apartment and demand to know why I have not called her, why she must learn what goes on from the lips of strangers rather than her own father's.

What could I possibly tell her?

I have come to wicked America. Where, if I breathe in too deeply, my nose burns and my skin itches. Where it is not just hot in the summer, but humid. Where the air is clammy. No wonder bad things happen here. The air is thick with spirits. Where I have never seen so many fair-haired pink people with too-bright eyes. Where the people who look most like me make the baboons of my homeland seem better behaved. Where no one greets an elder respectfully or gives them the right of way. Where the only time I hear the sound of the drum is on the international station. Kize keeps her radio tuned to it just for me. She prefers the noise they call R and B.

America is the land of hard gray streets, with its grass and herbs shut up behind fences the way farmers keep cattle. It seems to me only the cars run free. Hundreds of them, horns blaring, clog the roads and threaten to run over the foolish who pay no attention to the absence of a red light. The Cape buffalo is more predictable. Instead of chopping wood for a fire or pumping well water, I must turn on a light or a faucet. Whole families back home could have dined well on the wasted food I see dumped by my neighbors. The only welcome change I can find is in having a toilet. No one who has ever squatted over a muck-filled hole would blame me.

I sleep during the day. America is a land of many restless spirits and many unclean things. I can smell them. The stink of evil here does not wash off even with Ivory Soap and Tide. It does not matter how often I bathe my body or how often anyone else bathes their own. I can still smell it. Kize tires of my complaints, so I say nothing. She can tell from the look on my face what I am thinking. If someone were to give me a herd of shorthorn cattle, a magic broom, and a sharp *panga*, perhaps I could clean my street and all who lived on it. There is not enough blood to scrub this city, never mind America itself.

I come from a large village in Rwanda called Jambere. No one in the village called Roxbury has heard of it except for a Hutu who lives on the other side and a family of Tutsis who live in the village called Dorchester (they do not speak to me) and my daughter, Kize. We two are people whose bad fortune was to be caught in the fighting between Hutu and Tutsi. Kize, like so many others, thought to come here to escape. We have merely traded one danger for another. I think my neighbors do not like me because I am African. Because I remind them of what they have lost—language, religion, a sense of place. Before I came here, I was Rwandan. Now I know better. Here, I am the anxious stranger, the guilty one expecting to be found out and killed.

I listen to footsteps in the outside hall. They belong to Tawan's mother. The door to our building creaks. She is a large-bodied woman, the kind who gives her man joy to ride, to grasp her wide behind. She wears a damp T-shirt, shorts, and house slippers. Her straightened hair is wild on her head.

The night air thickens with death.

"M-my boy," she whispers at first. And then louder: "M-m-my boy!" She gathers his head into her lap and rocks him. I see no sign of her man. He is probably dialing nine-one-one. Silently, my neighbors file out and take their places about her. Their heads hang. I see them all: a retired minister and her husband; the postman and his girlfriend; a hairdresser; a graduate student; a young woman and her fiancé, the minister's grown son; a construction foreman; a single mother with another swollen belly full of baby; a crack dealer who keeps his trade off our street. The windows reveal the faces of children who have seen what they are not supposed to and manage to keep silent, as will the others. They do not even cry aloud, but I see the tears glinting.

The foreman says, "He's gone, Luwilla. Ain't nothin' more you can do for him."

Luwilla says, "Don't tell me that! He ain't supposed t'be!"

"The Lord has him," the minister's husband says. He looks meaningfully at his wife.

"Jesus will take away his pain," the Reverend Ames agrees.

"Died and gone to hell is more like it," someone else says. "Don't even play like Tawan was innocent or something. He knew."

Luwilla shakes her head. "No he didn't. He didn't."

"Shut your fool mouth, nigga!" says the postman. He's a tall, bony fellow, more skeleton than man. His clothes stick to him, soaked with sweat, as do everyone else's. He and the crack dealer are almost nose to nose like animals themselves, gleaming with fear on a hot night.

"Did they have to," asks Luwilla, "kill my baby?"

The hairdresser shrugs. "He was out there. It don't matter to them."

"He should'a known better," a student says. "He lived here."

"Didn't believe," another says.

The fiancée whispers, "They didn't take his soul, too, did they?"

Reverend Ames has no answer for her.

"The African," the minister's son says. "He couldn't sleep through this."

"He ain't 'sleep. He scared." The crack dealer jerks his chin in my window's direction.

"He won't tell."

"Better not," says the postman. "Them Skinned got good ears, you know."

An hour and a half after Tawan dies, the police show up. Two squad cars roll onto Graves Street, side by side. Sirens cut off. Doors swing open. A question fires into the night.

"*Whatthefuckhappenedhere?*"

One woman officer and three men stand around Tawan Charles. He lies twisted half on the sidewalk, half in the gutter. White bone peeks through his throat. The smell of blood and shit has not left yet. The streetlights show everything. Except the pale double sitting on the sidewalk with head in its bloody hands—Tawan's ghost.

I look out the window. I keep my lights off.

"Did you see what happened, ma'am?"

Luwilla has gone mute. She holds her son. Her man has his arms around her. He croons some nonsense song in her ear. She grunts.

"Mama," says Tawan's ghost. "I'm so sorry."

No one hears it.

A police officer asks, "Is that a no or a yes?"

"She's in shock," the female officer says.

"What about the rest of you—did you see anything?"

My neighbors shake their heads and mumble.

"By the time I got to the window," the postman says, "the pack was running away."

"How many?"

"Six or seven," says the young mother.

"Nine," says the crack dealer.

Others grunt in agreement.

"You sure?" the third officer asks.

"No, I'm not sure," says the postman. "The only thing I am sure of is that this boy is dead."

Tawan's ghost groans. It stands between the officers and my neighbors, waving its arms.

The police seem tired of their own questions. "You saw no other people on the street?"

"Just him." My neighbors speak as one.

I shake my head. They let this happen! I am ready to blurt it out. But I won't. I am not afraid of the Skinned for myself, but for Kize, who does not believe in such things. She lives here too, and she will listen to no talk about her neighbors. She refuses to acknowledge that the things we left back home could follow us here. She thinks where we are is ideal. Except for the few victims of the Skinned, there is no trouble on Graves Street— no drive-by shootings, no crack houses, no husbands beating wives or children, no prostitutes. Such a peace has its price. And from long before Kize and I moved here, these people have been willing to pay it.

The Skinned have claimed one of their own. Now what will they do? Will Luwilla forget herself and bring the Skinned to her door? Will it be someone else who cracks? Will the truth blaze its way past my chapped lips and to the ears of the police? Will they think me a crazy old man? My head sings.

I totter into the bathroom. By the fluorescent glow of the night-light, I stare into my own bloodshot eyes and hollowed-out cheeks. Sometimes a secret feeds on one. It steals all strength from a living body. It can be as evil as the madman who first unleashed the Skinned. Did I forget to mention someone made them?

I am aware of such means only because it was my trade to hunt down the inevitable products along with their makers. Someone who hates powerfully made the Skinned. Someone who could whittle the fat and fur off still-living canine bodies. Someone who smoked his victims so that the flesh would dry and preserve well, not caring if their eyeballs seared. Someone who buried nine animals on the land where these houses were built long ago.

All this I learned only because, from the first that I came here, I was disturbed. Because I am a *nganga* too, I can smell the work of witches. I can ask my *mkisi*, the trapped spirit in my pot, to tell me where a witch is or compel the witches to tell me their secrets. But I do not know who the maker of the Skinned was. It happened so long ago. One might think that the Native Americans, the original owners of the land, left them. But it does not feel like them. I do not think the juju of African slaves is responsible either. I would know that at once. No, the Skinned are something a white mind would imagine. I feel only admiration for what he or she has crafted. Every three moons, the Skinned must rise to claim another victim. They prowl the night streets unseen and unmolested until then. Bullets, blades, or fire will not hurt them. They are things of evil medicine. They are immortal. They are the Skinned. It is not possible to explain further. Evil takes as many forms as people have faces.

I am an old man. My body is bowed by time. My heart flutters in my chest. I am not long for this world. It should make my dilemma easier. I do not have long to put up with the evil gnawing at my soul. I can choose to die even now, but my dying will change nothing I have already done. Guilt eats away at me and leaves me only more guilty.

The Skinned do as they have been made to.

I must do as I am meant to. I will let no demons bind my tongue. I look to the clay pot with my *mkisi* inside it. Mine is very strong. With my *mkisi*, I have turned aside even bullets. I feed it with blood. I should take it with me. It would help repel the Skinned.

No.

This is a matter for men, not magic, my guilt says. Where were the invisible powers to defend your victims? It is not fair for you to move about protected while they could not. My eyes rest on another of my keepsakes from Rwanda. A nail-studded *masu*. With my *masu*, I broke open many a Tutsi skull. No, again. My guilt weighs down on me. Your dead had no such protection; neither should you.

I shuffle to my front door. I pull it open. My knee throbs. The dark hall yawns before me. Lightless. Empty. I head down the stairs sniffing, the smell of death growing closer.

My knee tries to hold me back. I ignore it.

My place is out there with the others.

The ghost rushes toward me. It knows I can see it. All the gory details. I shake my head. "Not now."

Tawan tries to grab my arm. I feel the cold.

"Not now!" I use a word of banishing on him.

With a wail, the ghost flickers into nothing.

The white officer is saying into his walkie-talkie, "I need the medical examiner's office to Nine-and-a-half Graves. We're securing the area."

The black officer says, "All right, people. There's nothing more to see."

Police fan out, gesturing for the neighbors to move back. My neighbors obey. They keep their guilty faces turned from mine. They know I know the truth. They trust me not to speak of it.

I hear my own voice. Quavering. Old man–sounding. I say, "I saw what happened."

The black policeman squints at me. His brows furrow as if he is disappointed by what he sees: this wizened elder. He does not know that in my youth I wore a uniform much like his. "And what did you see, sir?"

He called me "sir." Perhaps not all his people here are baboons. Here and there are those who remember something of how to carry themselves.

"The Skinned," I say. "I saw them."

The minister groans. Luwilla's eyes focus on mine, and then she closes them. The crack dealer begins to back away. One of the students looks around herself wildly. The hairdresser is already headed back into her unit fast as her thick legs can carry her.

"What?" asks the woman officer.

"He's some refugee from Africa," the postman says. "He sees and says things about what happened to him back there."

I shake my head. Wicked man! "I wish things were so simple. A boy lies dead because they all agreed."

The police glance at my neighbors. "Who all agreed?"

"Them. Even her." I point at Luwilla. She breaks into fresh sobs. Her man pulls her to her feet.

He says, "We don't need this. She's just lost her son, and you people are doing nothing."

"Wait a minute here," says the white policeman. "We have to follow up on every lead."

"You won't get nothing from him," says the foreman. He jerks his chin at me.

"We'll be the judge of that."

I continue. "The Skinned killed this boy as part of their payment. Usually, it is strangers. Tonight was a mistake, but it does not matter to the Skinned."

"The who?"

"The Skinned. Your dogs are not normal beasts. They are witch-things set loose."

The white officer's brows climb his forehead. I know he does not believe. I had no hope that he would. One of them must hear me. My guilt says, *See? Now you know what it is to go unheard.*

The black officer explodes. "Look! The sooner you come forward with what you know the sooner we can deal with this. Aren't you tired of the maulings every few months?"

"They should be," I say. "They should be weary with guilt." I know I am talking about my own guilt, but it seems easier to pass it off as theirs.

"He's crazy," says the minister.

Her husband says, "He doesn't mean no one harm."

The police become disgusted and send us all away.

I asked the minister, once, why she did not call upon her god to smite the Skinned. She said they were here long before she came. They'll be here after she dies or moves away. She said the first week she moved to Graves Street, the Skinned appeared. They followed her home every night, and no amount of Lord's Psalms would drive them away. They hung about her doorstep as if to say the street was theirs. She used to call the police on them, but they would fade away. Then, they tore apart her cocker spaniel while she watched. The Skinned had made their point. She knew then it would be her family next. One must deal with the invisible powers in terms they can understand. With power.

Tawan's ghost has vanished.

My neighbors left me outside alone on the sidewalk. They know I have made myself into bait. The houses slam their doors and seal their windows. My own door hangs open. I did not bother to close it. Or lock it. My *mkisi* is safe inside. Clamminess settles on me. Is it sweat or fear? I stand in front of my house watching the medical examiner's van drive away. It uses no siren, but the lights flash like a regular ambulance. The police cars follow. The vehicles disappear, leaving a chalk outline and dried blood in their wake.

No one even looks out a window to watch them go.

They already know what happens next. Now I die.

The shadows get longer. The invisible powers are invisible no more.

When the Skinned are near, even the cats keep from our street. I can hear the strays hissing a few blocks away. It is hard for me to tell if they are scared too. I listen to the thrum of city generators feeding the stick-trees. I hear a lone plane miles overhead. The light grows dimmer. I can smell the Skinned. They smell like wet dog and something dead at the same time. They make no sound. Not until they kill.

The streetlamps fail.

My game leg twinges. I can feel it cramp.

The Skinned form from the shadows.

Dark bodies.

Almost perfectly lightless.

I can see the reflected lights of their eyes.

Nine pairs.

The stink gets stronger.

I want to retch.

*Run!* my instinct tells me. My guilt holds me facing them.

I can't run. At best, I can only hobble.

The Skinned move as one, heads lowered, their tails curled. They prowl with the lopsided gait of animals in great pain. They seem too clumsy to be dangerous. Until they get close enough.

The leader lifts its head and bares needlelike teeth. Lots of people think that packs are ruled by males. That is not always so. It is a bitch who gives throat to the sound rattling around inside her. Her growl threatens to loosen my bowels.

I turn my back on them and walk away. Instinct wins. I may not have the right, but I will try to save myself. My guilt should have had enough fun.

I know I cannot get far.

My game leg catches at every step.

I will die inside my own house.

I keep moving forward.

Kize will know at once when she comes home what happened. Her own father will be one of the Dead, of his own free will. It is too bad I cannot explain myself to her. But then did my victims have the luxury of justifying why they died?

No one will believe Kize.

No one will help Kize.

No one.

There will be a chalk outline and a pool of dried blood on our carpet. I doubt the Skinned will simply let me close my door on them. Kize will see then that they exist. She may or may not seek the services of another *nganga* to defend herself from her father's fate.

Was it worth it? I wonder to myself. To tell the truth about one evil, when there are so many others gone unspoken in my long life? The

Skinned are no different than my abandoned *mkisi*. They are an impersonal force. They do what they do.

I hear them coming.

Clatter of paws on sidewalk.

Panting.

I step into my own doorway. I do not turn around. I make my way to my *mkisi*. I left it slumbering inside its pot near my front door. Will I have time to unwrap it from its leather pouch and bare it?

My hand closes on nothing. I have halted before my pot. Guilt reminds me of what I owe. I see the trap.

This is a matter of atonement.

I am no fearful American child.

I leave the *mkisi* alone.

I turn to see that the bitch has thrust herself into my door. My front room smells like rotted meat. She pulls back her slavering lips. An eager packmate almost shoulders her aside in its eagerness to tear at me. She snaps at it. It lets her enter first. She drags herself inside.

I step backward.

Reflex.

If I am meant to die—let it come now.

I know I deserve the terror.

I snatch up the *masu*. I swing it over my head, ready to bring it down on her skull. Even if I only bring her down, I might frighten the others.

The bitch lifts a leg and marks the corner where my *mkisi* lives in its pot. She sniffs the mess she has made deeply. Her cataract-covered gaze pins mine.

I stare back.

Something in her gaze compels. . . .

Around us appear the ghosts of my kills. Bloodied, broken-bodied fellow Rwandans rise up from my carpeted floor. They walk into each other and into the walls. They number by the hundreds. Children. Women.

Men. Westerners. One by one as quickly as they appear—they vanish.

The bitch wags her tail.

I am so shocked, I let the *masu* drop.

She limps over toward me, her eyes shimmering. She rumbles.

Should I trust her seeming change in behavior? Guilt welds me to the spot. Should she tear my throat open, I should welcome it. That, after all, is what I deserve. The invisible powers sense my weakness. I have allowed guilt to become my master, not they.

I remain still, even though the pain deep in my leg bone threatens to dump me on the floor. My *masu* lies still within reach. I do not move.

The only force greater than my instinct for self-preservation is my curiosity.

My lungs fill with stink.

The bitch sidles against me and butts her head into my thigh. She snuffles my crotch and wags her tail. My fingers glide over living dried sinews. The Skinned feels more leathery than like a once-fur-bearing animal. She rears onto her hind legs and lays her front paws upon either of my shoulders and glares deep into my eyes. I look back, ever guilty. Let her tear me from limb to limb and be done with it. My throat is only inches from her teeth. I offer it to her. Her breath takes mine away.

*I see you too*, says my guilt. *You are welcome to do what you will with me.*

The bitch bangs her forehead against mine, and I briefly see stars. Her claws rip the fabric of my shirt. She growls once at the rest of her pack, and they file inside silently. I am surrounded by the Skinned. They gaze up into my face with their seared-over eyes. The sniff me and the *masu*. Each one of them greets me with a nose in my crotch. The bitch licks her chops; her jaws open, and the sound coming from them is almost human laughter.

Laughter?

She licks my lips. She seems no different than a normal dog that does not realize that where its mouth has been is not welcome. She uses her full weight to make me kneel. The other Skinned crowd round, tails wagging. I curl into a ball before them. They rake apart my clothes, without harming me further.

The bitch lifts her leg again to spray. I do not move from the stream, just as I did not fight her in the end. I drown in liquid yellow bitter. It soaks my skin and runs down the length of my body, changing me. I feel my flesh liquefy. My bones crack and reshape. My limbs strain from biped to quadruped. I cannot explain the judgment of the invisible powers.

The Skinned leave me otherwise unharmed.

They know their own.

# DEATH'S DREADLOCKS

*Tobias S. Buckell*

**S**ometimes, late into the dead night, Old Ma takes the long locks of my hair and massages them between her callused yellowed palms. Such fine dreadlocks, she tells me. Such fine young shoulders they rest on.

But some of the old people are scared of dreads, she whispers into my ears. Don't mind them.

And I know why.

There was an old, very old, bush tale about the shadowy man some called Death. He was a fat giant who lived deep in the forest, teeth stinky with the smell of rotted flesh. In all of time he had never brushed his hair, and the knotted locks grew out into the underbrush for people to find.

It was a good story.

When I was young, out of the corner of my eye, sometimes I could see the long root of a tree, and just past it, I would just see the edge of a long, creeping dreadlock. I would avoid that space.

Once I got older, and times became hard, I saw more and more dreadlocks that sat right out in the open of the land. Old Ma's gift, and curse, to me.

And that is how I know why the few old ones left look at me with a strange eye.

Times, the old men said, were getting hard.

Really, we replied mockingly. They were easy before?

Old Ma lifted us up and away from the old men, their wrinkled

141

faces host to patient flies immune to leathery-handed swats, and she told us to hush.

Outside the bush the dust came and hung over the camps. And the wheels of Toyota minitrucks with Kalashnikovs welded to their beds and our brothers manning the wicked heavy guns with wide grins, the wheels of these vans kicked up even more dust.

Ho, Kuabi, we shouted.

Hey, little brothers, he yelled.

Good day, Mouwanat, we shouted.

Mouwanat ignored us, sitting with his new friends around a barrel with AK-47s spilling over the side. They spat in the dust and spoke of grown-up things.

That is the way it is with older brothers.

On the way home we passed the relief tent, dusty red cross on the side almost ready to lose itself in the gray fold flapping in the wind.

One of the workers, a pretty but very white lady with a red nose, asked us if we knew about the Lord Our God. Many of the relief workers had little pieces of paper with pictures waiting in their pockets. I'd even read one once with Old Ma, and we'd giggled and giggled. Who else but a white man would believe in a god born in the East, describe his looks in their holy writings as if he were an Arab, and then paint him as if he was what one of the older relief men called a hippy?

And apparently old white men don't even like hippies, Old Ma told us. Why would these men both love and hate their god so? I wondered.

Anyway, the relief workers didn't understand. We and Old Ma would never insult any god by believing in just one god, because that would leave all the other gods out. So like most other times, we thanked the worker for her interest in our souls, but pointed out that our own souls were really our own business, and none of hers. Which I think offended her, but no less than her own words offended us.

When we left with the rice Old Ma said, Well, at least they don't kill us for saying no anymore.

I'd laughed, thinking she was being funny. Then I remembered Old Ma was . . . very old. Maybe she remembered different times. I swallowed. Did they really used to kill people who wouldn't accept their god? Would their god even accept such souls?

Would you even want to spend time with a god that such people worshiped?

I shuddered.

Old Ma, I asked, were times better, back then?

Old Ma shifted the rice on her head and didn't look down.

Times, she said, shift around, go from here to there, and are often what you make of them. We've had worse times; we've had better times. No matter what times they are, there are always people outside the land who come in and tell us what times to have.

And with that she walked faster, her bare callused feet slapping the ground hard, kicking up small puffs of dust.

Old Ma was old. Very old. But she could walk like a demon. Sweat poured from my forehead, and I felt faint when we found our tent. There were many other tents all around us, and some men in jeeps asked us who we were, and where we were going.

They walked us to the tent, winked at Old Ma, then turned to me.

You are a little old to be walking with an old woman. You should ride with us. Be strong. Kill our enemies.

Who are our enemies? I asked. Old Ma smiled.

The men conferred among themselves, but could not come up with a single enemy. The enemy, they finally announced, are all who oppose us.

I would have said, Then since I oppose you, I must be your enemy. But it was a foolish thing to say. Old Ma saw my words even before I did, and spoke.

This one looks old for his age, she said. And I clamped my mouth shut.

The men laughed at us, then left to climb into their jeep and harass someone else. Old Ma shot me a nasty look, then crawled into the tent to start a dung fire and make us rice.

It is a hard thing to eat rice over and over and over again. The little brother and I left to hunt birds with a slingshot. A woman in red stripes stopped us at the edge of the tents.

Where is your mother? she demanded. She looked at my dreads with suspicion.

We have no parents, Little Brother said.

Then who takes care of you?

Old Ma.

Who?

Old Ma, I interjected. The old lady in the tent cooking rice. And we pointed Old Ma out, sitting with her legs crossed in front of the fire.

The witch takes care of you? The woman shook her head. You should not go out past the tents; you will die.

Not that easily, I protested. We can both see the dreadlocks.

The woman looked at us sideways, her hands on her hips, mouth slightly open.

Why do you think we never walk in a straight line? Little Brother laughed. And we ran out into the dust, leaving the woman to forget to scream at us.

Old Ma came out of the jungle during one of the wars, when Mom and Dad died. She took us under her flabby arms and told us stories, dried our tears, and fed us some soup. She tried to take us back to the forest one night, but Mouwanat started crying, and the relief workers found us.

Later, men in trucks packed us up and took us to the tents. There were explosions in the trees, making us so scared we cried until our lungs hurt, and Old Ma looked back out past our village clearing and cried with us.

The tent people didn't like her, because she had a necklace with bones and things on it. They would spit in her face, and Old Ma ignored them, muttering things under her breath and sighing to the old gods. The problem with casting at them, she told me, is that they don't believe, and so I cannot affect them.

But I believe, Old Ma, I would say.

I know, child.

So she would explain to me and Little Brother why, just under the surface of the infertile land, we could see the long, snaking black strands, the dreadlocks that coiled around everything.

When I saw them push into the trees and jungle, she told us, I knew Death came for me, and I had to follow them out. And that was when I found you! She would tell us about the old gods, and the story about Death and how his dreadlocks now draped out across the whole land like a spider's web.

We didn't find any birds to kill with our stones, and other boys were out looking. Tired and dusty, Little Brother and I returned. On our way back we heard gunfire, and the crackle of tents in flames.

Dreadlocks, black and sinewy, moved just under the ground away from the relief tents.

Stepping carefully over them, we walked to the tents. Men in jeeps rode around, and one of them recognized me.

See, he said. Ride with us, little one, and you will vanquish our enemies.

All around the white relief workers lay with dreadlocks curled around their bodies, the tightly wound hair soaking up the red blood oozing from their torn flesh. I recognized the pretty lady who had asked about our souls.

The men in jeeps spun more dust into the sky.

Late, late, into the night, I woke Little Brother up.

Times are going to get worse, I said.

He agreed with a nod.

The relief tents fed us, but now the rice is in flames. We are many miles from Old Ma's jungle. People are being crazy. I don't think any more relief people will come if they keep getting killed, and so we will starve.

Little Brother agreed.

So I must go out and find us a new place, or food, I said.

I will go with you, Little Brother declared.

No. I will go alone.

So Little Brother helped me pack, and then gave me a small portion of dried beef he had stolen from somewhere in the tents and hidden under his bedsack. I tried to make him keep it, but he insisted, and we cried together and hugged. Then I left.

Far from the tents, on my own in the morning cool, I watched the great ocher sun rise above the distant mountains and paid homage. I crouched on the sand and waited, and waited, for a plan.

As I watched, two vans chased a jeep across the flat dust. They shot and shot until the jeep exploded. They fired at it some more, then left. When I reached the jeep I recognized the men.

One stirred and looked at me with one eye.

Dreadlocks circled around and sniffed.

Is Death the instigator of all this, I wondered, or merely just circling around like a buzzard?

I followed the locks. I started at the burned-out jeep and ended up near the foot of the mountains. They stretched up toward the heavens above me. There was even some scraggly jungle around.

The dreadlocks all converged here. They all wound themselves toward a large bunker. The concrete was the same color as the hard earth around it.

When I walked in, the smell of rotting animals dizzied me. I steadied myself and walked on through many rooms. They were sumptuous rooms, tall and gilded with glittering objects, jewelry that must have once adorned beautiful men and women.

I followed the thick shanks of dung-smelling hair into a grand pit of a throne room. The air was dark, and dust hung still on everything. The hair all ran up into the center of the room, up the back and shoulders of a giant, as dark as the shadows. The giant's belly had rolls and rolls of fat that overflowed onto his crossed feet, and when he stirred, all the dreadlocks leading to the room shifted and coiled around the corners like snakes. It made me shiver, and I wished that times were different, and that I had never seen all the things that I had seen this day.

Hello, children, he said.

Who else is here? I demanded in a shaky voice. A small form stepped out from the hallway behind me.

My name is Kofi, the boy whimpered. Please don't hurt me. I followed. I was hoping I could steal some bread, or rice.

The giant, his dreadlocks shifting about us, laughed the deepest, most fetid-smelling belly laugh. A thousand TVs fastened to the walls flickered on, bathing everything in a cold blue light.

Of course I have bread, and rice, he said. But why would you want such boring and tasteless foods when I have much better?

He took from his side two large brown paper bags. They were stained on the bottom with grease. Kofi ran forward and snatched the bag, impossibly small against the giant's hand.

The bags smelled heavenly, and Kofi pulled a meat sandwich from his bag. There were more inside. He began to eat them rapidly. The giant flicked the other bag at me, and I caught it. As I opened it, my small stomach growling with excitement, I thought, *If those are Death's dreadlocks, then this giant is obviously Death. And if he is Death, then there is no doubt that something is not right about this food.*

I decided I would wait and watch what happened to Kofi. And as I watched Kofi, the giant, Death, also watched Kofi. Kofi ate and ate and ate, until he grew heavy with all the food and lay down against the side of the room.

If you will not eat, the giant said, why don't you enjoy yourself? And the TV closest to me started to show movies. Pick a movie, the giant said. Any movie.

So I watched men leap around buildings and fight each other, until the flickering made my eyes heavy, and against my will I drifted to sleep.

When I woke I found my wrists bound with a heavy iron. The giant chuckled to himself in the corner, and my heart thudded with fear.

What is going on here? I demanded.

The giant chuckled some more, and picked his teeth with a bone. He smiled at me, and his smile carried a rank, rotten smell. Like that of a man left in the desert to bloat and be picked at by carrion eaters.

You have pretty dreadlocks, just like me, the giant said. He leaned forward with a blast of a belch and touched the top of my head with his smallest finger. I wanted to vomit as the giant leaned back, still picking his teeth with the piece of bone.

Where is Kofi? I asked.

He went to play, the giant said. He snapped the bone in half and tossed it aside. I shuddered, for I knew it was most surely Kofi's last remains. I shook even harder, imagining what it would be like to die under the giant's greasy, chubby fingers. More than anything I wanted to run from the dank bunker out into the hot dust outside. But I was trapped.

Please don't eat me, I cried out, holding my manacled wrists into the air.

Why not? the giant demanded angrily. I can do with you as I please.

I thought hard and quick, looking to save my skin.

I have brothers! I yelled.

The giant was interested. His eyes gleamed, and I saw my chance.

I said, My brothers are warriors, and plump with victory and full of life. They are young and strong, with supple dark skin and tight curly hair.

The giant drooled and swallowed noisily. He pulled at my manacles with a dreadlock, like it was a tentacle of some sort, and I stumbled closer. I did not breathe, scared to smell his stench, as his nasty breath wet my face.

Bring them to me, he declared with moist lips, and I will spare your life.

When I returned to the tents my skin was dry and dusty, and my ribs showed beneath my skin. Little Brother grabbed my legs, and all my brothers stepped out from the tent. They hugged me and gave me water, then hugged me more.

I was surprised to see Mouwanat cry and hug me the most.

That is the way it is with older brothers.

Where have you been? Kuabi asked.

Who did this to you? Mouwanat demanded.

And Little Brother said in a small, wavering, voice, Old Ma is gone. She walked out into the night and never came back. We think men have killed her. Then we all hugged and cried again.

Brothers, I said, after grieving Old Ma. I was captured by a giant that showed me shows on TV, and gave me food in a paper bag.

Little Brother took the bag I pulled from my waist and looked at it. He wiped his forefinger on the grease and sniffed it.

Is that a bad thing? my brothers asked.

In response I opened my robes, and showed them the dreadlock that had lodged itself in the hollow place in my chest, just below my heart. For Death was not stupid; he had me just as surely as if I were still in the bunker with the blue light.

All raised by Old Ma, my brothers saw the dreadlock, and cursed and swore.

What shall we do? they all asked me.

You should follow me, I said. We will face Death.

For I had made something of a plan during the long trip back, all the while ignoring the evil-sweet smells of the bag on my waist. Old Ma had told us stories of tricksters who had been trapped by Death, and who had jabbed him with spears to kill him. We would do the same.

We drove back to the bunker after bribing a warrior with our bag of evil-sweet food. The man never saw the faint dreadlock clinging to the bag, and though we felt sorry for him, our compassion fled as we saw him eat the food so fast he grew sick.

As we drove we sang together. Old songs, new songs, and some in-between. We kicked up dust and drove over dreadlocks bravely. Here they were thick in the ground, and we could hear the sounds of war in the distance, feeding the ever-hungry fatness of Death. And when we drove up to the bunker with our truck, my brothers leaped from its sides and ran down into the darkness to face the giant, defiance in their eyes.

Ho, the giant said, dreadlocks squirming with eagerness among the sides of the walls. Little Brother's eyes opened wide, and he looked around at the TVs. A table filled with food and fruit sat near the giant.

Come, eat. The giant beckoned to us.

I turned to my brothers and nodded. We all turned weapons onto the giant. I fired a small pistol at the giant's face and watched his cheek shatter with a great gout of blood.

Kuabi threw grenades into the folds of the giant's belly, and the flesh flew apart with a great fart of sludginess.

Little Brother threw stones.

Mouwanat held his flamethrower forward, and a great stream of fire leaped out and struck the giant. Fat burned and slid to the ground, and the giant's arms beat against the sides of the walls. His dreadlocks slid up into his body, and kept sliding and sliding. Mouwanat turned his flame to them, and the dreadlocks lit up and spread crackling blue fire all over the bunker.

We burned and shot until there was nothing left to burn and shoot, and we walked out with smiles on our faces. We have killed Death, we celebrated among ourselves.

And saved our brother, Mouwanat said.

Outside, the dreadlocks had dried up, and were rusting into the sand.

If we killed Death, Kuabi thought out loud, aren't *we* immortal?

From by us came a loud chuckle. We turned, and there stood Old Ma, barefoot and sweaty, by the side of the truck.

You can't kill Death, children! She walked over to me and put a hand on my chest. She ran her hands through my locks and kissed my forehead. She put a salve on my chest, and it raised my spirits and let me breathe easier.

My brothers embraced Old Ma, and shouted and cried to see her alive.

But Old Ma, Little Brother cried, what about the stories you told us? Where they killed Death with spears?

Those, Old Ma said, turning away from me. Those were just stories. Stories to teach you, stories to help you be brave, stories to warn you, but still, just stories. Everyone tells stories. All over the world they tell stories, to help explain why things are just the way they are. Death will always be with us.

Kuabi said, If these were just stories, how could we see his dreadlocks?

Just stories? Old Ma snorted as she shooed us all back into the truck. Kuabi started to drive us off across the land. Crowded around her, we listened as she spoke.

Stories can build up an empire, or strike down a people. You can spell the most powerful spell, ease a friend's hurt, or break an enemy. Stories make you believe.

But how can we fight Death? Little Brother shouted, his eyes misting.

Old Ma took his hand. I told you a story to help you see the ugly Death in our land. But now you have to look for it on your own. There are other Deaths to face, other stories. Ones more cruel; others hopeful, kind. You have heard mine.

I looked around the truck. My brothers had left their weapons with Death. We jounced on through the dust.

I nodded.

Old Ma was right. She had helped us, come from the bush to guide us. And now we had our own story to tell.

Many miles passed, and Old Ma waved us toward the forest, where we could hide and be safe. As I looked all around us, the world seemed eerie and still. A dead quiet had fallen. Even the dust hardly dared stir.

We had been brave, and had faced Death. Now we had to be even braver and face the things that Death fed off. We could not fight Death with weapons. Death was not something we could burn, or knife. These things made it stronger, harder to see.

And we could never kill Death. We could only make it gentler, kinder, a friend who came after many years. But this Death would only come to us when we changed the current story, the one with Kalashnikovs, dreadlocks, and fear, with the dust heavy in the air as it was kicked up by wheels.

# ASUQUO
## or
# THE WINDS OF HARMATTAN

*Nnedima Okorafor*

A suquo followed her nose and used her birdlike sense of direction. All around her were men selling yams and women selling cocoa yams. She always knew where to find the good ones; they had a starchier smell. Her mother didn't believe her when she said she could smell specific vegetables in the market, but she could.

Asuquo was about to jostle past a slow-moving man carrying a bunch of plantains on his shoulder when an old woman grabbed one of her seven locks. The woman sat on a wooden stool, a pyramid of eggs on a straw mat at her feet. Next to her, a man was selling very dried-up looking yams.

"Yes, Mama?" Asuquo said. She did not know the woman, but she knew to always show respect to her elders. The woman smiled and let go of Asuquo's hair.

"You like the sky, wind girl?" she asked.

Asuquo froze, feeling tears heat her eyes. *How does she know?* Asuquo thought. *She will tell my mother.* Asuquo's strong sense of smell wasn't the only thing her mother didn't believe in, even when she saw it with her own eyes. Asuquo's face still ached from the slap she'd received from her mother yesterday morning. But Asuquo couldn't help what happened when she slept.

The man selling yams brushed past her to hand a buyer his change of several cowries. He looked at her and then sneezed. Asuquo frowned, and the old woman laughed.

"Even your own father is probably allergic to you, wind girl," she said in her phlegmy voice. Asuquo looked away, her hands fidgeting. "All except one. You watch for him. Don't listen to what they all say. He's your *chi*. All of your kind are born with one. You go out and find him."

"How much for ten eggs?" a young woman asked, stepping up to the old woman.

"My *chi*?" Asuquo whispered, the old woman's words bouncing about her mind. Asuquo didn't move. She knew exactly whom the woman spoke of. Sometimes she dreamed about him. He could do what she could do. Maybe he could do it better.

"Give me five cowries," the old woman said to her customer. She gave Asuquo a hard push back into the market crowd without a word and turned her attention to selling her eggs. Asuquo tried to look back, but there were too many people between her and the old woman now.

After she'd bought her yams, she didn't bother going back to find the old woman. But from that day on, she watched the sky.

**Asuquo was one of the last. It is whispered words, known as the "bush radio," and the bitter grumblings of the trees that bring together her story. She was a Windseeker, one of the people who could fly; and a Windseeker's life is dictated by more than the wind.**

Eleven years later, the year of her twentieth birthday, the Harmattan winds never came. Dry, dusty, and cool, these winds had formed over the Sahara and blown their fresh air all the way to the African coast from December to February since humans began walking the earth. Except for that year.

That year, the cycle was disrupted, old ways poisoned. This story will tell you why.

Asuquo was the fourth daughter of Chief Ibok's third wife. Though she was not fat, she still possessed a sort of voluptuous beauty with her round hips and strong legs. But her hair crept down her back like ropes of black fungus. She was born this way, emerging from her mother's womb with seven glistening locks of dada hair hanging from her head like seaweed. And women with dada hair were undesirable.

They were thought to be the children of Mami Wata, and the water deity always claimed her children eventually, be it through kidnapping or an early death. Such a woman was not a good investment in the future. Asuquo's mother didn't bother taking her to the fattening hut to be secluded for weeks, stuffed with pounded yam and dried chameleons, and circumcised with a sharp sliver of coconut shell.

But Asuquo was content in her village. She didn't want to be bothered with all the preparations for marriage. She spent much of her time in the forest, and rumors that she talked to the sky and did strange things with plants were not completely untrue.

Nor were the murmurs of her running about with several young men. When she was twelve, she discovered she had a taste for them. Her friend Effiom followed her to the river one day. He touched her between her legs, and the sensation made her ravenous. He smiled when she asked him to touch her again and again. Their activities resulted in a smooth transition to an act far more mature. He was the first of several.

Nevertheless, the moment a young man named Okon from a nearby village saw her, standing behind her mother's home, peeling bark from a tree and dropping it in her pocket, he fell madly in love. She'd been smiling at the tree, her teeth shiny white, her skin blue-black, and her callused hands long-fingered. When Okon approached her that day, she stood eye to eye with him; and he was tall himself.

Okon's father almost didn't allow him to marry her.

"How can you marry that kind of woman? She has never been to the fattening hut!" he'd bellowed. "She has dada hair! I'm telling you, she is a child of Mami Wata! She is likely to be barren!"

*My father is right*, Okon thought, *Asuquo is unclean*. But something about her made him love her. Okon was a stubborn young man. He was also smart. And so he continued nagging his father about Asuquo while also assuring him that he would marry a second wellborn wife soon afterward. His father eventually gave in.

Asuquo did not want to marry Okon. Since the encounter with the strange old woman years ago, she had been watching the skies for her *chi*, her other half, the one she was supposed to go and find. She had been dreaming about her *chi* since she was six, and every year the dreams became more and more vivid.

She knew his voice, his smile, and his dry-leaf scent. Sometimes she'd even think she saw him in her peripheral vision. She could see that he was tall and dark like her and wore purple. But when she turned her head, he wasn't there.

She knew she would someday find him, or he would find her, the way a bird knows which way to migrate. But, at the time, he was not close, and he was not thinking about her much. He was somewhere trying to live his life, just as she was. All in due time.

Her parents, on the other hand, were so glad a man—*any man*— wanted to marry Asuquo that they ignored everything else. They ignored how she brought the wind with her wherever she went, her seven locks of thick hair bouncing against her back. And they certainly ignored the fact that, though she was shaky, she could fly a few inches off the ground when she really tried.

One day, Asuquo had floated to the hut's ceiling to crush a large spider. Her mother happened to walk in, took one look at Asuquo, and then quickly grabbed the basket she'd come for and left. She never mentioned it to Asuquo, nor did she mention the many other times she'd seen Asuquo levitate. Asuquo's father was the same way.

"Mama, I shouldn't marry him," Asuquo said. "You know I shouldn't."

Her mother waved her hand at her words, her pleas. And her

father greedily held out his hands for the hefty dowry Okon paid to Asuquo's family.

Asuquo had been taught to respect her elders. Somewhere in the back of her mind, she knew her duty as a woman. So, in the end, Asuquo agreed to the marriage, ignoring, denying, and pushing away her thoughts and sightings of her *chi*. And Asuquo could not help but feel pleased at the satisfied look in her father's eyes and the proud swell of her mother's chest. For so long they had given her only looks of dismissal and shame.

The wedding was most peculiar. Five bulls and several goats were slaughtered. For a village where meat was only eaten on special occasions, this was wonderful. However, birds large and small kept stealing hunks of the meat and mouthfuls of spicy rice from the feast. On top of that, high winds swept people's clothes about during the ceremony. Asuquo laughed and laughed, her brightly colored lapa swirling about her ankles and the collarette of beads and cowrie shells around her neck clicking. She knew several of the birds personally, especially the owl who took off with an entire goat leg.

After their wedding night, Asuquo knew Okon would not look at another woman. Once in their hut, Asuquo had undressed him and taken him in with her eyes for a long time. Then she nodded, satisfied with what she saw. Okon had strong, veined hands; rich brown skin; and a long neck. That night, Asuquo had her way with him in ways that left his body tingling and sore and helpless, though she'd have preferred to be outside under the sky.

As he lay, exhausted, he told her that the women he'd slept with before had succumbed to him with sad faces and had lain like fallen trees. Asuquo laughed and said, "It's because those women felt as if they had lost their honor." She smiled to herself, thinking about all her other lovers and how none of them had behaved as if they were dead or fallen.

That morning, Okon learned exactly what kind of woman he had married. Asuquo was not beside him when he awoke. His eyes grew wide when he looked up.

"What is this?" he screeched, trying to scramble out of bed and falling on the floor instead, his big left foot in the air. He quickly rolled to the side and knelt low, staring up at his wife, his mouth agape. Her green lapa and hair hung down as she hovered horizontally above the bed. Okon noticed that there was something gentle about how she floated. He could feel a soft breeze circulating around her. He sniffed. It smelled like the arid winds during Harmattan. He sneezed three times and had to wipe his nose.

Asuquo slowly opened her eyes, awakened by Okon's noise. She chuckled and softly floated back onto the bed. She felt particularly good because when she'd awoken, she hadn't automatically fallen as she usually did.

That afternoon they had a long talk where Asuquo laughed and smiled and Okon mostly just stared at her and asked "Why?" and "How?" Their discussion didn't get beyond the obvious. But by nighttime, she had him forgetting that she, the woman he had just married, had the ability to fly.

For a while, it was as if Asuquo lived under a pleasantly overcast sky. Her dreams of her *chi* stopped, and she no longer glimpsed him in the corner of her eye. She wondered if the old woman had been wrong, because she was very happy with Okon.

She planted a garden behind their hut. When she was not cooking, washing, or sewing, she was in the garden, cultivating. There were many different types of plants, including sage, kola nut, wild yam root, parsley, garlic, pleurisy root, nettles, cayenne. She grew cassava melons, yams, cocoa yams, beans, and many, many flowers and sold her produce at the market. She always came home with her money purse full of cowries. She liked to tie it around her waist because she enjoyed the rhythmic clinking it made as she walked.

When she became pregnant, she didn't have to soak a bag of wheat or barley in her urine to know that she would give birth to a boy. But she knew if she did so, the bag of wheat would sprout and the bag of barley would remain dormant, a sure sign of a male child. The same went with her second pregnancy a year later. She loved her two babies, Hogan and Bassey, dearly, and her heart was full. For a while.

Okon was so in love with Asuquo that he quietly accepted the fact that she could fly. *As long as the rest of the village doesn't know, especially Father, what is the harm?* he thought. He let her do whatever she wanted, providing that she maintained the house, cooked for him, and warmed his bed at night.

He also enjoyed the company of Asuquo's mother, who sometimes visited. Though she and Asuquo did not talk much, Asuquo's mother and Okon laughed and conversed well into the night. Neither spoke of Asuquo's flying ability.

Asuquo made plenty of money at the market. And when Okon came back from fishing, there was nothing he loved more than to watch his wife in her garden, his sons scrambling about her feet.

Regardless of their contentment, the village's bush radio was alive with chatter, snaking its mischievous roots under their hut, its stems through their window, holding its flower to their lips like microphones, following Asuquo with the stealth of a grapevine. The bush radio thrived from the rain of gossip.

Women said that Asuquo worked juju on her husband to keep him from looking at any other woman. That she carried a purse around her waist hidden in her lapa that her husband could never touch. That she carried all sorts of strange things in it, like nails, her husband's hair, dead lizards, odd stones, sugar, and salt. That there were also items folded, wrapped, tied, sewn into cloth in this purse. Had she not been born with the locked hair of a witch? they said. And look at how wildly her garden grows in the back. And what are those useless plants she grows alongside her yams and cassava?

"When do you plan to do as you promised?" Okon's father asked.

"When I am ready," Okon said. "When, ah . . . when Hogan and Bassey are older."

"Has that woman made you crazy?" his father asked. "What kind of household is this with just one wife? This kind of woman?"

"It is my house, Papa," Okon said. He broke eye contact with his father. "And it is happy and productive. In time, I will get another woman. But not yet."

The men often talked about Asuquo's frequent disappearances into the forest and the way she was always climbing things.

"I often see her climbing her hut to go on the roof when her chickens fly up there," one man said. "What is a woman doing climbing trees and roofs?"

"She moves about like a bird," they said.

"Or a bat," one man said, narrowing his eyes.

For a while, men quietly went about slapping at bats with switches when they could, waiting to see if Asuquo came out of her hut limping.

A long time ago, things would have been different for Asuquo. There was a time when Windseekers in the skies were as common as tree frogs in the trees. Then came the centuries of the foreigners with their boats, sweet words, weapons, and chains. After that, Windseeker sightings grew scarce. Storytellers forgot much of the myth and magic of the past and turned what they remembered into evil, dark things. It was no surprise that the village was so resistant to Asuquo.

Both the men and women liked to talk about Hogan and Bassey. They couldn't say that the two boys weren't Okon's children. Hogan looked like a miniature version of his father with his arrow-shaped nose and bushy eyebrows. And Bassey had his father's careful mannerisms when he ate and crawled about the floor.

But people were very suspicious about how healthy the two little boys were. The boys consumed as much as any normal child of the village, eating little meat and much fruit. Hogan was more partial to udara fruits, while Bassey liked to slowly suck mangoes to the seed. Still, the shiny-skinned boys grew as if they ate goat meat every day. The villagers told each other, "She *must* be doing something to them. Something evil. No child should grow like that."

"I see her coming from the forest some days," one woman said. "She brings back oddly shaped fruits and roots to feed her children." Once again, the word "witch" was whispered as discreet fingers pointed Asuquo's way.

Regardless of the chatter, women often went to Asuquo when she was stooping over the plants in her garden. Their faces would be pleasant, and one would never guess that only an hour ago, they had spoken ill of the very woman from whom they sought help.

They would ask if she could spare a yam or some bitter leaf for egusi soup. But they really wanted to know if Asuquo could do something for a child who was coughing up mucus. Or if she could make something to soothe a husband's toothache. Some wanted sweet-smelling oils to keep their skin soft in the sun. Others sought a reason why their healthy gardens had begun to wither after a fight with a friend.

"I'll see what I can do," Asuquo would answer, putting a hand on the woman's back, escorting her inside. And she could always do something.

Asuquo was too preoccupied with her own issues to tune into the gossip of the bush radio.

She'd begun to feel the tug deep in the back of her throat again. He was close, her *chi*, her other half, the one who liked to wear purple. And as she was, he was all grown up, his thoughts now focused on her. At times she choked and hacked, but the hook only dug deeper. When her sons were no longer crawling she began to make trips to the forest more frequently, so that she could assuage her growing impatience. Once the path grew narrow and the sound of voices dwindled, she slowly took to the air.

Branches and leaves would slap her legs because she was too clumsy to maneuver around them. She could stay in the sky only for a few moments; then she would sink. But in those moments, she could feel him.

When her husband was out fishing and the throb of her menses kept her from spending much time in the garden, she filled a bowl with rainwater and sat on the floor, her eyes wide, staring into it as through a window to another world. Once in a while, she'd dip a finger in, creating expanding circles. She saw the blue sky, the trees waving back and forth with the breeze. It didn't take long to find what she was looking for. He was far away, flying just above the tallest trees, his purple pants and caftan fluttering as he flew.

Afterward, she took the bowl of water with her to the river and poured it over her head with a sigh. The water always tasted sweet and felt like the sun on her skin. Then she dove into the river and swam deep, imagining the water to be the sky and the sky to be the water.

Some nights she was so restless that she went to her garden and picked a blue passionflower. She ate it, and when she slept, she dreamed of him. Though she could see him clearly, he was always too far away for her to touch. She had started to call him the purple one. Aside from his purple attire, he wore cowrie shells dangling from his ears and around his wrists and had a gold hoop in his wide nose. Her urge to go to him was almost unbearable.

As her mind became consumed with the purple one, her body was less and less interested in Okon. Their relationship quickly changed. Okon became a terrible beast fed by his own jealousy. He desperately appealed to Asuquo's mother, who, in turn, yelled at Asuquo's distracted face.

Okon would angrily snatch the broom from Asuquo and sweep out the dry leaves that kept blowing into their home, sneezing as he did so. He tore through her garden with stamping feet and clenched fists, scratching himself on thorns and getting leaves stuck in his toenails. And his hands became heavy as bronze to her skin. He forbade her to fly, especially in the forest. Out of fear for her sons, she complied. But it did not stop there.

The rumors, mixed with jealousy, fear, and suspicion, spiraled into a raging storm, with Asuquo at the center. Her smile turned to a sad gaze as her mind continued to dwell on her *chi*, who flew somewhere in the same skies she could no longer explore. Each night, her husband tied her to the bed where he made what he considered love to her body; for he still loved her. Each time, he fell asleep on top of her, not moving till morning, when he sneezed himself awake.

Even her sons seemed to be growing allergic to Asuquo. She frequently had to wipe their noses when they sneezed. Sometimes they cried when she got too close. They played outside more and more and preferred to help their father dry the fish he brought home rather than aid their mother in the garden. Asuquo often cried about this in the garden when no one was around. Her sons were all she had.

One day, Okon fell sick. His forehead was hot, but yet he shivered. He was weak, and at times he yelled at phantoms he saw floating about the hut.

"Please, Asuquo, fly up to the ceiling," he begged, grabbing her arm as he lay in bed, sweat beading his brow. "Tell them to leave!"

He pleaded with her to speak with the plants and mix a concoction foul-smelling enough to drive the apparitions away.

Asuquo looked at the sky, then at Okon, then at the sky. He'd die if she left him. She thought of her sons. The sound of their feet as they played outside soothed her soul. She looked at the sky again. She stood very still for several minutes. Then she turned from the door and went to Okon. *When Okon gets well*, she thought, *I will take my sons with me, even if I cannot fly so well.*

When he was too weak to chew his food, she chewed it first and then fed it to him. She plucked particular leaves and pounded bitter-smelling bark. She collected rainwater to wash him with. And she frequently laid her hands on his chest and forehead. She often sent the boys out to prune her plants when she was with Okon in the bedroom. The care they took with the plants during this time made her want to kiss them over and over. But she did not because they would sneeze.

For this short time, she was happy. Okon was not able to tie her up, and she was able to soothe his pain. She was also able to slip away once in a while and practice flying. Nonetheless, the moment Okon was able to stand up straight with no pain in his chest or dizziness, after five years of marriage, he went and brought several of his friends to the hut and pointed his finger at Asuquo.

"This woman tried to kill me," he said, looking at Asuquo with disgust. He grabbed her wrists. "She is a witch! *Ubio!*"

"Ah," one of his friends said, smiling. "You've finally woken up and seen your wife for what she really is."

The others grunted in agreement, looking at Asuquo with a mixture of fear and hatred. Asuquo was staring in complete shock at her husband whose life she had saved, her ears following her sons around the yard as they laughed and sculpted shapes from mud.

She wasn't sure if she was seeing Okon for what he really was or what he had become. What she was sure of was that in that moment, something burst deep inside her—something that had held the realization of her mistake at bay. She should have listened to the old woman; she should have listened to *herself*. If it weren't for her sons, she'd have shot through the ceiling, into the sky, never to be seen again.

"Why . . . ?" was all she said.

Okon slapped her then, slapped her hard. Then he slapped her again. Only her *chi* could save her now.

Okon brought her before the Ekpo society. He tightly held the thick rope that he'd tied around her left wrist. Her shoulders were slumped, and her eyes were cast down. Villagers came out of their huts and gathered around the four old men sitting in chairs and the woman kneeling before them in the dirt.

Her sons, now only three and four years old, were taken to their aunt's hut. Asuquo's hair had grown several feet in length over the years. Now there were a few coils of gray around her forehead from the stress. The people stared at her locks with pinched faces as if they had never seen them before.

The Ekpo society's job was to protect the village from thieves, murderers, cheats, and witchcraft. Nevertheless, even these old men had forgotten that once upon a long time ago, the sky was peopled with women and men just like Asuquo.

Centuries ago, the Ekpo society was close to the deities of the forest, exchanging ideas, wishes, and words of wisdom with these benevolent beings who had a passing interest in the humans of the forest. But these days, the elders of the Ekpo society were in closer contact with the white men, choosing which wrongdoers to sell to them and bartering for the price.

Her husband stood behind her, his angry eyes cast to the ground. All this time he had let her go in and out of the house whenever she liked, he had never asked where exactly she was going. Who was she going to see? It couldn't have just been the forest. Who was she being unfaithful with? He had asked many of the women, and they'd all given different names. *Father warned me that she was unclean,* he kept thinking.

The four old men sat on chairs, wearing matching blue-and-red lapas, their feet close together, scowls on their faces. One of them raised his chin and spoke.

"You are accused of witchcraft," he said, his voice shaky with age. "One woman said you gave her a drink for her husband's sore tooth and all his teeth fell out. One man saw you turn into a bat. Many people in this village can attest to this. What do you have to say for yourself?"

Asuquo looked up at the men, and for the first time, her ears ringing, her nostrils flaring, she felt rage, though not because of the accusations. It made her face ugly. The purple one was so close, and these people were not listening to her. They were in her way, blocking out the cool dusty wind with their noise.

Her hands clenched. Many of the people gathered looked away out of guilt. They knew their part in all of this. The chief's wives, their arms around their chests, looked on, waiting and hoping to be rid of this woman who many said had bedded their husband numerous times.

"You see whatever you want to see," she said through dry lips. "I've had enough. You can't keep me from him."

She heard her husband gasp behind her. If they had been at home, he'd have beaten her. Nevertheless, his blows no longer bothered her as much. These days her essence sought the sky. It was September. The Harmattan winds would be upon the village soon, spraying dust onto the tree leaves and into their homes. She'd hold out her arms and let the dust devils twirl her about. Soon.

But she still couldn't fly that well yet, especially with her shoulders weighed down by sadness. If only these people would get out of the way. Then she would take her sons where they would be safe, and the caretakers she chose would not tell them lies about her.

"Let the chop nut decide," the fourth elder said, his eyes falling on Asuquo like charred pieces of wood. "In three days."

She almost laughed despite herself. Asuquo knew the plant from which the chop nut grew. In the forest, the doomsday plant thrived during rainy season. Many times she'd stopped to admire it. Its purplish beanlike flower was beautiful. When the flower fell off, a brown kidney-shaped pod replaced it. She could smell the six highly poisonous chop nuts inside the pod from meters away. Even the bush rats with their weak sense of smell and tough stomachs died minutes after eating it.

Asuquo looked up at the elders, one by one. She curled her lip and pointed at the elder who had spoken. She opened her mouth wide as if to curse them, but no sound came out. Then her eyes went blank again, and her face relaxed. She mentally left her people and let her mind seek out the sky. Still, a tear of deep sadness fell down her face.

The four elders stood up and walked into the forest where they said they would "consort with the old ones."

Those three days were hazy and cold as the inside of a cloud. Okon tied Asuquo to the bed as before. He slept next to her, his arm around her waist. He bathed her, fed her, and enjoyed her. In the mornings, he went to the garden and quietly cried for her. Then he cried for himself, for he could not pinpoint who his wife's lover was. Every man in the village looked suspect.

Asuquo's eyes remained distant. She no longer spoke to him—she did not even look at him—and she did not notice that her babies were not with her. Instead, she unfocused her eyes and let her mind float into the sky, coming back occasionally to command her body to inhale and exhale air.

Her *chi* joined her here, several hundred miles away from the village, a thousand feet into the sky. Now, he was close enough that for the first time, a part of them could be in the same place. Asuquo leaned against him as he took her locks into his hands and brought them to his face, inhaling her scent. He smelled like dry leaves, and when he kissed her ears, Asuquo cried.

She wrapped her arms around him and laid her head on his chest until it was time to go. She knew he would continue making his way to her, though she had told him it was too late. She'd underestimated the ugliness that had dug its roots underneath her village.

The elders came to Okon and Asuquo's home, a procession of slapping sandals, much of the village following. People looked through the windows and the doorways of their home; many milled about outside talking quietly, sucking their teeth and shaking their heads. Above, a storm pulled its clouds in to cover the sky. The elders came, and her husband brought chairs for them.

"We have spoken with those of the bush," one of them said. Then he turned around, and a young man brought in the chop nut. Her husband and three men held her down as she struggled. Her eyes never met her husband's. One man with jagged nails placed the chop nut in her mouth, and a man smelling of palm oil roughly held her nose, forcing her to swallow. Then they let go, stepped back.

She wiped her nose and eyes, her lips pressed together. She got up and went to the window to look at the sky. The three young women and two young men watching through the window wordlessly stepped back with guilty looks, clearing her view of the gathering clouds. She braced her legs, willing her body to leave the ground. If she could get out the window into the clouds, she would be fine. She'd return for her sons once she had vomited up the chop nut.

But no matter how hard she tried, her body would only lift a centimeter off the ground. She was too tired. And she was becoming more tired. All around her were quiet, waiting for the verdict.

The rumble of thunder came from close by. She stood for as long as she could, for a whole half hour. Until her insides began to burn. The fading light flowing through the window began to hurt her eyes. Then it dimmed. Then it hurt her eyes again. She could not tell if it was due to the chop nut or the approaching storm. The walls wavered, and she could hear her heartbeat in her ears. It was slowing. She lay back on the bed, on top of the rope Okon had used to tie her down.

Soon she did not feel her legs, and her arms hung at her sides. The room was silent, all eyes on her. Her bare breasts heaved; sweat trickling between them. Her mind passed her garden to her boys and landed on her *chi*. Her mind's eye saw him floating in the sky, immobile, a frown on his face.

As the room dimmed and she left her body, he dropped from the sky only thirty miles south of Asuquo's village of Old Calabar. As he dropped he swore to the clouds that they would not see him for many, many years. The wind outside wailed through the trees, but within an hour it quickly died. The storm passed, without sending down a single drop of rain to nurture the forest. No Harmattan winds shook the trees that year. They had turned around, returning to the Sahara in disgust.

A year later, on the anniversary of Asuquo's death, the winds came back, though not so strong. Reluctant. They have since resumed their normal pattern. Her husband, Okon, went on to marry three wives and have many children. Asuquo's young boys were raised calling the first of them "mother," and they didn't remember the strange roots and fruits their real mother had brought from the forest that had made them strong.

As the years passed, when storytellers told of Asuquo's story, they changed her name to the male name of Ekong. They felt their audience responded better to male characters. And Ekong became a man who roamed the skies searching for men's wives to snatch because he had died a lonely man and his soul was not at rest.

"There he is!" a boy would yell at the river as the Harmattan winds blew dry leaves about. All the girls would go splashing out of the water, screaming and laughing and hiding behind trees. Nobody wanted to get snatched by the "man who moved with the breeze."

Nevertheless, it was well over a century before the winds blew with true fervor again. But that is another story.

# THE HORSEMEN AND THE MORNING STAR

*Barbara Hambly*

The thing was, it hadn't been a bad year at all.

Maybe if it had been, the whole affair wouldn't have taken place. Hard times have their own rules.

But the sugar had cropped well, and only a pig or two had died, and Master Henri had gotten good advances on next year's sugar crop from the brokers in New Orleans. Ajax, who in addition to being the main gang driver could read and figure a bit, kept his eye on such things for the folks in the cabins, because Master Henri was a young man and eager to make his fortune with Bellebleu Plantation, and such enthusiasm could fall hard on a man's slaves.

But in New Orleans, Master Henri had met Amalie Deschamps, and was determined to make her his wife.

"She so beautiful, this Amalie?" asked Ajax's sister Flavia, when they were all sitting on the steps of the cabins one evening after the work was done—loading barrels and cutting drains, that time of year, making and mending to get ready to clear the fields for next year's crop.

"Curds an' whey," said Ajax, who'd heard this from Master Henri's valet Aristide. Aristide had been bought, trained to a hair, in New Orleans nine months ago and was far too grand to come down to the cabins. "Her papa's rich, and I think that's what Master Henri fell in love with. But being her papa's rich, she got her choice of husbands, and there's richer men and better looking than Master Henri."

It was shortly after that, that Leonidas Houbigant came to Bellebleu.

Leonidas Houbigant had gone to school with Master Henri in Paris (said Ajax); a Creole from Martinique, he'd settled in Rome. It was from Rome he came when Master Henri sent him a letter asking his help. The fields had been cleared and next year's sugar put in by then, with Master Henri driving to have extra fields cleared—he had no white overseer, the last one having died of black vomit a few years ago in '21. What with extra cutting and diking and breaking new ground everyone was exhausted from overwork. "He think one new field's worth of sugar going to impress Papa Deschamps?" asked old Dede, when Ajax gave the tree-clearing gang a rest though he wasn't supposed to, and the kids Cassius and Helen, who weren't old enough for heavy work yet, ran to get them water.

Old Dede was the oldest man in the cabins, and should have been let off the heavy work in Ajax's opinion, not that Master Henri asked it. White-haired, small, and spare, Dede was an Ibo from the Lake Chad country, and strong as a horse. But he'd started looking gray around the mouth when they'd hauled that last cypress trunk, so Ajax had told everyone to set awhile because the day was hot. "He's doing whatever he thinks he can, to impress Papa Deschamps," said Ajax. "No matter what it costs us."

The night Leonidas Houbigant arrived at Bellebleu, Aristide the valet came down to the cabins.

"There's evil in them boxes he brought," he said hoarsely. "Evil you can feel through the leather of the trunks, the brass of the locks. Evil that he won't let no one touch."

That Aristide would come out to the cabins at all was unusual enough to give Dede and Ajax, and Mambo Marie the cook, pause for thought, for after he was dismissed for the night the slender, light-skinned valet usually retired to his room in the attic and read French newspapers. But when Mambo Marie had finished her work in the kitchen that night and set up for the morning, Aristide had appeared and had walked with her along the path through the dark cypresses to the scatter of cabins where the slaves lived.

"I don't know what to do," the valet said, looking from Dede's face, to Mambo Marie's, to Ajax's in the low whicker of the pine-knot fire in front of the cabin where the single men slept. It was very late, and nearly everyone had gone to bed—the work had been hard that day. Master Henri was still driving everyone hard. Now that the sugar and the corn were in he was pushing to clear a road to a landing on the river where he planned to set up a woodlot, he said, and sell to the steamboats that were beginning to ply the Mississippi to the American towns upstream. He hoped to get a contract with one of the boat companies to be a regular supplier.

The valet went on. "After supper was over Master Henri tell me to take myself off out of the house. He and Master Leonidas had a job to do alone. When I looked in through the window they'd cleared out the study, and taken up the mats from the floor. They drew lines on the floor with chalk, and put up an altar like in a church, on the wall where Master Henri's desk usually sits, and golden candlesticks and little dishes of powder and jewels in each corner of the room. These are the things Master Leonidas brought in those trunks of his—those things and a big black book they read out of, calling on names in Latin. Calling on Asmodeus and Beelzebub, and Lucifer, the son of the Morning Star."

"They had me look out a black chicken this afternoon," said Mambo Marie, folding her hands around her skinny knee. She was nearly as old as Dede, and like Dede small, a Yoruba woman who had been beautiful as a girl and had suffered for it the way beautiful women suffer when they are made slaves. Her eyes were still beautiful. "They said don't kill it—Master Leonidas said. Just bring it alive in a basket." Her dark gaze stared out through the fire and into the night, as if seeing there the shadows of those who were drawn to the blood of black birds.

"I don't know this Asmodeus, or this son of the Morning Star," said Dede after a time. "But evil like this, it stays in a house. It stays in the people who touch it. This we need to watch."

Aristide had been baptized and wore a gold crucifix around his neck, but for good measure Mambo Marie made him a little bag of brick dust and horse hairs to tie around his ankle, to keep him safe. The next evening he reported that while Master Henri was out riding with his friend, he, Aristide, had slipped into the study and taken up the floor covering—mats of woven straw, for it was getting into the summer heat—and had seen where the chalk marks had been rubbed out, and where in places the cypress planks of the floor were spattered with fresh blood.

Two days later a letter arrived from an American steamboat company contracting for the use of the woodlot on the riverbank. Master Henri left at once for New Orleans, and when he came back, Aristide reported that Amalie Deschamps had undergone a change of heart, and found herself dreaming nightly (she said) of the young planter's splendid shoulders and ardent blue eyes.

Leonidas Houbigant stayed on in the house.

He spent part of his days reading, for he was a scholar, and a student of secret arts. The slaves didn't like him, mostly because of what he did to the girls he took to his rooms—the young girls, 'Machie and Cressy, couldn't work for a day or two after he'd had them. In one way or another he treated everyone the same as he'd treated the girls—not even like animals, but like machines, chairs, pieces of furniture that feel nothing. You sit down on them and get up off them and walk away. Even animals get taken care of, so they can be used to best effect. This tall man, with his dark slick hair and sallow handsome pockmarked face, walked the world like a visiting god and handled people as if they were pieces of money that could be traded for other, better things. He dealt with Master Henri this way, too, only the young man was so involved in getting wood cut for the lot, and clearing the swamp by the bayou for yet another cane field, and in adding and re-adding the columns of his ledgers, that he didn't notice.

Shortly after Master Henri came back from New Orleans with a contract for wood and Amalie Deschamps's scented handkerchief in his pocket, Sabine's youngest baby disappeared.

Sabine was Mandingo, a big strong beautiful woman who had birthed a child every year for a decade and a half and hadn't lost a one, doing work in the fields meantime while her mother looked after everyone's babies. That afternoon, though, the old woman had been called up to the house because one of the children had carved up the porch railing—though by the time she'd rounded them all up and questioned them, none could be found who'd admit to it—and when she'd finally got back to the cabins, little Hector was gone from the bed where he'd been lying asleep.

Sabine's mother sent Flavia's daughter Helen flying to the bayou where everyone was cutting wood that day, then went to the kitchen to get Mambo Marie. Mambo Marie checked the yard out in front of the cabin, and the cabin's dirt floor, for the marks of pigs' hooves, for those animals would sometimes molest babies. But she found none. She saw no sign either of panther or wildcat. The two old women, cook and slave-nurse, made a search of the vegetable gardens, and the woods out behind the cabins. Finally Master Henri came out and ordered Mambo Marie back to the kitchen. "I'm sorry about the child, of course, but I'm not going to have a guest of mine go hungry because somebody couldn't even look after a baby."

Mambo Marie enlisted every child able to walk easily, teamed them up in threes, and sent them out to search. But something in her heart told her there was a deeper darkness involved. In any case the children came back empty-handed. She wanted to question Aristide, but the valet had been sent off with a message to a neighboring plantation. The maid, a mulatto named Chloë, purchased like Aristide in New Orleans, had been set to polishing all the glassware in the house as soon as she'd finished doing the bedrooms that morning, and hadn't been out of the downstairs workroom all day.

An exhausted Chloë served the supper and was packed out of the house immediately thereafter. Aristide did not return to Bellebleu until late.

In the morning Master Henri and Leonidas ordered up a small work gang to follow them to an island in the river, where they spent the day in backbreaking digging. At length they unearthed a small hoard of gold and silver coins, legacy of the pirates who up until only a few years ago had plied the coast. In their absence, Mambo Marie and Aristide entered the study, which, like Master Leonidas's room, had been locked all the previous day. Beneath the floor mats they found fresh marks of chalked designs, and fresh stains of blood. The golden candlesticks Aristide had mentioned were gone, though dribbles of black wax beaded the small tables in the room's four corners. Though the tall windows onto the gallery were open, the curtains still reeked of incense and laudanum.

Nothing was ever found of Sabine's child.

The summer was a bad one. There were too few to work the new-cleared fields, and more wood needed to be cut than ever, for in addition to the extra cane there'd be at grinding time, the steamboats would be needing the wood Master Henri had promised. Ajax told Master Henri they'd need more men, four or five at least. But men were high in New Orleans that year, a thousand or more for a prime hand, and with his wedding to think about Master Henri grudged the cost. At length he bought two, when it was clear he'd not be able to keep up his commitment to the steamboat company unless he did. Aristide said he sat up most of the night with his friend Master Leonidas, drinking and cursing at the way of the world, that gave you money with one hand and took it away with the other. Master Leonidas only drank his cognac and said nothing.

In July, Xavier Deschamps and his daughter Amalie came on the steamboat to Bellebleu, along with his wife and a younger daughter and two sons and his maiden sister, to visit. All the men slept on the gallery while Papa Deschamps and his wife had Master Henri's bedroom, and Amalie and her sister the little cabinet where Master Leonidas had been, with the aunt in the cabinet on the other side of the house where the children of guests were sometimes put up. Aristide and Chloë had to double up with the maids and valets of the various members of the Deschamps family, because Master Leonidas's books and candlesticks and small jeweled censers were put into the third of the small attic rooms and kept under lock and key. Aristide—who was becoming more and more familiar with the folks in the cabins—told Dede and Mambo Marie that Amalie did poorly in the heat and talked a good deal about her father's property on Lake Pontchartrain, to which the entire family repaired after slightly less than a week at Bellebleu, in spite of Master Henri's protests that this summer was unusually hot.

"And you really ought to buy a couple more maids for this house, *cher*," Mademoiselle Amalie said as Master Henri handed her across the gangplank of the town-bound steamboat again. "Papa, you'll let Henri know when some good ones come up for sale in town, won't you?"

Old Papa Deschamps winked at his daughter's fiancé. "You know how girls are, eh, my boy? First they want a new dress, then a new maid; then they'll want a new house."

The steamboat whistle hooted, and the great paddles started to churn.

Two days after that, Flavia's daughter Helen disappeared.

Mambo Marie in her kitchen could feel the evil coming, as she felt the thunderstorms that rolled in off the Gulf in these hot, weighted August days. When Master Leonidas sent Aristide off in the morning with a message for Amalie at Lake Pontchartrain, the cook went to the children in the quarters and told them there was a bad moon rising that night, and they had best stay together and not let anybody be alone. But Master Leonidas rode out just after lunch, to check on the levee he said. Master Henri set Chloë to hemming all new sheets and curtains for the guest rooms, then came out onto the back gallery and told Helen to scat on out to the levee and take a message to Master Leonidas at once.

Mambo Marie, watching from the kitchen, tried to tell Cassius to go with Helen. But Master Henri said he had a job for Cassius too, and it was none of Mambo Marie's business to be ordering the children about anyway. Helen would make better tracks if she didn't have a friend with her to go looking for birds' nests with, he said.

Rain was coming on then, the hard downpour usual for summer afternoons. This came in sheeting torrents, driving everyone indoors. Looking out the open side of the kitchen, Mambo Marie couldn't even see the house through it, save as a pale blur through curtains of whirling gray. She thought she saw a black horse like the one Master Leonidas rode, standing by the stair that led up to the back gallery. But preparations for dinner kept her too busy to walk across and check, and when Chloë came to carry the dishes over to the house—with a weary-looking Ajax in tow, armed with an umbrella—the maid said she had heard nothing.

"Master Leonidas there, though," said Ajax.

"Come back here when you're done," the cook said.

It was still raining hard. The driver hadn't even changed out of his muddy clothes. When the others walked over from the cabins to get their rice and beans, Mambo Marie asked them if any of them had seen Helen since she'd been sent to look for Master Leonidas. Heads were shaken. Flavia, Sabine, and old Dede stood under the awning outside the kitchen, the women's bright headcloths black with wet and their skirts tucked up around their thighs, fear superseding the sodden fatigue in their eyes.

"She could be in the woods," said Flavia. "Rain could have caught her out there. If she was clear the other side of the bayou, it could be too high for her to come back."

"Master Leonidas, we could ask him if he'd seen her," added Sabine, her dread of the man clear in her voice.

"You think if he'd took her," asked Dede softly, "he wouldn't lie to you about it?"

They all looked at one another, then toward the tall rectangles of amber lamplight visible through the trees and the rain.

Flavia whispered, "What do we do?"

Dede's glance crossed Mambo Marie's, and held.

The slaves started slipping out of the cabins, making for the clearing by the bayou, before the rain let up. It was easing, though, and by the time they'd all assembled, the moon had broken the clouds. Aristide had left the wine-cellar keys with Chloë that morning, and she brought a bottle of rum. Those whose help they sought were fond of rum.

In spite of the laws against slaves owning drums, Judas the barrel maker brought one, small and double-headed, thonged around the sides to vary the pitch. The only house near enough for the sound of it to carry was to Bellebleu itself, and at Bellebleu, Mambo Marie knew, the blankittes would be occupied with other things. She herself brought part of a pound cake and two pieces of brown candy, and red rags to tie on the branches of the trees. Dede, pale and rather shaky from the day's labor cutting wood, emptied from his pockets a dozen candle ends gleaned from the workshop next to the kitchen. The two new men, though like Ajax both were Louisiana-born, brought crucifixes and horse brasses to decorate the makeshift altar, and one of them added a handful of sassafras and tobacco leaves, native to this land. Their fragrance sweetened the murky air.

They lit the candles, and torches made of pine knots, smoky in the dense wet heat of the night. Crickets and cicadas made an eerie chorus in the dark. Somewhere on the bayou an alligator bellowed, answered by the steady, throbbing peep of the frogs. Far off, like a single glowing apple seed of flame, the windows of the Big House burned beside the river, where Leonidas Houbigant worked to summon that which promised white men—European men—gifts in return for allegiance and innocent blood.

In the dark of the trees, the folk from the quarters began a summons of their own.

Judas beat his drums. Mambo Marie drank a little of the rum, then took another mouthful and spat it at the altar, the way she'd been taught. Dede took none at all, only swayed, dancing as if he had not been almost unable to walk for weariness an hour and a half before. Chloë the maid was swaying too, between Flavia and Sabine and Sabine's old mother, who were casting their head scarves away to let the long curly masses of their hair swing like the shadows of the rough sea. As she danced Mambo Marie thought about Helen, thought about those diagrams she'd seen chalked on the study floor and all the rituals the white men followed to summon the one they called the Lightbearer, the son of the Morning Star. It would take them time, to make all ready.

Many times in the past, the folk of the cabins—Ibo or Yoruba, Songhai or Mandingo or a mixture of those tribes—had opened themselves for the spirits of their gods. Had offered themselves as mounts for the unseen horsemen: to hear their advice, to solicit minor help . . . sometimes only to touch the hands of the gods and know they were still there. Only to know that the gods still watched over them.

The priests in town all said those gods were powerless, were only minor spirits, scruffy and quarrelsome and acting too much like humans to be taken seriously. And though all of this was true, it was still good to know they were there, good to know they still watched out for those whose families had worshiped them in the African lands.

This was the first time the folks on Bellebleu had sought them in such deadly need, facing such evil as Mambo Marie sensed was being summoned in the Big House. She wasn't entirely certain they would come.

But they did.

Gradually the dancers' purpose, though it never slipped from their minds, became secondary to the dance itself. The calinda's rhythm took them by the bones and the hearts, and weariness loosened from them, and fell away with their tattered clothes. Their anger, their desperation, their fear, melded and changed with the drumbeat and the cicada voices into something else, something clear and burning and perfect, bright as the core of the sun.

And then he was there.

An old man in rags, molded out of the night. Some people couldn't see him at all, and others said they saw the trunk of the cypress, the glitter of the moonlit bayou, right through his thin arms and lined, intelligent face. He leaned on a crutch, and the coal-bright gleam from his pipe was like a third eye, no brighter than the two that watched the dancers. Some said later that he wore a bunch of keys on a string around his neck. Nate, one of the new men, cried "Saint Peter! It's Saint Peter!" but though this was true in a way, Mambo Marie recognized him at once as Papa Legba, the guardian of the crossroads, the one who watches over the gate between the worlds.

They called him Legba here, a Dahomey name.

She'd seen him many times before.

Past his shoulder it seemed to her that she could see through the gate itself. The phosphor glim around him was sometimes the flicker of moonlight on the bayou, and sometimes eye. The restless stir in the dark could have been ground mist or shapes the wet-slate hue of shadow, moving to the echo of the drums. A serpent flowed through the grass at his feet, Damballah bearing his silent messages from one world to the next.

Mambo Marie held out her hands, trying to explain, but only harsh noises came out of her mouth. She closed her eyes, and let come into her whoever would.

Old Dede cried out, jumped and flinched like an unbroken horse feeling the first touch of a rider's weight. Hands caught him, supported him, his friends controlling his flailings lest he hurt himself, for he was an old man and brittle in his bones. At the same time Ajax screamed, and collapsed to the ground, twisting and kicking. Nate and Sabine got him up, propped his back to a tree while his head lolled and his white-rimmed eyes stared out in horror.

In the darkness Mambo Marie heard Papa Legba say, "That's a big evil being summoned to that house, folks." He had a very deep voice, and spoke in some African tongue that wasn't the Yoruba of Mambo Marie's childhood, but she understood it anyway. "All the magic from over the sea and down through time, being called up by those greedy evil men. Being called by their promise of a young girl's blood. You need strength from the earth. We're far from our home, on this new ground, so we need some spirit that grew up and grew old in this land."

He held out his chalky-knuckled hand to Ajax, and his teeth flashed like fangs in a dark grin. "Hey there, Manitou, big Bear from these woods! The Choctaw, the Natchez, the Houmas all gone, who used to worship you. But you still here?"

The Bear stood up from the foot of the tree, pushing aside the man and the woman who'd helped when the Bear had mounted into the man. He couldn't speak, being a bear, but he spread out his great shaggy arms and roared, and his eyes were like the red fire in the fields when they burned the cane-trash in winter.

Papa Legba laughed. "There's one Beelzebub gotta worry about! But Beelzebub, he clever. He the Morning Star, but he also the Lord of the Flies. He got the graveyard wisdom, drunk from the brains of all those that die and go to him. Our Bear gotta have somebody to guard his back."

"Old Beelze-prick not the only one got the graveyard wisdom," said a thin voice like wind through bones. "He's the Lord of the Flies 'cause he's the Lord of Stink, and he'll find that out 'fore he's another night older." Tall and thin the next god came forward, riding the frail old Ibo Dede whom he'd chosen for his horse. But Mambo Marie did not see Dede. All she saw was the jaunty skeleton in the long black coat, flaps of fat and gristle holding together brown-stained bones. He tipped his tall black hat to her and grinned—he could hardly help grinning—and whether there were eyes behind the spectacles he wore she couldn't tell, but if he'd had them he'd have winked at her. "Ain't that right, sweetheart?"

"No sweetheart to the likes of you, Baron Cemetery," Mambo Marie heard herself retorting. But it wasn't she herself who spoke, and when she flipped her shoulder at him she saw it young and soft and silken, and in that moment knew she had been mounted; she was being ridden herself by a god, and she knew who that god was.

Known by one name or another since the beginning of time, she was a god who'd act differently depending on her name and circumstances, like all women do. But like all women she was in her heart the same: the Lady of the Water, who kept boats from sinking; the lady of fruits and roses and bitter tears. Flirt sometimes and mother sometimes, and sometimes just an old cook who knew what the right words were. She said, "My child is in danger."

"Ezili," someone said, and looking down Ezili saw a woman she knew as Flavia kneeling before her, holding out a rosary to her. Ezili took it, and placed the brownish glass beads around her neck. She smiled down at Flavia.

"We get your daughter," she said softly. "We get her back safe and sound. The demon the white men summon with blood, it won't get her." She turned back to the Baron Cemetery, who was polishing off the rum on the altar. "You get those skinny bones moving," she said briskly. "We got work."

He came toward the house from the levee, and the wet grass hissed in the prints of his hooves. Wind blew around him, tainted with brimstone, dry and harsh with desert dust, and all the night was filled with the rank stench of carrion and the buzzing of flies.

Behind the three gods, lamps burned in the study of the Big House among the cypresses, the only light now that the clouds had covered the moon once more. Coming rain breathed in the air. Even through the darkness Ezili saw him, and though the horse she rode had never seen such a thing before—was shocked and terrified and crying out, *What the hell is that?*—the goddess knew. Indeed, the goddess had always known the Lord of the Morning Star.

The goatish flanks were unchanged, bones and filth tangled in the matted hair; the huge purplish genitals thrusting forth; the thick slabs of muscle under the crimson skin of his man half; the three horned and grinning heads. The demon as the blankittes saw him, the whites who'd written the rite now being spoken in the Big House to summon him into this world. Baron Cemetery remarked, "Smells as sweet as ever, don't he?" and the Manitou Bear growled, hating him as animals instinctively hate what is evil. The Lord of the Morning Star saw them, lined up before him on the lawn between house and river, and laughed . . . or perhaps it was only the echo of thunder, rolling in from the Gulf.

"And what's this?" he chuckled, and the lights from the house gleamed on the bloody matter that clotted his teeth. "Three little godlets, come to . . . what? To save some little bitch's life, so she can be fucked to death and worked to death by the time she's nineteen? Or will you be around then as well, to pull her arse out of the coals?"

"We might be," said Ezili. "We do take all kinds of forms. And we're generally always around." Her gesture reached toward the house, and the cabins beyond—maybe to the cities beyond those. "These horses we ride—these beings of flesh and soul and love and hate—they're stronger than you give them credit for."

He laughed again, scorning the bodies the three gods chose to wear, the tangle of human-beingness that shaped them and called them and gave them life. "I've known them as long as you have, I know what they're made of, and how they're made."

"And still they're stronger than you think." Wind stirred her hair back, a black Isis robed in the shadows of the sea.

"Maybe not as strong as you hope, Woman." He spat the name at her like a curse. "But you're too much like them yourselves to know that, aren't you? You think you can stand up to me? You're barely more than humans yourselves, and human in your hearts, squabbling and loving and hating—*pah!* I am one thing, and all in one: Lucifer, Asmodeus, and Beelzebub all three: Intellect, Senses, and Strength."

"Or Pride, Greediness, and Violence," replied Ezili. "But only half of those three things—the evil half, the half that fights only for itself. If we're like humans, good and bad mixed together as they are, then when we fight for good, we're fighting for something other than our own pride, our own greed, our own bad tempers. And that's why we say to you: better you go back to Hell, and leave that child in there alone."

Behind her Ezili was aware of the two men in the study, genuflecting ceremoniously before the altar they had raised. The traced lines upon the floor focused the powers of the earth and air, concentrated the wills of the men to evil, and fed that power to the thing on the lawn, the demon they had called. Ezili was aware—and through her, clearly and with a kind of remote attentiveness, Mambo Marie was aware as well—of twelve-year-old Helen lying naked on the altar, her breathing thick with the drug-induced dream in which she'd lain since Houbigant had seized her in the woods that afternoon. The magic that filled the night smelled of the girl's blood, and the blood smell seemed to glitter in the demon's six red eyes.

"Go back!" Lucifer laughed again. "Best you go back yourselves, if you don't want to be pulled into Hell with me yourselves, to do my bidding and be my slaves! You think the bodies of those fools who've called you into them can stand up against my power? Do you think their flesh is strong enough to survive my anger?"

"Do you think your spirit is strong enough to survive theirs?"

With a roar like the shattering of lightning the Manitou fell upon the demon, biting and rending with iron claws. Lucifer screamed, and tore at the Bear's flesh with his own great nails, ripping at ears and eyes and snout. Great snakes of lightning tore the sky apart around them, and were hurled aside by the Baron's hoarse cry—for it was true that the Baron was the Lord of Magic as well. Things half seen curled into life from the dirt all around them, snapping and gouging at the Bear's legs and back with poisoned fangs, and the Baron flung fire at them from his fleshless hand, chasing them away.

The demon hurled the Bear to the ground, but the earth of this country gave him back his strength, for the earth of this land was the dust of those who'd worshiped the Bear and had no reason to love the blankittes either. The Bear tore at the demon, though the demon's blood striped the fur from his paws and seared the flesh beneath, and the hurricane winds screamed in from the river and flayed them both. Whatever magic the demon would call forth, Baron Cemetery would hurl back: rain where the demon called fire to burn the Bear, and when the demon summoned snakes, the Baron called Damballah-Wedo, the Grand Zombi, the biggest snake of them all, to eat them up.

And meantime in the house the two men in their chasubles of black Italian silk walked back and forth and made signs of pentacles and crosses reversed, chanting words from Houbigant's books. Now and then they'd pause, and glance at one another, wondering at the delay, while all the winds of Hell howled outside.

At last the Bear hurled the demon back against the levee, and the ground shook under the blow. Lucifer climbed to his feet, wings torn, hairy flanks matted with blood. There was rage and murder in his glowing eyes.

"This is enough," said Ezili, and stepped through the trees. Flavia's rosary sparkled on her neck like jewels. "You two could fight all night until dawn, and though you'd probably kill the Bear's horse"—and her own and the Baron's, she thought, for the mental effort at channeling her own strength and the Baron's into the Bear was almost more than she could endure—"who knows how long your two friends inside the house are going to keep walking back and forth in front of that altar? You have your plans for them already. Just tell them to release the girl."

Lucifer bared his teeth at her, and spat bloody gobbets. But the three raggedy godlets stood as they'd stood in the beginning: the bespectacled skeleton, though his tall hat had been crisped by the lightning; the blood-streaked Bear with eyes like the Milky Way; the beautiful woman robed in the night sea.

"Your word," Ezili said. Though the demon will lie to men, he cannot lie to gods, even to minor gods who act like human beings much of the time.

"My word," Lucifer scoffed. "Keep the little bitch, then. She'll grow up to spit on your names."

Ezili smiled. "You think that will make her less our child?"

Baron Cemetery added, "How many of your most faithful servants swear every Sunday of their lives that they have no truck with you?" He doffed what was left of his hat and stepped aside, and Lucifer swept to the house like the dry killing wind that had been his avatar from earliest days.

The three gods followed him, and stood on the dripping gallery outside the windows, watching while the core of light formed up within the pentacle. The two devotees cried out in wonder as the light glowed in rainbow colors, and took the shape of the Lord of the Morning Star.

In his shape as Asmodeus he was exquisitely beautiful, girlish, slender, the image of desire. The part of her that was the flirt and the patroness of lovers warmed in Ezili at the thought of kissing those pouting rosebud lips, and she laughed at herself, admitting the desire but knowing what she knew. Of course Houbigant, as an adept of forbidden magic, must know too what the demon truly looked like, but in his eyes was the entrancement of love: Ezili knew he saw only what he wanted to see. Houbigant raised the knife he held above the throat of the drugged girl on the altar, and Asmodeus waved a negligent hand.

"Leave the worthless bitch go," he said, in a light voice whose very tone was music. "It's not her blood I want, but only proof of your love."

Master Henri looked uneasily at Houbigant. The adept inclined his head and said, "You have always had that, my lord."

"Then kiss me," smiled Asmodeus, "and I will reveal to you that which you sent for me to ask."

He spoke so sweetly, so winningly, that Houbigant stepped forward at once, over the protective boundary of the pentacle, and pressed his lips to the lips of the demon, who was, Ezili observed, extremely practiced in the act. Master Henri, on seeing his friend come to no harm, stepped forward as well.

"There," said the demon, in the wounded reasonable tone of one who has been accused of cheating at cards. "That's all that I ask."

"Like hell," murmured Baron Cemetery on the gallery, and Ezili nudged him in the ribs, almost putting her elbow between them as if they'd been slats of a fence.

"The great treasure which the pirate Teach took from the Spanish is buried on Point des Chênes, downriver from here, which was an island in his time," the demon said. "Since the landmarks have all changed I'll leave this with you, to show you where it lies." He took from Master Henri's coat pocket the young man's watch and fob, and detached the golden seal from the fob. He held it for a moment in one white, feminine hand, then gave it back, and Henri nearly dropped it in pain.

"It's hot!" he cried, and looked at Houbigant in fear.

"Not going to lose your nerve now, I hope?" purred the demon. "It's hot only by way of contrast, Henri. Walk the ridge that cuts off the tip of Point des Chênes between moonrise and midnight, and the seal will turn cold when you pass over the treasure. But you must be alone. Only you two must know of your expedition to the point. Tell anyone, even the slaves, and you'll have nothing to show for your walk but sand in your shoes. Agreed?"

"Agreed!" breathed Henri, blue eyes already shining with anticipation of a bigger house, a place on Lake Pontchartrain to which he could carry his bride . . . the dowry of the bride herself and the position in the world that such riches would bring. "No one will know where we go, Leonidas, but you and me!"

Hard times have their own rules. Greed does, too.

Perhaps it was because he'd kissed the demon, but Ezili saw a strange gleam spring to Leonidas Houbigant's dark eyes.

The three gods followed the men when they carried Helen out into the rain-soaked woods and left her; Ezili, and the Manitou Bear, and even the Baron stayed watching her until dawn. Then they slipped away out of the bodies they rode, and Ajax, and Dede, and Mambo Marie carried her back to the quarters. Ajax nearly had to carry old Dede, too, for the old Ibo was gray-faced and trembling. Mambo Marie put a poultice of mold and spiderweb on the unexplained cuts that marked Helen's arms, and on the wounds that Ajax bore: he carried the scars to his grave. Mambo Marie herself was exhausted, with strange memories that she might have thought were a dream, save for those parallel gashes that marked the face and back of her friend.

She wondered how she would explain those wounds, and her own exhaustion, to Master Henri, but she need not have worried. In the small hours of that rainy morning, Master Henri and Leonidas Houbigant both departed, leaving orders about the work to be done with Aristide.

It was Mambo Marie who told Ajax where to look for them, three days later when neither of the white men returned.

They found both men within a dozen feet of the deep hole dug in a thicket of laurel bushes on Point des Chênes. A broken oak box lay beside them, and there were dirty gold coins, ropes of pearls, jeweled cups, and handfuls of gems scattered among the tangle of shrub and weed. Master Henri had been stabbed in the belly with the short sword-cane that Ajax recognized as part of Leonidas Houbigant's luggage; enormous bloodstains in the sand showed how long it had taken for him to die. The pistol that had killed Houbigant was still in Henri's hand.

Foxes, buzzards, ravens, and ants had been at them both. The air was alive with the thick drone of flies.

Mambo Marie, Ajax, and old Dede stood for a long time on the trampled sand, looking down at the gold and the blood.

"The devil . . . put his mark on that gold," said Mambo Marie slowly, the dreams of lamplight coming back to her, of looking through the study windows at Master Henri in a black silk robe stepping across chalk lines on the floor to kiss someone whose face she could not recall.

"He did it to trap them," said Dede, folding his arms as if chilled despite the heat of the day. "He told them to come here alone, without no one knowing. He did it for spite. Maybe he did it to trap us, too."

They looked at one another, remembering or half remembering why the devil would have a spite against them, though they had only been the horses of the gods. There were old kings, Mambo Marie remembered hearing, who used to kill not only the messenger who brought bad news, but the horse he rode in on.

And they looked at the gold.

"Gold is freedom," said Ajax, and his dark eyes burned with a somber light. "How else could a man take a child and drug her, and hide her in his house, and later plan to kill her knowing that child's mother couldn't even ask to search? Just because he bought them both with gold." They were all remembering not only Helen, but Sabine's baby Hector as well.

The flies droned, singing their lord's name as they ate.

"His family'll know they was fighting over something," pointed out Dede, after a long time of thought.

"Then we leave half where it is," said Mambo Marie. "We leave half the gold, and all the jewels—we couldn't sell the jewels for cash anyways. But we hide our half of the gold, hide it deep. And in a year we bring out enough for Ajax to buy himself free. He goes to New Orleans, and a little at a time, so no one suspects, he buys out first one person, then another, whoever in the quarters needs it first and most."

Ajax glanced at her sharply, and for a moment she saw in his face the wanting to take it all, the thought of what he could buy for himself and do for himself with that much, and what were the rest of them but slaves anyway?

Then he laughed, and touched the half-healed claw rakes on the side of his face, and shook his head, throwing the thought aside as he'd thrown down the Lord of the Morning Star. "Be a long time for the last man on the list," he said. He glanced at old Dede as he said it, and at the cook, as if he guessed that neither would live to be bought with that gold.

"Greed and hurry is what started all this," said Mambo Marie. "You see what that gold cost Master Henri and Master Leonidas, Manitou Bear." And for a moment her smile was the smile of the Lady. "You're the only one who'll be safe holding it, until it's all turned to good again."

"A year's a long time. How do we be sure no one finds it before then?"

"Wherever we put it," said Dede, "we write Papa Legba's sign over it, the sign of the crossroads: the sign of gates and doors and things that are hid. If it's in our best interest that the gold stay hid until we can use it for good, Papa Legba'll know that, and keep it safe. If not—if the mark of the Morning Star still lies on that gold—it's better out of our hands. We can earn our freedom some other way."

Those that got bought out by the money over the years were Helen and Flavia and Sabine and Sabine's mother and four of Sabine's children; Judas the barrel maker and Cressy the maid and Aristide the valet, and

Mambo Marie herself, who sold pralines in the market in New Orleans until she turned a hundred and one. Ajax married Flavia, Helen's mother, and had his own work gang on the wharves of New Orleans, and with the money he made from that he bought free three or four more. Though the girl Helen, as Lord Lucifer had said, became a good Christian and turned her face away from the African gods that had saved her, still Papa Legba kept a good eye on the gold, for it was never found.

Master Henri's brother-in-law, who took over Bellebleu Plantation, might have been a bit profligate about some of the remaining gold and the jewels that were found by Master Henri's body—he gave expensive gifts to everyone in his family and sent his daughter to school in Europe—but a good deal of it he put back into the land. He proved a more patient man than his predecessor, and less greedy. Nearly a quarter of what was found by the bodies on Point des Chênes he simply gave to the Chapter of the Cathedral in New Orleans, where Master Henri and Leonidas Houbigant were buried, with orders that it be used for perpetual masses for their souls. Ajax sometimes went to the masses, on his way to boss his work gang on the levee, but he personally doubted whether that or anything would be enough to remove from their souls the kiss of the Morning Star.

# SHE'D MAKE A DEAD MAN CRAWL

*Gerard Houarner*

I t wasn't the black man, or the white one. It wasn't me before I came to be what I am. But she doesn't care. She's past caring about anything at all. That's what breaks my heart. Nobody thought I had a chance with her before, but now that she's gone, even I know it.

There's nothing worse than a dead man with a broken heart. That's past blue, long into black.

I woke up at the crossroads. The old one, where the Choctaw trace cuts across the slave trail from what's left of the Blanchard Plantation to Miller's Creek. Mosquitoes were out, of course, but they weren't biting. Just buzzing, like they were mean from hunger. The last slice of moon was balanced atop the sycamore, what they used to call "the hanging sycamore," and the stars were soft in the humid air. The cloud or two passing through said nothing about rain.

She was there. With the dog.

The dog spoke first.

"What do you need to learn?"

"What am I doing here?" I asked. The last thing I recalled was sitting at my table early Sunday morning, before even the reverend was up rehearsing his sermon, with an empty bottle in front of me, and a dirty glass. There were cards on the table; but Trey was long gone, and I still hadn't picked up his last hand to see if he'd bluffed me or not. I hadn't heard the crickets all night, though they'd been going. When they stopped, the quiet nagged me. I heard a sound at the window. I started to turn, letting the breeze chill the sweat coming down the side of my face. Then it got dark and cold.

A bottle with no label stood full between the dog's front paws. Beside the dog lay a dead rooster. A silver fork, glittering just a bit in the thin shine of moonlight, stuck up from the ground between us. The dog stood, knocked the bottle over, gnawed at the rooster. That's when I could tell it was a male.

"He isn't here to learn," Phebe said. "He's here to do what I tell him." Her voice was honey in my head. It filled me with hope and yearning and more happiness than all the liquor I ever drank. I wanted it to be day so I could see the smooth, polished brown of her skin, the fall of her blouse over her breasts and the hug of her skirt around her hips; so I could see all of her, not just the shape of her head, the hint of her face, as she crouched at the crossroads next to the dog.

I wanted to move across the way to feel that skin, cool and warm at the same time, silk and stone, and maybe kiss it like I'd never been able to, and even take her in my arms and hold her to me, like I always dreamed of, because waking up to her made it seem like that was what was supposed to happen next. I'd always felt like I belonged to her, even if she'd never paid me any mind before now, but this was the first time I ever felt like, maybe, she belonged to me.

"Good evening, Phebe," I said. I would've asked after her family, and how things were going for her at the factory, but my voice didn't sound like my own, and talking made my throat hurt.

I couldn't feel my heart beating, which it normally did fast and loud whenever I was around Phebe, and breathing took an effort that hardly seemed worth the trouble. I thought maybe I was sick, and had wandered out of my bed, and Phebe had been walking a new dog and found me. Maybe, in the best of a fevered dream, she'd been home taking care of me, and had woken up to find me missing, and had gone out to catch me in my sleepwalking, and found me passed out at the crossroads.

"Shut up," she said, and turned her head. One of her hands went to her face, over her mouth and nose. The other swatted at the mosquitoes. I wanted to kiss the fingers over her face, taste the salt of her sweat and the dirt from her labor. What there was to see of her eyes made me want to jump into them and keep falling, forever.

"He's not giving the crossroads the right question, anyway," the dog said, glancing up at me. "And he hasn't been here enough times to earn the right to ask. Sorry. Got confused, with the two of you here. Usually it's just a guitar or a pair of dice *one* of you is supposed to bring to me to learn about."

I remembered dogs shouldn't talk, and what people said about the crossroads, and about the rider, or the Black Man, the devil, or the dog that came when you'd gone to the crossroads enough times at the right hour. I didn't want to think about that, especially with Phebe there, and me having her all to myself. "Can't you be nice to me?" I asked. I should've gotten up to sit beside her. That's the kind of thing a man does, after a question like that. But I was tired.

"I don't have to be nice to you, anymore. I just have to tell you what to do, and you're going to do it. Because that's what I need."

I looked to the dog, but he said nothing as he licked blood from the rooster. I noticed a few more bodies, maybe a couple of squirrels, maybe a cat, a little up the roads, both High and Low, like they'd been thrown there after being hit by a truck. Or a poor try at something that shouldn't have been done.

"Now I want you to get over to the Gateses' place, and see if you can find anything from this list." She took a folded piece of paper from a pocket in her skirt and held it out.

I found the strength to go over to her. I let my fingers glide over hers before taking the paper. She was so warm, I wanted to lay my head down in her lap and bury my face in her belly. She snatched her hand away as soon as I touched the paper.

"Why don't you go get them yourself?" I asked, watching her stand. "He likes you."

194

"I already tried," she answered, brushing herself off. She stooped to gather a few things—jars and tin cans and satchels—that had been hidden behind her, placing them in a bag hanging around her shoulders.

I felt a chill at the sight of her belongings, like she'd plucked them out of me.

"Doesn't seem likely he'd keep anything from you that you wanted, knowing how much he likes you." I admit to jealousy. Alex was family, distant though it was, and he had land and an education and things to offer a woman like Phebe. He didn't care about their differences, like most people might, and with what he had he could take her to places where people might not care about what separated them. If he really wanted to.

"It's not him I want; it's what he's got," she said, short and hard. "Get to it."

Hearing her say she didn't want Alex took the edge off of the way she sent me on. People don't talk to each other that way, not around here, not even across the lines that keep everyone where they think they're supposed to be. I hardly held it against her that she never once called me by name. Of course, I realize now that she'd probably worn it out right before I woke up.

It took nearly all day to get to Alex's place. Walking was slow, and I stayed off the roads because the sun was hard on my back and the cool under the trees was inviting. I cut across a field or two, but no one saw me. I waited to get hungry, but I never did, and I thought I'd come down sick, which explained why I moved so slow.

I didn't bother knocking on Alex's door. I knew where he kept the key, so I just let myself in—after ripping out the telephone wire. His wife screamed and went for the telephone, like I knew she would, but when he came down he took the phone from her and hung it up as if he knew what I'd done. Or maybe he knew I didn't answer to no man-made law.

His kids gathered along the upstairs rail, and he sent her to take them in the bedroom and wait for him to come up.

By the time they were gone, he'd drifted over to the front hall closet where he kept a .22 rifle, a shotgun, and a machete.

"What are you doing back, Henry?" he asked.

"I've got an errand to run."

The sun was coming in through the sitting room windows, filling the first floor with golden sunset that made the Blanchard Plantation antiques scattered here and there look like they were in a museum postcard. The house wasn't part of the original manor, of course. It wasn't anywhere as big, except for that grand portico with tree-tall pillars, and nowhere near the Indian mound on top of which the wreck still stood, surrounded by land that couldn't do anything but break the plow because there was too much sorrow in it. Alex had just built the place to look like it might have been a shadow of what was, and he'd bought and restored furniture from the time to complete the look. I think his affection for Phebe was a part of those same traditions he liked to keep.

"You shouldn't be here," Alex said.

"Heard that before. I just need a few things." I still didn't sound like myself, but talking hurt a little less. And Alex understood me; that was clear.

"You're looking in the wrong place."

"We're still family."

"I don't have no gandy dancers or Pullman porters or submarine cooks on my side, Henry."

"We used to get together. If I recall right, my side helped build this house. Funny as that may seem."

"You know, there was a day when your dad would've been strung up for what he did, and maybe your ma, and maybe even you."

"I know that, too, Alex. I never asked anything from you."

"Then what are you doing here?"

"Phebe sent me."

Alex sagged like he'd taken a bullet, and suddenly he looked a lot older and fatter than people thought he was underneath his wrinkle-free pants with the creases that never faded and the polo shirts that never showed him sweating. That gave me a chance to take a step, so that by the time he'd opened the closet and put his hands on the .22, I had my hands on him. He put up a fight, but not much of one. In the end, he went down hard, and I didn't feel a thing.

I went through the house and collected the things Phebe had on her list. Most I found in his den, a couple in the garage, in a trunk where he kept things from when he was young. Phebe had been younger still in those days. I studied the pictures for a while, caught up in how small she looked next to Alex.

I had to go upstairs for some personal items. The wife poked out a .45 and shot me as I passed by in the hall. Once. I staggered back, nearly went over the rail. But I didn't bleed. When she saw me still standing there with a hole in my gut, she closed the door. Slow. It shut with a snick, loud in the quiet after that big bang. I went on about my business, but in the end, I had to go into that master bedroom, where the wife and kids were hiding and whimpering.

I had to bust the door down, but I left them alone.

I got back to the crossroads that night. The walking went faster, in the dark, without the sun and the heat wearing me down. Phebe was waiting. The dog was gone, but I felt something at the back of my neck, like a lost gust of Canadian air that dipped too low and lost its way, or a farewell kiss from a wandering Cherokee haint, and I figured that dog wasn't far.

I gave her a little bag with all the things I'd taken: papers, a video and a couple of audiotapes, pictures, a computer disk. What was on them, I didn't know or care. Except for some of the pictures. I would've liked to keep one or two of them, if only to imagine myself in Alex's place. But my hands wouldn't let me keep nothing. And besides, the ragged suit I wore had its pockets sewn up.

She put everything in a plastic bag, and the bag went into a hole she'd dug in the middle of the crossroads. She told me to cover it up. It wasn't much of a hole, so it only took me a minute. Then she gave me another list and said, "Randall."

The name carved a hollow in me big enough for another heart. Alex was one thing, hurting me because he was blood, and because he had things I'd never have, which he used to get ahead of me to Phebe. But I didn't have an answer for Randall. He got to her because he was just a better man. He was the closest thing she had to a true lover, and everybody knew it.

I went right to it. I didn't think of sleeping until I reached Randall's cabin, off a dirt road, between some birch and hickory. He wasn't home, so I got what she needed, except for a single little thing. I thought of waiting for him to come home, but the urge to get what she wanted done took hold of me, and I went out to look for him. I was down by Miller's Creek, watching the water run by, a little brown from all the dead leaves along the sides. A cottontail jumped out with a rustle. The trees were thick, the air quiet.

"I just like to see them run," Randall said, coming out from cover. He wasn't out shooting rabbits with the load he was carrying.

I didn't say a thing, only looked at the piece of red flannel sticking up out of his trouser pocket.

"Damn, she really *can* make a dead man crawl," he said, staring at me hard, seeing who I was for the first time. He slipped the shotgun out his arm cradle, put his finger on the trigger.

"What are you doing with those conjure bags, Henry?" he asked, glancing at what I had tied to my belt.

"Taking them, Randall."

"And what are you doing out here?"

"There's one more I was sent to get."

The look on his face was the same I'd seen when someone too full of whiskey would come up to him at the bar and say they'd find his stash, or hijack his shipment, or cut a better deal with his buyers. I don't know if they ever told him that when no one else was around. "You know, she's the one that killed you," Randall said, slow and even. A warbler started up, stopped just as quick, as if realizing it was interrupting something it wanted no part of. "She laid a foot-track trick at your doorstep, Henry, and sprinkled Goofer Dust all around your house. I know; I helped. Of course, she's not really the patient kind to wait for the poison to work. Not after all these years. I guess, not after all those broken promises she was left with."

"I never broke any promises to her. I never got a chance to make any."

Randall squinted, like a ray of sunlight had come through the canopy and pierced his eye. "She was the one at the window that put a bullet through your heart."

I guess I knew that, but hearing it still made me make a sound like a slaughtered pig's last grunt. "Why?"

"You were a damn embarrassment."

"No more than you, or any of the others."

"We knew our place, and hers. You're the one who showed up everywhere, anywhere, at any time, just to get a look from her, like nobody could see the black side of your ass when you wanted to be white, or the white side when you had to be black. You were the most pathetic thing I ever saw."

I took a step toward him, setting my sight on that last bag he was carrying. "Maybe she believes I can be more use to her dead. More use than you alive."

"Yeah, there's that, I guess. I sure wouldn't be fetching for her, dead or alive."

He took his shot after another step. I fell down, got up, but he didn't fire again. I don't know if it was the sight of me carrying almost all his luck and protection on my belt, or what I looked like after he blasted me, but he didn't bother with the gun again. Instead, he drew that bowie of his and ran up to me, getting me good between the ribs on the first try. It wasn't until I lost some fingers on that edge that it occurred to him he might get farther by chopping rather than cutting or stabbing.

But by then he was bleeding and in some places broken, and pretty soon the bowie came out of his hand and he couldn't pick it up anymore.

I took what he was carrying out of his pocket without bothering to see what kind of mojo hand was inside. It hadn't helped Randall any more than his other mojo.

I had to wait a while for Phebe to come to the crossroads that night. It was pitch black under the sycamore, and after a while I wondered if I really had died and this time not woken up. But she came along, lighting her way with a lantern, and she took what I gave her and buried it with the rest, having me dig and cover up, this time. When I was done, she handed me another list and told me to go to the graveyard.

She didn't shine her light on me once. But I got a long look at her, and that brought me peace while I worked, like I'd gone to paradise and didn't ever have to leave it.

The cemetery wasn't a long walk, since she meant the local churchyard, where the graves were marked and men and women and children of our times rested, not the slave graves or the Indian burial ground deep in the woods, where hardly anyone went, and never at night. I didn't catch a chill walking over the graves, but I had to wait until dawn to read the names, so I could gather up the dirt from under the proper headstones and put them in envelopes she'd already marked. Lifting that many headstones, I could see why Phebe had had me do this job. One grave I came across had been dug up. I only saw the first name on the headstone before I understood I didn't have to be bothered with it and moved on. There wasn't a Henry on her list.

That was a long day waiting for Phebe, and it bled into a longer night when she didn't come. I put the envelopes in the hole, digging with my bare hands, skinning them raw until they should've bled. Then I sat under the sycamore and listened to an owl hoot and to the brush rustle with an occasional opossum or whitetail. I might've smelled some of what was growing around me if my own stink hadn't taken up all of what was left of my nose.

Somewhere, a steam whistle blew, though there hadn't been a train on the rails making that sound since before I was born, except for tourist runs, and they didn't come out here.

An old man came up on me. Or rather, he was there one minute, out of the dark. I could see his white beard and hair, the skin stretched over bone, the toothless smile, all clear in the dark; and I could see through him, too. He sat down next to me and started talking about the river, the boat he worked, and how the rails put them all out of business. I tried to ask him a question, but he talked right through me. I asked his name, but he didn't answer. After a while he faded away, and another took his place, this one crying instead of speaking, pointing at a thick limb from the sycamore stretching over the Choctaw Trace coming up on the crossroads. Then someone else took his place, ranting and preaching and throwing brimstone words at someone who wasn't there. And then another, screaming in terror until I felt the cold of his voice touching the back of my neck, and another chanting in a tongue I couldn't recognize. And more, drunk and shot and burnt and one or two laughing at something I felt sure wasn't funny. None of them answered me, or seemed to even know I was there, except for the one who came to stand and stare at me, or at the spot I was sitting in, with envy, or in sorrow.

When the sun came up, the visitors stopped. But a knocking started up close by, and I thought it was Death at the door come for me. But it was only a 'pecker getting an early start.

I thought about where Phebe might have gone, and all that came to me was her going to Randall's cabin to help him clean up and mend. I wanted to cry, but I didn't have the tears. She was probably with someone else I might have to fetch something from soon, anyway. I ached to see her, but I didn't dare go by her house. I didn't like the feel of the sun on me at all, and I didn't really want to see what she was up to if I did catch her at home. At least I knew what to expect from my heartache.

The day went by quietly, and no one came until later, after nightfall. Phebe came by with her lantern again, under a gentle rain, and when she saw I'd done the burying she gave me another list and told me, "Mrs. Wilkerson."

As I left the crossroads, I thought someone was watching me, but when I turned Phebe was already gone. None of the previous nights' visitors had come back. I figured it was the dog.

I took my time strolling through the damp, coming up on places I felt were familiar, but never could remember. Like they belonged to someone else.

Mrs. Wilkerson watched me come out of the dusk, a shotgun in her hands, her back to a sunset made brighter by the blanket of clouds still overhead. But she didn't shoot me when I stopped in front of her. Her dogs watched from the doorway of her trailer. They didn't come out or bark. Horses worried in the barn.

"Looks like Miss Phebe did get the devil to raise you," she said, looking up at me from underneath those big, white brows. Her head was covered in a hat, and she wore jeans and boots, like she'd been out riding. The wrinkles of her face were caked with dust.

"It wasn't the devil, and I don't think the one who came did anything but show her a few things."

"It doesn't matter. She lost her soul, like I always knew she would."

"Don't think she lost anything, just became more of what she always was."

"Don't contradict me, boy. You're lucky I let you on the property—

you know I'd have shot you if you'd taken after your father."

"I know. I know I work cheap, too."

"Don't get fresh with me, either. It's this very behavior that's made me be particular about who I let on my property. I don't want any of your kind playing tricks on me."

Randall's words came back to me. I knocked the gun out of her hand while she was still thinking of what to tell me next, like the fence needed mending or the stalls cleaning. I must've run into her while I was going through her trailer, because when I turned to leave she was laid out on the floor, a dog on each side of her. When I stepped over them, she was still breathing. The lock of hair was the last thing I took.

Phebe kept me waiting another night and a day. The woods weren't so quiet this time. Men and dogs came through the crossroads. The dogs wouldn't have any part of me, no more than Mrs. Wilkerson's animals. I lay down in the rot under the trees, and no one could see me.

The men came in every size and, in a sight I'd never seen before, every color. Black and brown and white and red and even yellow, all of them calling out my name and Phebe's, hunting the both of us. I don't know where they all came from. I never knew about, or maybe I never saw, all their kind getting together like that before. Not at any bars I went drinking to. Certainly not working together. It made me think Phebe had gotten around, and men were scared enough of her, and me, to put aside differences to help each other survive.

I always thought the world came in two colors, and that the only woman I could ever love was Phebe, and that there was nothing after life but death. I guess I was wrong two out of three times. I didn't add any more thoughts I might've had, like the one about Phebe one day loving me back. At least we were together in a lot of people's eyes.

She came late the next night, once the posse had moved on. This time I'd waited for the shovel to dig out the hole and bury the satchel of china, picture frames, a canister of funeral ash, and the lock of hair. The moon was out, and its light filled Phebe's eyes until I thought she might've fallen from the sky. I caught sight of a turn of her thigh, through the dress that was nearly as ragged as my clothes. She hadn't cleaned herself or done her hair in a while, either. She looked like she was working harder keeping herself alive than I was staying dead.

It almost made me glad I was already dead, that look of hers. It almost made me wonder if I was already in the place she was heading, and if that meant I'd have a chance with her, after all, if she came passing through where I was after getting everything she wanted and was grateful for my help.

She handed me another list. A long one, on a couple of folded pages. "Zilla," she said, and I knew I hadn't started working hard, yet.

"So it *is* you," Zilla said when I came through the front door to her wood shack. She was sitting by the window, where she'd seen me coming, probably for a long time. I'd had to stay low and move carefully, but Zilla had a way of knowing where and when to look for what was likely to show up. "I thought they were calling the dog on me when some boys came through here looking for you and told me how busy you'd been. Don't you know any decent folk?"

"Sure I do, but they don't know me too well." I could've said, *And Phebe has no business with them, so it isn't likely they're going to get to know me anytime soon.* But didn't. Of course, Zilla knew all of that already.

"Where've you been hiding?" she asked. Candles burned all around her, filling the room with smells that were sweeter than me, and with shadows that kept moving and got on what was left of my nerves.

I got stuck staring at her for a while, like I was a child again staring across a fence at a carnival resting for its next show. Her long, pleated dress showed only her dusty ankles and moccasins as she shifted in her rocking chair to look up at me. Her blouse had no sleeves, showing off long, bony arms covered halfway to the elbow with bracelets. An old conch belt was slung over her hips, and her nation bag hung low, resting in her lap. Silver glistened from her belt, rings, bracelets, and the necklaces intertwined around her neck until they looked like a single piece of braided rope. Bits of turquoise, garnet, ruby, amethyst, and amber glistened like colored dew among the beads and bones of her jewelry, and against the folds of dark cloth. Her smooth skin didn't say anything about her age, and the gray hair tucked back into a braid lied about her years, as well. It was her eyes—large like an owl's, sharp as an eagle's—that said she'd been around for quite a while.

She was what Phebe wanted to be, but the girl hadn't stayed with Zilla anywhere near long enough to know how to carry it off. And she didn't have the years of living, and watching others die, behind her, either.

The silence between us gave me a nudge. "I was at the crossroads," I answered her, like I was young again and it was her business to know.

"Is that right? What did she ask to be taught, to raise the dead?"

"I don't know. She didn't say."

Zilla stood gingerly, but I didn't believe she was that delicate. The look she gave me made me stand ready for anything. "You're a little stuck between worlds, aren't you?"

"Always have been."

"Yeah, I guess so." She shook her head and shuffled past me to a counter, jingling from the Mercury dimes in her nation bag to her silver bracelets. She poured a drink from a jug into a tin cup, took a sip. "What this Phebe's doing is way beyond what anyone's thought or dared to do before," she said, after licking her lips. "If there's a devil coming to the crossroads, it's her. And she's the one taking souls."

"You taught her," I said, with a streak of meanness. "Maybe you're responsible. Or jealous." I didn't regret the words, no matter what people said about angering Zilla. I couldn't help but think of what might have been, if Phebe hadn't learned what she had, if Zilla hadn't felt the need to pass along what she knew after all her years.

What was she going to do to a dead man?

Zilla finished what was left in the cup, licked her lips, turned her back to me. "I don't envy what's coming to her," she said.

And then I felt the cold that was my flesh and bones, and darkness closed around me, again, and this time I could smell the earth, hear it tapping on my coffin as the diggers filled the grave, and I could feel the worms kiss and caress me, their mouths as eager and tender as the lover I knew only in my dreams.

Zilla put the cup down. Turned. I expected her eyes to be burning and her lips to be shaping more terrible truths for me to understand. But there was only a tear, which she wiped quickly, as if surprised by its appearance. She pointed at my hand. "Is that for me?"

I gave her the list. She read it, smiled, then broke into a laugh like she'd finally seen a fresh bit of foolishness after a long dry spell, then gave the paper back, shaking her head from side to side. "She doesn't want to miss a thing, does she? Some of that's in the back. I'll go get it for you while you start on what's in here."

"Aren't you going to try to stop me?"

"Why should I? The only way to stop that woman is to give her what she wants."

Zilla went through the back door, which opened to the hillside cave hidden by the shack.

I found a duffel bag, emptied the few things in it on the floor, and started loading up on what Phebe had asked for. It took a while to find what I could. Zilla had accumulated a lot of things during her life.

I got stuck going through a book called *The Weary Blues*. Poems. Langston Hughes. 1926. My hands tingled when they touched an old 78, with an Okeh label declaring it was Mamie Smith's "Crazy Blues." Then there were the stacks of labels for Zilla's brand of mojo oils and sachet powders. Supplies were tucked away everywhere: bottles of Florida Water and Hoyt's Cologne, tins of sulfur, rattlesnake eggs, sugar, salt, red flannel and yellow silk, John the Conqueror and devil's shoestring root, a packet of two-dollar bills, a bag of lodestone, a collection of charms in a chest, a bag of rabbit feet.

I did find the buckskin shirt, and the set of carved wooden masks with feathers and opossum fur and carved bone teeth, a red kerchief, and the piece of wood with the handprints I recognized were made in blood.

"That's from my grandfather's house. From when they burned it down. He was a freedman." Zilla tossed a canvas bag at my feet. "I'll come claim what's left when she's done."

She frowned a little at the duffel bag when I tied it closed. "I'll be taking that back, too, when this is all over. That was my son's, when he came back from Korea."

I didn't ask whatever happened to her son.

Phebe didn't come to the crossroads that night, and neither did anyone else. The moon was out, reborn and growing stronger. A dog howled in the night. I lay there with my back against the sycamore and waited.

The next night was the ninth since I'd come back, by my count. The dog came before Phebe.

"What do you need to learn?" the dog asked. He sat on his haunches in front of me, tongue lolling.

"What?"

"You sat at the crossroads for the appointed time. That means you need to learn something. What is it?"

"Don't you have to have an offering?"

The dog came up to me and sniffed my leg, crotch, and up to my neck. I gave him a rub behind the ear. "Seems like you're dead enough," the dog said, then licked me. "What do you need to learn?"

"I want Phebe."

"I can't teach you anything about that. Sounds like you already know everything about wanting her."

I thought about what the dog was asking, about what Phebe

might've asked to know and about her hand in my dying and coming back. I told the dog what I'd always wondered about: "How can I make her love me?"

"Don't you want to learn the guitar, or how to gamble, like everyone else?"

"Not really."

"I suppose there's no accounting for what a dead man might want to know how to do. Though I did think you might be interested in seeing if I could teach you how to live again."

"No. I want to know how to make her love me."

The dog trotted back to the middle of the crossroads. "I can do that," he said, tail wagging.

"What's the price?"

"You know that's not how it goes. The learning is its own price. Bring what you took from the old woman out here."

I got up, dragged the duffel and canvas bags after me. "What's your name?"

The dog bowed his head, yawned. With a shake of his head, he said, "Prometheus."

I set the bags down. "That's a big name."

"It's someone else's. Like devil. Might as well call me Mercury, or Legba. Names don't matter out here. Come on. Dig up what you buried."

I looked at the broken ground, and at my hands. I started digging, and when everything was laid out next to Zilla's belongings, I looked to the dog.

"You've got to use what you've got," the dog said.

I looked down at myself. "That isn't much."

"Not that. What you got for her. That's what she wants." He tapped the edge of the hole with his paw.

"What can I do with that, other than give it to her when she comes for it?"

"If you want, I can show you."

"You're going to have to do that."

"Like this," he said. He took a picture in his paws, and suddenly they moved like they had fingers, and he folded the picture into a tiny square and tossed the morsel into his mouth. He chewed a couple of times, swallowed.

"Neat trick," I said. "Better than talking."

"You try."

I took Zilla's buckskin out of the duffel bag, folded it as tight as I could, pushed it into my face. Of course, I couldn't do anything with it. Even worse, flesh kept flapping off my fingers from all the digging I'd done.

The dog walked over to me. "Get down here," he said. He put his paws over my hands. I don't know exactly what I did, or how a dog can show a man how to do something. I remember my fingers working like they were on strings and someone was pulling them along. After a while, I was able to fold the shirt some more, until it was no bigger than a pea. I popped it in my mouth.

The shirt had no taste, and it didn't fill me at all.

The wood mask was a lot tougher, but once the dog got my hands working right, I was able to bring it down to the size of a nickel and swallow it without a splinter. I finished most of Zilla's things, but stopped at the red kerchief, which I tied around the dog's neck.

He gave me a look that made me want to take him home and give him food.

"Nobody ever thought of doing that before," the dog said.

"You never met anyone like me before."

"That's a fact."

And with that, the dog got up and left me. "Hell of a night," I said, maybe to the dog, maybe to the moon. Or maybe to all I'd had to eat.

When I was done, I filled the hole back up and sat down with my back against the sycamore. When I was alive, I know I would've been good for a nap.

When Phebe showed up, she didn't stop at where all the things she'd had me get should've been buried. She came straight to me with eyes big as saucers of spilt morning coffee. She put her arms around me like I'd always dreamed she would, and those big eyes turned wild, like an animal's feeling its slaughter. She gave me kisses; then soft, tender licks; and finally nibbling little bites. I tried to give back what she gave, but she wasn't interested, and I let her have her way. We rolled around on the ground, with me trying to work both my pants and her skirt off while she kept herself busy with that mouth of hers. And I can't say I minded a bit.

Until she sank her teeth into my cheek and tore off a chunk of my face. She came back for more, and I threw her off of me. Again she came, and I hit her hard enough to sit her down. But Phebe wasn't sitting down for long. She showed her teeth, and that Cheshire grin closed in on me before I could get out of her way. She grabbed my arm when I swung it again, took a knuckle from my hand.

I had to kill her. She didn't want me, just the things inside me, the ones I'd eaten, the things I'd become. I choked the life out of her as she tried to devour my arms and hands like they were made of sugar and honey. She slumped against me when it was over. She didn't join me in the place I was, the spot between life and death where she'd put me, like I'd hoped. She just kind of slipped past me, and went someplace else.

So it wasn't the black man that she wanted, and it wasn't the white one, either. It wasn't any of those other men and women she'd had me visit, and it wasn't me before I came to be what she made. It was the me that I made myself up to be in the end, full of the things she sent me to get, that she came to want for whatever power she thought she'd have over the people who made and owned them.

Phebe doesn't care anymore about what she learned to do at the crossroads or all the things I brought back for her or what she was going to do with them. Neither do I. She's past needing and wanting and caring about anything at all.

All I got left is my broken heart, now that I know there's no chance. My heart's all over the ground, in bits and pieces, melting into the earth like the rest of me, feeding the brush and the trees and the squirrels and mice and birds and bugs that come along. Some days I feel I should crawl around to find those pieces of my heart, thinking maybe one day I'll find them all and put them together and be a man again. A living man.

But my crawling days are done.

I'm still at the crossroads, the one hardly nobody ever comes to, underneath the sycamore. Not even Zilla, though her things are leaking out of me, along with all the rest I ate, now that I'm fading away. I don't mind. I got a taste of what I needed, learned everything I wanted to, and more. Lately, I've noticed the magnolias and wild azaleas are blooming again, out of turn, and the woods are filled with the songs of kites and tanagers and hummingbirds and flycatchers. In the shade, with the scent of fresh blossoms and the songs, it feels a little like paradise. The moon passes by, and sometimes I think it'll keep going and I'll never see it again because it's heard this story so many times. But it always comes back for a listen, like it can't believe a dead man really can tell a tale. The dog paid a visit, once. He gave me a lick, but didn't offer to teach me anything, and I didn't ask.

When he left, I understood he wasn't the devil, or any of those other names he mentioned. Never had been. Those were just names folks put on mystery. He was just the one that comes along to show us all the way.

To show each of us our own way home.

# COOKING CREOLE

*A. M. Dellamonica*

**A**t seventeen, it was music. Guitar.

Then, at twenty-four: speechmaking. Rabble-rousing, his mother had called it. Binding a group of listeners—big, small, middling—with his voice. Inspiring the local grocery clerk to dump her useless husband. Selling roses in boxes on lonely street corners. Swaying a strike vote at a fish-packing plant on the East Coast.

Stupid, dangerous skill. What had he been thinking?

Reinventing himself again at twenty-seven, he took up gambling. Rake in the green, he figured, and the rest would fall into place. For a time he was about nothing but the ins and outs of cards and billiard cues, the snap of dice in his wrist and the chuckle of roulette balls going around and around.

Now Steep Dover had finally figured out what he wanted to do with his life.

At thirty-five, he looked close to fifty on his bad days, with taut, light-catching strands of white wired through the close-cropped black hair against his scalp. The lines on his forehead and around his eyes were prematurely deep. Instead of wearing the slow erosions of age, he'd been fractured by upheavals: heartbreaks, riot cops. When he faced the mirror in the mornings, he saw himself icing over. Only when he smiled—or so women told him—did he look like the young man he still was.

Tonight, though, he felt childlike: vitally awake, keenly excited, and more than a little scared.

He was picking his way along the side of Vancouver's Lougheed Highway to a crossing point that looked—except for the whizzing trucks and fast commuter cars—like it should have been out in a country town somewhere. Squeezed between a shopping mall two hundred meters back and a scattering of machine shops up ahead, a barely paved and rutted lane transected the busy Lougheed. An abandoned gas station occupied the northeastern corner of this crossroads, unconvincing evidence of human occupation in a wilderness that was otherwise nothing but traffic noise and curving hillsides of blackberry brambles. Narrow grooves of trampled grass bracketed the road—a path for anyone on foot who had business there, though what there was to bring an ordinary pedestrian into this no-man's-land, Steep couldn't say.

The intersection had no traffic light, no sign or marker, not even a pullout lane for the gas station. A pocket of remoteness in the midst of an urban bustle, it sat in the industrial wildlands between the Lougheed and its sister highway, the Trans-Canada, its gas station dark, its blackberries fat and oiled over with fuel emissions, its pathways abandoned and yet never quite overgrown.

It was just after nine. The mall had closed, and the sun was setting; on the road, commuters were headed east to Coquitlam and Port Moody. Higher up, crows were commuting, too—sharp charcoal animations, they glided by the thousands across a palette of darkening blue.

Steep sat on a halved oil drum. It was still warm, heated through the sunny day that was now passing into dark. He took an Anjou pear from his pack and chewed it slowly, only distantly aware that it was a little tough, not quite ripe.

Up above, the crows kept coming, a first sign of the world bending into the wrong. The birds should all have been roosting by now, coating the flat roofs of the warehouses lying to the east like a lumpy black blanket.

An hour or so before midnight, he opened his backpack again, laying out its contents with a care usually accorded to surgical instruments. A cooking knife first; then a stewpot, a book full of Creole recipes, a small sack of groceries, and a separate, smaller bag filled with okra. Moving deliberately, he selected an onion and began to strip its skin.

Overhead, the crows were slowing.

Flapping and flapping above Steep Dover, they were suddenly going nowhere. They flew in place over the crossroads, an ever-more-dense flock that chipped away the sky. They blotted out the thin fish-scale clouds, the peeking stars behind them, and the rising moon. The thin amber glow of the city reflected back at him off their bellies, leaving Steep to chop his vegetables in a faint haze of orange light and the glow of headlights cast by the passing trucks and cars.

He squinted at the book, sliced peppers, added things steadily to the pot.

Traffic continued to blur past, creating a hot yellow streak that lit the road. Beneath the tires, its surface seemed altered—not asphalt anymore but cobbled, bumpy shale. Steep kept cutting, glancing up occasionally, awakening to a distant awareness that his backside was growing sore. He noticed that the grime on the windows of the gas station formed patterns, delicate lines tracing out the shapes of piled bones. The meridian between the east- and westbound traffic lanes— sidewalk-wide, just barely—curved upward in a smooth marble hump. A signpost thrust upward from its tip, a metal tree trunk with no foliage and viciously sharp edges at its crown.

The whisper of a road that crossed the Lougheed in this place had become a strange mixture of foreign material; mixed in with the chopped-up bedrock were shards of fossil, dead barnacles, shaved bits of rust, ground lumps of chalky drywall, broken strips of zippers, fragment upon fragment of crumbled eggshell, knots of ginger root, broken bolts, child-sized teacups, bits of wire, and plastic knobs and switches.

At midnight the motion of the crow wings above brought a hot wind downward, swirling the road dust into tiny whirlwinds, raising ghost-shapes on the road. It gusted down at Steep in short panting breaths.

The blackberry bushes, silent barbed guards of the sides of the highway, rustled loudly.

Steep froze in the act of reaching inside the okra bag as the gnashing of brambles intensified. Berries rolled off the bushes, bouncing gaily onto the pavement to get squashed by the humming tires. Their juices pressed in instant fermentation, making blackberry cordial spiced with dirt and motor oil. The fruity machine-shop odor made him want to gag. He focused on the feeling of the feathery green pod in his hand, on the tattered cookbook and the sack of food—and tried to ignore the puddle of liquor spreading blackly to cover the crossroads. Rippling, smooth, it washed out and around the thin meridian, lapping at its edges like the calm leading edge of a flood.

Then, suddenly, a shuddering sound of brakes and a truck paused in front of him. Creaking, it slowed almost to a stop; then its engine roared and it sped away, taking the rest of the traffic with it.

It left a man behind in the intersection.

He was nine feet tall, with lacquered crow feathers for skin and shiny bird eyes. He wore a tailored suit, a stylish jacket woven from blades of autumn grass. His tie was a puzzlework of automobile air fresheners: lemon, pine, cherry, and new-car scented felt, all crushed together into silk and emanating chemical perfumes.

The new arrival stood, arms crossed, the expression on his face most distinctly a glare. Meeting that gaze, Steep felt his stomach melt to acid. His lips curled back from his teeth, and it took all his will to bend them into a smile.

No response—just that hostile, steady gaze.

Clumsily he stuck the knife into a thick wedge of potato and lifted the potful of vegetables. Tucking the Creole cookbook under his arm, he started forward.

As he reached the edge of the road a motorcycle whipped into view. Oblivious to Steep, it bounced into a nearly invisible groove in the pavement as it roared past. Blackberry cordial washed over him in a gravel-laced spray, coating him from toes to midthigh. A warning? Black Man telling him: go on home, learn to cook the old-fashioned way?

But he couldn't do that, not with a head full of music, pretty phrases, and card-counting.

Steeplechase Dover stepped into the crossroads.

Sticky wet steps: one, another. Excuses were marching in his head, pleas and arguments. *This time it's something I love*, he would say. *This time, I'm settling down.*

His gut burned, unconvinced.

He'd cooked short order in a dozen cities before starting at Muldeen's place. Why he'd ended up staying he hardly knew; there was something in the old woman that unnerved and delighted him, an atmosphere in her restaurant that made every diner a house guest, every meal a family gathering. But Deeny's feet wouldn't hold her up through a day anymore. She needed a partner, someone to run the kitchen. Steep wanted to do it with the ease—the soul-gotten genius—that came to him when he was playing the guitar or drawing an inside straight.

An unromantic dream, maybe, but more honest than the other boons he'd begged.

He was close now, craning up to meet the pitiless inscrutable eyes. Holding the book and the stewpot out, he opened his mouth to speak. Then something hot and big raced past him on the road. The splash of cordial soaked his back, and the words dried on his tongue.

"Steeplechase Dover." The Black Man's voice was a gnashing of small rocks. "Why do you waste my time this way?"

Another answer rose to his lips; another car whizzed behind him. This time the rushing beast made contact, a bumper that felt like bone kicking out the backs of his knees. Chopped vegetables bounced across the road as he fell hands-first, losing the pot. The potatoes went airborne, propelled like soft shrapnel by the edges of oncoming car tires. They struck Steep in a quick hail as he braced himself on the rise of the meridian. He was drenched; thick toxic cordial tickled through his hair. A spreading bruise on his chin was haloed with potato mush.

His companion bent, rescuing the kitchen knife, and then began sharpening it on the tines of the signpost. "Do I look like a community college?"

Steep managed a muttered negative without getting sideswiped again.

*Shhh-shhing!* Whisk of the knife against metal. The cookbook had gone flying too, and now one taloned toe tore loose from its fine Italian shoe, flipping through the book's juice-stained pages.

"Creole cooking," he said in disgust. "Aren't you from Michigan?"

Steep pulled himself closer to the signpost. "It's the last time."

Traffic snarled back and forth in response to this, roaring eighteen-wheelers with no clue he was there. Steep clung to the post, holding himself on the curved and slippery meridian, and shouted again. *"Please!"*

Bird eyes regarded him. Something sideswiped the stewpot, setting it clanging back and forth in the road, bouncing off car doors. It whizzed past him as he clutched the slender steel tether, conscripted into a deadly game of road tennis.

What could he do? Dripping, stinking of cordial, Steep started talking.

At first it was the usual breezy bullshit, tales he'd told about himself a hundred times in a dozen cities. Half-truths about having to get out of music because people were using him. About how his speechmaking landed him in jail and in hospital. How the gift of gambling was a disaster if you lacked the nerves.

It all came down to nerve, really. The more he had, the less he'd been willing to lose.

And it all came out pretty, because he'd learned to speak from the best source there was, and though the deadly missile of the stewpot came close to hammering him off his perch a dozen times, it never seemed to make contact. He laid out a patter, lost himself in it, and all the while the Black Man sharpened the cooking knife, the trucks roared past, and waves of berry cordial lapped at his ruined running shoes.

Then he thought he was done, and it turned out he couldn't shut up.

"I never fit anywhere," he heard himself say, and that, suddenly, was full truth. "I grew up in Michigan with parents from Georgia, and I hit school talking funny. I couldn't lose that accent fast enough. Then we'd go to Granny's in Habersham and I was the next thing to a Yankee."

"Boo and hoo, Steep." The eyes were pitiless.

"I was always too something. In music: too political, too apolitical, too loud, too soft, too slow. . . ."

"Too greedy."

"In the union: too soft, too chicken, too conciliatory."

"I say flighty! If you'd just stuck with something!"

"I was a kid. I didn't know what I wanted."

"That's all you have to say to me? You chose wrong; you didn't know where you fitted, and now you're up here—"

"Northern boy with a Southern accent. American among Canadians, black among whites," he murmured, appalled at himself. What did this have to do with anything—and why did it hurt so much to say it? "Always just a bit out of place."

"But now you belong somewhere." Black Man's voice rang skeptical.

He shook his head. There were no words for the feeling at the restaurant. "You know how when you're putting a jigsaw puzzle together—"

"Son, I have good uses for my leisure time."

"It's going hard, and you're frustrated, so you stick two pieces together because they look right. They almost fit, but there are these tiny empty spaces where the knob meets the groove. . . . And you mash them together and pretend, for a second, that they work. But they don't, and sooner or later you have to admit it."

"But you put in the right piece, it's effortless. This restaurant, it's . . ." He stopped, uncharacteristically at a loss for words.

"So take yourself to cooking school."

"There's no room," he said. "I wake up hearing music. I try to think about recipes, and suddenly I'm putting words together to describe how the food's going to taste. I'm supposed to be making roux and instead I'm reckoning the odds on finding a two-yolked egg in the next shipment."

"And whose fault is that?"

He shook his head. His chest ached, and every inhalation seemed too short to make up for what he was pouring out.

"This is another whim, Steeplechase."

He felt a heavy, fearful weight in his gut. "Can't be. I can't keep moving around aimlessly. I have to stop. I want to stop."

"I hope you're sure," the Black Man said, and for a moment his voice was almost kind.

*I do too*, he thought. It was too easy to imagine himself packing up again in a couple years, and the thought made his knees waxy, while his upper body went lead-heavy and strained to bring him down.

The blackbird toes started picking through the few remaining chopped vegetables on the road, choosing a bit of this, a bit of that.

*Ssshhh sshiing!* One last swipe of the knife. And *clang!* The stewpot, red-hot with friction, a ground-level meteor burning itself against the velvety summer air, rebounded off an SUV. It rattled like a pinball on a bumper through the wheel well of a tiny Ford hatchback, and then bounced up to smash hard against the windshield of an oncoming semi. From there it came at Steep like a spiked volleyball, red-hot and lethal. . . .

But the nine-foot-tall man caught it just millimeters short of his head. Steep had flinched away from the blow as it came; now he felt the heat of the pot up near his cheek, smelled his whiskers scorching and curling.

"One last gift, you say?"

"I swear," he replied.

"You've tried to throw off everything I ever gave you," the Black Man said. The traffic had dwindled again, and his words seemed to doppler in the sudden quiet. "But it could be that I'm fond of you. Could be I'd overlook that."

Steep was seized by an overall shudder. He tightened his grip on the post and swallowed.

Whistling, the Black Man dropped a fat handful of onion into the glowing pot, sending a healthy kitchen stench rising into the air. His feathered hands pulverized cloves of garlic to liquid. He raked the small collection of rescued vegetables off the road into a pile, adding them to the brew. Hot roux, Cajun napalm, dribbled off the backs of his wrists as he took up the bag of okra and chopped it up fast, sending white seeds everywhere.

The avian eyes blinked once. "Didn't you bring me anything else, Steeplechase? Can't make gumbo without meat."

Squeezing the post with his knees Steep pointed, shakily, to the grocery sack with its cargo of hard-shell crabs and chicken necks, sausage and oysters.

Instead of retrieving it, the massive head bent close. "Got some cooking secrets for you, son."

Fear had set his teeth chattering, and he kept them clamped as he answered. "I'm listening."

"Buy local. Check the produce yourself. Never settle for crappy tomatoes. And always, always . . ."

"Yes?"

"Marinade." The knife seemed to come out of nowhere, slicing through the remains of his clothes like a razor blade through paper, unzipping Steep's stained and sticky skin from his left collarbone to his right hip. His flesh dropped open in a flap, bloodlessly, revealing the redlubed workings of his body. Heart, lungs, stomach, pulsing and healthy.

He pulled back involuntarily, and the taloned foot seized his neck, tossing him on his back into the road, pinning him supine on the wet alcohol-soaked asphalt. A station wagon zipped out of nowhere, spattering cordial into his exposed body cavities.

Steep's shriek was cut off by the crushing weight on his larynx.

"Let's see . . ." The red-hot pot clanged down beside his head, sending up clouds of sweet cordial steam. The knife hovered far above him; the feathered hand that had held the pot, now freed, poked at his innards with heated fingers.

Then the knife dipped in, out. A grub-sized hunk of meat was displayed in the Black Man's hand. "Haven't been playing cards much of late, have you?"

He tried to swallow, couldn't. He could see his organs reflected in the bird's-eye gaze.

In and out again, and another nugget came up on the knife, this one plumper, lined with one nice streak of fat. "But you have been on the guitar some."

The grip on his throat eased. "Deeny likes it." He chunked out the words like he was vomiting ice cubes.

"Audience of one." Disgust in the voice, and blackberry stench roiled over Steep's face in angry waves.

Then the Black Man's expression gentled. He reached inside Steeplechase Dover and cut out a fat chunk of prime meat. "And here's the gab. Who you wasting that on? Bankers? Health inspectors?"

He didn't answer.

The Black Man juggled the three hunks of meat, dicing them in midair and letting the pieces fall into the gumbo. A rich meaty smell rose from the cooking pot, and he raised it to his feathered lips and drank deep.

Belching, he curled up the knife like an accordion, tucking it gently into Steep's opened body. Then he took a handful of leftover okra pods, rubbing them fast between his hands until they were a wet, silvery paste. He glued the incision shut with it, fixing the skin into place with blackberry thorns.

"You're a hot-shit Creole chef now," he said. "Happy?"

"I . . ." Still pinned, he couldn't look away. Instead, he fought against a series of retches.

"Don't try to thank me. Cooking's a gift, the last gift. As for the rest, you're keeping what you've tried to throw off. Understand?"

He managed to shake his head slightly.

The Black Man glowered. "I'm gonna have a little of this stew tomorrow. And the day after. And the next. It's up to you to make sure there's meat in my pot."

He chilled. "If you mean . . ."

"You saw where it came from." The face was close to his again. "Sing songs, Steep. Roll dice. Talk up a storm; get people whipped up; start trouble. Do it all; do it often; do it up fine. Don't oblige me to come looking for something else I can cut from you."

Breath whistled out of him. For a ludicrous, brazen instant, he was even about to protest. How could he do everything—speak, game, sing—and still keep a restaurant afloat? Gambling alone would ruin it sooner or later. . . .

Then he remembered where he was, lying on the eastbound yellow line of the Lougheed Highway, with talons clamped around his neck and the sound of approaching traffic humming in the road beneath him. The backtalk withered in him, died.

Belching, the Black Man lifted Steep to his feet, setting him lightly beside the sack of crabs and chicken parts in the gas station parking lot. He turned his back on the shaking, patched-together supplicant. The traffic steamed back into full visibility, howling past indifferently.

Maybe if we keep everything in Muldeen's name, Steep thought, find me some way to own the restaurant without owning it. Shaking, he bent to lift his pack, and by the time he'd straightened up the Black Man was gone.

Good thing I gave up on asking him to teach me to box, he thought, remembering the single day when that had seemed like a sort of answer. The thought brought first a sickly laugh and then another case of the heaves. He retched dryly over the oil drum, once, before forcing himself to move.

"Things to do," Steep muttered. Sing. Gamble. Shower. He smelled like a head-on collision between a bachelor party and a gathering of student engineers. His clothes were stained and resinous, and the blackberry thorns in his chest itched and tickled, pushing against the places where the Black Man had carved out his dinner.

But he still couldn't seem to leave the crossroads.

Then a startled cawing drew his eyes upward. The crows frozen overhead were caught in a moment of night-blind confusion as they eased into renewed motion. Flapping madly for the roosts in the warehouse district, they drew back from the night like a curtain to reveal the sky and the stars.

Mouth tingling with a sudden and intimate knowledge of Southern flavors, Steep took first one wavering step and then another in the direction of the sleeping shopping center.

# WHITE MAN'S TRICK

*Eliot Fintushel*

**O**nisabe Oduduwa went walking with a white woman on an August afternoon. Her arm circled his waist, they said. The heat was like ravens' beaks pulling through one's pores—I remember the afternoon. Before a shop window on Sixth Avenue,x Onisabe paused to mop the sweat from his face. His eyes rolled up; he made a slight choking noise; and then, so they said, he collapsed to the pavement.

According to the papers, he had been wearing a dashiki and a round blue cap decorated with images of leopards. The police who cut through the gathering crowd found the leopard cap but no body. Yes, the black man had collapsed. But was he dead? Maybe he had just sneaked away. The police rang phones, knocked on doors, collared informants, and excuse-me-sirred diplomats, but the earth seemed empty of him. The white woman, too, had vanished.

Onisabe Oduduwa had been known in the theater world as a promoter and performer of the works of his countryman the famous Nigerian playwright Wole Soyinka, famous for his concern, "fundamentally African," says Compton's, "with 'numinous' boundaries: those between the human and the divine, between life and death."

It was a time when the issue of blackness was white-hot, and the blackest damn thing a sensitive person could be was white. It was a time when young black men burning with intelligence and curiosity would approach white men in train stations and ask them without preamble, "Why do you hate black people?"

But once, at a bus stop in Albany, I met three young black men who told me enigmatically, "You're ready." They promised to show me "what niggers do downtown at night" and gave me the address of a poolroom.

Late the next night I walked through the Albany ghetto looking for them, a white boy in the yellow light of streetlamps with broken globes—light, shadow, light, shadow—walking down hot summer streets dangerous to white boys. Two children wagging their legs over the side of a glider on a porch above me called, "Hey, honky, the fuck you doin' here?" The whole street watched, catcalled, laughed. That's how it was all the way to the poolroom, where my guides to the underworld, as it happened, were not. "Hey, honky, the fuck you doin' here?" I ran home through steaming moonlight cannibal shadows and the smell of blood.

Me, I still thought it was all one place, mind. I still thought we were all one smell, one blood. I always thought that. It's what I always said. I just had had a bad night, is what I figured. It wasn't me, really, I figured: that's what kind of a time it was, was all.

Next month there were riots.

My friend Clarence told me about Onisabe's disappearance over the telephone from Cleveland. Clarence was in Cleveland, and me, I was in the cheap hotel in lower Manhattan where I had holed up after Regina, another Onisabe find, had dumped me via perfumed stationery:

*. . . It's like not being able to breathe in, dear Larry—dear, dear Larry—but only out. With you I'm only half a person and emptying more by the heartbeat, by the breath. . . .*

Yes, I was right in town, but Clarence had heard about Onisabe's disappearance first. Though farther away, he was closer to Onisabe. He had had a deal going with Onisabe to put on a new play in the converted garage that housed his small black theater company in Cleveland.

I'd called Clarence to tell him about the new power I was developing, the power to open my hotel room window from a distance of six feet and six inches, just by looking at it a certain way and thinking a certain thought. Then you didn't have to climb over the edge of a sullying distance, see? You were as if back-to-back with the thing, whatever it was and however "far away," see?

I almost had it down. I only needed to complete this thought with a tiny essence, a flavor, a mood, a lost chord, like a floating astigmatism that, by its very nature, flees one's focus but is near, near—if only I could complete that thought, then . . . everything. It had something to do with water, travel by water, something like that, see? Concentrate. I was close.

What kept throwing me off was the fear of intrusion, I told Clarence, like a fly buzzing around your head as you try to read or reason: there was a door connecting my room to the neighboring one, and me, I kept breaking my concentration to look at it, even though I knew it was bolted, see? I heard movement in the connecting room, and my mind, pressed as it was to an extraordinary purpose, played tricks with it, like air leaking from a teeny-tiny crack in an overfilled tire. See, my mind put the neighbor's random sounds into a beat, a beat, a beat—an illusion, surely, but it broke my train of thought.

Clarence interrupted me before I was done explaining this to tell me that our friend and director Onisabe was dead. Dead, he said, sure of it.

Me, the first thing that came to my mind at the news of his vanishment was the Möbius strip I'd shown Onisabe, a thing with no boundaries. That had been backstage in an Albany theater. We'd been doing a regional gig in the troupe he'd hired me and Clarence into. I gave a sheet of paper the half twist, taped the ends together, and said, "See? Only one side." I traced the line that proved it, all the way along both "sides" and back to the beginning without picking up the pencil.

Onisabe frowned and shook his head. "You know what we call that where I come from?" (English, to Onisabe, was a drum to beat, and he struck it as he would.)

"No, what?"

"A white man's trick."

It's a funny thing that what put me in mind of it to show to Onisabe was a postcard I'd just received in the mail from Clarence nearly three years after he had sent it. That postcard had been all over the universe, seemed like, before it caught up with me care of the theater in Albany, New York. It was sealed inside one of those big transparent envelopes in which the United States Postal Service sends you items that have been mangled in the rain, snow, sleet, hail, or gloom of night. The thing inside was spindled and crushed so you couldn't tell one side from the other. Smashed into the fibers along one edge, there seemed to be what they call a tête-bêche: two stamps, one heads-up and one heads-down, both ten-centers, connected.

I pried the half-pulped card apart as carefully as you would coax a Band-Aid from a baby's pink bottom. Within its calyx (Or had this been the outside originally? I mean, top. I mean, bottom.), dog-eared, water-stained, scaly as with eczema, was a blurry mass of postmarks, one over the other, like those time-lapse photos of the midnight sun. Careless how they stamp them, swiftly completing their appointed rounds, obscuring the text. Stamp them; stamp them at every angle, upside down and even front to back, it looked like, but that must have been the ink fading through the soaked paper. You can't really stamp something front to back in the paucity of dimensions the good Lord gave us.

But me, I knew it was from Clarence all right. A word here and there told me so: "upchuck . . . Coney Island . . . Loop-de-Loop. . . ."

Me and Clarence had met at the Equity office in New York—he there from Ohio, looking for high-profile gigs—and we hit it off somehow. I liked being with the dark man—there has always been some healing feeling for me in seeing black and white conjoined. Well, Clarence was not black, really. I mean, he was the same degree darker than the mean as I was lighter. I guess I wasn't white exactly, either. Who is? It's a continuum, isn't it—between every two shades, always another? That's what I always thought. There was solace, anyway, in being near my other-shaded other, carried by his slipstream, buoyed on his joie de vivre. It emptied me nicely, like a spirogyra draining gametes into its conjugant. Free at last!

We had taken a train to Coney Island, where we scarfed some foot-long hot dogs with everything. Then we went on the Loop-de-Loop. Sinuous, neon-lit, blinking, it looked like a gigantic knot, parallel steel ribbons between which cars screamed—tracks above, tracks below—and people screamed too, losing up for down. Clown faces decorated the upper and the lower tracks. The carny, like a hooded executioner, clamped the bar down on our laps, and we began by ratcheting in through the mouth of a Fratellini whiteface. Clarence was grinning and gobbling handfuls of popcorn from a crinkly yellow bag. "You're gonna love this, Larry." I watched the clown faces creep, then roll, then zip past, blending and gyring. Periodically our car slowed for a corkscrew turn, and I saw the same clown faces leering down at me or up at me. I think that ride must have been a Möbius strip, two Möbius strips, in fact, with the cars in between. That would explain how top and bottom traded as we moved around the track. In that setup, between the nested strips, when you come half the length of the combined tracks ("roof" and "floor," call them, but who knows?) you find yourself in the same spot, but upside down.

That would explain it.

But me, I'm not entirely sure, because pretty soon I felt woozy. I leaned out over the edge of the car and motioned frantically to the executioner. Actually he was a lanky teenager in a muscle shirt and cutoffs with a Yankees baseball cap shoved down over his eyes. He shrugged: we had passed the point of no return.

So I vomited. As Clarence shoveled it in, I heaved it out. I let centrifugal force push the masticated hot dog meat up out of my stomach and flinching esophagus ("Wrong way! Wrong way!") into the neon glow between the tracks. Shamelessly, I moaned.

Loss of support is one of the few fundamental instinctual fears.

When your orientation is screwed up, anything can happen—even the protoplasm knows that. Any minute, you can die. You don't know if you're eating or being eaten, for Christ's sake. My vomit was everywhere, spattered across the blasted-ass grins of the Augustes and the Pierrots and the Zannis above—or below?

Clarence held my shoulders from behind as I heaved. It should have steadied me. Instead, I felt that it was Clarence pushing the guts out of me—you know how crazy nausea can make you, walking that tightrope between thoughts as you strive to keep your stomach on the right side of your mouth. Me, I felt that he was trying to slip between my bones to replace my insides with his own. Blood pounding in my temples, wheels rattling and grinding bebop earth to sky, I kept shaking him off, and he kept grabbing me again in his misguided kindness.

Afterwards he led my green-gilled ass onto the beach. We sunned ourselves and looked at women. He wanted to take me to the Apollo that night, but me, I was wasted. My sense of balance and of life returned slowly. Clarence disappeared up the tubes to Jersey, where he said he had a girl who owed him something, leaving me in some dark underground hole wondering which staircase led up to the street and which went down darker to the uptown trains.

I keep going forward and backward, and I can't keep track. Or the track I keep is fooling me. It's like using a map printed on paper so thin that sometimes you read it straight and sometimes you read the flip side by accident, because it's showing through the front, backlit by the sun. Now the road you read is in another city entirely, but it seems to connect to the first one, a kajillion miles away. Front to back to front to back, forward and backward—all depending on the weight of the bond and the hour of the sun.

That's the sort of thought that opens windows for you at a distance of six-foot-six, joining outdoors and in. That's what I filled my mind with—and sashes shuddered, see? That and one thing else—something dark and far away, an ocean away, centuries away, not to be wrapped and ribboned in white-boy words. Me, I couldn't say what exactly, but this rang a bell: travel by water.

I keep going forward and back.

Another time, we were driving together to New York City, me and Clarence, two poor actors, each to his separate New York City host. It was just for a lark on a black weekend (no shows, I mean) out of Schenectady.

Clarence had just facilitated a confrontation group where the idea was to teach white people what it meant to be black. "You've got to face yourself, you white people. You've got to face your hatred and your fear of the black man, Larry. You've got to share everything, expose everything—exorcise it, see?" Clarence's eyes were as bright as branding irons lifted from the fire.

"Show me how, Clarence. Tell me what to do." We were driving into the Lincoln Tunnel at that point, a very long, dark tunnel that goes under the Hudson River or the East River or some river: they all empty into the Atlantic anyway. Why do they give them different names? They all join there, at the Atlantic, and they all loop into the mountains and up through the sky, steaming, clouding, twisting down again, and if you try to say one part is separate from another, you're a damn liar. You can't find a border between them anywhere, except what a person's mind has made, and for no reason.

Clarence gathered his thespian nimbus. In the staccato lamplight from little sconces along the tunnel wall, I could see his face harden into a mask of histrionic contempt. "Fucking white asshole!"

"Black bastard!" I tried. My heart wasn't in it. I'm not all that great of an actor, I confess; frankly, it surprised me when Onisabe took me into his company. I never understood why he did, why he took me or why he took Regina either. There were plenty better.

"Jesus, Larry, that the best you can do? You want me to believe that's the depth of your racism? Bullshit, it is! You got your race hate with mama's milk, white milk, and your mama got it from her mama, back and back to your slaving ancestors. You hate our guts and you know it."

"Shut the fuck up!" Passion, when it's called for, can make even a bad actor look good for a moment. Me, I couldn't quite tell whether I was acting or not, and it made me nervous.

"That's more like it, Mr. Nicey-nice. Now we're seeing the face of the beast. Fuck all you honky hypocrites and your phony morals! Yes, yes, you can be as liberal as you like, money in your pockets and smiles on your faces, with all your noble causes, only we darkies better not invade your neighborhoods and schools and families, no, no. 'Don't step over onto our side.' "

"Come on, Clarence; there's only one side." I always said that. Me, I'm no scrapper.

"Dammit, Larry, you gonna do this thing or not?" he yelled. We were underneath the river, in pitch black but for the headlights and the bullets of light from along the tunnel wall. "Come at me, you white sonuvabitch."

"Okay. Okay. I hate you. I hate all of you jungle bunnies, you niggers. I hate your black asses. Damn you!" Funny to hear myself say words like that. "Damn you! You think you know it all, you goddamn black fucks, but you only know what we let you know. You're nothing but bones in black bags, and baby, you are dispensable. Me, my side's the side that counts. Plenty more where you came from, little prick. Talk about my mama and my mama's mama back and back? Your mama and your mama's mama back and back go back to a pen where they hunched and sweated and stank till a white man bought them, pulled their black asses out the cage door, and showed them how to live." It was dark. The acoustics were funny in the Lincoln Tunnel. I didn't know how loud I'd been shouting until I saw the shock strobing across Clarence's face. The mask was gone.

Something bright, dense passed between his eyes and mine; compared to it, our brains were milkweed fluff. Me, in the dark of the Lincoln Tunnel, I was black. But Clarence's teeth and tears sparkled white. We didn't say anything else to each other that weekend except "Good-bye," and back on the tour upstate, it took us a couple of weeks to stop being polite to each other.

It was via the Actors' Equity office in New York, one of the many places Onisabe had held auditions, that Clarence and I had found our way to the Albany company, but Regina was a local; she had never done any professional theater until Onisabe recruited her. Regina, it must be emphasized, was white, was white—was very, very white—unit albedo, and I'm not talking about her albinism now. She was completely reflective; nothing penetrated at all. She had no room inside for anything more; she was already struggling at the edge of sanity. Overwhelmed by her own nervosity, she taught everyone around her equanimity and calm—one learned these skills or else one did not survive Regina.

It was like being afloat on a tipsy skid. Guy moves right; you've got to move left. Guy leans in; you've got to lean in too, to compensate. Otherwise, the skid tips and you all fall in. That's what human society is all about. In the presence of a firebrand, you tone down your rhetoric. Save it for when you're with someone less dangerous. A crazy person in the room makes everybody else very sane—very, very sane. It's a sensitively balanced system, human society. People are not so much individuals as valences, roles, variables in an equation that we are constantly called upon to balance. You could be this or you could be that, up the scale, down the scale, all around the clock, depending what the other guy is.

Unless you want to get wet.

It was the year of Biafra. White Regina wanted to help, of course. She saw the footage of starving babies. Those ugly sores moved her. The videotaped crying and moaning echoed in her mind, stained her awareness, constantly threatening to push her right past the firewall of her nervosity into the land of genuine psychosis. She found some measure of relief in activity: Regina was the regional organizer of the food drive to save the Biafran civil war victims. She knew the genocidal Federalists were moving in, the evil Muslims of the Nigerian northlands versus the gentle Christians of Biafra.

Onisabe laughed. Ha! Ha! Very big ha! It was very white of Regina, of course, to help the poor black Christians, but did she not know that the Federal leader was himself a good Christian? That the rumors of Nigerian genocide were circulated by the French, who were cultivating Biafran partnership in exploiting oil reserves there? And these ships of Regina's loaded with merciful edibles—the food was rotting at the harbor. The Biafrans were lactose-intolerant. They didn't know what to do with the canned vegetables. Spain was an enigma to them. Post Toasties were unfathomable. Ha! Ha! Stupid Americans! Onisabe knew it wasn't generosity. Onisabe knew it was all political. Very big ha!

Regina shook with rage, unable to speak. Me, I almost thought she would faint on the spot. Her shoulders dipped with every breath: a little kid squaring off against the big guy. She clenched and unclenched her fists. She stuck her snoot right in Onisabe's, then fell back to lean against the wall as he laughed.

Clarence jumped in. "The Ibo—you don't know it, with your Coca-Cola and your Motorola and your blinky board on Times Square, ha—you don't know it here in Ah-merica, but the Ibo and the Ibibio invented all your Ah-merican magic. Black men invented all the white men's tricks. Invented them, tossed them off—what did they care, fertile as they were, like the rain forest?—tossed them off like shavings from a whittled doll, and where they fell they took root. The black men don't care; they got a jillion more, like the rain forest, snakewood and resurrection lily and begonias, zoom, curl, climb, and twine from where those shavings hit, and the white men cry, 'Look what I've made here. Wonderful!'

"The Ibo and the Ibibio, they made Biafra; they seceded to protect their magic. Priest magic. Oracle magic. Aro magic men with bloodred palm oil torches down in the gorge of Aro Juju, bristly and thick as a bitch's cunt! And the talking drums—*Boowong! Boowawawong! Boowongongong!*—and the dried gourds painted like missionaries' skulls with their white brains shriveled to a bead and rattling around inside—sh-sh-shake shake shake! Sh-sh-shaky-shake . . . !"

Dirty and daft as were his words, me, I knew this to be Clarence's choirboy voice. He was parroting these words, secret teachings, terrible things the African African had told the mere African-American, things Clarence reverenced and couldn't help crowing, as American Jews of that same epoch aped the Hebrew sabra dicta of Israeli Jews. Gone topsy-turvy now was the old Negro social order, inspired by Massa, in which lightness of skin was coin in the kingdom. "He so black he purple," I used to hear black kids joke of other black kids, spurning them. "I don't hang around with those black folks," a black man told me once, long, long ago, trying to befriend me. "I've got all nice white friends." In the new order, upside down and backward, blackness was nobility, pedigree, authority.

I could feel all that in Clarence's grinning sycophancy, even before Onisabe, eyeing me sidewise as a sign to the brother, said, "Shh!"

Cowing the taller man. Clarence folded like a blushing geisha. What, I wondered, had Clarence been saying that Onisabe didn't want shared with white foreigners?

Worried about her, I pressed Regina's hand, but she didn't look at me. She was staring at Onisabe. Her hand was cold.

One day, listening to Onisabe's foreigner ironies for the umpteenth time backstage at a Catholic school in Guilderland, Regina exploded, and I defended her as vociferously as my white-boy tonsils would allow. Me, I was half twisting toward Regina at that time, so to speak. I felt a mystic kinship with her: a past life acquaintance, I figured. I was beginning to feel her charm and trying to make her feel mine. Somewhere in the middle of all that, I found her hand in mine. God bless international politics. Clarence came in alongside the Nigerian and nearly had his Equity card taken away for the kinds of noises he made right up to curtain time—and that audience, boy, having heard our ruckus, was stunned and blanched, and we managed to milk neither laugh nor sigh from the lot of them as we snarled our lines at one another, doubling meanings all over the stage and house.

One black night at my place in Albany, before he disappeared on Sixth Avenue, Onisabe pulled open the neck of the loosely knitted sack he carried—orange, purple, blue, and checkered with hints of faces that never quite coalesced, as if it were the sea of inchoate moods, airs, and passions around which, anciently, human faces formed. He reached into that polychrome throat from which he would sometimes pull a handkerchief, a chocolate, a driver's license, a knife, and this time pulled out a marionette.

It was a rude jointed figure with the dark of the tree still upon it, whittle scars on all its limbs. Its head was a Janus figure, two faces back-to-back. One was elaborately tattooed, dense with fine lines like those pen-and-ink hatch lines that are supposed to make white black, but these made the dark wood whiter. The opposing face was simply black, black. Both were faces, me, no one I know would want to be caught in: too simple, too raw, too revealing of the soul, faces bone-deep. They were the faces to which our faces compose when all the civilization, like silicone from a teat, drains out: grooves along a single brutal grain and, in between, dumb dark plateaus; yours, mine, anybody's, all the same under the lineaments of culture.

Onisabe danced the thing. Me, I would have expected a pro thespian like Onisabe to play the duet: the marionette as two characters relating to each other, turn and turn again, like a mime playing Pantaloon and Harlequin, changing masks as he chases behind a screen.

But no: it was just the same dance, now the black, now the white, clacking lead-weighted heels against the tabletop while Onisabe worked six strings—knuckles, knees, head, and tailbone—and punctuated: "Ha! Ha! (very big:) Ha!" Strange to say, this angered Clarence. "Onisabe Oduduwa, you can't make a white man dance like a black man."

"See I do!"

"No. No." Clarence vised his face; centuries of racism torqued the handle; starved black flesh rotting on the bone in the nauseous holds of slave ships—flesh of kings, sages, beauties, simpletons, no matter— black souls raked and rotted by white overlords nearly convincing them of their nonexistence while granting their Negroes marvelous gargantuan phalli, as if to compensate. Grimacing so painfully his facial muscles seemed to grind and squeak, Clarence hit the table, making the marionette jump (but Onisabe kept dancing it and laughing). "No. A white man won't dance that way.

"Everything about the white man is different, Onisabe. Sorry to have to spell this out in front of you, Larry, but the white man talks different, sings different. I can tell in one second flat when I hear a singer on the radio if he be white or black. I can tell it from the horn he plays, from the sound of his breath, or the squeak of the Dobro on his guitar strings. I'm telling you, the white man is different through and through. Fucks different, dies different; everything about him is different from us black men. We're from older stock, deeper down, see?" He took me head-on now, burning eye to eye, struggling up a frayed rope ladder from the rank dark hold, beating back demons—me, who wanted to subtract his soul and add it to the length of his meat. "You Europeans have history—*his*-story, see? But we have *my*-story—mystery."

Then to Onisabe: "You, dammit, dance it different back or front. You know that 'We the same' shit just honky jive."

"Mystery, ha ha! Very big ha, gentlemen!" Onisabe stuffed his marionette back into the magic bag. "Yes, the black man and the white man are completely, utterly different, like left and right. And like left and right, gentlemen, are we not utterly the same?"

"No. It's deeper than skin, deeper than blood, deeper than bone, deeper, deeper. Before you're born, back and back, to the seed and the seed's seed, man, you're white or you're black."

Onisabe smiled. Me, I didn't say anything. I offered him and Clarence a Coke.

For the Albany show I'd had to play a frame drum, and Onisabe showed me how. All Nigerians are drummers; it's in the soul, something that rides with the seed down through generations. Me, I had the hands, the ear, the brain, but not that. It was a humbling experience; everybody had always told me how musical I was, yet here was Onisabe laughing at my efforts and throwing up his arms: "No, no, no!" I couldn't for the life of me tell what I was doing wrong. I thought I was drumming exactly as he did. Sometimes I thought he was playing a black man's trick on me, punishing Whitey for the sins of racist European colonists. Other times I believed that Onisabe's rhythms, even when they seemed simple, were just too subtle for me, that before Onisabe—when it came to African rhythms, though I felt like a pro—I was a dilettante.

Yes, all Nigerians are drummers, blood-deep; and me, I was a dilettante, I thought. Of course, I'm not just talking about drumming per se, but about all that drumming implies, all that's savage and rhythmic and deep. "Full of passion, pulse, and power," is what Whitman said, androgyne, bisexual, polysexual, in whom, I always have thought, all life met itself, and turned. Of course, he was no Nigerian—was he?

Take the way Onisabe drummed women. I caught him at it once. I was looking for him to go over some stage directions I was mixed up about, because the house we were playing next day, in Watervliet I think, had seating on three sides, which screws up all the blocking. The tour manager got us all rooms in the same ratty hotel; I was just down the hall from the Nigerian. I knocked at his door, but he didn't answer. I heard drumming inside, so I figured that that was it—he didn't hear me for the loudness of his drum. I tried the knob—his door was unlocked. I slipped it open. "Onisabe?"

Steamy in there. *Open the windows, Africa man*, I thought, but he probably liked it that way. Let the wallpaper peel; bugs nest under the flaps; mold spread up from the mopboards, down from the wainscot, hotel room to rain forest; ceiling paint bubbling, cracking, dripping, warping the floorboards, feeding the insects and the mold, then steaming up again. Thirty-five dollars the night and check-out time ten-thirty, weekly rates available at the desk, *boomlay boom!*

It was a strange drum the man was playing—*boomlay boom*, like Vachel Lindsay—maybe with water inside, or with metal bands I figured, the way some are, twanging or *wow-wow*ing with every stroke. "Onisabe?" I wandered in.

Inside, against the wall opposite the hall door, there stood an old mahogany-veneered dresser—mahogany from the groves near the Gulf of Guinea, who knows?—with a mirror mounted on top. Angle of incidence equals angle of reflection. Thirty degrees between the line of my chin and the plane of silver, splotchy as an albino's arms and rippled like a forest pool clogged with twigs, catkins, scats. Thirty degrees the other way between the mirror and Onisabe Oduduwa drumming his box springs and a white girl, her face between his legs, his face somehow in her buttocks, but I didn't see exactly, me, didn't stick around to figure it out, did the best I could with the blocking I remembered, was out of there. . . .

Me, I keep going forward and backward, I know, and I can't keep track, but this is the sort of "can't keep track" that will open a window for you six feet, six inches away, eventually. Don't you feel it? The operative thought is in this; you'll see. But maybe it were better locked shut.

• • •

Wait. Let me take this back to my hotel room where I was recovering from Regina. It's right here—you don't have to go over an edge. Back to the window sash microscopically rising, but rising, be sure, six-foot-six away, like land sighted at the edge of a roiling ocean. Back to dead gone Onisabe. (Or is it forward?)

I had mobiles of Möbius strips hanging from the ceiling of my cheap hotel room in lower Manhattan: red, blue, black, newsprint, construction paper, pizza-box cardboard, double strips loop-de-loop, linked bisected strips, and concentric strips, every one of them endless, every one of them magically one-sided—if you can believe a white man. I used subway maps sometimes—they were free, and the paper was strong and veined with interesting branching lines: red, blue, green, and black; uptown, downtown, local, and express. Regina's Dear John, half twisted and joined at the ends, spun alongside a Brenda Starr. That's how I spent my days, me, when I wasn't levitating the sash.

Yes, I set about the fabrication of mobiles. String, masking tape, white paste, a pair of scissors or a knife, a bunch of junk paper you can scavenge anywhere—you're all set. I became adept at intricately balancing mobiles. Distance times weight is the principle, just as in a lever. Levers in levers in levers—that's the idea of a mobile. That—and spin. But the spin part is mystical. Who can analyze that? Only God. Nudge. Blow. Watch it go.

I couldn't have Regina.

"He's dead, man. Onisabe is dead. Fuck your magic powers. I'm damn glad you called, though, Larry. We have to talk. You were the brother's friend too. He respected you, man. He respected you enough to take you into his troupe."

"Mystery to me! Anyway, he took Regina too—where's that at?"

"Don't doubt Onisabe Oduduwa's judgment. You know how great an actor the man was himself. Listen, you're in New York. I want you to find the bastard who killed him."

"What?" I'd been distracted by a rhythmic pounding in the connecting room: paranoia. Funny how you can know it's that, and yet it still casts its spell. "Killed him? What makes you think someone killed him? What makes you so sure he's even dead?"

"You think he just dropped, just like that, thirty-three years old, smart as an owl and strong as a bull?"

"Could it have had to do with Onisabe's bowels?" I said. Now I thought I saw a little dust fly from the window sash. The movement could be that small at first—this is how I figured it—that you couldn't perceive it exactly, but you could see its effects, even from my six feet, six inches, like dry caulk powdering from the slight upward pressure—

"His hanh?"

"Bowels. He asked me if I had glycerin once, you know. It was when we were playing that opera house in Buffalo, the one with the slanted stage—"

"Don't be stupid. That wasn't for his bowels. It was for his soap bubbles."

Now it was my turn: "Hanh?" I looked away from the window, and into that old middle distance. "Onisabe blew bubbles?"

"He didn't blow them. You couldn't blow them. That kind of bubbles, they were too delicate. If a person across the room breathed, they'd bust on you. Say, I'm not talking about some kiddy bubble wand, Larry. This was Aro priest magic—your phone isn't bugged, is it?"

"Me, nobody knows I'm here but you—and Regina maybe."

"Listen up. I'm going to forget you're a white man and lay a jewel on you: Onisabe Oduduwa was an honest-to-God African magic man. Think about it—you ever see him eat?"

That stopped me. I realized I had not. He never ate with the rest of the cast, never snacked in the greenroom, never drank with us. There was so much about him that, to an American, was odd, nobody would ever think to single out his eating habits. "What are you telling me, Clarence?"

"No Aro priest will be caught dead eating in public. It's his training, Larry. It's too human a thing to be seen doing, understand? It would undermine the people's respect."

"But he ate, right? Onisabe did eat, didn't he?"

Clarence didn't answer. I heard a few breaths against the telephone in Cleveland, and when he spoke again, it was about something else. "Onisabe had this way of bending a piece of spring wire or the wire from a spiral pad, joining up the ends so it was a circle with a loop inside— sacred secret magic—and when he dipped it into the bubble soap at the end of a rod, it was just amazing; the liquid hung there, curving in here and out there, looping round and glistening, all so fine and delicate. . . ."

"A Möbius strip, you mean. I thought that was supposed to be a white man's trick."

Clarence horselaughed. "You don't know shit, Larry—no offense. You think Onisabe Oduduwa was going to tell a white boy Africa magic secrets like he told a Brother? You think he was going to let on he knew your paper tricks up and down, before and after, and make you dangerously curious? Something else you don't know: all through the upstate tour, my man, Onisabe and I were working on another script."

"Another script? A different play?"

"It wasn't Soyinka. It was deep-down Africa magic. He was teaching me lines that no one would dare write down."

"What was that play about?"

Clarence cleared his throat. "I don't really know. I got it piecemeal. We were supposed to put it all together when he came to Cleveland—that was my understanding. But now this. When I hit the city, I'll fill you in on some things, Larry. It wasn't his bowels killed Onisabe Oduduwa."

Me—back to the window sash at my six-foot-six. Clarence was raving.

"Oh yeah? What, then?"

"He had enemies. . . ."

"Ah!"

241

It's an actor's exercise, contrapuntal argument: nothing easier for an actor than to have his mind on one thing while he talks about another. Me, I was all window sash and willpower, but I managed the phone and Clarence, no sweat.

". . . FBI. They did it to Martin Luther King, my man. Hell, Onisabe Oduduwa's threads would give old J. Edgar night sweats, never mind that play of his. You know what the man was wearing when they vanished him?"

"Wearing? Clothes. Me, how should I know?" Travel by water—that was the key. Burrow deeply into that thought, like a rat into a slaver's hull, see? Soon—an open window.

"Rhetorical question, Larry. It was in the goddamn AP filler. Reporter thought it was colorful: dashiki and leopard hat. . . ." Clarence's voice was dim as a swab's chantey to a slave's ear down in steerage.

"Sure, oh yeah, I remember that hat." Could be heat waves rippling the window view. Could be heat waves; could be me.

"You never saw the inside of it. They didn't mention the inside in the papers either. FBI made sure nobody saw it. They snatched him and his magic-man hat before anybody could glimpse it and suspect maybe that this was not, which it was not, a goddamn simple-as-shit heart attack or a stumble on a Coke can.

"Design knitted into the fabric, Larry: three naked dead men lying butt up next to their severed heads, hands bound behind their backs. Ringing the inside of Onisabe's hat: three dead men—and one live one, a priest, lying faceup, in a robe and a conical hat. He's got a torch or staff or something; Onisabe never told me what. Oh, and there's a raven, looks like, at the live man's feet; it's eating the eyes and brains out of one of those severed heads. That's what Onisabe wore. Must have scared old J. Edgar shitless."

"Oh, really? Onisabe showed you that?" Travel by water: they die all around you and are hauled away. It's only life. Part of the contrapuntal argument. A person still has things to do, thoughts to think, windows to open. . . .

"I'm a black brother, Larry. Onisabe serves Juju Himself, quiet as it's kept; Juju is the dark side of the Ibo god. Dark, man, dark—no good to you white meat! Onisabe is an Aro priest."

"Was, you mean?" The stench in the hold. The waves rocking. A thought like this may take generations to hone, but then there is escape.

"Whatever." Yelling: "Are you listening to me, man?"

I started. The ship vanished, the sash still down. "What do you want me to do, for Chrissakes, Clarence? I don't know anything about Juju or dead people, faceup or facedown, with or without their heads."

"Fuck it. I'll come to New York and follow this through myself. I just need you to put me up."

"Clarence, I have this sleazy hotel room on Seventh Avenue. I pay by the night. I pee in the sink. . . ."

"What's the address? You put me up, Larry. You can do that much for me, can't you? I need you, man. I'll be there in two days." Pause. "Oh, how's Regina?"

"Dumped me."

"Better off, man."

"No sweat."

"Don't say that, Larry. Don't put me on. We're past that, aren't we, you and me? Remember the Lincoln Tunnel?"

"I didn't think you'd want to."

"What do you mean? You're ready, man." He paused. Me, I felt I was supposed to say something, but I couldn't think what. "Two days."

I told him the address, and two days later he was there. Claustrophobia. At the hour of the wolf, the night before Clarence's arrival, I woke up sweating. My room felt as small about me as a CAT scan tunnel. The pipes under the sink dripped, dripped. The dark could have been my throat for the heartbeat pounding through it. To calm myself, I turned on the light and set about shortening the buttonhole threads by which my mobiles were suspended: Clarence was six inches taller than I, and I didn't want him screwing up my elaborate white-man symmetries. Then I fell into a chair and slept without dreaming—well, without fantasy, anyway. My mind kept calculating lengths and balances, weights shifting as levers gyred through the extravagant geometries of Nod, till the knock at the door.

"What the hell is all this?" Clarence charged in and swept his hand across the ceiling, tangling half a dozen mobiles his first heartbeat in my room. "You getting over the love affair, huh? In Nigeria when they're getting over a love affair, they play mbira, which some South African white man stole and squared the corners of and mass produced and called kalimba. Hmmph! Ka-lim-ba! That what you doing, Larry, my man?"

"I've been experiencing things that are going to change the nature of this universe, Clarence."

"Why do you always have to do that, Larry? Woman dumps you and you gotta make metaphysics. It's not meant to be, is all. She and you don't go. Get over it, man. You don't need this crap."

He located and began to wolf my sesame rice crackers. The can of Multi-Protein Food on the ledge above my sink/pissoir he cursorily lifted, inspected, and slammed back in place with a withering nose wrinkle. "You got anything else to eat in here?"

"No."

"I hate New York." He sat down on my bed. I gave up trying to untangle the mobiles and sat down opposite him in the metal folding chair by my desk or settee, depending how you looked at it. He leaned back—*boowongongong!* "Let's get down to business. Larry, can you show me exactly where Onisabe was murdered?"

"Yeah, I guess. If that's what it was."

And we were walking down Sixth Avenue. We threaded through tourists, shoppers, businessmen, and ragged street people smelling of musk, of old salt, of jasmine, of onions, of gasoline. The street was a solid wall of cars, like Sambo's tiger turned to butter. Brake pads squealed and horns sounded. A man in a wheelchair offered us religious tracts; when we passed without taking any, he swore at us.

When we came to the spot where Onisabe had fallen Clarence wouldn't let me say a word. "We're being followed." I was just supposed to sort of nudge him.

I nudged him. There was a narrow alley down which a body might have been spirited away. There was a fire escape it could have been dragged up and a storm cellar it could have been dragged down. You would have to be strong, though, with a heart like the Manhattan pumphouse, and fast: through the crowd and out of sight before the police arrived.

Clarence's eyes did the hokeypokey. "Just keep on walking." We walked to a subway station, crossed the street underground, then made our way up again. We headed back in the direction of that gallery, but now it was on our left instead of our right, of course.

Suddenly I realized something, and I had to sit down. I felt as if I were on Coney Island again with a gut full of Nathan's, round and round and round: that shop was on our left instead of our right, all right, but by the sun and by the numbered streets, we were walking in the same direction as before. It was like seeing your thumb on the wrong side of your hand.

"No, we are not walking in the same goddamn direction. Get up off the curb, Larry. You're attracting attention. No, we're not, or else it was on the left before, too. What does it matter? You been eating okay, man? Let's get some food somewhere. Get up, man. I'm buying, okay? Where's a deli?"

Back at my hotel, after throwing away the hot dog Clarence bought me, I had to stop at the desk and pay for another day. The desk clerk was a tall woman, masochistically slender, with pink makeup so thick it made you think of palette knives. She took my money with her muscular long-fingered hands of pale brown; with nails like hers, you have to be careful not to cut people. Then she asked me if "that girl" had gotten hold of me.

"Me? A girl?"

"Me, a girl?" she mocked me. "She only been comin' every day for the last week. What you bein' so coy about? This the woman you talkin' to, honey; ain't nothin' I ain't seen.

"She thought you maybe checked out, and she axed me, do I know where you went? Do I know where you went! I told her, 'Honey, I don't ax questions. If he don't come back, that mean he checked out. Go leave him a note in his room if you want to take the chance. You know where it is.' Then I had to go powder my nose, so I figured she gone out already while I was busy, and you maybe bumped into her."

"You say she's been up there before?"

"Well, honey, look at you. Maybe you don't know her. Maybe she been seein' some other white man on your floor. Maybe it just your turn. Hell, maybe she live here." The woman horselaughed. "I didn't check her in, I tell you that. I just fill in mornings for, uh, Uncle Harry." She pursed her lips but couldn't scotch the smile. "Maybe Uncle Harry checked her in. I gotta have me a talk with old Uncle Harry about that little piece of action."

Clarence turned away from her. He closed his eyes and shook his head with a look of unutterable disgust.

"Did she say what her name was?"

"She didn't leave no name. Why you don't read the note, if there be a note? Maybe she signed it—if she got a name. Here your change. Don't you be spending it all in one place, honey."

"It's all one place anyway," I said. I always said that.

"Honey, if that be true," the desk clerk said, "it broken to pieces, ain't it?" She hit a pack of Kools against the counter to settle the tobacco, and she started to peel it open with those red manicured nails as sharp as scissor blades. "Say, that girl, she a 'bino, she got those pink glasses and shit?"

The stairway beside the broken elevator smelled like urine, sweat, and Lysol. Clarence labored behind me—"Slow down, man"—but I wanted to see that note from Regina, the note begging reconciliation. She couldn't live without me, she had realized.

*It's like not being able to breathe in, dear Larry—dear, dear Larry—but only out. Without you I'm only half a person and emptying more by the heartbeat, by the breath. . . .*

But there was no note. I fished out my key to open the door— maybe she had slid the note under it—when I noticed that it wasn't quite closed. I pushed it open, and there was Regina sitting on my bed, twirling Möbius strips. She smiled.

"I knew you'd be back," I said. "How did you find me?"

"It's not like that, Larry."

Clarence squeezed into the doorway beside me. As soon as he laid eyes on her, his mouth dropped open. I had seen the middleweight Archie Moore like that once while the ref gave him a standing six-count. "Now I get it. You here to cut a deal with us, Regina? Now I get why a great black man was all over a gray bitch like you." Then to me: "I hate to have to be the one to tell you this, Larry, but Onisabe and Regina screwed each other blind."

I smiled like an idiot. I started to shiver. I didn't know what to do or what to say. I thought, *Regina's going to come apart. She's going to have her psychotic break right here under my mobiles. She's going to faint or scream or come after Clarence, all fists and feet.*

She didn't, though. She just sat there on my bed, staring back at him. "Let's not be crude."

Clarence eyed Regina and nodded slowly. "FB-fucking-I. You drugged him, didn't you? I know what you people are capable of. You drugged him; you pumped him dry; then you killed him down on Sixth Avenue and dragged him away to Juju knows where."

Muscles and blood, Clarence set his jaw and started to bull toward her. Me, I caught his elbow, and he stopped. It was the touch, not the force, that stopped him. It was his choirboy scruples. The breath hissed through his nostrils. He snapped to face me.

"Clarence, you're crazy," I said. "Onisabe and Regina upstate?"

My hand still on his elbow, Clarence clutched my arm at the biceps and held tight. "Every position, man, every hole."

I remembered the mirror on the fake mahogany bureau in the steam of Onisabe's hotel room, the white girl in his bed: 69, with the twist. "You think Regina killed him?"

"Hell, yes."

Regina laughed. "Ha! Ha! Very big ha!" she said in an Onisabe voice. "Why don't you two monkeys come in here and close the door behind you? Unless you want to do a show for the whole hotel."

We had been frozen at the threshold. I stepped inside now, and Clarence, like a Siamese twin, came in with me, side by side. I reached back for the door and closed it, just as Clarence did the same—two hands on one knob, darker hand, lighter hand. The rub of his arm on mine thrilled me. Travel by water. Down in the hold—bodies rubbing; men, women, vermin. The rolling of the boat. The window was going to open. The electricity between our skins completed the telekinetic mind-state—I was sure of it.

That, or I was just excited by Regina's being there.

"How did you get in?" I asked her.

"The cleaning lady was doing towels and bedsheets. I came in, is all. She thought it was my room. She left, and I stayed."

"Is what Clarence said true—that you were fucking Onisabe?"

She pursed her lips in a way that told me that behind those tinted lenses she was making a calculation. She crossed her legs. She uncrossed her legs. She leaned forward in apparent exasperation. "Of course not."

Regina wore a sheer white blouse with long sleeves and a skirt the color of buttercups. Her eyebrows curved above the rose lenses like little apostrophes—my little apostrophes; I'd kissed them so often I saw them with my lips. I saw with my lips the eyes quivering underneath them too, small puddles where a sparrow dips its beak. She reached up to fuss with her hair: stage business.

I didn't want Clarence to be there. "I saw you, though, Regina, you and Onisabe—in the hotel in Watervliet."

She squirmed on the bed. She looked down, pulled down a hem. Amateur. "It wasn't me." I thought she smiled.

"Sex!" Clarence shouldered past me. "The sex doesn't matter. Onisabe is dead. What are you going to do, kill us too, Regina? For your FBI bosses?"

I grabbed him by the shoulders. "Shut up, Clarence. She's no FBI agent. You're paranoid."

He shoved me away. "Go levitate a window. I'm paranoid—hah!"

I turned to Regina. "What's going on?"

She began to cry. "Hold me, Larry."

Clarence sneered, but me, I went to her.

She buried her head in my chest. "I was his slave, Larry. He beat me, threatened me. He would have killed me. He was crazy. You have to believe me. He said he was some kind of a priest, an Aro priest, and it was all for God. I was out of my mind. He made me his slave. All those arguments we had upstate, remember? I was struggling with it. I was already bound to him, infatuated, and I would get into those little fights, because part of me was resisting, and I had to make a show of it, but in the end, he won me. I loved him. I loved him."

She rubbed her nose against mine. It was an old gesture between us. I glimpsed her albino eyes behind those perpetual specs of hers, blue eyes jittery as jello on a plate. Me, tears welled. "We'll tell the police." I felt my words dissolve as soon as I had spoken them, like the words of a child or a fool. Regina tightened her arms around me until it was hard to breathe. Me, I thought of boa constrictors and funnels in witches' mouths—but I didn't want to move.

Clarence snarled, "Best acting job I've seen you do yet, Regina."

Still clutching me with one hand, Regina reached behind her on the bed and pulled out something she had been hiding there. She looked up at Clarence, and I felt her grow foreign against me, flesh become stone. I thought of a fisherman snapping the line taut against a hooked flounder. She handed the thing to Clarence. "Gift."

He took it into both hands. It was a leopard hat just like Onisabe's. He turned the hat inside out and rotated it, headless man by headless man, past the raven, past the priest, and, terrified, looked up at Regina.

"Clarence? Regina? What's going on?"

Regina laughed, but it wasn't her laugh: it was Onisabe's. I wanted to rear back to get a good look at her face—I was too close now to really see—but her arm noosed me. I couldn't budge. Then she growled at Clarence in Onisabe's voice, "Open the door." She nodded toward the connecting door.

"It's locked on both sides," I said. "It's always locked. Nobody'd open it. You can't open it."

The leopard hat shook in Clarence's hand. He looked at the hat, at the connecting door, at Regina, at the door again, then walked to it, unbolted it, and pulled it open.

Slumped in a fat chair against the wall opposite us in the connecting room, between a dusty mirror and a cheap painting of a little white girl with big, big eyes, Onisabe Oduduwa drooled and babbled. At the opening of the door, he reared up and shouted in a woman's voice, "Give me back my body!"

I looked at him. I looked at Regina. "Ha! Ha! Very big ha!" She smiled.

"Onisabe?" I said to her. Then, turning to the man in the connecting room, "Regina?"

"The white man's trick." Clarence steadied himself against the wall.

"Yes, the white man's trick," said Regina.

I said, "You mean the Möbius strip?"

"Shush. Not that. That's just a piece of paper." The tears were gone. Her softness was gone. She was having a conversation with Clarence now.

"Yes, so that's it." Clarence moved from the wall as if he were diving into a cold sea. He seemed to grow pale. His fingers twitched as he spoke, like so many flicking tongues. His eyes mirrored my windows, two little closed windows.

"That's it. We are talking about human beings. They shipped them first to São Tomé, remember, Clarence?"

"Who shipped who?" I tried to see the connecting room again, but Regina torqued me away, tightening so hard I squealed.

"Remember, Clarence?" She beat the drum of her words just as Onisabe would. "It's time to perform that play we were working on, you and I. Do you remember your lines, hm?"

Clarence sweated. His face seized up, knots around his eyes and mouth. His voice deepened, and he fell into what I took to be an Onisabe riff:

*"Who can follow the river?*
*"In the marshes of Macina*
*"The Niger River branches out*
*"Like fibers of a soaked smashed burl.*
*"Who can follow its channels?*

*"Who can name its lakes,*
*"Lakes that suck it*
*"Like a Yoruba whore giving head?*
*"Only the Nun, the Forcados, and the Escravos*
*"End in the Gulf of Guinea.*

*"The other channels—*

*"Whither do they wend?"*

After the first few words, Regina had joined in, reciting Onisabe's riff word for word with Clarence, a syllable or two behind until the very end, when they joined in unison to say, "Ha! Ha! Very big ha!"

They exchanged a deep look, to me inscrutable, like an estuary dully pulsing, mixing waters with the sea. Then, while Onisabe, in the far room—if he was Onisabe—babbled in Regina's voice, now blubbering, now cursing brokenly, Regina—she who held me—went on alone:

*"Down in the Aro Juju gorge,*

*"Where the earth sweats and fucks and heaves*

*"While cicadas shrill dead men's names,*

*"The oracle said,*

*" 'Gather Me men to sell as slaves.*

*"I would extend My children's dominion*

*"To a far land.'*

*"Then snaked the Aro priests*

*"Through desert, rain forest, and savannah.*

*"They enticed men into servitude*

*"With a certain dirty promise. . . .*

*"On the coast,*

*"At Calabar, Bonny, and Elem Kalabari,*

*"Towns redolent of dried fish,*

*"Streets sparkling with sea salt,*

*"Men's heel bones drummed the gangplanks*

*"Bound slaves bound*

*"For America.*

*"But the word of the Aro was good:*

*"In the West Indies, by the power of Juju,*

*"These slaves would change bodies*

*"With the men who bought them,*

*"Black for white—*

*"The white man's trick."*

"The white man's trick," Clarence echoed her, eyes focused on a spot thousands of miles and hundreds of years remote. "The blacks who had been slaves in Africa were going to wear the masters' skins in America."

Sibilant, obscene, the words wet with meaning, Regina said: "I knew you would come. I was counting on it. I was waiting like a man who sees a ball in the sky and puts out his hand to catch it.

*"In the Indies one white-come-black,*

*"A slaver caught in an African's husk*

*"After the white man's trick, escaped.*

*"Like scum in a drained cistern,*

*"Language, thoughts, and memories clung,*

*"White thoughts in a black skin:*

*" 'Stow away!'*

*"He hid among rats in sodden crates*

*"In the hold of a ship to Africa.*

*"There, he hid from the Aro priests:*

*"They might recognize his skin*

*"And guess its new inhabitant.*

*"For generations, his family after him*

*"Kept their distance from the Aro,*

*"Until the matter of the white man's trick*

*"Was a dimly remembered tale—*

*"To all but that man's descendants."*

"That's crazy," I said, as much to myself as to Regina. "If there was such a man, he was an African to begin with, gone mad in the pens, in the Indies. He thought he was white. It's crazy."

"No.

*"This was my ancestor, white-come-black.*

*"I in my black carapace,*

*"Onisabe Oduduwa, white-come-black,*

*"In skin come down to me*

*"From my boonswaggled ancestor,*

*"I entered the Aro Juju gorge.*

*"I petitioned the oracle,*

*"Ate brains and blood with the raven,*

*"Learned the spells,*

*"Attained the leopard hat,*

*"And became an Aro priest,*

*"The first white Aro priest,*

*"I in my black hull.*

*"Ha! Ha! Very big ha!*

"Now I have returned. I shall white-man's-trick them all back, all the whites-come-black."

"No!" Clarence flinched. His face trembled. He ripped himself from Regina's gaze and fell back against the wall as if he had been thrown there. "Why you want to be this pale bitch? You're Onisabe Oduduwa, a powerful goddamn Black Africa magic man, a world class goddamn drummer, the greatest goddamn actor I ever met—"

"Don't mistake the role for the actor, Clarence. The shaman is not the tiger. In every man a soul dances; it wears his body and mind as a shaman dancing the tiger wears the tiger mask. But the shaman is not the tiger, Clarence. The shaman has his own deep form. So the soul, its own deep form. Regardless of what it wears, the soul in itself is black or white. I am no black man. My soul is white, Clarence—just like yours."

"No." I didn't mean to shriek, but it was all my throat would do. "Souls have no color. We're all the same under the skin." I always said that. Everybody says that.

Regina merely inclined her head, and Clarence came toward her, away from the wall, as if he were peeling out of his defiance, leaving it stuck to the wallpaper. "In you, Clarence, was the seed of my white brother. You bought humans in the West Indies. Larry and Regina carry seeds from enchanted blackies. You think it was crazy luck that you came to my auditions, mine, a famous Nigerian's? Come to that, you think it was crazy luck that you were actors to begin with, wearing roles like second skins?

"No, the mind, my friends, is like a dead dog's tail: however you straighten it, it curls again. The false whites seek me the way criminals seek the hot seat of their sin. You, Clarence—you sought me like a lost man wandering back and back and back to the baffle where he lost his way."

"It's true. It's true. Deep down, I always knew it."

"That's not why I became an actor," I tried to say—snowflakes in a furnace. They didn't seem to hear.

"I did Regina," Regina told him. "You do this one now. Do Larry. Black-come-white. You were working on Larry all the time, and you didn't know what you were doing." She threw back her head and cawed. "You were like a man fucking in his sleep, Clarence. This is what I came here for."

Her fingers sank into his forearms like logs into swamp water. "We are the masters, we whites. Do him. Hold him." She stood. She thrust Clarence down beside me and looped his arm around my waist like so much rope.

His gaze broke over me. "Yes!" he said, or someone said. "Black-come-white. We almost pulled it off in the Lincoln Tunnel once, didn't we, black man?"

I pulled my eyes away, beast in a bear trap gnawing off its leg. I looked toward the window.

A certain thought was coming to fruition. In me my mother and her mother and centuries of mothers before her sat up at attention, faces limned behind my eyes, staring through my sockets. It wasn't a window we saw, but a trapdoor, and we were looking up at it, not across. Dust, starlike, tumbled in rays that seeped between its boards.

Oh, let me unlatch the devil hatch by the power of my mind. Oh, Juju! Oh, let me fly through to the deck and freedom. The sea doesn't frighten me as much as this endless stinking dark, knee-deep in death.

A thought like that, thrust so hard, may fly for generations, mind to mind, like bloody vengeance. Behind my eyes, we heaved.

Me, I thought: this is all wrong. We're all the same under the skin. Black past or white past is all past. What's it to me? Below decks or above the deck, whipped or whipping, Moses or pharaoh, it's all us same human beings, isn't it? That's what I thought, me, and my own mind hushed me as Regina had hushed me. I felt my thought dwindle like a snowball in hell while the souls of my ancestors bellowed the other, older thought:

*Oh, Juju!*

The sash flew all the way up. The window banged open. The counterweights clacked inside the casement. The old tar-patched screen peeled up like a zipper, shredding at the frame. Clarence and Regina looked at me.

Me, I had not known that there was a fire escape outside it, but when I threw Clarence aside—*boomlay boom!*—tumbled him from my bed and squeezed feetfirst out the window I had never touched with anything but my mind, and when I then felt not air but metal bars beneath me, I was glad. I scrambled across the landing and made for the stairs.

Yes, the Middle Passage. Yes, the long hot way from the island of São Tomé across the Atlantic with the slavers. Yes, the Aro had enlisted us with promises of transformation and release. Hundreds died bone to bone with the living until the sailors weeded out their stinking corpses and threw them into the sea.

Yes, at port in the British West Indies they herded us into pens, and the ticket holders grabbed us out like so many sides of beef.

There at last the magic half twisted us.

Ha! Ha! Very big ha!

"Larry, what the hell?" Clarence has scrambled across the bed; I see him at the window. I am clanging down the iron steps.

They grabbed us in the pen, yes, but the pen was the place of the half twist—ha, ha—and those who grabbed us emerged from there black men and we blacks became white, with slavers in our arms. Free at last! Free at last! The men who had sold the tickets smiled at us, and we nodded, smiling back. We were not the same men to whom they had sold the tickets, the fools. Those men were in our grasp, white-come-black, male-come-female, tight-come-loose, high-come-low.

"Larry, honey," Regina calls.

I won't look back. "Shut up. I know who you are, Regina—Onisabe Oduduwa. She fought it and fought it, but you were too near. Me, no half twist is gonna get me, babe."

Even as I say this a voice in me shrills, *This is all wrong. I know this is all wrong. It's all upside down. What I always say is true, that we're one.* It shrills at the top of its tiny voice, but none of the rest of me gives one-half of a half-twisting good goddamn, because no one—no one, goddammit—is going to put me in that blood-stinking hold. I run.

"Get the jungle bunny." Regina bangs the sash.

Clarence vaults and scrabbles down the iron rungs above me. "Now you're mine, boy. How many hundred years don't matter. You pulled a fast one in the pen, all right, but now everything's come round, down through the sperm"—*clang!*—"down through the egg"—*clang!*—"coupling after coupling." *Clang!* "And here we are, Massa, but Massa is me."

I've reached the pavement now—three sliding, clanking runs of metal rungs ahead of him—but Clarence jumps. I feel the crush of him landing on my shoulders. I collapse to the ground with an ache so fierce, head to heels, toes to nape, nipples to butt, twist, twist, that I can hear it like a chant, like a scream, like a *boomlay boom!*

When I open my eyes I see myself lying below my black butt. The body beneath me, the white man I thought was me, springs up laughing.

He leers at me with such carnivorous glee there's drool seeping from the corners of his lips—or my lips, somebody's lips. I'm on the wrong side of me. He lays both his white hands on my chest and shoves. I stagger back, staring at my black hands, black fronts, black backs. I am crashing into garbage cans and boxes brimming with spoiled fruit. He leaps up the fire escape hand over hand to where white Onisabe, Onisabe in Regina's husk, beckons, beckons to his ancient kinsman.

I'm shambling on strange feet through fractured crates, ankle-deep in wormy fruit meats. I half lunge, half fall toward the iron railing. I grab it. Through the heel of my black hand I feel the pulse of the white man's footfalls going up the rungs.

"Come back, Clarence, brother man," I shout. "Come back. Under the skin we're the same, you and me! You can't leave me here like this!"

"Call me Larry—nigger."

Hour by hour my new skin claims me. My new mind wraps itself around the old kernel. Soon, soon, *boomlay boom*, all I was will seem a madman's tale.

Me, I've nearly vanished to myself, when Regina takes pity on me. She comes to me in the alley where I lean against the fire escape mumbling and crying.

"Calm down, Clarence. Everything's okay, man." She takes me by the hand and walks me up and down the streets as far as Sixth Avenue, a black man and a white woman on an August afternoon.

# THE TAWNY BITCH

*Nisi Shawl*

**M**y Dearest Friend,

This letter may never reach you, for how or where to send it is beyond me. I write you for the solace of holding you in my thoughts as I would that I could hold you in my arms. So rudely as I was torn from the happy groves of Winnywood Academy, I can only conjecture that you also have been sent to some similarly uncongenial spot. Oh, my dear, how I hope it is a better one, even in some small measure, than the imprisonment forced upon me here. I inhabit a high garret: bare of wall, low of ceiling, dirty-windowed. Through the bleary panes creeps a grey light; round their fast-barred frames whistles a restless wind. Some former inmate has tried to stop up the draughts with folded sheets of paper, and these provide the material platform on which stands my fanciful correspondence with you.

My pen is that which you awarded me, my prize for mastering the geometric truths of Euclid. Sentiment made me carry it always with me, next my heart. How glad I am! It is now doubly dear to me, doubly significant of our deep bond. As for the ink, I must apologize for its uneven quality, due entirely to its composition. In fact, I have rescued it from my chamber pot. Yes, love, these words are set down, to put the matter quite plainly, in my own urine, a method imparted to me by my old African nurse, Yeyetunde. It has the advantage, in addition to its accessibility, of being illegible, almost invisible, till warmed above a flame. As I am allowed no fire of any sort, I may not see to edit my words to you. I hope my grammar and construction may not shame me, nor you, as my preceptress in their finer points.

But I believe I will soon cease to trouble myself about such things.

Whom do you suppose to have betrayed us? I am inclined to suspect Madame, as she was the only one, probably, who knew of our attachment. Certainly none of the other pupils was in a position to do so. Though Kitty was most definitely set against me on account of my race, and pretended not to understand the difference between mulattoes and quadroons such as myself, she had no real opportunity to do us harm.

It vexes me that I made no attempt to buy Madame's silence when I had plenty of gold at my disposal. She dropped the most enormous hints on the subject, which I see quite clearly now, in hindsight.

I must school myself not to fret about these matters, over which I have no control. There is enough with which to concern myself in my immediate surroundings. If I spend my days fussing and fidgeting, I will wear out my strength, both physical and mental. My first concern is to preserve *all* my faculties intact.

When I came to myself in this place, I did doubt my senses. I had lain down to rest on a bed of ease, confined, it is true, as a consequence of our discovery, but still with my own familiar toys and bibelots ranged round me. I awoke with dull eyes, a throbbing head, and a fluttering heart, in these utterly cheerless surroundings.

Well, some evil drug, perhaps, subdued me to my captor's power. He has yet to reveal himself to me, and my two gaolers say not a word in answer to my inquiries, but I have no doubt as to who it is: my cousin John. When informed of our behavior, he must have once more assented to be burdened with my maintenance. Certainly he could not have hoped to have kept me in school much longer, the backwardness ascribed to my race and Colonial upbringing having by now vanished under your tender tutelage. I have thought much of these things during the two days I have spent here, there being little else to occupy my time, and I believe it must be so.

But now I have the comfort of writing. To hold intercourse with you, even through so attenuated a medium as this, will give me strength to endure whatever trials lie ahead.

I continue with the description of my prison. I believe I neglected to mention that the walls are washed a stark white; harsh, yet tainted, soiled with the careless print of unclean hands. The floor is a mere collection of loose boards. It is there that I shall hide this letter, and any other secrets my time in this place vouchsafes to me. Gloomy pillars rise at intervals to the rough rafters above, and a brick chimney from which proceeds all the warmth afforded me.

The windows, barred and begrimed, afford an ill view of the countryside. That I am in the country I deduce from the silence surrounding me, unbroken save for the moaning wind and the monotonous nightly barking of a solitary dog. The glass is so befouled as to disguise all distinguishing visual characteristics of the neighborhood.

I have just formed the project of cleaning it, when left on my own as now, that I may perhaps ascertain my whereabouts. There, you see how good you are for me, what a salutary effect so slight a contact with you even as this can have upon me? Then do not chide yourself for the predicament in which I now find myself, love. The danger may yet be won through, and the rewards have been so richly sweet as to defy description. No need; you know them. Back, then, to the present.

One door only serves my prison, and it is a heavy barrier, much bolted. It opens twice a day to a brutish pair, whom for a while I thought to be deaf-mutes, so little did they respond to my pleadings for release. But just this morning— Stay! I hear

I have been honored by such a visit, such attentions as would surely drive me to destroy myself, were adequate means within my reach! No, I remember my promise to you, and there shall be no more attempts of that sort, whatever the goad, however easily the weapons were to come to my grasp. But oh, the insult of his touch! The vileness of the man, the ghastly glare as of his rotting soul, shining through the bloodshot eyes with which he raked me up and down, the moment he stepped in the room.

"Ho," said Cousin John (for it was he), "the little pickaninny loses what small comeliness she had. Martha, Orson, does she not receive good victuals? Remember, I pay all expenses, and shall have a thorough accounting made."

The shorter of my gaolers, a man (presumably Orson), replied that I consumed but a small portion of my meals. This is true, for who could be tempted by a nasty mess of cold beans and bloody sausages, or a bowl of lumpy gruel?

My cousin then turned back to me and said, "So you would starve yourself, would you, my black beauty? Well, that's no good, for then your fortune will revert to that b——— Royal Society. And though I am your guardian until you come of age, your father made no testamentary provision for me upon your death." These last words were almost murmured, and seemed to be addressed to himself. He sank into a silent revery, which lasted a few moments, then roused himself to his surroundings.

"Now Martha! Orson! You must bring up some refreshment, and the means with which to partake of it. And a chair or two would not be amiss." (For the lack of any furniture in my description of this room is not owing to your correspondent's negligence.) "I dine with the young lady. What! Why stand you gawping there? Be off about your business!" Orson muttered something about the danger in which his master stood should I try to escape.

"Nonsense! This twig of a thing harm me?" And he laughed aloud at the idea, a heavy, bloated laugh. And indeed, he is much larger than me, and stronger, too, as he had occasion to prove at the conclusion of our interview.

For the moment, however, my cousin was all affability. He surveyed the sparseness of my accommodations and shook his head, saying, "Well, 'tis a sad comedown from Winnywood. But you have been a very naughty puss, and must learn to repent your errors before you can be allowed anything like the liberality with which you have been used to be treated. I must not throw away money on the cosseting of a spoiled, sulky, ungrateful schoolgirl."

*Why should I be grateful?* I thought to myself. *The money is mine, though you seem inclined to forget this.*

As though he had heard my unspoken words, my cousin showed himself somewhat abashed. He crimsoned, strode away, and hemmed and hawed for a moment before trying a new tack. The gist of this was, that by my shameless behavior with you, I had ruined for myself all hope of any respectable alliance with a man. He veered from this presently by way of allusions to the unacceptableness of my "mulatto" features, the ugliness of which also unfitted me as a bride.

He paused as if for breath, and I spoke the first words I had dared to utter in his presence: "Love, affection of any sort, then, is quite out of the question? My fortune forms my sole—"

"Love! Affection!" interrupted Cousin John. He seemed astonished that I should dare to feel their want, let alone speak of it. "After giving way to the unnatural perversions which have reported themselves to my ears, Belle, you ought to be grateful for common civility."

He went on in this vein for some time. I confess that after a while I paid his lecturing scant heed. It put me in mind of my father's scolds to me when, as a child, I showed myself too prone to adopt the quaint customs of Yeyetunde and the other blacks about our place. As Cousin John prated away I seemed almost to see my parent stand before me in his linen stock and shirtsleeves, urging rationalistic empiricism upon a child of ten. Of course I was eventually brought to Reason's worship. But well I remember the attraction to me of the island's cult of magic, with its grandiose claims to control the forces of nature which my father sought only to understand. The brightly colored masks and fans and other ceremonial regalia, surrounded by highly scented flowers; the glitter of candles in dark, mysterious grottoes; hypnotic chants and sweetly chiming bells—all clamored at my senses and bade me admit in their train the fantastic beliefs with which they were associated. Then, too, I felt these practices to be connected somehow with my mother, of whom, as I told you, I have no true, clear, conscious recollection. Yet her presence seemed near when I was surrounded by these islanders, to whom the barrier between life and death was but a thin and permeable membrane.

Indeed, I can still dimly picture the altar which Yeyetunde instructed me to build in my mother's honor. It was a humble affair of undressed stone, with a wooden cup and a mossy hollow wherein I laid offerings of meat, fruit, and bread, and poured childishly innocent libations to her spirit.

My thoughts had wandered thus far afield when I was roused to my senses by the sudden seizure of my hand. Cousin John knelt, actually knelt on one knee at my feet, and held me in a grip firmer than was pleasant. Ere I had time to discover what he meant to be about, came a knock on the door, and the sound of its several bolts and chains being shifted about in preparation for someone's entry.

My cousin with difficulty regained his feet, and the man Orson entered the room, bearing with him two chairs, followed by Martha, who carried a collapsed, brass-topped table.

I have not yet made you see these two, I think, fixtures though they are in my prison. Both are tall, stout, loose-fleshed, and grim of countenance. Did they for some reason of deviltry trade clothes, one would be hard-pressed to note the change, for they are distinguishable otherwise only by the female's slightly greater height, Orson's face being smooth-shaven.

In bringing in their burdens, this pair left open the door. I stepped round as noiselessly as I could to obtain a view through it, that I might determine what chance I had of making off. None, it appeared, for the door's whole frame was filled by a large, bony, yellow dog, a bitch. She eyed me suspiciously, and her hackles rose, and a low growl erupted from some deeper region, it seemed, than her throat. Martha heard it. "Come away from that!" she ordered harshly, whether speaking to me or the bitch, I could not tell. I backed away anyhow, and the bitch held her place.

I realized that in this apparition I had an explanation of the tiresome barking which plagues my dark hours here, and bids fair to keep me from ever obtaining a full night's sleep.

But my light and my ink both fail me, and I must postpone the telling of my thoughts and the rest of the day's events till morning.

I cannot recall exactly where I left off in my account. The door was open, I believe, and I had discovered it defended by the tawny bitch. . . . Yes, and I had just remarked how I believed her the source of the irksome barking which, together with the poorness of the pallet provided (Martha or Orson brings it in the evening, and it is removed on the arrival of my dish of gruel) and the uncomfortably chilly atmosphere, conspires to ruin my nightly rest. The barking goes on literally for hours: low, monotonous as the drop of water from some unseen, uncontrollable source. It is tireless, hopeless almost in its lack of change in tone, pitch, or volume; in frequency just irregular enough that one cannot cease to remark its presence. With daylight, it ends, but so soon as I am able to fall into a broken slumber, my gaolers appear, remove the pallet, and the miserable day commences. No wonder, then, that this animal and I viewed each other in instant and seemingly mutual detestation.

"Come away from that," cried Martha (have I already said?), and not knowing to which of us she referred, I retreated anyway. The two servants dropped their burdens and took turns in bringing in the food and other necessities, then shut the door and proceeded to set before us our dinner. This was much nicer than I usually get, consisting of a baked chicken, boiled potatoes, a side dish of green peas, and a steaming hot pie, fragrant of fruit and cinnamon. I could not but imagine that Martha and Orson had designed this for their meal, and my mouth fair watered at the sight and smell of such good things. But Cousin John would have none of it at first, and raised a fit, asking for soup and fish, jellies, cakes and such, and demanding that all be taken away and replaced with something better. However, there was nothing else, Orson told him, be it better or worse, so he was forced to make do with what was before him. But he did demand wine to drink, and two bottles were brought, and the servants then dismissed.

I made quick enough work of the portions on my plate, and surprised and pleased my cousin by requesting more. He helped me to it, refreshing himself with great draughts of wine between his labors. "That's the dandy!" he said, spooning forth a quantity of gravy. "Mustn't have you wasting away, merely because you are under a punishment." Well fed, I felt an increase of courage. How long, I asked him, must my punishment continue? "Why, till you repent your sins, little Belle, and show that you are truly sorry for them." As he said this he gave a heavy wink. Then he bellowed for Martha and Orson, who cleared the dirty dishes and broken meats, close-watched once more by the bitch, which confined itself, nonetheless, to the passageway. Orson would have taken the wine with the other things, but his master bade him leave it.

Then we were alone, without hope of interruption. I had not drunk my wine, but lifted my glass now as cover for an inspection of my cousin's face. I hoped to reassure myself by tracing in his blurred, reddened outlines some coarse resemblance to the beloved features of my father. I saw puzzlement there, and thick, unaccustomed lines bent the brow in frowning thought. I lowered my eyes, and when I looked up again upon setting down my glass, his expression had shifted to a false grin.

"Come, Belle," said he, "you are not so unseemly to look at when you smile a little, and let down your guard. Black but comely, a regular Sheba, one would say. As for your schoolgirl episodes, I could bring myself to set all that aside. Many a man would not have you, but for myself I say you're as good as a virgin, and a blood relative besides. Thicker than water, eh? You want no more than a proper bedding, which your little adventure proves you anxious to receive. I'm not proud; I'll take you to wife, let the world say its worst."

"No more you will," I muttered through hard-clenched teeth. In the next instant the tabletop was swept aside with a crash, and my cousin on his feet, dragging me to mine.

He seized me in a horrid, suffocating embrace, mauled me about with two fat, hairy paws, and breathed into my shrinking face a thick, wheezing lungful of tobacco-scented, wine-soaked breath.

Half swooning, I yet fought with ineffectual fists for my release. The monster loosened his grip, but only to change the angle at which he held me, leaving more of my frame subject to his inspection. And not with his eyes alone did he examine me! But with eager hands he sought to undo my bodice, and gain sight of what its strictures denied him. Busied thus, he failed to notice my slow recovery, until I *made* him know it! He stooped to bestow upon my bosom a noxious kiss and received a sharp bite on the nose! Alas, not sharp enough, for no blood flowed, but a torrent of curses and ugly expressions of wrath.

I took advantage of my attacker's pain and distraction to extricate myself from his hold, and with trembling hands tried to restore somewhat of my customary appearance. When he saw this, he laughed. "Don't bother yourself with that business," he sneered. "I've not finished yet." In a most sinister manner he advanced, and I retreated to the utmost corner of my prison, protesting uselessly. A bully and a tyrant I called him, and other fine epithets, but it must have gone hard with me if not for intervention of a most unexpected sort. A great noise arose at the door: a confusion of banging, barking, scratching, scraping, howling and I know not what else. Though loud enough to herald the arrival of a pack of hellhounds, it proved, upon Orson's opening the door, to proceed solely from the tawny bitch. The beast rushed past him to a position which would have forced my cousin to engage with her in order to come at me. Though she is an ill-favored brute, I admit an obligation to her for this timely interruption. A few blows quieted her, and gave vent to most of my cousin's spleen. This was further relieved by cursing Orson, and demanding to know what he was about to keep such an unruly animal. And why had he not better control of it, and what meant he by unlocking the door to it, and exposing my cousin to its attack?

As he restrained the barely subdued dog, Orson seemed somewhat puzzled to defend himself, and made out that the bitch was not his own, but his master's. Hadn't he seen it trotting up behind my cousin's carriage as he arrived that afternoon?

"Mine?" cried Cousin John. "Why should I saddle myself with such a wretched-looking animal as that? Put it out. Have it whipped from the grounds!" And that he might supervise the execution of these orders, he left me to soothe my disordered nerves and recover from his attack as best I could on my own. No apology or inquiry as to my well-being came either that day or the next, today. Only I cannot think he was successful in barring the tawny bitch from the property, for again last night I heard her constant, irritating bark.

But perhaps it is not the same dog. These disturbances have gone on ever since my arrival here, and according to Orson, the bitch came with my cousin.

Now afternoon, I think. Cousin John has not approached me all the day. Perhaps he may be gone away again. If not, if he should once more assault me, what shall I do? How shall I defend myself? Should I agree to marry him in order to gain some measure of freedom? I do not think that in a case of coercion, the contract would be valid. Yet, I hesitate to take such a step, uninformed as I am of my rights here in England. Who could tell them to me? Who would deign to defend them? Escape is a better tack to try.

I contrived this morning to retain a damp cloth from amongst the meagre provision for my ablutions. With this I have been rubbing at the windowpanes—at least, as much as I could reach of them through the iron bars. Of course, a great deal of the dirt is on the outside, but I do think I have made an improvement. In one corner, I can see a bit of the landscape. From this I judge that the house in which I am confined is in a hollow, for a dingy lawn sweeps up almost to a level with this window, topped by a row of dreary firs. A road, very rough, little more than a cart track, falls gradually along this declivity, till it disappears from sight around the house's corner. All is grey and forbidding, and altogether Northern in its aspect.

Forgive me, my friend; I know you love this land, even its rural solitudes. You, in your turn, are as sensitive to my longing for the smiling skies of St. Cecilia, for the loss of which you comforted me so sweetly. But now, separated alike from my home and my dear solacer, and ignorant as to how long this separation lasts—oh, my spirits are abominably low. I cannot go on writing in this vein. Besides, it grows too dark.

Very low. No plan as yet. My situation seems very bad, though still without sign of Cousin John. Left alone to brood on my wrongs. The food is as inedible as formerly. If it continues so, I shall not have to weigh my promise to you. Starvation will put a period to my troubles.

I try to think on happier times. It is now five days since I have been here. Allowing time for travel, and for the effects of the drugs I believe to have been administered upon me, it is perhaps not much more than a week ago that we were together.

Do you remember the delight with which you caressed my hair, likening it to rain clouds, and the weightless fluff of dandelions? How you loved to twist and smooth and braid the dark masses, remarking on their softness and compactability! And how I loved your touch there, so gentle yet so thrillingly luxurious. . . . I had not known such tender attentions since the sale of my nurse, on my father's death and the breaking up of our household. It frightened me sometimes, your tenderness; it seemed but a fragile insulator for the energy of your passion. As if, the more delicate its outer expression, the deeper and more primordial its final essence. Exactly so did I find this essence, when at last it was unveiled to me. And in its echoing through the sad hollowness of my orphaned heart I heard, I felt, music, rapture, bliss! To hold with all my might this joy, and to enfold my own within it, to wrap myself around you and your fierce love, to feel you yield it to me with such voluptuous uncontrol, and in your pleasure afford me mine, oh my dearest, it was right, it was good and inevitable. My maiden hesitancies melted all away in these heated storms, as a summer downpour annihilates the hard pellets of hail strewn before it.

I know that you believe our separation to be a judgment upon us. So much I was able to divine from your hasty note, though I read it only a few times the night I received it, and could not find it on waking here. I understand your assertion, but I *deny* it. We have harmed no one, have behaved only according to our natures. This time of trial is troublous; but hold fast, and it, too, shall pass. My cousin may confine; he may persecute me—but over the passage of time he can have no control. In a few short months I shall be twenty-one, and mistress of my fortune. Better if I spent those months free from this confinement, but however slowly they may slip away, whatever horrors or privations I may have to endure, I will live to come of age. Nothing, then, can divide us. I will find you; I will

A carriage has come up along the road. A sound so unusual stood in need of investigation, so I ceased my writing for a moment, to see if I could catch a glimpse of the equipage. I just made out the closed top of a smart brougham, giving no hint of its occupant as it wheeled swiftly by.

I cannot contain my hope and curiosity. The sound of the carriage's movement ceased abruptly. Has it brought rescue? Another prisoner, perhaps? Perhaps—my love, could it be *you?* I am agitated; I think I hear signs of an approach—

• • •

So very wretched a turn things have taken, that I cannot bring myself to write for long. Dr. Martin Hesselius is the name of this new visitor; a proud, sparely fleshed man with a Continental accent and a cold eye, and an even colder heart. My entreaties for release engrossed him but as symptoms. He has been persuaded of my insanity, and sees in me a rare opportunity to exercise his theories on the causes of, and effective treatments for, mental disorders.

Upon examining me he was greatly surprised that I spoke the Queen's English, and never seemed quite possessed of the idea that I could understand it. He made many offensive remarks on my physiognomy and physique, as of their primitive nature, and was deeply derogatory of my mother, hardly less so of my father, citing his "degenerate lust" and her "cunning animality." Any protest I uttered against his infuriating statements was made to stand at no account, except that of proving my madness.

And then, my friend, Cousin John brought in his report of our doings. It was sickening to witness the happiness with which he made sordid-seeming all that I hold in my memory as sacred. And much worse was the light in which Dr. Hesselius received these tidings. I take it now that for a woman to love a woman is more than just a crime; it is the very definition of insanity. . . . How shall I ever, ever win my way from here?


Distracted. Bitch barking throughout the entire night. Early in the morning, just at dawn, I detected the sound of a carriage leaving, but I take no heart from that. By something I overheard Martha say to Orson, I believe Dr. Hesselius has left, but only temporarily, in order to procure some "medicines" and "instruments" for my torture—he would have it, for my cure.


Somewhat better now. I have had a meal, the menu of which was decided by the good doctor: boiled lamb, finely minced, and asparagus. I had some difficulty in eating this, as I am no longer entrusted with cutlery, nor any implement more dangerous than a wooden spoon, even under the watchful eyes of my guards. The meal was not ill-prepared, though, and I did it some justice. The whole washed down with great lashings of green tea, of which, I am told, I am to have any quantity I like, this dietary regimen being a part of Dr. Hesselius's recommended course of treatment.

Three other changes are to be instituted as a result of his prescription. I learned of them through indirect means, as neither of the servants will answer my questions even now that I can call them by their names. But Orson complained to Martha of having to draw and haul the water for my baths, which I gather I am to be given daily from now on. Martha retorted that she was just as much put upon by the order to accompany me on my airings in the garden. Then there are "salts" to be administered, which I hope will prove harmless when they arrive. I believe there are other points in the doctor's program, with which I must wait to acquaint myself till his return.

The idea of being able to walk out of doors fills me with an almost unhealthy excitement! At last, I shall be able to look about me and form some estimate of possible means of escape. To abide in my cousin's power any longer than necessary, even though he make no further advances upon me, is an uncountenanceable thought. I am not mad, to be so confined, nor a naughty, impetuous little girl. I have full and clear possession of all my faculties.

Just returned from my first, highly anticipated airing. It was not much in the way of what I had expected. Martha wrapped me round with a rough, woolen shawl and hurried me out to a dull little plot of grass divided by a gravel walk. Along this she proceeded to lead me back and forth, under skies in that irritating state of not-quite-rain, and between thick, tall hedges which retained just enough of last year's leaves as to make it impossible to spy out any significant features of the landscape barely glimpsed between their branches.

Still, I managed to obtain some intelligence from this outing. From the general air of dirt and neglect visible on my quick trip through the house, I am strengthened in my belief that it has probably no other inhabitants than myself. Martha, Orson, and (if he yet remains) my cousin. There is no one else, then, whose sympathies might be won to aid me in my plight. However, one may also say that there is no one else to hinder any efforts I am able to make on my own behalf.

My evening walk and meal differed slightly from those of earlier in the day. Celery stalks substituted for the asparagus, and a muffler made an addition to my walking ensemble.

As we stepped rapidly along the gravel, I noted a peculiar effect occasioned by the stems of the hedges which we passed. Lit now by the pale, watery yellow of the declining sun, they alternated with their shadows in such a manner as to produce the illusion of *something*— some animal, perhaps—keeping pace with us on the hedge's further side. It was most marked. My eyes were able to discern that the effect rose to a height somewhat equal to my waist, in a blurry, irregularly shifting mass. That it was an illusion, and not an actual animal, was proved by the precision with which it matched our speed and direction; pausing where we paused, hesitating, turning, and recommencing along with us in an exactitude not to be explained otherwise.

I amused myself by imagining to which natural laws my father would ascribe this curious phenomenon, from the wisdom accumulated through his naturalistic inquiries. He had studied thoroughly many occurrences which our islanders saw in a supernatural light, always assuring me, when I became frightened at one of old Yeyetunde's tales, that there was a rational explanation for everything to be encountered in . . .

Such an uproar as there was last night! No one thought to inform me as to the cause of the hubbub, and I racked my brains in sorting out its details, trying to see how they might be made to fit together to accompany a reasonable sequence of events.

First came the sound of an approaching carriage. Or was the noise sufficient for two? I got up and strained my eyes to look through the dark, dirty windows. There were lights, as of coach lanterns, but briefly glimpsed and not steady enough for me to count their number.

The horses halted. Muffled shouts, cries for assistance, came in coarse, workmen's voices. Then a furious gabble of frightened screams, heavy crashes, and ferocious barks. Now canine, now human tongue predominated, till at length came a lull, followed by the sounds of a carriage in movement again. This soon ceased as well, so presumably the vehicle was just led round to the stables. Then came a long silence. Then the sharp report of a pistol.

Nothing further disturbed the night's calm, not even the customary plaint of the tawny bitch.

I am left to surmise that she attacked the arriving carriage, or its occupants, perhaps dislodging some heavy piece of luggage, and for her sins was shot. The sadness with which I greet this conclusion surprises me. Dogs are lowly animals, as my father taught me, unworthy of their fame as faithful, noble creatures. "A wolf," he would often say, "is somewhat noble. A dog is a debased wolf; an eater of human waste and carrion, fawning, half-civilized, wholly unreliable." The islanders, too, hold dogs in very slight esteem. Their use in the tracking of runaway slaves, perhaps, has led to their general abhorrence.

I am not sure whether any were sent after my mother. She was not a slave, because married to my father. Somehow she wandered away from the plantation and became lost. The exact circumstances leading to her death were never spoken of.

Yeyetunde, with that patient obstinance so typical of the African, said only that my mother had met her fate deep in the forest, after being missed at home for more than a day. What was she doing there? Who found her? And how came they to know where to look? I could not induce her to answer me, save with the stricture that such things were for my father to tell me, if he would.

He would not.

Oh, he spoke of my mother, and that frequently enough. Almost, I could believe his memories my own. Her beauty, her skin described in a multitude of hues such as amber, honey, and the pure light of dawn; her genius for discovering rogues and ill-wishers amongst his pretended friends; the portside hostelry where first they met; the speed and ease of her confinement and my delivery; with these I am more than familiar. They only serve to make the blankness following less bearable.

In time I grew so used to my father's evasions and silences on the subject of my mother's death, I began to conclude that the occurrence had been excruciatingly painful, and that he omitted to recount it not from any conscious design, but from his positive inability to do so.

Still, I learned to note one peculiarity in his responses, which, however, I am yet uncertain as to how I might interpret it. For hard upon his silences, or at the heart of any irrelevancies with which my father might choose to distract me, came the subject of dogs: their viciousness, their unruliness, and their unpredictability, especially when dealt with as a pack.

I grow weary of lamb. Asked of Martha if there were no other provision to be had. She answered me with stony and insolent silence.

The tea is good, and very warming after my cold immersion baths.

If last night's arrival was the doctor, or my cousin, I have not heard from them nor received any word of their coming. How annoying to be dependent on the doings of servants for my augury of what goes on around me! Orson has been absent, all my needs being met this morning by Martha, even the toilsome task of hauling up and filling the tub for my bath. Was he injured in last night's fracas? Or perhaps another was hurt, and requires his attendance. That would make of the present an opportune moment for my escape. I wish I knew.

Gathered no further intelligence from my morning's excursion, save that the odd phenomenon of the shadow beyond the hedge seems not to confine itself to evening hours. Mentioned this to Martha, who took it just as she takes all I say: with no further notice than an evil, impertinent look. But I noted her eyes trained nervously on the blur as it accompanied us, and I believe our exercise was curtailed as a result of its effect upon her. I shall not mention it aloud again, for I grudge every step denied me. I must keep up my strength. It would not do to come upon a chance to flee, and be physically incapable of taking advantage.

Languid all the day. This must be the consequence of my perpetually disturbed rest. The bitch is back. That expressionless bark, as of a monotonous lesson learned by rote—I cannot sleep, but I begin to think that nonetheless I dream, for words fit themselves to its untiring, evenly accented rhythms. Admonishments, warnings, injunctions to take up unclear duties, the neglect of which foreshadows danger, yet the accomplishment of which is impossible. The whole effect is one of unbearable tension. I rise and pace, barely able to keep myself from rattling the barred windows, the bolted door—I *dare* not give way as I should like to do. I must remain in possession of my faculties, that I may engage the belief and sympathies of whomever I first come across on breaking free of my captivity. It may be the keeper of a nearby inn, or some pious and upright local divine; for their sakes, I must retain a rational appearance.

I must escape while I have the wit to do so.

Violation! Oh, foul and unwarrantable assault! To live and endure such a burden of shame, oh, my friend, how? How can I?

My hand shakes; I have not the strength to write. But if I do not, I may be moved to relieve my outraged feeling on myself, and I have sworn to you—

I have a further thought that these words, so poorly penned, will yet stand witness to my sobriety. In order that I might give the lie to my cousin's claims as guardian of an unhinged mind, I will recount here all I recall. The sickening details—

The bed—I cannot bring myself to rest there. It is a symbol of my humiliation, with its awkward headboard and thick, stiff straps. When it arrived in my prison this afternoon, I thought I might perhaps be able to recoup some of my lost sleep, and so fight off the half-dreaming state that recently has plagued me. The straps repelled, but the thick mattress was more welcoming than my poor, vanished pallet. I had just lain down to test its softness when my gaolers made an unexpected return, wheeling with them a strange apparatus. A large, inverted glass bottle hung suspended from a tall rack. At its neck dangled a long, flexible tube, and on the end of this—oh, it is of no use, I cannot . . . yet I will go on—a hard, slick nozzle, fashioned of some substance such as porcelain: white, cold; horribly cold. . . . I fought, but Martha and Orson together managed to restrain me to the bed, strapped in so that I lay stretched out on my side. Beneath me they tucked a piece of thick, yellow oilcloth. As they did this they lifted and disarranged my skirts, and draped sheets over my head and shoulders, and also about my knees. Thus I lay with my fundament exposed, while I had no way to see anything further of what passed.

Imagine my sense of shame, then, when I heard voices approaching and recognized the tones of Dr. Hesselius and Cousin John! They entered the room discussing my case as though I had not been there. Far from protesting this rudeness, I maintained a foolish, cowardly silence. A child with her head hidden beneath the counterpane, avoiding nightmares; that is how you must picture me.

Dr. Hesselius spoke of how a host of substances he termed "mortificacious" had deposited themselves throughout my inner workings. "I deduce that they have chiefly attached themselves to the lower end of the patient's digestive system."

My cousin cleared his throat. "Mmm. Er—how did you arrive at this conclusion, sir?" He sounded a great deal embarrassed.

"You intimated that the patient's studies progressed well—exceedingly well, in fact, for one of her primitive origins. This indicates that the head's involvement is only a partial one. As the mortificacious material tends to gravitate to its victim's polar extremities . . ." So much I am sure he said, and a quantity of other quackish nonsense besides. My attention was distracted by a clatter nearby, as of glass and metal rattling together. Then came a liquid sound, like water running into a narrow container. I cannot convey to you the sense of unreasoning dread these noises aroused in me.

Suddenly, gloved hands seized me upon—no. Seized me, I say, and I was forced—forced to accept the nozzle. My shame and confusion were such that not for several moments did I realize another's howls of pain and outrage were mingled with my own. As this was borne in upon my suffering consciousness, I subsided into sobs, listening. The other sounds quickly died down as well, though a low, near-constant menacing growl made evident their author's continued presence.

The good doctor had ceased his ministrations at the clamor's height. He now ventured to ask my cousin why he had not done as requested, and shot the d——— bitch?

Cousin John replied that he had done so, "and at pretty near point-blank range. But the revolver must have misfired, for the beast got up and ran away, and I suppose it was only wounded."

"A wounded animal is all the more dangerous," Dr. Hesselius informed him. "I have already paid to your hellhound my tithe of flesh. Better take care of the problem at once."

Only my cousin did not chance to have any weapon handy, so that these two brave, bold gentlemen were required to cringe in my prison with me while Orson was sent forth into the now silent passage armed with a board torn from the floor. Meanwhile, I lay in my sodden clothes, half naked, half suffocating in a cooling puddle of noxious liquids. After some moments, the quiet continuing, Martha was ordered to unbolt the door again and go in search of the other servant. From her hallooing and remarks subsequent upon her return, I deduced that the house appeared empty.

that this filthy, soi-disant treatment is to be inflicted weekly. I do not intend to remain a captive here for so long.

The hedge-haunter is no spectre, but live, flesh and blood. It is the tawny bitch who has followed me on my daily walks. I saw her outline quite clearly through the hedge this morning, despite the rain. Orson accompanied me; I fancy Martha has taken a dislike to her duties, or to my other escort. I know not why, for the poor beast cannot help her looks. As for temper, the only signs she has shown of that have come upon threats to my well-being. I could almost love her.

Walked again with Orson this evening. I made sure he noticed how marvelously close the tawny bitch was able to follow our various paces. He liked it not.

Barking commenced earlier, at sunset, long before dark. Text: How sharper than a serpent's tooth it is, to have an ungrateful child, etc., etc. Well-laid arguments, but I cannot see anything apposite in the quotation. Does it contain some hint as to how I may make my escape? I must reflect on this.

Oh, my friend, my best and most beloved friend, soon now I shall be able to confide my heart unto your very bosom! I have quite a clear presentiment that it will be so.

This evening I was let out to accomplish my walk on my own. Martha's eyes were ever on me, it is true, as she stood in the entrance to the kitchen garden, with all the long gravel walk in her plain sight. But she could do nothing to prevent my plan.

It came to me because they would give me so much lamb. And the poor thing looked so thin, gliding along outside the hedge. And indeed she must have been quite wasted away, to have slipped through those tight-packed branches and come to me. I coaxed her to take the meat straight from my hand. Such a pet! I called her my honey, and kissed her cool, wet nose, and collared my arms about her soft, smooth-furred neck. Goat's meat would have been preferable. I remember that from Yeyetunde's teachings. It was goat's meat I placed upon her altar as a child. But the lamb was quite acceptable.

Twice more shall I make my offerings. I can hardly contain my great joy, but soon the barking will begin, so steadying to my nerves. So reassuring, to know that she is there.

Afternoon. This morning I have given unto her the portion brought to me to break my fast, and she has shown me the passage she is preparing for my escape. Thin as I am, the hole will yet need widening. My feeble hands have not been of much help. I am to leave this evening. She says she can dig all the day, and that it will be ready. Of course I shall have to crawl, and become fearfully dirty. So much the better if my light clothes are thereby darkened; they will not so easily betray me to my pursuers.

Pursuers I shall have, but she says she can distract them. I do know that she can set up an awful cacophony at will. But would she actually turn back to attack them? If so, she shall no longer fight alone. Together we will tear, we will savage

*The preceding text has been assembled from a collection of fragmentary writings discovered during the demolition of an old country house. Their presentation is as complete and chronologically correct as my efforts could make it. The veracity of their contents, however, has proven somewhat difficult to determine.*

*Penmanship and internal references (Dr. Hesselius drives a brougham; oilcloth rather than a sheet of India rubber is used during the enema's application) lead to the conclusion that the events narrated took place between 1830 and 1850. This very rough estimate I narrowed a bit further by deeds and entitlements pertaining to the purchase of the property, in 1833, by a Mr. John Forrest Welkin, presumably the narrator's "Cousin John." Parish records show his death as occurring in 1844. He would, at this time, have attained forty-eight years; he was not young, but certainly he fell far short of the age at which one dies suddenly and without apparent cause, as seems to have been the case. He was single, and had no heirs of the body.*

*Of the locations described by the author, only this house's "high garret" is of unquestionable provenance. The papers were found secreted beneath the loose flooring of just such a bare, comfortless room. The house itself had been uninhabited for half a century, commencing early in the reign of our Queen. The place has a bad reputation in the district as being haunted, and reports of various canine apparitions are easily obtainable at the hearths of all the neighbouring alehouses. Of course such superstitious folklore can scarcely be credited. No two "witnesses" can agree as to the size or number of the pack, though as to colouring there seems a fair consistency. To the rational mind, however, the house's situation down in Exmoor, halfway between South Molton and Lynmouth, and its less-than-luxurious appointments, ought to be enough to account for its long state of tenantlessness.*

*Turning to those proper names revealed by the text, often so fruitful of information for the careful investigator, my researches became more and more problematic. Winnywood Academy may possibly have been located in Witney, near Oxford. A relevant document, a six-year lease, apparently one in a series of such contracts, has been uncovered. It stipulates an agreement between one*

*Madame Ardhuis and the fifth Viscount Bevercorne for the use of Winny Hall. Contemporary records also indicate a pattern of purchases by this Madame Ardhuis at stationers, chandlers, coal merchants, and the like. Quantities and frequency are sufficient for the type of establishment sought.*

*Though the narrator writes of the "smiling skies of St. Cecilia," there is no trace of such an island in any atlas. Santa Cecilia is a small village in the mountains of Brazil (26°56′ S, 50°27′ W). Also, there is a Mount Cecilia in Northwest Australia (20°45′ S, 120°55′ E). Neither of these satisfactorily answers the description. We are left to make do with the uncomfortable knowledge that place-names do change with time, and local usage varies.*

*In reference to most of the persons depicted above, none but Christian names are used: Belle; John; Martha; Kitty; Belle's old nurse, Yeyetunde. Four others are referred to only by title: Father, Mother, Madame, and the document's intended reader, "my friend." The research involved in matching all these references with actual historical personages is beyond the scope of a lone amateur. Belle may have sprung from the loins of the irresponsible Hugh Farchurch, a connection of Welkin's on the distaff side. In postulating this, equating "Madame" with Madame Ardhuis, as seems reasonable, and achieving the identification of "Cousin John" with Welkin, I have done that of which I am capable.*

*In the case of Dr. Martin Hesselius we have a surname, and corresponding historical linkages. The doctor was well known during his professional career (1835–1871), and his presence would seem to vouch for the text's authenticity. But Hesselius's character as represented here is quite at odds with his reputation. He was known as a layer of mental disturbances, not as one who raised them into existence. Moreover, the few details of his personal appearance given us do not tally. We are left with the distinct impression that in this matter someone has been imposed upon.*

# BITTER GROUNDS

*Neil Gaiman*

## 1 | "Come back early or never come"

In every way that counted, I was dead. Inside somewhere maybe I was screaming and weeping and howling like an animal, but that was another person deep inside, another person who had no access to the face and lips and mouth and head, so on the surface I just shrugged and smiled and kept moving. If I could have physically passed away, just let it all go, like that, without doing anything, stepped out of life as easily as walking through a door, I would have. But I was going to sleep at night and waking in the morning, disappointed to be there and resigned to existence.

Sometimes I telephoned her. I let the phone ring once, maybe even twice, before I hung up.

The me who was screaming was so far inside nobody knew he was even there at all. Even I forgot that he was there, until one day I got into the car—I had to go to the store, I had decided, to bring back some apples—and I went past the store that sold apples and I kept driving, and driving. I was going south, and west, because if I went north or east I would run out of world too soon.

A couple of hours down the highway my cell phone started to ring. I wound down the window and threw the cell phone out. I wondered who would find it, whether they would answer the phone and find themselves gifted with my life.

When I stopped for gas I took all the cash I could on every card I had. I did the same for the next couple of days, ATM by ATM, until the cards stopped working.

The first two nights I slept in the car.

I was halfway through Tennessee when I realized I needed a bath badly enough to pay for it. I checked into a motel, stretched out in the bath, and slept in it until the water got cold and woke me. I shaved with a motel courtesy kit plastic razor and a sachet of foam. Then I stumbled to the bed, and I slept.

Awoke at 4:00 A.M., and knew it was time to get back on the road.

I went down to the lobby.

There was a man standing at the front desk when I got there: silver-gray hair although I guessed he was still in his thirties, if only just, thin lips, good suit rumpled, saying, "I *ordered* that cab an *hour* ago. One *hour* ago." He tapped the desk with his wallet as he spoke, the beats emphasizing his words.

The night manager shrugged. "I'll call again," he said. "But if they don't have the car, they can't send it." He dialed a phone number, said, "This is the Night's Out Inn front desk. . . . Yeah, I told him. . . . Yeah, I told him."

"Hey," I said. "I'm not a cab, but I'm in no hurry. You need a ride somewhere?"

For a moment the man looked at me like I was crazy, and for a moment there was fear in his eyes. Then he looked at me like I'd been sent from Heaven. "You know, by God, I do," he said.

"You tell me where to go," I said. "I'll take you there. Like I said, I'm in no hurry."

"Give me that phone," said the silver-gray man to the night clerk. He took the handset and said, "You can *cancel* your cab, because God just sent me a Good Samaritan. People come into your life for a reason. That's right. And I want you to think about that."

He picked up his briefcase—like me he had no luggage—and together we went out to the parking lot.

We drove through the dark. He'd check a hand-drawn map on his lap, with a flashlight attached to his key ring; then he'd say, "Left here," or "This way."

"It's good of you," he said.

"No problem. I have time."

"I appreciate it. You know, this has that pristine urban-legend quality, driving down country roads with a mysterious Samaritan. A Phantom Hitchhiker story. After I get to my destination, I'll describe you to a friend, and they'll tell me you died ten years ago, and still go round giving people rides."

"Be a good way to meet people."

He chuckled. "What do you do?"

"Guess you could say I'm between jobs," I said. "You?"

"I'm an anthropology professor." Pause. "I guess I should have introduced myself. Teach at a Christian college. People don't believe we teach anthropology at Christian colleges, but we do. Some of us."

"I believe you."

Another pause. "My car broke down. I got a ride to the motel from the highway patrol, as they said there was no tow truck going to be there until morning. Got two hours of sleep. Then the highway patrol called my hotel room. Tow truck's on the way. I got to be there when they arrive. Can you believe that? I'm not there, they won't touch it. Just drive away. Called a cab. Never came. Hope we get there before the tow truck."

"I'll do my best."

"I guess I should have taken a plane. It's not that I'm scared of flying. But I cashed in the ticket; I'm on my way to New Orleans. Hour's flight, four hundred and forty dollars. Day's drive, thirty dollars. That's four hundred and ten dollars spending money, and I don't have to account for it to anybody. Spent fifty dollars on the motel room, but that's just the way these things go. Academic conference. My first. Faculty doesn't believe in them. But things change. I'm looking forward to it. Anthropologists from all over the world." He named several, names that meant nothing to me. "I'm presenting a paper on the Haitian coffee girls."

"They grow it, or drink it?"

"Neither. They sold it, door to door in Port-au-Prince, early in the morning, in the early years of the century."

It was starting to get light, now.

"People thought they were zombies," he said. "You know. The walking dead. I think it's a right turn here."

"Were they? Zombies?"

He seemed very pleased to have been asked. "Well, anthropologically, there are several schools of thought about zombies. It's not as cut-and-dried as popularist works like *The Serpent and the Rainbow* would make it appear. First we have to define our terms: are we talking folk belief, or zombie dust, or the walking dead?"

"I don't know," I said. I was pretty sure *The Serpent and the Rainbow* was a horror movie.

"They were children, little girls, five to ten years old, who went door-to-door through Port-au-Prince selling the chicory coffee mixture. Just about this time of day, before the sun was up. They belonged to one old woman. Hang a left just before we go into the next turn. When she died, the girls vanished. That's what the books tell you."

"And what do you believe?" I asked.

"That's my car," he said, with relief in his voice. It was a red Honda Accord, on the side of the road. There was a tow truck beside it, lights flashing, a man beside the tow truck smoking a cigarette. We pulled up behind the tow truck.

The anthropologist had the door of the car opened before I'd stopped; he grabbed his briefcase and was out of the car.

"Was giving you another five minutes, then I was going to take off," said the tow-truck driver. He dropped his cigarette into a puddle on the tarmac. "Okay, I'll need your triple-A card, and a credit card."

The man reached for his wallet. He looked puzzled. He put his hands in his pockets. He said, "My wallet." He came back to my car, opened the passenger-side door and leaned back inside. I turned on the light. He patted the empty seat. "My wallet," he said again. His voice was plaintive and hurt.

"You had it back in the motel," I reminded him. "You were holding it. It was in your hand."

He said, "God *damn it*. God fucking *damn* it to hell."

"Everything okay there?" called the tow-truck driver.

"Okay," said the anthropologist to me, urgently. "This is what we'll do. You drive back to the motel. I must have left the wallet on the desk. Bring it back here. I'll keep him happy until then. Five minutes, it'll take you five minutes." He must have seen the expression on my face. He said, "Remember. People come into your life for a reason."

I shrugged, irritated to have been sucked into someone else's story.

Then he shut the car door and gave me a thumbs-up.

I wished I could just have driven away and abandoned him, but it was too late, I was driving to the hotel. The night clerk gave me the wallet, which he had noticed on the counter, he told me, moments after we left.

I opened the wallet. The credit cards were all in the name of Jackson Anderton.

It took me half an hour to find my way back, as the sky grayed into full dawn. The tow truck was gone. The rear window of the red Honda Accord was broken, and the driver's-side door hung open. I wondered if it was a different car, if I had driven the wrong way to the wrong place; but there were the tow-truck driver's cigarette stubs, crushed on the road, and in the ditch nearby I found a gaping briefcase, empty, and beside it, a manila folder containing a fifteen-page typescript, a prepaid hotel reservation at a Marriott in New Orleans in the name of Jackson Anderton, and a packet of three condoms, ribbed for extra pleasure.

On the title page of the typescript was printed:

*This was the way Zombies are spoken of: They are the bodies without souls. The living dead. Once they were dead, and after that they were called back to life again.*

Hurston, *Tell My Horse*

I took the manila folder, but left the briefcase where it was. I drove south under a pearl-colored sky.

People come into your life for a reason. Right.

I could not find a radio station that would hold its signal. Eventually I pressed the scan button on the radio and just left it on, left it scanning from channel to channel in a relentless quest for signal, scurrying from gospel to oldies to Bible talk to sex talk to country, three seconds a station with plenty of white noise in between.

*. . . Lazarus, who was dead, you make no mistake about that, he was dead, and Jesus brought him back to show us—I say to show us . . .*

*. . . what I call a Chinese dragon. Can I say this on the air? Just as you, y'know, get your rocks off, you whomp her round the backatha head, it all spurts outta her nose. I damn near laugh my ass off . . .*

*. . . If you come home tonight I'll be waiting in the darkness for my woman with my bottle and my gun . . .*

*. . . When Jesus says will you be there, will you be there? No man knows the day or the hour, so will you be there . . .*

*. . . president unveiled an initiative today . . .*

*. . . fresh-brewed in the morning. For you, for me. For every day. Because every day is freshly ground . . .*

Over and over. It washed over me, driving through the day, on the back roads. Just driving and driving.

They become more personable as you head south, the people. You sit in a diner, and along with your coffee and your food, they bring you comments, questions, smiles, and nods.

It was evening, and I was eating fried chicken and collard greens and hush puppies, and a waitress smiled at me. The food seemed tasteless, but I guessed that might have been my problem, not theirs.

I nodded at her politely, which she took as an invitation to come over and refill my coffee cup. The coffee was bitter, which I liked. At least it tasted of something.

"Looking at you," she said, "I would guess that you are a professional man. May I enquire as to your profession?" That was what she said, word for word.

"Indeed you may," I said, feeling almost possessed by something, and affably pompous, like W. C. Fields or the Nutty Professor (the fat one, not the Jerry Lewis one, although I am actually within pounds of the optimum weight for my height). "I happen to be . . . an anthropologist, on my way to a conference in New Orleans, where I shall confer, consult, and otherwise hobnob with my fellow anthropologists."

"I knew it," she said. "Just looking at you. I had you figured for a professor. Or a dentist, maybe."

She smiled at me one more time. I thought about stopping forever in that little town, eating in that diner every morning and every night. Drinking their bitter coffee and having her smile at me until I ran out of coffee and money and days.

Then I left her a good tip, and went south and west.

## 2 | "Tongue brought me here"

There were no hotel rooms in New Orleans, or anywhere in the New Orleans sprawl. A jazz festival had eaten them, every one. It was too hot to sleep in my car, and even if I'd cranked a window and been prepared to suffer the heat, I felt unsafe. New Orleans is a real place, which is more than I can say about most of the cities I've lived in, but it's not a safe place, not a friendly one.

I stank, and itched. I wanted to bathe, and to sleep, and for the world to stop moving past me.

I drove from fleabag motel to fleabag motel, and then, at the last, as I had always known I would, I drove into the parking lot of the downtown Marriott on Canal Street. At least I knew they had one free room. I had a voucher for it in the manila folder.

"I need a room," I said to one of the women behind the counter.

She barely looked at me. "All rooms are taken," she said. "We won't have anything until Tuesday."

I needed to shave, and to shower, and to rest. *What's the worst she can say?* I thought. *I'm sorry, you've already checked in?*

"I have a room, prepaid by my university. The name's Anderton."

She nodded, tapped a keyboard, said "Jackson?" then gave me a key to my room, and I initialed the room rate. She pointed me to the elevators.

A short man with a ponytail, and a dark, hawkish face dusted with white stubble, cleared his throat as we stood beside the elevators. "You're the Anderton from Hopewell," he said. "We were neighbors in the *Journal of Anthropological Heresies.*" He wore a white T-shirt that said "Anthropologists Do It While Being Lied To."

"We were?"

"We were. I'm Campbell Lakh. University of Norwood and Streatham. Formerly North Croydon Polytechnic. England. I wrote the paper about Icelandic spirit walkers and fetches."

"Good to meet you," I said, and shook his hand. "You don't have a London accent."

"I'm a Brummie," he said. "From Birmingham," he added. "Never seen you at one of these things before."

"It's my first conference," I told him.

"Then you stick with me," he said. "I'll see you're all right. I remember my first one of these conferences, I was scared shitless I'd do something stupid the entire time. We'll stop on the mezzanine, get our stuff, then get cleaned up. There must have been a hundred babies on my plane over, IsweartoGod. They took it in shifts to scream, shit, and puke, though. Never fewer than ten of them screaming at a time."

We stopped on the mezzanine, collected our badges and programs. "Don't forget to sign up for the ghost walk," said the smiling woman behind the table. "Ghost walks of Old New Orleans each night, limited to fifteen people in each party, so sign up fast."

I bathed, and washed my clothes out in the basin, then hung them up in the bathroom to dry.

I sat naked on the bed, and examined the papers that had been in Anderton's briefcase. I skimmed through the paper he had intended to present, without taking in the content.

On the clean back of page five he had written, in a tight, mostly legible scrawl, *In a perfect perfect world you could fuck people without giving them a piece of your heart. And every glittering kiss and every touch of flesh is another shard of heart you'll never see again. Until walking (waking? calling?) on your own is unsupportable.*

When my clothes were pretty much dry I put them back on and went down to the lobby bar. Campbell was already there. He was drinking a gin and tonic, with a gin and tonic on the side.

He had out a copy of the conference program, and had circled each of the talks and papers he wanted to see. ("Rule one, if it's before midday, fuck it unless you're the one doing it," he explained.) He showed me my talk, circled in pencil.

"I've never done this before," I told him. "Presented a paper at a conference."

"It's a piece of piss, Jackson," he said. "Piece of piss. You know what I do?"

"No," I said.

"I just get up and read the paper. Then people ask questions, and I just bullshit," he said. "Actively bullshit, as opposed to passively. That's the best bit. Just bullshitting. Piece of utter piss."

"I'm not really good at, um, bullshitting," I said. "Too honest."

"Then nod, and tell them that that's a really perceptive question, and that it's addressed at length in the longer version of the paper, of which the one you are reading is an edited abstract. If you get some nut job giving you a really difficult time about something you got wrong, just get huffy and say that it's not about what's fashionable to believe, it's about the truth."

"Does that work?"

"Christ yes. I gave a paper a few years back about the origins of the Thuggee sects in Persian military troops. It's why you could get Hindus and Muslims equally becoming Thuggee, you see—the Kali worship was tacked on later. It would have begun as some sort of Manichaean secret society—"

"Still spouting that nonsense?" She was a tall, pale woman with a shock of white hair, wearing clothes that looked both aggressively, studiedly Bohemian and far too warm for the climate. I could imagine her riding a bicycle, the kind with a wicker basket in the front.

"Spouting it? I'm writing a fucking book about it," said the Englishman. "So, what I want to know is, who's coming with me to the French Quarter to taste all that New Orleans can offer?"

"I'll pass," said the woman, unsmiling. "Who's your friend?"

"This is Jackson Anderton, from Hopewell College."

"The Zombie Coffee Girls paper?" She smiled. "I saw it in the program. Quite fascinating. Yet another thing we owe Zora, eh?"

"Along with *The Great Gatsby*," I said.

"Hurston knew F. Scott Fitzgerald?" said the bicycle woman. "I did not know that. We forget how small the New York literary world was back then, and how the color bar was often lifted for a genius."

The Englishman snorted. "Lifted? Only under sufferance. The woman died in penury as a cleaner in Florida. Nobody knew she'd written any of the stuff she wrote, let alone that she'd worked with Fitzgerald on *The Great Gatsby*. It's pathetic, Margaret."

"Posterity has a way of taking these things into account," said the tall woman. She walked away.

Campbell stared after her. "When I grow up," he said, "I want to be her."

"Why?"

He looked at me. "Yeah, that's the attitude. You're right. Some of us write the best-sellers; some of us read them. Some of us get the prizes; some of us don't. What's important is being human, isn't it? It's how good a person you are. Being alive."

He patted me on the arm.

"Come on. Interesting anthropological phenomenon I've read about on the Internet I shall point out to you tonight, of the kind you probably don't see back in Dead Rat, Kentucky. Id est, women who would, under normal circumstances, not show their tits for a hundred quid, who will be only too pleased to get 'em out for the crowd for some cheap plastic beads."

"Universal trading medium," I said. "Beads."

"Fuck," he said. "There's a paper in that. Come on. You ever had a Jell-O shot, Jackson?"

"No."

"Me neither. Bet they'll be disgusting. Let's go and see."

We paid for our drinks. I had to remind him to tip.

"By the way," I said. "F. Scott Fitzgerald. What was his wife's name?"

"Zelda? What about her?"

"Nothing," I said.

Zelda. Zora. Whatever. We went out.

## 3 | "Nothing, like something, happens anywhere"

Midnight, give or take. We were in a bar on Bourbon Street, me and the English anthropology prof, and he started buying drinks—real drinks, this place didn't do Jell-O shots—for a couple of dark-haired women at the bar. They looked so similar they might have been sisters. One wore a red ribbon in her hair; the other wore a white ribbon. Gauguin might have painted them, only he would have painted them bare-breasted, and without the silver mouse-skull earrings. They laughed a lot.

We had seen a small party of academics walk past the bar at one point, being led by a guide with a black umbrella. I pointed them out to Campbell.

The woman with the red ribbon raised an eyebrow. "They go on the Haunted History tours, looking for ghosts. You want to say, 'Dude, this is where the ghosts come; this is where the dead stay.' Easier to go looking for the living."

"You saying the tourists are *alive?*" said the other, mock concern on her face.

"When they *get* here," said the first, and they both laughed at that. They laughed a lot.

The one with the white ribbon laughed at everything Campbell said. She would tell him, "Say 'fuck' again," and he would say it, and she would say "Fook! Fook!" trying to copy him. And he'd say, "It's not *fook*, it's *fuck*," and she couldn't hear the difference, and would laugh some more.

After two drinks, maybe three, he took her by the hand and walked her into the back of the bar, where music was playing, and it was dark, and there were a couple of people already, if not dancing, then moving against each other.

I stayed where I was, beside the woman with the red ribbon in her hair.

She said, "So you're in the record company too?"

I nodded. It was what Campbell had told them we did. "I hate telling people I'm a fucking academic," he had said reasonably, when they were in the ladies' room. Instead he had told them that he had discovered Oasis.

"How about you? What do you do in the world?"

She said, "I'm a priestess of Santeria. Me, I got it all in my blood; my papa was Brazilian, my momma was Irish-Cherokee. In Brazil, everybody makes love with everybody and they have the best little brown babies. Everybody got black slave blood; everybody got Indian blood; my poppa even got some Japanese blood. His brother, my uncle, he looks Japanese. My poppa, he just a good-looking man. People think it was my poppa I got the Santeria from, but no, it was my grandmomma—said she was Cherokee, but I had her figgered for mostly high yaller when I saw the old photographs. When I was three I was talking to dead folks. When I was five I watched a huge black dog, size of a Harley-Davidson, walking behind a man in the street; no one could see it but me. When I told my mom, she told my grandmomma, they said, 'She's got to know; she's got to learn.' There was people to teach me, even as a little girl.

"I was never afraid of dead folk. You know that? They never hurt you. So many things in this town can hurt you, but the dead don't hurt you. Living people hurt you. They hurt you so bad."

I shrugged.

"This is a town where people sleep with each other, you know. We make love to each other. It's something we do to show we're still alive."

I wondered if this was a come-on. It did not seem to be.

She said, "You hungry?"

"A little," I said.

She said, "I know a place near here they got the best bowl of gumbo in New Orleans. Come on."

I said, "I hear it's a town where you're best off not walking on your own at night."

"That's right," she said. "But you'll have me with you. You're safe, with me with you."

Out on the street, college girls were flashing their breasts to the crowds on the balconies. For every glimpse of nipple the onlookers would cheer and throw plastic beads. I had known the red-ribbon woman's name earlier in the evening, but now it had evaporated.

"Used to be they only did this shit at Mardi Gras," she said. "Now the tourists expect it, so it's just tourists doing it for the tourists. The locals don't care. When you need to piss," she added, "you tell me."

"Okay. Why?"

"Because most tourists who get rolled, get rolled when they go into the alleys to relieve themselves. Wake up an hour later in Pirates' Alley with a sore head and an empty wallet."

"I'll bear that in mind."

She pointed to an alley as we passed it, foggy and deserted. "Don't go there," she said.

The place we wound up in was a bar with tables. A TV on above the bar showed "The Tonight Show" with the sound off and subtitles on, although the subtitles kept scrambling into numbers and fractions. We ordered the gumbo, a bowl each.

I was expecting more from the best gumbo in New Orleans. It was almost tasteless. Still, I spooned it down, knowing that I needed food, that I had had nothing to eat that day.

Three men came into the bar. One sidled; one strutted; one shambled. The sidler was dressed like a Victorian undertaker, high top hat and all. His skin was fish-belly pale; his hair was long and stringy; his beard was long and threaded with silver beads. The strutter was dressed in a long black leather coat, dark clothes underneath. His skin was very black. The last one, the shambler, hung back, waiting by the door. I could not see much of his face, nor decode his race: what I could see of his skin was a dirty gray. His lank hair hung over his face. He made my skin crawl.

The first two men made straight to our table, and I was, momentarily, scared for my skin, but they paid no attention to me. They looked at the woman with the red ribbon, and both of the men kissed her on the cheek. They asked about friends they had not seen, about who did what to whom in which bar and why. They reminded me of the fox and the cat from *Pinocchio*.

"What happened to your pretty girlfriend?" the woman asked the black man.

He smiled, without humor. "She put a squirrel tail on my family tomb."

She pursed her lips. "Then you better off without her."

"That's what I say."

I glanced over at the one who gave me the creeps. He was a filthy thing, junkie thin, gray-lipped. His eyes were downcast. He barely moved. I wondered what the three men were doing together: the fox and the cat and the ghost.

Then the white man took the woman's hand and pressed it to his lips, bowed to her, raised a hand to me in a mock salute, and the three of them were gone.

"Friends of yours?"

"Bad people," she said. "Macumba. Not friends of anybody."

"What was up with the guy by the door? Is he sick?"

She hesitated; then she shook her head. "Not really. I'll tell you when you're ready."

"Tell me now."

On the TV, Jay Leno was talking to a thin blond woman. IT&S NOT .UST T½E MOVIE, said the caption. SO H.VE SS YOU SE¾N THE AC ION F!GURE? He picked up a small toy from his desk, pretended to check under its skirt to make sure it was anatomically correct. [LAUGHTER], said the caption.

She finished her bowl of gumbo, licked the spoon with a red, red tongue, and put it down in the bowl. "A lot of kids they come to New Orleans. Some of them read Anne Rice books and figure they learn about being vampires here. Some of them have abusive parents; some are just bored. Like stray kittens living in drains, they come here. They found a whole new breed of cat living in a drain in New Orleans, you know that?"

"No."

SLAUGHTER S ] said the caption, but Jay was still grinning, and "The Tonight Show" went to a car commercial.

"He was one of the street kids, only he had a place to crash at night. Good kid. Hitchhiked from L.A. to New Orleans. Wanted to be left alone to smoke a little weed, listen to his Doors cassettes, study up on chaos magick and read the complete works of Aleister Crowley. Also get his dick sucked. He wasn't particular about who did it. Bright eyes and bushy tail."

"Hey," I said. "That was Campbell. Going past. Out there."

"Campbell?"

"My friend."

"The record producer?" She smiled as she said it, and I thought, *She knows. She knows he was lying. She knows what he is.*

I put down a twenty and a ten on the table, and we went out onto the street, to find him, but he was already gone. "I thought he was with your sister," I told her.

"No sister," she said. "No sister. Only me. Only me."

We turned a corner and were engulfed by a crowd of noisy tourists, like a sudden breaker crashing onto the shore. Then, as fast as they had come, they were gone, leaving only a handful of people behind them. A teenaged girl was throwing up in a gutter, a young man nervously standing near her, holding her purse and a plastic cup half full of booze.

The woman with the red ribbon in her hair was gone. I wished I had made a note of her name, or the name of the bar in which I'd met her.

I had intended to leave that night, to take the interstate west to Houston and from there to Mexico, but I was tired and two-thirds drunk, and instead I went back to my room. When the morning came I was still in the Marriott. Everything I had worn the night before smelled of perfume and rot.

I put on my T-shirt and pants, went down to the hotel gift shop, picked out a couple more T- shirts and a pair of shorts. The tall woman, the one without the bicycle, was in there, buying some Alka-Seltzer.

She said, "They've moved your presentation. It's now in the Audubon Room, in about twenty minutes. You might want to clean your teeth first. Your best friends won't tell you, but I hardly know you, Mister Anderton, so I don't mind telling you at all."

I added a traveling toothbrush and toothpaste to the stuff I was buying. Adding to my possessions, though, troubled me. I felt I should be shedding them. I needed to be transparent, to have nothing.

I went up to the room, cleaned my teeth, put on the jazz festival T-shirt. And then, because I had no choice in the matter; or because I was doomed to confer, consult, and otherwise hobnob; or because I was pretty certain Campbell would be in the audience and I wanted to say good-bye to him before I drove away, I picked up the typescript and went down to the Audubon Room, where fifteen people were waiting. Campbell was not one of them.

I was not scared. I said hello, and I looked at the top of page one.

It began with another quote from Zora Neale Hurston:

**Big Zombies who come in the night to do malice are talked about. Also the little girl Zombies who are sent out by their owners in the dark dawn to sell little packets of roasted coffee. Before sun-up their cries of "Café grillé" can be heard from dark places in the streets and one can only see them if one calls out for**

**the seller to come with the goods. Then the little dead one makes herself visible and mounts the steps.**

Anderton continued on from there, with quotations from Hurston's contemporaries and several extracts from old interviews with older Haitians, the man's paper leaping, as far as I was able to tell, from conclusion to conclusion, spinning fancies into guesses and suppositions and weaving those into facts.

Halfway through, Margaret, the tall woman without the bicycle, came in and simply stared at me. I thought, *She knows I'm not him. She knows.* I kept reading though. What else could I do?

At the end, I asked for questions.

Somebody asked me about Zora Neale Hurston's research practices. I said that was a very good question, which was addressed at greater length in the finished paper, of which what I had read was essentially an edited abstract.

Someone else—a short, plump woman—stood up and announced that the zombie girls could not have existed: zombie drugs and powders numbed you, induced deathlike trances, but still worked fundamentally on belief—the belief that you were now one of the dead, and had no will of your own. How, she asked, could a child of four or five be induced to believe such a thing? No. The coffee girls were, she said, one with the Indian rope trick, just another of the urban legends of the past.

Personally I agreed with her, but I nodded and said that her points were well made and well taken, and that from my perspective—which was, I hoped, a genuinely anthropological perspective—what mattered was not whether it was easy to believe, but, much more importantly, if it was the truth.

They applauded, and afterward a man with a beard asked me whether he might be able to get a copy of the paper for a journal he edited. It occurred to me that it was a good thing that I had come to New

Orleans, that Anderton's career would not be harmed by his absence from the conference.

The plump woman, whose badge said her name was Shanelle Gravely-King, was waiting for me at the door. She said, "I really enjoyed that. I don't want you to think that I didn't."

Campbell didn't turn up for his presentation. Nobody ever saw him again.

Margaret introduced me to someone from New York and mentioned that Zora Neale Hurston had worked on *The Great Gatsby*. The man said yes, that was pretty common knowledge these days. I wondered if she had called the police, but she seemed friendly enough. I was starting to stress, I realized. I wished I had not thrown away my cell phone.

Shanelle Gravely-King and I had an early dinner in the hotel, at the beginning of which I said, "Oh, let's not talk shop." And she agreed that only the very dull talked shop at the table, so we talked about rock bands we had seen live, fictional methods of slowing the decomposition of a human body, and about her partner, who was a woman older than she was and who owned a restaurant, and then we went up to my room. She smelled of baby powder and jasmine, and her naked skin was clammy against mine.

Over the next couple of hours I used two of the three condoms. She was sleeping by the time I returned from the bathroom, and I climbed into the bed next to her. I thought about the words Anderton had written, hand-scrawled on the back of a page of the typescript, and I wanted to check them, but I fell asleep, a soft-fleshed jasmine-scented woman pressing close to me.

After midnight, I woke from a dream, and a woman's voice was whispering in the darkness.

She said, "So he came into town, with his Doors cassettes and his Crowley books, and his handwritten list of the secret URLs for chaos magick on the Web, and everything was good. He even got a few disciples, runaways like him, and he got his dick sucked whenever he wanted, and the world was good.

"And then he started to believe his own press. He thought he was the real thing. That he was the dude. He thought he was a big mean tiger-cat, not a little kitten. So he dug up . . . something . . . someone else wanted.

"He thought the something he dug up would look after him. Silly boy. And that night, he's sitting in Jackson Square, talking to the Tarot readers, telling them about Jim Morrison and the cabala, and someone taps him on the shoulder, and he turns, and someone blows powder into his face, and he breathes it in.

"Not all of it. And he is going to do something about it, when he realizes there's nothing to be done, because he's all paralyzed. There's fugu fish and toad skin and ground bone and everything else in that powder, and he's breathed it in.

"They take him down to emergency, where they don't do much for him, figuring him for a street rat with a drug problem, and by the next day he can move again, although it's two, three days until he can speak.

"Trouble is, he needs it. He wants it. He knows there's some big secret in the zombie powder, and he was almost there. Some people say they mixed heroin with it, some shit like that, but they didn't even need to do that. He wants it.

"And they told him they wouldn't sell it to him. But if he did jobs for them, they'd give him a little zombie powder, to smoke, to sniff, to rub on his gums, to swallow. Sometimes they'd give him nasty jobs to do no one else wanted. Sometimes they'd just humiliate him because they could—make him eat dog shit from the gutter, maybe. Kill for them, maybe. Anything but die. All skin and bones. He do anything for his zombie powder.

"And he still thinks, in the little bit of his head that's still him, that he's not a zombie. That he's not dead, that there's a threshold he hasn't stepped over. But he crossed it long time ago."

I reached out a hand, and touched her. Her body was hard, and slim, and lithe, and her breasts felt like breasts that Gauguin might have painted. Her mouth, in the darkness, was soft and warm against mine.

People come into your life for a reason.

## 4 | "Those people ought to know who we are and tell that we are here"

When I woke, it was still almost dark, and the room was silent. I turned on the light, looked on the pillow for a ribbon, white or red, or for a mouse-skull earring, but there was nothing to show that there had ever been anyone in the bed that night but me.

I got out of bed and pulled open the drapes, looked out of the window. The sky was graying in the east.

I thought about moving south, about continuing to run, continuing to pretend I was alive. But it was, I knew now, much too late for that. There are doors, after all, between the living and the dead, and they swing in both directions.

I had come as far as I could.

There was a faint *tap-tap*ping on the hotel-room door. I pulled on my pants and the T-shirt I had set out in, and barefoot, I pulled the door open.

The coffee girl was waiting for me.

Everything beyond the door was touched with light, an open, wonderful predawn light, and I heard the sound of birds calling on the morning air. The street was on a hill, and the houses facing me were little more than shanties. There was mist in the air, low to the ground, curling like something from an old black-and-white film, but it would be gone by noon.

The girl was thin and small; she did not appear to be more than six years old. Her eyes were cobwebbed with what might have been cataracts; her skin was as gray as it had once been brown. She was holding a white hotel cup out to me, holding it carefully, with one small hand on the handle, one hand beneath the saucer. It was half filled with a steaming mud-colored liquid.

I bent to take it from her, and I sipped it. It was a very bitter drink, and it was hot, and it woke me the rest of the way.

I said, "Thank you."

Someone, somewhere, was calling my name.

The girl waited, patiently, while I finished the coffee. I put the cup down on the carpet; then I put out my hand and touched her shoulder.

She reached up her hand, spread her small gray fingers, and took hold of mine. She knew I was with her. Wherever we were headed now, we were going there together.

I remembered something somebody had once said to me. "It's okay. Every day is freshly ground," I told her.

The coffee girl's expression did not change, but she nodded, as if she had heard me, and gave my arm an impatient tug. She held my hand tight with her cold, cold fingers, and we walked, finally, side by side into the misty dawn.

# SHINING THROUGH 24/7

*devorah major*

**H**ola, Glow, you got company. Says he knows you from before."

When she heard Chino's sandstone voice call through her trailer window, Glow looked up from the fluorescent Marine Blush polish that she was painting on her big toe.

"Don't know anybody from before."

Glow had grown comfortable with the small circle of folks that accepted her, although most of them accepted her from a couple of arm lengths with a lead apron in the middle. She had made peace with her life. Chino was a real friend. So was the cook, Tillie. They would eat some of their meals with her. Chino had even slept with her a couple of times. Life was tolerable, almost good.

"Glow, he says he's a friend."

"Ain't interested."

It was then that she heard Dusty's scratchy voice ring out, "That is you, Joline! Well how 'bout you get interested?"

Glow smiled in spite of herself. He had been a friend, once. But he wasn't a friend the last time she saw him ten years ago. In fact the last thing she remembered was his shadow hovering over her twisted, retching body before he ran out of the basement apartment in the abandoned building that they called home.

She smiled and moved toward the door. "Dusty? If I open this door for you, you got a hug for me, even though you know how I am?"

"Yeah, girl, you got one for me?"

Joline opened the door and stood hands akimbo dressed in a cream-colored sweat suit, her hair tied up under a pale pink scarf, her neck and face and hands letting off a faint apple-green mist.

"I was damn happy to find out that you were still alive . . . and workin' it too." The man stared at the ground as he talked, brushed his hand across a thick mustache that covered most of his top lip. Glow looked at him. He had picked up some weight and only had a few strands of gray to show that he was closer to fifty than he would admit to any of the young honeys that caught his fancy. Dusty did not return her gaze. He stood sideways and continued to stare at the broken tarmac as he laughed and talked. "I was working on a construction crew in East Palo Alto and I saw a flyer for 'The Neon Sensation.' Purple and red was painted all around this sexy brown-skin gal with big round eyes. To tell you the truth, last time I saw you it was more yellow-orange, and a sheet a paper couldn't fit between your skin and your bones. But those eyes, all round and dark, all the time looking, I knew it was you. Well"—he chuckled to himself—"that and the neon. You know." Dusty covered his mouth at this last part and winced slightly. "Anyway it's good t'see you doing better. Joline, you inviting me in or what?"

"Say it's good to see me? What I look like to you, Dusty. You got your face turned all sideways. What the hell I look like to you? Not some damn flyer—me?" She spat the last few words out with the edge of tears in her voice.

Dusty walked up three steps and wrapped his arms around her. Chino started to come up the steps in back of Dusty, but Glow waved him away as Dusty kissed Glow on each cheek and then pulled her close again. Joline could feel him trembling.

"You look pretty good. Finest I ever saw you." Dusty pulled out of the hug as he spoke and covered his mouth as he smiled. He was dressed in his red velour sweats and sporting a new haircut, square at the top and faded from the top of the ears. His hands were gloved, and his face seemed to be covered with a thick layer of burnt-umber foundation.

"You put on some weight, girl."

"Yeah. You got a little weight on you too."

"You still got the glow on I see."

"Name says it all." She shrugged.

"Naw girl, not all of it. Fact is I came to get the rest of the story, to get a better understanding of what happened . . ." His voice trailed off.

"As I remember, last time I saw you, you weren't too interested in finding out the four-one-one. Didn't even have time to help out a sick friend. Just had time to hightail it out the door."

"Well I got some time now. Even brought some beer. But I can go get something else if—"

"Don't much drink anymore." Glow sighed. "But come on in, Dusty. Let's drink it up for old times' sake. How come you don't have a mask on? You know they say I spill radiation. You're supposed to put on the metal apron and stand behind the glass." She motioned for him to sit down on the straight-back chair that stood near the window. She settled back down on the couch.

"You know I'm radiation-proof," Dusty said as he sunk into the chair. "But, I was wondering, Joline, does your thing shine, too?"

"See that? Ain't seen me in fifteen years and just as crude as ever. What it matter to you? Just 'cause I gave you some when I was cracked out, sure as hell doesn't mean I'll give you some now. That's why you came?" She attacked her words like a sideshow barker. "See the freak. Get your glow on here. A miracle of radiation disease. No cancer, no rotten skin, just a yellow glow that turns orange when she gets angry. Crack that whip; watch her shine!" As she spoke a smell of curdled milk came from the chair, and everything around her got brighter, orange rays falling across the Naugahyde seat cushions and onto the floor. Even the curtains had a new tint.

307

Dusty moved to the couch and sat down next to Glow and handed her a beer. "Here's to staying alive." As he did so Glow thought she saw some yellow flash from his mouth. "So Joline . . . or you want me to call you Glow now?"

"Whatever suits you, suits me fine."

Dusty looked down at the floor and smiled. "Now girl, that's what I've always wanted to hear. Because maybe now we could kind of suit up each other. Y'know, I wear a metal apron and you take it off; and you wear one and I take it off. And then after the apron we can work on to—"

Glow broke out laughing. "Dusty, you must be real hard up to come looking for a radiation mama to hang with. Last time I saw you, you was trying to get away from me as fast as you could."

"Joline, you were glowing orange all over you, and it was alive. You were throwing up and spitting. I'll never forget the way the spit ran out of your mouth and onto the floor. It flattened out and then rolled itself into a ball and rolled onto the leg of your jeans, and I swear it found some open skin at your waist and dug right back in you. You expect me to stay around and watch? I might be a damn fool, but I'm not stupid."

"Well, you could've seen if I was all right."

"Damn, Joline, you weren't all right. Even a blind man coulda seen that."

"Well, while you were running out the place, I was busy vomiting and foaming at the mouth for two or three days. Folks came by to visit you, but they'd open the door and see me lying in a pool of vomit and shining like a damn Las Vegas casino, and they'd hotfoot it outta there."

"What the hell made you like that? That's what I need to know. I mean—"

"I spent those three days trying to remember myself what happened. Trying to understand what happened. Round 'bout eleven I was trying to get me a little sumpthin' sumpthin', you know. And I headed over to the blocks. I figured I could check out some cars. You know, maybe find an open door and get something I could sell, or some change in the ashtray, something.

"Well, like it was just waiting for me there is a car with a window down a little way, and what looked like a brand new baby seat sitting in the back, and a kinda nice CD player in the dashboard. I start after the car seat cause I know that's five, maybe seven-fifty. So I get in the backseat, and I start unhooking the seat, and I'm about to get it out. Then this big ole yella woman wearing all kind of bracelets and expensive stuff dangling from her head and waist come yelling, what am I doing in her car. It was the lady used to live around from my stepdad, Lou. You know, always telling fortunes, spitting on folks' feet, and throwing powder.

"So there I am, kinda sideways half in and half out the car, you know, with one foot on the street. It was one of those old Volvos, big old backseat, easy to get in and out of fast. So just like that I pull out and start to haul ass, but she sticks out her leg and trips me. And I'm there on my butt and the car seat is hanging out the car, and my arm has got the seat belt wrapped around it. I'm trying to get loose, all the time talking about how I thought it was my cousin's car and I was just helping her out."

Dusty cut into her story. "You always did tell the weakest lies. . . ."

"And a whole lotta times folks go for them." Glow smiled back. Other than Chino she had never told the whole story to anyone. "Yeah, some people go for almost anything, but not this woman. I'm whining about how my cousin tole me to get in, and how I was just doing what I was told, and how I'm sorry. All the time I'm trying to get up and on down the block, but then it's like she was just burning me with her eyes. Just pressing me down. Seemed like I couldn't get my legs steady under me or get loose from that strap.

"First she's looking at me real mean, but then she soften up and talk to me real soft but at the same time cutting into my head: 'You Lou's child, ain't you, baby. I remember before he spun out he brought you around. Tried to get me to do a blessing. Your daddy always asking for something he already has, and trying to get full off of something he don't need. And now here you are just like him. But you deserved to be given more than you got, so I'll help you out of that hole you dug yourself into.' Then she spit on the ground and stamped four beats with her left foot and three times with her right. And then when it gets time for the eighth beat she spits again and starts talking about how it's time for me to give up the pipe and at the same time acting like I'm causing trouble for her.

"Then she smiled like we old friends, talking about she's going to be kind to me and distract the snow queen so she'll let go a my belly. She says not to worry, I won't ever crave no more kinda drugs. She says, 'Next time you see me, I don't want to hear nothing out you but *thank you kindly*. You hear me, girl? That's what you pay me for this gift I'm going to give you. Just a thank you kindly.' Then she laughs and reaches out her hand to help me up. She says something else, but I didn't understand a word 'cause suddenly she's talking all gibberish. I mean the words are all in English, but they don't fit together in a way that made sense. Then I see her reach into a pouch that's hanging off her belt. See, she had this wide sash look like it's all kind of bits and pieces of rags braided together tight, and she's got little sacks hanging all around it like charms on a bracelet."

"I remember her now," Dusty said. "She could walk up on you quiet as could be, but when she got there, she'd be a pile of noise what with bells ringing, and shells crackling against each other."

"Yeah," Glow interrupted him, impatient to get back to her story. "But see, you only hear all that stuff if she's going into her bags. I remember when I was a child, I heard one rattle and asked her what was inside, and she told me bones. And I asked her what kind, and she told me to never mind what I didn't need to know. But I remember she kept those bones inside a leather pouch, only I didn't know it was leather then. In fact, I asked her what was the pouch made out of, and she said just as sweet as could be, 'Animal skin, of course. Why baby girl, skin and bones always go together. You remember that. You don't want to put bones in silk or canvas, only some kind of leather.' Like I was going to be doing anything with a bone 'sides chewing on some barbecued ribs or something. Anyway, here I am trying to get up, and I see that same leather pouch hanging from her sash, and another one look like some cheap cotton, and one look all Chinese with birds and flowers on it, and one was just some kinda plastic. Well, she puts her hand in the flowery one and takes out some powder and blows it in my face. Then she says some other words and spits on the ground itself. Then she goes back in her belt and is opening the leather pouch. But that one . . . that one got stuck, and she get so involved with it, she let her gaze offa me. Well, that was all I needed to break away. Dusty, I just took off running. But she's not chasing me. She's talkin' about I didn't let her finish, talkin' quiet in my ear, right next to me, but she ain't nowhere close. You know what I mean?"

"Yeah, Joline. Smoke dreams."

"Naw. But that's not the point. The point is before you know it I am all the way on the edge of the shipyards. And out by the water I see this fire. It ain't like nothing I ever saw before. It was bright blue, and pea-green smoke, and yellow-orange too. Like greasy overcooked peas, and this bright, bright yellow-orange like my cousin Eunice liked to wear. Burn your eyes out. And it smelled too. Smell like rubber and blood, smelled like it could just melt your fat right off your bones."

"So it was a good thing you didn't have none, hey Joline."

Joline didn't even blink the corner of her eye at him. "Henry D was out there. You know, the old man always wore a navy cap and always pushing a cart. Sometimes he's got bottles, sometimes radios. You know the one. Like some piece of polished wood that's been around like a thousand years. That's what he looked like."

"He died of cancer, all in his glands, four, five years ago." Dusty shook his head.

"That's a damn shame." She crossed herself and continued, "Bless him for trying to warn me. Even though I didn't listen. That day when it happened he was waving at me. I remember hearing him tell me turn around, don't go that way. He knew they were burning poison. He told me it had been going on for two weeks. He said the sunsets weren't regular out there, but even though folks were talking about it, no one seemed to do anything. He told me he had seen people already coughing up all kinda colored spit. The ones that get too curious and get too close. Then he spat into the ground and kicked some trash over it. I heard him out, and kept running.

"See, I thought I still felt that woman, like she breathing down my neck, so I get closer and closer to the fire. And when I see the flames, they start to looking just like the smoke I'm wanting to breathe; I can almost see a giant glass stem and the smoke just licking round the edges of the bowl. I slowed down and started walking, thinking how close I could get. I just got to get closer till I can't even smell the stink, till I can't feel no heat, just looking at the fire and breathing in deep as I can and hearing that ole woman's voice just cackling in my ear. Then the wind shifted, and I was full of the smoke, painted with it. And it was like it was alive. I felt like little ants were just crawling all over me looking for something. Then they'd find a hole and they'd crawl inside me. Funny colored smoke slinking across my hands and up into my nose and my mouth all full of it. By this time I don't care about what's chasing me. I'm scared of what I have inside, and I start running back.

"I don't know where I got the strength, but I tell you it was like iron in my thighs. My lungs, they just opened up and let the air through, and I ran back up to the street but everybody I pass starts running away when they see me. They say I glow, say I'm not human no more. And I pass that ole lady, and she just laughing and rocking. I'm crying, and she's saying, 'Don't worry; you'll live, little girl. You'll live to tell the story. But you gonna be sorry if you don't let me finish up.' I keep running and hear her just laughing in back of me and in front of me at the same time. 'Just like your daddy, got the answer in front of you and won't see its truth.' "

Joline started crying. Yellow-orange drops came out of her eyes and then went right back in the open pores on her cheeks and nose. "Anyway, I keep running, and before you know it I ran over to your place. Figured you'd at least let me have a hit so I could calm down and figure out what had just happened to me."

Dusty shook his head and pulled his hand across his mouth, muttering into his palm, "I remember you walking in the door, glowing with an orange light around you flashing. And sweat pouring down your face but then getting swallowed back up. And I wanted to get up outta there, but I couldn't move exactly. It's like I was stuck. I was about to light up, and you just reached over and grabbed the pipe. And I didn't do anything but watch you, and instead of smoke coming out of your mouth after you sucked in, you started frothing at the mouth, and your eyes rolled back, and a kinda neon blue mixed in with the yellow and the orange, and I thought you were sho 'nuff dying. Then you started flashing an even darker orange and getting brighter and brighter with this kinda sour-milk stink coming out of you.

"After you started foaming and coughing the pipe fell out of your hands and would have broken if I hadn't caught it. What was left of the rock rolled out of the bowl, and the entire stem and mouthpiece was a sickly colored green. You think I cared? Shit, I ran up the alley and lit up in the first boarded-up doorway I saw. When I leaned back and looked down at my hands, which were buzzing, I saw some yellow-green drops on the ends of my fingers. I didn't know then, but it got my teeth and tongue and nostrils too." Dusty reached into his mouth and pulled out a full set of dentures. Underneath, his gums glowed green. "I had them all pulled. Waste a money, and now I don't have any damn teeth, but it still looks like Christmas off in there. Most times I just talk kinda closed-lip and don't take my teeth out too much." He put the false teeth back in his mouth and pulled off his gloves. All the fingers on his left hand and the thumb and first two fingers on his right also flashed in light yellow.

"Like you might imagine it's hard getting work. So I saw this poster of you, you know. And I thought, maybe you'd like a partner."

Glow's mouth fell open. She took Dusty's hand in hers and rubbed the inside of the palm softly. "You not as bright as me, but you definitely have some shine on you. But Dusty, I fly solo. I mean we cool and alla that, but I fly solo. Anyway, what I got, it's only a piece of a life. Only reason I'm back here is to try and find that old woman. I asked people about her. Thought I could find her since she knew my folks and all. But most of those folks dead, dead or gone on. But I know she's around, and I know if I could just talk to her I could get her to, you know, fix me up. Make it all right.

"I want to get out of this racket. I just want to stay in one place and maybe have a couple of songbirds. Can't keep no pets now. They all die. It's a damn shame. We get close enough to Frisco for me to take a couple of days and look for her about once a year. This my tenth trip out. I know I'm gonna run her down this time."

Dusty stood up. "Well now, that's even better. Let's you and me hit the streets and try and find her. I got a car, a tank full of gas, and as much time as it takes."

An hour later they were at the shipyards in San Francisco's Hunters Point district. A shopping center stood where the old shipyards used to be. New housing developments reached up and around the surrounding hills. They drove up and down the streets. For two days they searched, spending the nights leaning against each other in the front seat of the car. On the third morning they were awakened by a knock at the window. It was her. She was standing there dressed in white, except for the multicolored sash hanging from her waist. She had rows and rows of shiny colored beads wrapped around her neck and going up her arms. Standing next to her was a young woman who looked like she was in her early twenties, She had a white cloth wrapped around her head with the edges of hennaed dreadlocks poking out, but she was just wearing jeans and a T-shirt. The young woman seemed to be giggling.

Dusty and Glow untangled themselves and jumped out of the car, leaving the doors wide open.

The old woman laughed. "Haven't learned to close a car door yet, I see. Seems to me last time we met you were hanging out a car door too. Only that time, if I remember right, you were trying to steal my youngest great-grand's car seat. You've been back here every year for the last ten years asking everyone about me, and getting close as I was willing to let you get. But Cowrie"—she indicated the young woman standing next to her and chewing on the inside of her cheek to keep from laughing— "Cowrie seems to think it's mean watching you flicker in distress. But baby, the truth is, I can't do a thing for you. You had to let me finish back then. You didn't."

"What about me?" Dusty spoke out. "I didn't go out to the fires like she did. I was just a bystander."

"From the look of your mouth you were more than that. Why'd you get your teeth pulled? You about a fool. Listen, you tell me the name of that unscrupulous dentist and I'll put a little knot in his string if you like. I'm mostly retired now." She smiled so broadly it lit up the young woman standing next to her. "What I used to do, my daughter or one of my grands or great-grands take care of." The old woman put her arm around Cowrie. "Isn't that right, baby girl?"

Cowrie nodded but didn't say anything. She seemed to be humming a tune under her breath.

Dusty and Glow both started to approach the two women but then jumped back, and then like they were puppets in a show Dusty clasped his hands and began to beg, and Glow hung her head, avoiding the old woman's eyes, and echoed his words.

"Please, we are real sorry."

"Real, real sorry."

"We really need your help."

"Really . . ."

The old woman lifted up Glow's head and looked into her eyes. "Thank you kindly. That's the only words I'm supposed to hear coming out of you." The old woman was laughing and rocking.

Joline's words stumbled out. "It's not that I'm not thankful. . . . I mean, I just want it to be all the way right."

"Thank you kindly, end of story." The old woman stamped her feet and began to walk away, leaving her great-granddaughter, who continued to hum but was taking a small bag out of her pocket.

Dusty yelled at the old woman's back, "If you could help us we would do whatever. I mean we could work for you, or cook for you, or do whatever you like. I mean . . ."

The young woman started chortling very softly. It almost sounded like songbirds dancing around her words. "Well, we really don't know how to do it. Grandma didn't want to admit it to you. I mean she has the knowledge she has, and it's a whole lot more than most people. And she really could've helped you through, but not after you ran away. Not after you mixed the spirit voices; you mixed the powders and got turned all neon. That part wasn't her doing, see; that was you and the fire. She thought maybe, if you had've stopped, *maybe* she could've done something. But she didn't really know. I mean, when the first ones got the knowledge and passed it down, what did they know about crack and pollution?

"We've been seeing you come out here. My great-grandma and me. She's been teaching me, and every time you come she tells me the story about how you got that glow. And every time she always turns a corner right before you see her. Walking, riding in a car—one time we were even on the bus. I thought you saw us that time. Anyway, Grandma, well, she high past eighty-five, and I just really realized that she was really taunting you. I decided this year when you came, we would stop you and tell you."

The old woman was halfway down the block by this time. "Cowrie, I believe we said all that had to be said."

Glow ran to the old woman and reached out her hand to pull her around. "Is it true?"

Before her fingers could touch the edge of the woman's blouse, the old woman turned her head sharply, and her voice cut out like a jagged piece of glass. "Back off, child. Had X rays for my teeth already this year. Don't need you spilling that stuff into my delicate skin." And then the old woman broke into a girlish giggle.

Glow became angry and began to shine a brighter orange. "Is it true, old woman, that you don't even know how to take this away?"

"Never said I did. Said I could help you. And I did. Said next time you saw me you should have some manners. And you didn't." With that the old woman turned back and continued walking away. She looked over her shoulder and called out, "Cowrie, I am taking myself home. I did what you asked, and now I am taking myself home."

The young woman wordlessly moved toward her great-grandmother. Then she stopped and sang a few words. She took out some powder from the bag she had taken out of her pocket and stamped her left foot three times. She spat and made a small circle with her right foot. Then she sashayed right up to Dusty's and Glow's faces and blew the powder into their eyes. "Won't be seeing you," Cowrie repeated three times in a singsong voice and with a broad smile walked up to her great-grandmother.

The old woman cackled. "Child, your soft heart is going to make you die young. Forgetting powder?"

"Just a little veil. Make them stop looking for us." She kissed the old woman on the cheek. "Grandma, what you say we drive down to the docks and watch the herons fly out?" She put her arm around her great-grandmother's waist, and the two of them began to sing as they walked.

Dusty and Glow saw the two women move away. Glow looked at Dusty and trembled a bit. She could not even remember how they got there. Dusty looked at Glow and wanted to ask her what they were doing there, but he didn't want to sound like a fool. They stood there looking at each other for a few minutes saying nothing. Finally Glow broke the nervous silence. "Dusty, why'd you want to bring me out here?"

"What do you mean? I never come back down this way. How many colored folks you see out here now? They moved most of us out years ago. You're the one wanted to show me how the neighborhood changed," he answered with long spaces between his words, not sure why they were standing on a curb near the shopping center on the edge of San Francisco at the crack of dawn. "And now that you seen it and see there's nothing for us here, what you think?"

"Think about what?"

"About what we was talking about, about you and me hooking up?"

"Is that what we were talking about?" Glow tried to reach back. "Well, like I was saying, it's only a piece of a life, Dusty. When I started out I was 'The Glowing Nubian from Outer Space.' Or in some cities they called me 'The Boom Box Alien.' After a while Chino helped me figure out a better act, always in the dark, dancing behind different-colored glass walls that flash and make designs. I turned into 'The Neon Surprise.' But even though I keep glowing the flesh still started to sag after I hit thirty-five. So it's thicker glass and iron-framed see-through girdles, and I'm the revamped 'Neon Sensation.' Most folks don't even eat with me. I can't go nowhere public without the heavy getup; everyone throws me out. I'm always moving. And I glow all the time. I swear sometimes the glare keeps me up at night. And worst part I can't get high 'cause it just makes me sicker, and almost nobody is willing to even lay down with me and do the nasty. Tell you the truth I'm getting tired of it. It's a life, but it's not all the way living."

"It's not like we were all the way living before, Joline. Besides, look at the good sides."

"Like what?"

"Betcha don't ever need a flashlight."

"Yeah, pretty safe walking around in the middle of the night. Thief or rapist don't want to get close enough to grab anything. But on the real, Dusty, I don't think they could handle two like us. They can barely handle me."

"What, you got quotas in the human light-show department? Anyway, from what you saying, you need a new gimmick."

"Hell, Dusty, what you gonna do?"

"Introduce you. Grin. Blow bubbles. Come on, Joline, we could figure something out. You know, 'Dusty and the Glow,' or 'The Glow and the Dustman,' or—"

"Glowdust . . ."

"I like that. Glowdust—shines in the dark."

"You know the score."

The two of them got back in the car and drove back to the carnie, laughing all the way, their car windows lighting up with flashes of yellow and pale blue, sometimes blending into a metallic sparkling green.

# NOTES FROM A WRITER'S BOOK OF CURES AND SPELLS

*Marcia Douglas*

*Work into the night,* mi *love—*
*letters small and tight—*
*until the moon, eating her own flesh,*
*disappears.*

## 1 | Conjuring Mafunda

First you start with her belly—a large mango seed that you wash with rainwater, then leave on the zinc roof to dry in the sun. After three days, lean your ladder against the wall and climb back up to take a look. The seed will be shrunken and bleached white. Hold it carefully in your palm; feel it warm as a fresh egg.

Use your penknife to make a thin slit through the seed's side; then soak it overnight in a half cup of white rum. Next morning, check on it again before leaving it to dry on the roof once more. After four days, you will see that the slit has widened, the inside a faint yellow.

Sit at the kitchen table and stuff the belly well with ground pimiento, thyme, salt, pepper, and a little rosemary; then write the word "speak" on a piece of tobacco paper, folding it tight and sliding it inside. Tie the stuffed belly with a strip of muslin, winding it securely.

The head is to be made from a guinep seed. After it is washed and sun-dried, write your character's name—Mafunda, Mafunda, Mafunda—around and around in tiny letters; then wear it tied tight right over your navel. After seven days, take it off and attach it to the mango belly.

The arms and legs are next—twigs broken from a tamarind switch. Spanish moss will do for her hair and two seashells for her breasts. A bag of glass beads makes perfect embellishment. Attach them one by one—red and green and blue; then adorn with gold thread as you see fit. Paint a generous mouth and two eyes wide open; a single cowrie should hang from her hair.

## 2 | Pouring Libation

Feed Mafunda with white rum and yellow cornmeal. Place fresh bougainvillea at her feet along with a bowl of uncooked rice filled with coins. When you are ready, tie a red ribbon around a ballpoint pen. Put it in your bag along with a loaf of bread, a bottle of soda, a packet of powdered milk, a kerosene lamp, two red candles, and a small hand mirror. Go outside and keep on walking until you come to a place where the road splits like your legs pushing out a child. Choose the path with the most gravel. To the left there will be a julie mango tree with a snake carved into its bark. When you see this, switch your bag to the other shoulder and keep on going. You will need to hurry if you are to make it to the river before sundown. The last thing you need is for your shadow to beat you there, snatching away the words waiting at the water bottom.

As soon as you arrive, take the bread from your bag; break it into small pieces and cast it in an arc upon the water. Open the bottle of soda and pour it slowly; sprinkle the milk powder and watch it disappear downstream. This is the time to light the red candles and the kerosene lamp. When at last you reach for the pen, the ink will ooze like shed blood. Do not lift your hand from the page. Do not stop to scratch your scalp, slap the mosquito at your ankle, or brush the fly from your chin.

Most of all, do not worry about the crocodile eyeing you from the other side of the river. Cut your eye, spit over your shoulder, and keep on writing. You must write until there is no more ink left in your pen.

## 3 | Signs and Wonders

Later, when the moon appears, the dogs upstream will begin barking. You will know when Mafunda is ready, her chest softly rattling—*took-took*, *took-took*—like so many seeds. From the corner of your eye, catch a glimpse of her sitting on a warm rock to the side, her face in her palm. Know that she has traveled from a long way—two hundred years through cane fields, swamp, grass-lice, wind, rain, and mango blossom. See how twigs fall from the nutmeg tree each time she blinks to adjust her eyes to river light.

She has come to observe your hand busy as a small bird, reminding her of a night long ago, when she leaned against a moonshine windowsill, scratching on wood and dry leaf with a pen stolen from Massa and marked with his initials. How she hungered for words then, devouring them wherever they could be found—the bottoms of cracked plates, the inside soles of shoes, the rims of old biscuit tins. She worked into the night, tiny letters like soldier ants, racing across bark.

A quick glance at Mafunda, and see how she cranes her neck, closes her eyes, listening to the rhythm of your pen. Someone is probably throwing stones into the river, trying to distract you, but do not look up or you will break the spell, the ink turning to scab before it reaches the page. Concentrate instead on the two flickering candles with long red tears, for it is your busy hand that keeps Mafunda breathing, and whatever you do, you must not lose her. Write write write her name over and over, bringing her back to the next morning, her fingers stained night blue and hidden in shallow pockets against her thighs. When Mistress called, she quickly took the egg basket and scurried away so she could wash with water from the chicken trough. She washed and washed, but the blue remained. Two brown eggs fell onto the floor. A door banged shut; footsteps approached from across the yard.

As you write the word "yard," fireflies circle the kerosene lamp, and you notice a man's foot on the rock beside you. Resist the temptation to run away. There is no escape now; Mafunda has taken you all the way back—two hundred years through the smell of molasses. Hold your head still as the man sharpens his machete. Pretend to be interested in crushed corn on the ground. Leaves rustle underfoot, and you hear Mafunda scream, her voice high-pitched and broken in the evening sky.

This is the scene in which blood trickles everywhere, words lodged in your throat like fresh bone. As Mafunda's amputated fingers are hurled through the air, stuff your scarf in your mouth to stop your lips from trembling. Grab the fingers quick before the dogs arrive. Bloody nails dig into your skin now, and you want out of this story, as far away as you can possibly hide. You almost dash your pen to the ground, but then for one brief moment, Mafunda's eyes meet yours.

Remember a woman who got stuck in story, wandered around and around and never came back? They found her shoes by the edge of the river with a note inside which read, *The word made flesh.* . . . Better to have stayed at home—hung the clothes on the line, stirred the cornmeal porridge, swept under the bed. But you cannot change your mind anymore; you are too far gone. A small crow cries in the lime tree behind you.

## 4 | Closing the Space

This is the time for the hand mirror in your shoulder bag. Reach for it with your left hand and lean it against the rock in front of you. The mirror sees trouble before you do and will always remember the way back home. Mafunda still screams a trail of red, and you must hurry before she disappears. Chase the trail all the way through the bush; howl if you must, your voice joining hers; follow the course of the river as she runs downstream.

You will see Mafunda pause at the river's mouth; note how she beckons you with her bottomless eyes. Late as it is, the moon has almost eaten all its flesh; the crocodile sleeps at the water's edge. In the square of the hand mirror, glance back down the path from which you came. Way at the end of it, you will see your little yellow kitchen, the table set with clear glass plates. A lizard stretches on a straw mat by the stove. Sugar ants cluster around crumbs on the windowsill. As Massa's hungry dogs race towards Mafunda, spell out her name; press into the page as you urge her on, your pen almost empty.

You have heard stories of slaves in flight, flying back to Africa, but this is not that story. You have heard stories of women walking out into the ocean, drowning themselves, but this is not that story.

In this story, you must follow Mafunda's heels until the river falls into the waiting sea. In wee morning light, the Caribbean is thick as dark ink. You wade into the water, and it licks your flesh with a warm blue tongue. Massa's three dogs arrive only inches behind you, hesitating at the water's edge. Mafunda turns around and grabs at your collar, pulls you down flat against the ocean floor. You hold on to each other, plaits afloat in blue fluid. When you open your eyes, you see the dogs' paws paddling above. Your lungs are swollen, and you cannot hold your breath much longer; soon you must rise up for air. You turn to look at Mafunda and notice her face: The sockets of her eyes are generations deep; the pupils like searchlights burrow into yours. As your head fills with yellow light, you recognize each other as next of kin. She pulls a string from her navel—two hundred years long—coils it into a ball, presses it in your hand. You want to reach her, to make some gesture—

But you are out of air. Somewhere a whip cracks, and you rise from the water, arms extended. As your blood pumps faster, the dogs hurl themselves at Mafunda's flesh. Do not try to save her—there is no more time and not enough ink for indecision. Keep one eye on the mirror and turn now, go. Run back down the gravel path, past the julie mango tree and back to the place where the road splits like your legs throwing away a child. Dry your tears on your sleeve and keep on going. Do not look back; this scene cannot be revised.

As you enter the yard, the little ball unravels behind you, expanding in the wind like a long red cloth. Fold it carefully before you enter the house; then write your name in the middle of your hand. Trace the lines of your palm, crisscrossed and dusty. Call yourself out loud—hear how your voice has changed.

# HOW SUKIE CROSS DE BIG WATA

*Sheree Renee Thomas*

**B**efore you begin, before you fix your lips to tell the lie, let me see if I can take this tale and bend it straight. I was there when her bloodline first arrived, when her mama folk emerged from tree-born ships, 'cause I carried them on my back, carried them from the door of no return in the land they call Mother, and I been carrying them ever since. Sayna, 'cause the wood is a witness, and I ain't talking 'bout no slippery elm or no weeping, whimpering willow tree. Sayna, I'm talking 'bout baobab, mahogany, banyan, mapou, and ebon tree-born ships that carried those that did not fly away, carried those that did not jump across bloody bows and plunge deep into my depths. Ain't talking 'bout those who walked back 'cross my neck to their fathers' shores but those who come 'cross the waters on spiritwood, on my turtleback and limbs outstretched to the land they call Taino, the land in the back door of what they call New World.

These lives I carried while the hollerwood splintered and echoed, their groans creaking like split bone in the wood. I carried them, her people, 'cross the big watas, and I carried her like I carried the rest—generations 'cross the crying watas to these bitter shores.

So when she dipped her long blacktoe in my throat, the part they call Sippi—*and the child did not speak*—I asked her did she know my name. *Child,* I say, the muddy waters carrying my words to the riverbank where she stood, *do you know me?* She blink like she ain't sure she heard right, so I send a cold current swirling round her toes. *Child,* I say, and I say it again. *Do you know your own name? Do you know your mama name?*

At the mention of her mama, this woman-chile look like she want to sink, not swim, so I send a warm current to tickle the blackbottom of her feet. *How you gon' cross over these watas so wide and dip into that other world, if you don't even know yourself? If you can guess my name, I will tell you a story. And if you listen true, you will know when I am bending it and when I am telling it straight, 'cause like a river, every story got a bend. So, listen, child, and I will carry you, carry you clear over, like I carry all the rest. Carry you from where you come, to where you must go. And this how the story begin . . .*

• • •

She has many names. Aunt Nancy, Sukie Diamond, Diamond Free, but her navel name was Stella or Dinah, depending on who tell the tale. I'm telling this, and on my end of the river bottom, we called her Stella because no matter who come after her, she always managed to steal away. Now, some folk say Stella mama was a real bad seed, contrary kind of soul, always running. Say the last time she run, her white folks dug a hole in the ground and put her in there, belly baby-swole and all, and beat her till she couldn't do nothing but grunt. Say when she come out of that hole that night, she was spirit talking, whispering words ain't nobody live long enough to know the meaning to. Saying,

"Stee la dee nah
"nah dee la stee
"stee la dee nah
"nah dee la stee
"steeeela! deenah!
"Steela! Steela!"

Whispering then shouting and yelling them words—part African, part Indian—till folk turn a pot over to hold in the song, whispering and shouting till she didn't speak no more and her body come still. But her baby, that baby Stella just a kicking in the belly. Folk say they could see her little arms and legs just a waving under the cold dead flesh of her mama. Say Stella birth herself in her own time, say she come on out kicking, and swinging too, and been swinging ever since.

Say when she was born her eyes was wide open, not shuteye like most babies but bright as two harvest moons. Say she leaned back, took in her world, saw her mama tree-stump dead—the spirit still fresh on her breath—and didn't drop no tears. No, Stella didn't cry. Stella leaned back, smacked the old granny that held her, and snatched back her navel string. Say she'd bury it her own damned self. Say she'd rather carry her destiny in her own hands than trust it to some strange bloodtree, cut down 'fore its roots can grow, like her mama and all her kin that come before. And some folk say she been carrying that string in a mojo band round her waist ever since.

But that night, the night Stella birthed herself, they say she looked round and saw the others' faces and said just as loud for anybody to hear, "I'll eat the clay of my own grave 'fore I'll slave a day in this life or the next for any man, woman, child, or spirit—white, negra, or other." She say this and then she was gone.

Stella walked right down the path to massa's house, spit and set the Big House afire. Then the fields, then the tool shack that held every hoe. She kept walking till she come 'cross overseer, running crook-legged and buck-toe from all them burning fields.

Now, overseer was looking mighty 'fraid till he see Stella standing up in the row, buck naked with the backside of a smile on her face. When he saw Stella frowning down at him, he dug his rusty heels into the ground and puff up his chest till his black muscles gleamed 'neath all the sweat and dust.

"Where you think you headed, gal?" he asked, like the aim of Stella's long toes wasn't cuss clear. "Who yo' people?"

Now, overseer didn't recognize Stella, but he look her up and down like he thirsty and want a taste. At first sight, Stella didn't say nothing, but her eyes walked all over his face. Seem like she knowed he was the one put her mama in the belly hole and beat her till she spoke in spirit tongue. (What overseer didn't know was that Stella remembered what most forget, on the trip to this world from the next. She knew why she'd been sent, just not how or when or where. She reckoned she'd just put one foot 'fore the next till they carried her to a place that felt like home. But when she come out that night, she knew that belly hole wasn't it.)

Finally, after a long, hard spell, Stella say, "My mama folk come from heavy-boned ships. . . ." She spit, and sparks fly. "They's the kind the slavers couldn't half handle. . . ." She spit and mo sparks fly. "And if you couldn't handle my mama"—spit, she moving now—"what make you think you can handle me?"

When she say this, overseer look like he grab the wrong end of a rattler. "Who yo' mama, girl?" he ask, backing up all a sudden.

"Bet you know when I give you this kiss," Stella say, pressing her full lips on his rusty jaw. Burnt off half his face. Overseer cry so loud, his voice seem to come from a hundred throats, distant but close like.

"*Steela!*" he cry. She watched him in silence and frowned. Seem like her name in his mouth called down the rain. Stella stood under the baptism a moment, the sky a red sinking ball afire; then she picked up her long feet to go.

After, Sukie walked down to massa's house, spit and set the Big House afire, then the fields, then the tool shack that held every hoe. When overseer come tumbling down the row, jaw looking like a big ole greasy piece of fatback, folk was ripping and running so, nobody had time to see Stella make her way down the road, through the gates, and on into them woods. And that's how Sukie come free. She walked her way into freedom, carrying that navel string in her hand.

But that night, the sky was full of cloudsplitters, and the rain felt like heavy hands pounding the earth. In the woods, the tree branches made dark arches, and Sukie ducked beneath them till her feet carried her across upturned roots and thorny thickets to an elderspirit tree whose branches curved just so.

Back then, the woods stayed full of negras, spirits, and haints. Folk running all the time, even if it only for a few days or a week or two, till they hear the Word—that being that massa wouldn't turn a lick if they come back within a day of his calling. In them time, a negra could come back when massa say or get the nine and thirty—lashes, that is. Come back or run away for good.

Now, Sukie didn't run. She walked. She walked right on through the plum thickets and bilderbrush weeds and climbed up in that elder tree. Guess she knew then not a bull had been born or a lash made evil enough to break the hard skin on her cold black flesh. She chuckled to herself, 'cause poor overseer never got a chance to give her back a taste. Still, Sukie shut her eyes for a spell and dreamed till she woke to see a screech owl sitting on her branch. Owl was just a fidgeting and whispering, shaking his great head. Owl say,

*"Oooh wee Sukie*
*"Oooh wee Sukie*
*"Sho'll be in trouble now.*
*"Oooh wee Sukie*
*"Oooh wee Sukie*
*"Massa done sent bloodhounds.*
*"Better get gone*
*" 'fore trouble get grown.*
*"Your scent all over de ground.*
*"If they find you*
*"You know what they gon' do—*
*"Nine and thirty lashes*
*"Oooh wee oooh!"*

Now, Sukie stretch and yarn, blink back remnants of the day. Look old Screech Owl dead in his face and spit. The branch spark and sizzle a li'l in the drizzling dusk. Sukie say she ain't worried 'bout no lash 'cause ain't n'am person gone lay a finger or a scar on her back or leg. Say she heal 'fore the blood rise warm. And can't no man—slaver, teacher, or preacher—claim the back room of her body, mind, or soul. Say she walk in the guts and scales of Holy Rollers and got a mojo bone buried deep in her breast. Say she come here, head so full of figurin' and words so old and new, the books still waiting on the seeds to take root—let alone the trees. Say she don't need no pass or no word from massa. Sukie say she go where she very well please. She say massa got more than her flat feet on his mind. Say massa still be stomping out that big ole fire she start, long after she come and gone. Sukie say this and smile, like she know a secret, and Screech Owl hoot, too. He knowed can't nobody get ahold of Sukie 'cause she a dangerous kind of hussy, a negra gal, damn near one of the most dangerous of all.

Screech Owl knowed this, but still he worry. He knowed Sukie watn't nothing but a day old, and a young'un sitting in newborn skin—no matter how thick and spirit-blessed—still needed a mother's wing in the world.

True, though Sukie had birthed herself in her own time, climbing from her mama's bone-still womb, and she'd come out kicking and swinging, too. Not shuteye like most natural-born babies but eyes wide open like *boop!* sitting up in the sky. Sukie had spoken her first words with a mouth full of teeth and not a tear in her eye, breaking the stunned silence of the others who'd watched her walk away to her doom—or so they had thought. And she'd spoken in spirit-tongue, as her mama before her death, rising from the belly hole to take her freedom, her long feet leading her straight to Screech Owl's elderspirit tree.

Now, Sukie done all that in a woman's full-grown body that ain't yet seen one day of sun, let alone two, but inside, her heart was grieving. Seem like the li'l sleep she got was nothing but a drop of sorrow, the taste as bittersweet as wada root and all them big words in her mouth. And for the first time since Sukie climb out her mama womb, seem like she could barely breathe. Her chest felt tight, the breasts heavy with mama ache and the phantom weight of stolen freedom. She knew there wasn't but one place she could go to relieve it.

'Fore Screech Owl could blink and turn his big wobbly head, Sukie was up stretching her long limbs, shaking the elder bark out of her ears, brushing the grief from her eyes and her thick, tangled hair. She was headed for the belly hole, where they'd buried her mama.

"Owl, I thanks you for the company," Sukie say, "but I'ma have to see 'bout my way."

Sukie leaped from the elderspirit's dark, knotty branches and landed on moist fertile ground. Turned her straight back to go.

Screech Owl could tell by the curve of her hip sway that Sukie wasn't going to turn back. Still he hopped down to a lower branch, his big ole eyes blinking in the dark, crying,

*"Aaah Sukie, aaah Sukie*
*"Know it's yo mama you mourn*
*"But you better turn west*
*"Where your fortune be best*
*"Or them pattyrollers*
*"Gone make you wish*
*"You watn't born!"*

Now, Sukie turn her back on Screech Owl's warning, didn't want to hear another mumbling word, but when she got back to the belly hole seem like somebody call her name, and it watn't no owl either. The call echoed from the pit of her own belly, sound like sweet spirits sangin'. Then Sukie felt a kiss—soft full lips on her temple, the place where the spirit rest—and she knew it was her mama come to visit.

Sukie shut her eyes, head bowed as blue flames licked her brown skin and slowly spread round the curve of her jaw to her throat. She felt strong arms round her, a bosom that pulsed not with blood but with will, and shoulders as wide as her own.

Sukie stood there, among the elder trees in the south bank of massa's land, embracing the body that, for a time, had sheltered her own from a world that would make her unfree. Sukie stood there, cradling her mama's head in her arms, breathing—*one Mississippi, two Mississippi, three Mississippi, breathe.* Then her mama spirit disappeared, and Sukie was alone in the world again. She turned her face toward the earth, listening with strained ears for the sound of many movements, sounds dragged off like heavy bales of cotton.

Overhead, the sky opened up as if to welcome her mama spirit, washing the bloodstains of each moment she'd breathed from the soil. Sukie rose from her square knees and drank skywater, fat drops glistening on her chin.

Soon, she knew she must leave that place. The Sippi couldn't hold her body no more than it could her mama spirit. The air around her grew dense, thick with spirits, the ancestors pressing against her skin, pushing her forward. Sukie moved as if invisible fingers were gently coaxing her to go. She moved with heavy feet, allowing the black dirt so full of cottonseed, blood, and bone to fall heavily to the earth through her stiff fingers.

She moved with purpose, flinging more of the black mud with each step, until all that remained of her mama's charred body were a few dark smudges on her fingertips and lips.

Some folk say when Sukie got to the river, she turned herself into a stone. You know the kind, smooth and polished and slick. The kind of rock that'll slip out of your fingers if you ain't careful, bust you in your own head. Well, one of them pattyrollers, surprised not to find Sukie barefoot and bleeding on the water's edge, seized a stone just like that one and chunked it clear 'cross the water, clear to the other side of the river, saying that's how he'd bust that negra gal's head if he ever caught sight of her again.

Now, when the stone reached the other side and settled in the dust, it turned into Sukie's straight back again, and Sukie just wiped the dust off her long feet and smile and pointed her long toes west, sangin',

*"Steela Deenah Steela*
*"Steela Deenah Steela*
*"Sho'll be glad to put Sippi to rest*
*"Guess these feets is heading west*
*"There's a wagon train calling my name*
*"Leaving Sippi, won't be back again*
*"Call me Sukie Diamond*
*"Changed to a stone*
*"Skipped 'cross the river*
*"And now I'm gone*
*"Diamond to a stone a stone turned to gold*
*"On my way to the Oregon road"*

And that's how Sukie left Sippi. She skipped her way clear 'cross the river.

*The nail ain't broke*
*The nail just bent*
*And that's the way*
*The story went*

# About the Contributors

**Jenise Aminoff** is a freelance science journalist currently covering the robotics industry. She successfully escaped from a physics degree at MIT by writing a poetry thesis and, thus prepared, emerged from the Clarion '95 Science Fiction and Fantasy Writers' Workshop relatively unscathed. A native of New Mexico, Jenise now gardens, sings, tutors, plays games, and refines the perfect chocolate-chip scone in a cohousing community in the Boston area with her husband, Alex. This is her first professional fiction sale. For more information, see www.jenise.com.

**Barth Anderson**'s stories have appeared in *New Genre*, *On-Spec*, *Strange Horizons*, *Talebones*, *Rabid Transit: New Fiction from the Ratbastards*, and *Asimov's Science Fiction*. His work has received Honorable Mention in *The Year's Best Fantasy and Horror*. Barth lives in Minneapolis.

**Steven Barnes** was born in Los Angeles, California, and has been a professional writer since 1979. Since that time he has published over two million words, and been nominated for the Hugo, Cable Ace, and Endeavor Awards. His "A Stitch In Time" episode of *The Outer Limits* television show won a Best Actress Emmy for Amanda Plummer. His most recent novels include *Lion's Blood* and its sequel, *Zulu Heart*. He lives in Longview, Washington, with his wife, novelist Tananarive Due, and his daughter Nicki.

**Tobias S. Buckell** is a Caribbean-born speculative fiction writer who has published in magazines like *Analog Science Fiction and Fact* and *Science Fiction Age*, as well as a number of anthologies. He is a Clarion graduate, a Writers of the Future winner, and a nominee for the Campbell Award for Best New Writer in 2002. He now lives in Ohio, which is why he feels comfortable writing about strange things happening to seemingly normal people.

Born at the tail end of the 1960s, **A. M. Dellamonica** had the kind of action-packed childhood that most people dream of, featuring actual plane crashes and the occasional really long car trip. After catching her first fish at the age of six, she realized she was ready to fend for herself in the wild, though in the end it took her eleven years to pack her books and depart. Her fiction began to appear in print in 1986, and despite repeated washings, remains in circulation in a variety of print and on-line locales, including the *Tesseracts8* anthology, Scifi.com, and *Isaac Asimov's Science Fiction.*

**Marcia Douglas** was born in England and grew up in Jamaica. Her fiction and poetry have appeared in literary journals nationwide. She is the author of a novel, *Madam Fate*, as well as a poetry collection, *Electricity Comes to Cocoa Bottom*. She teaches creative writing at the University of Colorado, Boulder.

**Tananarive Due** won an American Book Award for her latest novel, *The Living Blood*, and her short fiction has been included in two Best of the Year science fiction anthologies. She is the author of three supernatural suspense novels and a historical novel, *The Black Rose*, based on the research of Alex Haley. She and her mother, civil rights activist Patricia Stephens Due, recently coauthored a family civil rights memoir, *Freedom in the Family*, and her next supernatural novel, *The Good House*, will be published in the fall of 2003. She lives in Longview, Washington, with her husband, novelist Steven Barnes. Her Web site is at www.tananarivedue.com.

**Andy Duncan,** winner of two World Fantasy Awards and a Theodore Sturgeon Memorial Award, is the author of *Beluthahatchie and Other Stories* and coeditor, with F. Brett Cox, of the forthcoming anthology *Crossroads: Southern Stories of the Fantastic*. He lives in Northport, Alabama.

**Eliot Fintushel** is a traveling performer of mask and mime shows. He has won the National Endowment's award for Solo Theater Artists twice, and made millions and millions of children laugh, a few hundred at a time. He lives in quiet dignity near the Sonoma County fairgrounds, between the horse stables and the muffler shops. Eliot's short fiction has appeared in *Asimov's Science Fiction*, *The Ohio Review*, *Science Fiction Age*, *Amazing Stories*, *The Whole Earth Review*, and various anthologies in and out of genre. A story of Eliot's was a 1999 Nebula finalist.

**Gregory Frost** has been writing and publishing stories of fantasy, horror, and science fiction for two decades. He is the author of the recent novel *Fitcher's Brides* and the much-acclaimed novelette "Madonna of the Maquiladora," which appeared in the May 2002 issue of *Asimov's Science Fiction*. His story "How Meersh the Bedeviler Lost His Toes" was a finalist for the 1998 Theodore Sturgeon Memorial Award for Best Short Science Fiction. He has twice taught in the intensive Clarion Science Fiction and Fantasy Writers' Workshop at Michigan State University. His shorter work has appeared in *The Magazine of Fantasy & Science Fiction*, *Asimov's Science Fiction*, *Whispers*, *Realms of Fantasy*, and numerous anthologies.

**Neil Gaiman** is English, but he lives in America. He wrote *Sandman* and *American Gods* and *Neverwhere* and *Coraline* and other things. For recreational purposes he grows pumpkins, or fails to, both of which occupations can keep him happy for hours. He has won more than his share of awards, and, guiltily, neither dusts nor polishes them.

Born in 1951, **Barbara Hambly** is a native Californian, though she spent a year of college at the University of Bordeaux, France. She attended University of California, Riverside, obtaining a master's degree in medieval history and a black belt in karate, both of which have been equally useful in the writing of fantasy novels. She has taught high school, assisted aerospace engineers with their grammar, modeled, and clerked at an all-night liquor store; she has written horror, fantasy, science fiction, comic books, historical whodunnits, and scripts for Saturday morning cartoon shows. In her spare time she sews, does carpentry, hikes, and dances. She is a widow who lives in Los Angeles.

**Nalo Hopkinson** was born in Jamaica and lives in Toronto, Canada. She is the author of *Brown Girl in the Ring*, *Midnight Robber*, and *Skin Folk* and the editor of the anthology *Whispers from the Cotton Tree Root: Caribbean Fabulist Fiction*. She has received numerous awards for her writing. She has been scaring and thrilling herself by reading folktales since she was a child, and she's very pleased to be able to pass on some of the chills, thrills, and knowledge.

**Gerard Houarner** is a product of the New York City public school system, attended the City College of New York, where he studied writing under Joseph Heller and Joel Oppenheimer while sneaking into William Burroughs's hallucinogenic classes, and attained a master's degrees in psychology from Teachers College, Columbia University, so he could make a living. After publishing over two hundred short stories, four collections, and three novels, he must occasionally remind people he only works for, and does not actually reside in, a psychiatric center. For the latest, visit his site at: www.cith.org/gerard.

**devorah major** became the third Poet Laureate of San Francisco in April of 2002. She won the PEN Oakland Josephine Miles Award for Literary Excellence for *street smarts* and the Black Caucus of the American Library Association First Novelist award for *An Open Weave*. She has a second novel published, *Brown Glass Windows*, and a third book of poetry, *with more than tongue*. Her poems, short stories, and essays are available in a number of magazines and anthologies. She has taught poetry and creative writing as a community artist-in-residence and/or college adjunct professor for over twenty years. She is currently working on a speculative fiction novel, *Ice Shadows*.

**Nnedima Okorafor** is a writer from Chicago. A 2001 Clarion graduate, Okorafor's first novel, *Zahrah the Windseeker*, will be published by Houghton Mifflin in 2004. Her short story "Windseekers" was a finalist in the L. Ron Hubbard Writers of the Future contest and was published in *Writers of the Future Anthology* (volume 18). In 2001, Okorafor was a winner in the Hurston/Wright Awards, for her story "Amphibious Green." She also received honorable mention in *The Year's Best Fantasy and Horror* (14th ed.) for her short story "The Palm Tree Bandit." Okorafor is currently working on her Ph.D. in English at the University of Illinois, Chicago. Learn more at Nnedima's Web site at www2.uic.edu/~nokora1.

**Kiini Ibura Salaam** is a writer, painter, and traveler from New Orleans, Louisiana. Her speculative fiction has been included in *Fertile Ground*, *Dark Eros*, and *Dark Matter*. Her essays have been published in anthologies such as *Colonize This!*, *Race Matters*, and *Men We Cherish*, as well as magazines such as *Essence*, *Ms.*, and *Utne Reader*. She is currently crafting *Bloodlines*, her first novel. She is the author of the KIS list, a monthly e-report on life as a writer. More of her work can be accessed at www.kiiniibura.com.

**Nisi Shawl**'s short stories have appeared in *Asimov's Science Fiction*, *Wet: More Aqua Erotica*, and the first volume of *Dark Matter: A Century of Speculative Fiction from the African Diaspora*. Her first professional publication (in company with William Gibson, J. G. Ballard, and other notables) occurred in 1989, in *Semiotext(e) SF*. For over a decade a practitioner of the West African–based tradition known as Ifa, Nisi belongs to Oakland, California's Ile Orunmila Oshun. She lives in Seattle, Washington, on a direct bus route to the beach.

**Jarla Tangh:** Once upon a time, in Boston, there lived a nearsighted young woman of primarily African descent who haunted the Fantasy and Science Fiction sections of bookstores. She kept looking for stories about people who shared her heritage. She didn't find too many. In a rage, she took to a sturdy #2 pencil, then graduated to a ballpoint pen, then a typewriter, and then to a Mac computer. (Once her writer friends got tired of reading her chicken scratching and faint, typewritten copies.) Born Carla Jean Johnson, she writes under the pen name Jarla Tangh to avoid vengeful creations.

**Luisah Teish** is the author of several books, notably *Jambalaya: The Natural Woman's Book of Personal Charms and Practical Rituals*. She is an initiate elder in the Ifa/Orisha tradition and holds a chieftancy title (yeye'woro) from the Fatunmise Compound in Ile Ife, Nigeria. She is the founder of the School of Ancient Mysteries/Sacred Arts Center in Oakland, California. Teish is internationally known for her storytelling performances, multitraditional rituals, and community activism. Web site: www.jambalayaspirit.org.

**Sheree Renee Thomas** is the editor of *Dark Matter*, which won a World Fantasy Award and a Gold Pen Award, and a cofounder of *Anansi*, a literary journal. She is the publisher of Wanganegresse Press and works as an editorial consultant. A 1999 Clarion West graduate and a Cave Canem Poetry Fellow, her short fiction and poetry is collected in works selected by Ursula K. Le Guin and Elizabeth Alexander and appear in several anthologies, including *Role Call: A Generational Collection of Social & Political Black Literature & Art*, *2001: A Science Fiction Poetry Anthology*, *Bum Rush the Page: A Def Poetry Jam*, as well as numerous literary journals. A member of the Beyond Dusa Women's Collective, Thomas is a native of Memphis and lives in New York with her family.